UnCaGe me

BLEAK
HOUSE
BOOKS

Published by
BLEAK HOUSE BOOKS
a division of Big Earth Publishing
923 Williamson St.
Madison, WI 53703
www.bleakhousebooks.com

Printed in the United States of America
12 11 10 09   1 2 3 4 5 6 7 8 9 10

978-1-60648-015-1 (hardcover)
978-1-60648-016-8 (paperback)
978-1-60648-017-5 (evidence collection)

Dianne and Drea,

without whom I would be imprisoned or insane

Contents

IntroDuCtiOn
John Connolly

TO PARAPHRASE COLE PORTER, in olden days a glimpse of stocking might have been considered shocking, but now, quite frankly, almost anything goes. I say "almost" because, of course, Porter was wrong to conclude that there were no longer any limits on behavior, although we can forgive him because he was less interested in making an irrefutable statement than in fitting words to a good tune. It's probably asking a lot to expect him to be more than broadly socially and philosophically accurate as well.

Boundaries and limits—legal, moral, national, aesthetic, sexual, racial, and physical—still exist, but it is a facet of the modern (or even postmodern) world that they are being challenged at an ever accelerating rate. But those challenges are not entirely negative in their connotations; rather, they can be seen as an effort to establish the nature and extent of those limitations. Thus, acts of transgression should not be viewed as destructive by nature. To approach them in this way is to misunderstand them, for their relationship to the society that gives rise to them is far more complex than might at first appear.

The word "transgression" enters the English language for the first time in the sixteenth century, but it comes weighted with negative spiritual meaning. Perhaps the first great act of transgression is the decision by Adam and Eve to eat forbidden fruit, thereby violating their pact with God. Yet with this act comes a certain liberation, albeit at considerable cost. Admittedly, the Church fathers did not see it in this way, and so transgression becomes associated with evil, with St. John telling us that "Whosoever transgresseth, and abideth not in the doctrine of Christ, hath not God" (2 John 9).

It is worth noting, in passing, that Eve bears the primary burden for disobeying God's will, and subsequently tempting her partner. Here, the seeds are sown for an abiding distrust of women, and the demonic associations that came to be made with feminine qualities. Thus it was that the female body, by the time of the Renaissance, was the subject of constant surveillance, and was regarded as, in a way, grotesque. It was a body that potentially exceeded any boundary or limit, and was thus regarded as transgressive by its very nature. Something of this sense of the threat posed by the feminine mystique survives in the femmes fatales of film noir, who are, in their way, all descendants of the lady Eve.

As time progresses, though, some of those earlier spiritual connotations fall away, and "to transgress" becomes more general in its meaning, covering any kind of deviation from the norm, as well as non-physical acts of aggression against the person. Finally, it begins to refer to the crossing of boundaries, whether moral, legal, or, indeed, artistic and aesthetic, which is where we should perhaps locate it for the purposes of this volume.

In fact, creative and artistic endeavors provide an apt proving ground for notions of transgression. As the writer bell hooks puts it: "Art, and most especially painting, was for me a realm where every imposed boundary could be transgressed."

The use of the word "imposed" raises an interesting question. Are constraints entirely imposed from the outside? If we transgress, do we do so purely against some external authority, whether human or divine? I would argue that we do not, that there is a personal element in our responses to moral imperatives, an element of subjectivity that brings with it a desire to transgress, even a necessity to do so. Societies find a way to channel and express this desire: mythologies are one such channel, acts of mockery another, or what Bakhtin described as "the laughter of the carnival." Such laughter is collective, universal, and ambivalent, but it is not destructive, and here is where our relationship with the notion of transgression becomes really interesting.

Transgression is both an act of affirmation and denial. It recognizes the existence of certain limitations or boundaries, even as it seeks to overstep those marks. In fact, it requires the continued existence of such boundaries for its effect. If the act of transgression shatters the boundary entirely, then what is left? As St. Paul put it, "Where no law is, there is no transgression" (Romans 4:15).

Transgression is not the same as disorder. It does not invite chaos. Even Georges Bataille, the twentieth-century writer whose work is perhaps most closely associated with the notion of the transgressive, for whom erotic transgression was the archetype, the *sine qua non,* of all transgression (albeit linked, by violence, to death), understood the necessity of suspending, rather than removing, sexual constraints. A taboo might be violated, but not terminated. "The sacred world," wrote Bataille, "depends on limited acts of transgression."

One might argue, then, that transgression is not in itself necessarily subversive. It seeks to question boundaries and limitations, not destroy them. It is not an overt challenge to the status quo; it is instead an interrogation, a questioning. In that sense, it is complicit in that which it critiques, but it is not blindly accepting of it. Instead, it recognizes that every limitation contains within it the the possibility of its own fracture. The instruction to obey carries with it the potential for disobedience. In cultural terms, it prevents stagnation by forcing us constantly to reassess the rules governing our society, while at the same time reaffirming the necessity of those rules. It may lead to a reordering, but not to the absence of order at all.

Still, the tension between what may be perceived by one side as legitimate questioning that may possibly lead to change, or even just a different perspective, and by another as a threat to the established order, goes some way towards explaining why the relationship between art and the law is so fractious. It's worth recalling the furor that initially greeted Howard Brenton's play *The Romans in Britain* when it was staged by the National Theatre in London in 1980. Intended, in part, as a commentary on the situation in Northern Ireland at the time, it included a scene of homosexual rape that led a "moral guardian," Mrs. Mary Whitehouse, to take a private prosecution against the play's director for procuring an act of gross indecency. (Mrs. Whitehouse declined to view the play herself, fearing corruption of her soul. Sir Horace Cutler, by contrast, who was a board member of the National Theatre, walked out in disgust, informing a journalist that his wife had been forced to "cover her head" during the scene in question, although nobody seemed entirely sure how, precisely, her concealment was achieved.) The trial was eventually halted with both sides claiming victory: the Attorney General was said to have ended the case because it was not in the public interest to proceed, but the judge did rule that the Sexual Offences Act could be applied to events on a stage, and to simulated acts of indecency.

When the play was revived in 2007, critics reflected nostalgically on the earlier controversy, but no comparable outcry greeted the revival. Time and the emergence of an even more permissive society perhaps both played their parts in this, but there was also, I think, a recognition that the law had no further role to play in this discussion.

The law is rarely successful in its attempts to police art. The tension between law and art is too great. A moralist will argue that art has no special privilege, and art that transgresses against, for example, the laws of decency should be punished. Artists, according to the moralist, have no right to greater license than any other section of the population. Artists, generally, beg to differ.

The nature of transgression in art, as in life, is intensely problematical. It has been argued that one of the roles of art is to conquer taboos, which brings with it the assumption that such taboo-breaking is always good, and anyone who objects to it is automatically narrow-minded, misguided, and guilty of oppressing the artistic imagination.

Yet not all restrictions are necessarily bad in themselves, just as not every act of transgression is worthy of note simply by the fact of its existence. Bad art does not enlarge the imagination, and an artist or writer who creates it is open to censure. Offensive and transgressive are not the same thing. Similarly, finding a piece of art objectionable is a perfectly valid critical response to it; seeking to suppress it on that basis is not.

Yet transgression in art is not limited to questions of moral or sexual license, although the subject is most frequently raised in public in such contexts. Literature is subject to certain constraints, some physical and material, others related to the nature of the form. Can we not look at Lawrence Sterne's *Tristram Shandy* and say that, in its questioning of the received notions of storytelling and its steadfast refusal to abide by what was expected of the novel in the middle of the eighteenth century, it is a profoundly transgressive work, a postmodern novel before there was any "modern" to be "post" about? Or what of B.S. Johnson's 1969 novel *The Unfortunates,* which was published in a box containing twenty-seven separate chapters, one of which was marked first, one last, with twenty-five others that could be shuffled around as the reader wished? It is experimental, certainly, but is it not also transgressive in its attempt to overcome the limitations on the formal structure of a printed work? In other words, for the writer, as for any artist, transgression may not merely be a matter of subject, but of form. The transgressive abhors that which is self-enclosed, and rejoices in openness. It rejects the notion of purity, and instead revels in mongrelization. It is the art of the hybrid, of broken things.

More recently, there was the controversy over Salman Rushdie's novel, *The Satanic Verses,* first published in 1988, which led to a *fatwa,* a sentence of death, being declared on Rushdie by Iran's Ayatollah Khomeini because of the novel's perceived slighting of Islam (and arguably Islam continues to be the single most significant cultural, religious, and social boundary that artists may transgress, even at peril of their lives). Looking back, what is fascinating about the Rushdie controversy is the variety of responses it provoked from Rushdie's fellow authors. Their support for him was far from universal, with Roald Dahl and John le Carré being among the loudest of the dissenting voices. Clearly, it seemed, transgression was not something to be defended on principle, even by one's own peers.

There is one significant act of transgression that I have deliberately left until the end of this introduction, precisely because it is so relevant to some of the authors that follow, and that is crime. A number of the contributors to this volume are best known as mystery writers, but there are some difficulties in presenting crime as a purely transgressive action. In part, this is because the definition of an act as "criminal" is a matter of law, but at the same time it is difficult to deny the element of choice involved in the commission of certain crimes, or the fascination, even appeal, that criminal behavior may hold for us. A crime of passion is not necessarily transgressive, even if one might take the view that it breaches the taboo of unjustly taking a human life, because it lacks control, or perhaps planning and intent. It is born out of a rush of blood, an excess of feeling. Similarly, a starving woman who steals a loaf of bread could be considered to have done so out of necessity in a moment of weakness governed by blind appetite, not will.

But those criminals who choose to kill, to steal, to break, who, in the words of J. Katz in *Seductions of Crime* (1988), "take pride in a defiant reputation as 'bad,'" are of a different breed, and their actions resonate with us precisely because they are a dark shadow of the desire that lies within each of us to breach, however occasionally, the constraints imposed upon our behavior, and glimpse for a moment the possibility of the infinite. To quote Katz again: "Perhaps in the end, what we find so repulsive about studying the reality of crime . . . is the piercing reflection we catch when we steady our glance at these evil men."

There may be stories in this collection that you find difficult to like, or of which you may actively disapprove. There will be stories that may remind you of your own past acts, and stories dealing with acts that you believe you could never commit. Yet each of them touches upon the basic human urge to trangress, and in this you will find a certain sense of commonality, however uncomfortable it may be. Remember, after all, the words of Terence, which were inscribed upon the ceiling of the great essayist Montaigne:

"I am a man: nothing human is foreign to me."

Love me

Ten Gallons of Infected Saliva, or, The Cuckold, Avenged
Scott Phillips

You couldn't join the projectionist's union without experience you couldn't get without being in the union, but I wanted to be one so bad I persisted until finally Barney Sack, a wizened old pro from the Fox Twin downtown, took pity on me and told me that the union would count hours worked at certain select non-union theatres.

"Which non-union theatres?" The notion baffled me, since I'd applied for work at every movie theatre in town and been rebuffed at each for lack of a union card.

"Fuck movies," Barney said. I thought he was cursing the entire medium; I must have had a blank look on my face, because after a few seconds he squinted and hit me on the shoulder. "You know. Dirty movies. Raincoats and Kleenex. Kind of thing you watch with your pants around your ankles. The Air Capital out west on Kellogg's got a special deal with the union."

"I don't think that would be a good job for me," I said, thinking mostly of what I'd tell my parents, who were already worried I was going to quit college and start associating with a low crowd. We were in the booth waiting for a reel change on *The Deer Hunter* in Cinema One.

"One of their guys just quit. If you go in with my say-so they'll take you on. Keep it to yourself but I jerryrigged their changeover system myself, under the table. I don't imagine they pay for shit but that's what you get when you're a fucking scab."

I STOPPED IN THE AIR CAPITAL CINEMA the same afternoon, emboldened by the certainty that my bad fortune would persist, and that I could at least tell Barney I'd given it a shot. The manager was behind the combination box office and concession stand, selling dirty playing cards and prophylactics alongside the popcorn and Good & Plentys. His robin's egg-blue tuxedo was a much larger version of the one I'd worn to my Junior Prom, and remarkably clean considering that he must have worn it almost daily.

His distracting wheeze I put down at first to lung disease, until I figured out that it was just the strain of moving his bulk from one leg to the other; when I asked him months later why he didn't get a swivel chair to sit on he muttered something about the unhealthiness of the sedentary American lifestyle.

His name was Hurd Mackey, and though he had good things to say about Barney and the union, he ignored my question about why the Haven and its sister theatre the Pageant were allowed to remain union free. "You've operated a projector, I assume."

"A sixteen millimeter one, at Wichita State."

"Pfft. You know what Werner Herzog says? 'Sixteen millimeter is an amateur medium.' Come on upstairs, I'll show you the works and introduce you to Anders, the other projectionist."

The stairs were disastrously steep, which spared me having to ask my next question, which was why he was working concessions and box office instead of the projection booth. He heaved and panted as he climbed ahead of me, lurching so badly I thought at one point he was having a heart attack and actually took a couple of steps downward to get out of his way. At the top a man of sixty or so wearing overalls and nothing else stared at me while we both waited for Hurd, his muttonchops glistening and plastered down with sweat, to catch his breath.

"New man, Tuesday, Wednesday, Thursday nights," Hurd managed, then went back to gasping.

Anders nodded and returned his attention to the window. On the screen a chesty blonde was getting mounted from behind by one guy while she sucked off another. Though I'd spent my adolescence enslaved to various titty mags, this was my first introduction to real hard-core smut. That the print was badly scratched and faded to a thin blue, and the sound tinny as an AM radio, hardly mattered compared to the fact that sexual intercourse was happening unsimulated onscreen.

Anders had started paying close attention to the screen, then he bared his teeth, reached down and yanked hard on a big wooden knob with a screeching noise that must have been audible in the seats below as the projector on the left started rewinding.

"Why don't you put some oil on that fucking thing," Hurd said.

"I oil it once a week. That's the way Barney made it."

"Hey, Barney's the one sent the kid over. What's your name again?" he asked me.

"Ace," I said. It was Amos, but I was trying to build a new persona, and I was tired of being known, as I inevitably was in any circle I ended up in, as "Anus."

"All right, Ace, you start Tuesday. Come in at six and you can train with Anders here, then Wednesday you're on your own. Refreshments are free but you got to pay for any adult materials, 30 percent off."

I glanced around the moldy booth. In one corner was a table stacked with what looked like hardcore magazines, and next to it was a kleenex box and a trash can. I couldn't help noticing that there wasn't any place to wash your hands up there.

THE PASSENGER WINDOW of my sleek red '77 Opel came down, and my girlfriend of only three weeks expectorated a mouthful of my semen and her saliva in a graceful arc onto the drive-in pavement. I took advantage of the awkward aftermath to tell her about the job, unsure of what reaction to expect.

"It's just a union thing." Old and unmaintained though it was, the speaker hanging off my window provided a clearer, brighter tone than the PA at the Air Capitol Cinema. "I'm not sure what I think about porno."

To my considerable relief Sandy gave me a snort of derision. "Didn't we just watch Fonda getting off on the legless guy a minute ago, there?"

"They're pretending. Jane Fonda wouldn't have real sex on camera."

"Looked pretty real to me." She straightened herself up in her seat and returned her attention to the movie.

"We can go now if you want," I told her. Having seen the dirty part, and my knob having been swabbed, my interest in the whole drive-in concept was pretty well exhausted.

It was a hot night and I'd stripped off my t-shirt for the blowjob, and she reached for it off the backseat. "I want to see the rest of it." She wiped her mouth with the shirt, tongue and inside cheeks included, and I snatched it away.

"My shirt's not a cumrag."

"Fine. It's great for my mouth, but not on your shirt."

"It's my Jim Morrison shirt."

"I'm sure it's not the first time he's wiped spunk off some coed."

"We've both seen this already, let's go."

"I want to see the part where Dern calls her slope-cunt and walks into the ocean."

"I'm going to get a Coke then."

"Get me a Sprite, you owe me now."

I put my cum-stained shirt back on and hiked back to the refreshment stand. The night was sticky and buggy, half the cars rocking to the tune of teenage intercourse, and the saliva on the shirt actually felt pretty good against the heat.

While I waited in line behind a stoned couple who couldn't decide what they wanted though we'd been in line a good ten minutes, my friend Tad poked my shoulder and asked me how the job search was going. He was thrilled at the idea of my working at a place we often discussed but had never actually had the nerve to visit, but his lip curled when I asked him how his own work was going.

"I broke an old lady's jaw today."

"Accidentally or on purpose?"

"They sent me on my first solo housecall. I was stapling the jaw shut and I'd only done it a couple times before and never on an old lady with osteoporosis. Fucking lower jaw just snapped inward into two pieces."

"She probably didn't care."

"Her family sure did. I thought her grandson was going to fuck me up good."

He'd been fired from three jobs since tenth grade, all of them for major fuckups: a co-worker burned with fryer grease, a totaled delivery van, a two-hundred dollar funeral spray crumpled into salad beneath a dozen crates of roses. The unfairness of it rankled more than the job losses themselves; Tad was a hard worker, dedicated and possessed of a sterling work ethic. I on the other hand hadn't ever lost a job, despite a deep-seated disinclination toward making anything but the slightest token effort.

"Think you could get me some hours there? I may not be long for the Mattingley Brothers."

"I'll ask," I said, wondering what kind of damage Tad could do at a porno house.

"There's another reason I may not last at the funeral home." He bounced up and down on the balls of his feet, a deranged grin on his face. "I'm slipping the meat to Mrs. Mattingley."

"One medium Coke and one medium Sprite and a large popcorn, extra butter," I said to the counter girl. She looked at Tad and blushed, which he didn't seem to notice.

"Did you hear what I said? I'm fucking the boss's wife."

"I heard," I said, fairly impressed. Skinny, bug-eyed Tad had a way with girls I could only put down to his supreme self-confidence.

THE JOB AGREED WITH ME. By September I could do pretty much any job that needed doing at the theatre, and I was only in the projection booth my original three nights a week. The rest of the time I ran the ticket counter and concessions and cleaned up, which left plenty of time to do homework. "That's okay with me," Hurd said when he first found me doing math problems sitting behind the counter. "Long as you keep the spunk cleaned up off the crapper floor."

Hurd started disappearing earlier and earlier in the evenings, so I was locking the place up some nights. He didn't have a phone at home, and if any problem arose that I really couldn't handle I was screwed. But the theatre was a pretty quiet place most of the time, and the only melodrama usually involved some guy trying to jack some other guy off who didn't want to be jacked off, not by another guy anyway.

Sandy came up into the booth with me to screw a few times those first weeks, thrilled at the thought of doing it in a house of filth, but the thrill wore off soon after that and I started going to her apartment straight after work. The relentlessly masturbatory atmosphere of the Air Capital Cinema made the thought of jerking off became tedious and finally distasteful, and with Sandy as a sexual outlet I stopped masturbating entirely (at least for a while). This didn't hold for everyone; the available evidence pointed to Anders jerking off constantly during his shifts. Once I caught him beating his meat to a magazine entitled *The Wonderful World of Assholes*. He claimed he hadn't heard me coming up the creaky stairs and seemed not in the least embarrassed to have been interrupted, which I suppose made sense considering that there was an auditorium below us filled with guys more or less openly doing the same thing.

IN NOVEMBER Tad called me up at the theatre. "I'm bringing her in," he said, laughing.

"Bringing who in?"

"Beth, dumbass. I'm bringing her in to watch a porno. She's never seen one before."

"Who's Beth? She a new one?"

"Beth Mattingley. The boss's wife."

I DIDN'T TRY TO TALK HIM OUT OF IT, but I didn't encourage it either. It got weird when women came in. For one thing we had to watch out for prostitutes, since that could get us busted. For another, some guys got flustered when a woman came into the theatre and skulked out. And then one time a middle-aged guy with a lot of gold chains and aviator sunglasses (indoors, at night) came in with a younger woman with elaborately teased blond hair and a lot of real-looking jewelry. They went in to the feature and fifteen minutes later came out screaming at me. Once I calmed them down enough to speak coherently I understood that someone sitting directly behind them had ejaculated onto the top of the lady's hairdo. Whoever it was had apparently de-camped, and all I could offer was a refund and an apology.

TAD SHOWED UP AT NINE FIFTEEN with a woman on his arm. I guess I expected her to be some kind of cross between Mrs. Robinson and Jennifer O'Neal in Summer of '42, but she was a pretty average look-ing lady of forty or so, kind of skinny, with a purple dress on and shoes that matched it exactly. Her hair was auburn and straight down to her shoulders with a flip, and she looked really excited, like she and Tad were robbing a bank or something. There was a little smudge of lipstick on her uper left incisor, and I couldn't stop glancing guiltily down at a run in her pantyhose. She had nice legs, actually, and while we stood there talking I started thinking she wasn't so bad looking after all. She was drunk, too, and giggling. "She has three kids," he'd told me once. "All being groomed for the priesthood or the mortuary industry." Tad looked back at me and grinned as he led her into the auditorium to enjoy our current feature, *Up the Ass with People*.

I SETTLED BACK, looking at a copy of *Lesbian Dildo Bondage*, number 7. It was a title we weren't allowed to carry in the shop next door, part of an unwritten agreement between management and the Vice Squad, but a copy had been sent in a shipment by mistake and I was think-ing about taking it home to Sandy, who liked me to describe the smut I'd watched at work, even though she didn't like watching it herself. The door opened and a slender, worn-out looking guy in a heavy over-coat came in.

"When's the feature start?"

"It's continuous."

"What do you mean continuous?" The idea seemed to infuriate him.

"It runs all the time, when it stops we start it again."

"When's the beginning going to happen? I hate to walk in in the middle."

"I don't know."

"How can you not know? It's a movie theatre."

"Look, mostly people just go in, watch a little bit and come out when they're done."

"What do you mean, when they're done?"

"When they've had their fill, you know."

He was taking in little short breaths through his nose and tapping his left toe against the counter in a rapid tattoo. This was my least favorite kind of customer, the kind who's really disgusted and outraged by the thought of fuck flicks, but buys a ticket anyway. They were probably the ones who got the biggest thrill out of the whole enterprise, though.

"You mean when they're done masturbating."

"No, sir." One of the first things Hurd had drummed into me was that we never, ever acknowledged to any outsider that we were aware that the sin of Onan was practiced in our theatre. "I don't think that's what they do."

"Like hell," he said. "They're jerking off in there right now, and worse, I bet."

"Are you going to buy a ticket, sir? Admission is seven dollars."

"Seven bucks? You're out of your goddamned mind. A movie's four, four fifty."

"Seven dollars, mister."

He reached inside his overcoat and pulled out a revolver. It looked heavy, and he waved it around, never quite pointing it at me but scaring me shitless nonetheless. He took it into the auditorium, and I sat there for a minute trying to think what to do. Finally I picked up the house phone and rang the booth.

"What is it?" Anders said.

"Guy just busted into the auditorium without buying a ticket."

"What'd you let him do that for?"

"He had a gun."

Anders was quiet. "Shit."

"Should I call the cops?"

"Never, ever call the cops, boy, unless a crime's been committed of the kind we can't deal with ourselves."

He hung up on me, and I debated calling the cops anyway. I stood up and walked to the doors, pulled one of them open slightly. I thought I could see the guy, seated toward the back in a row by himself. In the front sat Tad and Mrs. Mattingley, wrestling, while the rest of the audience watched them as attentively as they did the movie.

I sat back down on my stool at the booth and started doing my homework in a distracted way, memorizing dialogues in German about going to the lakeshore and renting a boat. It was a good ten minutes later, as Monika und Hans were discussing the possibility of a second day on the lake, that the shot went off, explosive and cracking, followed by a woman's scream.

A customer blew out the doors with his dick hanging out his pants. "Hey, mister, what was that?" I asked as he disappeared through the front door without answering.

The phone rang, and not knowing how else to react I picked up.

"What the fuck was that?" Anders said. "That your buddy with the gun, shooting people?"

"He's not my buddy. Think we should call the cops?"

"Fuck, no," Anders said. "I'll put on the house lights and you check it out."

INSIDE THE AUDITORIUM most of the audience was cowering on the floor, including Tad and Mrs. Mattingley. They were starting to peer up over the seats to see where the shot had come from, and I heard a few groans of disgust and horror as they registered the sight of the dead man in the overcoat, revolver in hand, braincase blown two rows behind him, bone and blood all over the back of the theatre. God-damn it, I was the one going to have to clean this shit up.

People started standing. Mrs. Mattingley, the only woman in the whole building, screamed again when she saw the body, the scream transforming itself slowly into keening as she stumbled up the aisle toward the corpse. When she reached it she threw herself on it, sobbing, her clothes slick and sticky with fresh blood. In front of the screen, upon which a wholesome-looking blonde girl was taking it up the poop chute from a guy dressed as a sailor, stood Tad, looking for once like he wasn't in on a secret joke, and I pushed open the auditorium doors to buzz Anders upstairs and ask if it was okay to call the cops now.

No Thanks, Please
Declan Burke

Heads turned, half-curious, then full-faced in horror. A man started towards her, one hand out as if reaching to catch a low driven ball, but she walked on, turning up off the river under the arch at Christchurch and on down Patrick Street.

A condom in the gutter with a used teabag inside. A Labrador puppy cocking a leg at its reflection in a puddle. Italian names on car tires. Each new thing reminded her why she was looking in these places for the first time. Not to avoid the shame she would see mirrored in their eyes or the degradation she might glimpse in some angled shop window. It simply hurt too much to roll her right eye up against the bruising. So she kept her head down and her shoulders hunched, arms loosely folded to cradle her ribs.

Now her feet began to hurt. At first the pain was a sharp pinching where the stiff leather folded across the knuckles of her small toes, but soon it became a chafing and melted down in a raw burn. She realized the blisters had burst but she did not stop. She thought that if she stopped walking she would fall down and die. This was who she was now: a woman who might die if she ever stopped walking.

She tried to remember her name.

HE RATTLED THE PAPER IN FOLDING IT, then slammed the pen down. This was his quiet time, mid-afternoon, a time for the crossword, a smoke. He crossed the apartment in two strides and jammed a forefinger against the red button.

"Yes?"

But all he heard was the intercom hiss and a low, rasping breathing. "Look," he said, "if I have to go down there ..." Then he heard the faint, choked-off sob.

"Janey?" His stomach churned. "Janey? Is that you?"

The sob broke.

He didn't open the door wide enough and slammed his shoulder on the frame on the way through.

HE MINISTERED TO HER CUTS AND BRUISES using paper tissues and Dettol. But it was awkward, leaning in from so far away. She would flinch back even before he touched her.

"I'm not going to hurt you, Janey. I just want to———"

"I know," she whispered.

She had bawled at first, raw and honking until the whiskeys seeped through. Then she had whimpered, shoulders shaking with rage and fear and the tremors of a pure adrenaline charge. Now she seemed blank and dry, like old cardboard. "I just," she said, "I ..."

He waited for her to finish but she only winced and hunched forward, arms folded below her chest.

"Janey, I really think we should get you to the ER. Those ribs should be———"

"It's too late now." She nodded at the empty glass. "It's the first thing they'll ask, was I drinking."

"But I gave you the whiskey, to calm you down. I'll be your———"

"Jay? James?"

"What?"

"Can you run me a bath? Can you do that for me? A warm bath?"

"But shouldn't you wait until after you get ...?"

But she was rocking herself, features flinty and set against the world at an impossible angle. He put the paper tissues on the arm of the chair and left the room.

WHEN SHE SAID, "I'll need you to help me get undressed," he could almost taste the loathing that coated her tongue.

"Of course," he said. "Whatever. Janey, just ask. Anything you want."

She nodded, staring at a fixed point between the coffee table and who she used to be.

"You can stay here, no worries," he went on. "He won't get in here." He ground his teeth. "He can fucking try, but he'll be leaving backwards, in three fucking body bags."

She made a sucking sound, ran her tongue between her teeth and her split upper lip. "Jay? Did you leave the bath running?"

"Fuck."

HE MOPPED THE FLOOR WITH DIRTY TOWELS, poured in a handful of fizzy salts. Called her from the bathroom door and watched her lurch down the hallway like an aging monster. She turned her back to him and he eased her t-shirt up over her shoulders, unhooked her bra, slid her denims over her hips and down past her knees. He experienced the frisson he had been dreading but when it was past he was unable to say if it had been the expected sexual rush or a profound reaction to engaging with the most vulnerable intimacy he had ever known.

The abrasion on her back ran from one shoulder blade almost to her kidneys. It looked as if he had attacked her with a wire-wool scrub. He quivered, felt his jaws lock in place.

"I'll be right next door, Janey," he said, retreating. "If there's anything, just shout."

"It hurts when I talk."

He closed the door as gently as he knew how and backed away down the hall wondering what his next move should be. The grating of the key was a kick in the gut.

HE SLIPPED OUT to the small Spar on Patrick Street. A pizza, garlic bread, a bottle of vodka, a carton of orange juice, some Panadol. At the checkout a stout middle-aged woman leaned across the counter to the young bottle-blonde till jockey. He edged closer until they could no longer ignore him. The older woman turned and drew herself up.

"Can we help you?" she asked. Dry pink powder grouted the corners of her mouth.

"My friend was beaten up," he said, nodding at the armful of groceries. "She's a woman," he explained. "Her husband beat her up."

Their eyes glazed over, tiny pools freezing fast.

"She's taking a bath," he added, as if that might help them thaw.

"You left her alone?" the bottle-blonde said.

"She locked the door."

"You shouldn't have left her alone," the stout woman said. "God love her." Her hand was a hummingbird as she blessed herself, bringing her forehead down to meet the fingers, the wicker carrier-bag heavy on her elbow. "How bad?" she said.

"I'm going to kill him."

The stout woman stood back to allow him to put the armful of groceries on the counter. "Now hush," she said. "That's no way to talk."

"How?" the bottle-blonde said, waving the pizza at the side of the till until she heard the beep of barcode recognition. He stared at her. "How are you going to kill him?" she said, picking up the orange juice.

"Now, Tricia," the stout woman said.

"I'm going to eat his fucking throat out," he said.

The bottle-blonde bagged his groceries and put out her hand. "Don't just say it," she said. She rang up the transaction, returned his change. "I don't believe you," she said.

SHE ATE STEADILY, without interest or appetite, and he despised himself for having to look away from the loose gaping of the bathrobe. She took two more painkillers and sipped her vodka-orange and stared vacantly at the TV.

"Are you sure you don't want to ring the cops?" he said.

She nodded.

"And you definitely don't want to go to the hospital."

She nodded again, weary.

"Are you going to stay here tonight?"

"No." The word deader than stone.

"You're going back?"

She nodded.

"Jesus, Janey …" Her eyes flickered away from the screen and came to rest on his. "If he's done it once he'll do it again. Go back now and you're telling him it's okay. You're giving him the *right*, Janey."

"Don't you think that's a bit simplistic?"

"What's so complicated about being kicked in the head?"

She waited. "This is about me," she said quietly.

"It's you I'm trying to help."

Her eyes flickered back to the screen.

"At least let me ring Caroline," he said. "What's her number?"

"She's minding the girls," she said. She drained her vodka-orange and stood up slowly.

"At least they weren't around to see it," he said, and just like that, as if she had suddenly seen it through her daughters' eyes, a thin orangey vomit spewed.

"AT LEAST," he said, re-hooking her bra, "let me come in with you. Just so he knows you're not alone."

"So he knows there's someone like him, just ready to go."

"Fuck sakes, Janey …"

"You can come in," she said. "If you can admit that you need to come in for you, then you can come in."

"Okay," he said. "I'm only doing it for me. So my conscience is clear. Happy?"

"No," she said. She walked to the car barefoot.

HE DROVE UP PAST THE CANAL, out through Donnybrook, taking the N11 all the way to Foxrock. He vaguely remembered the estate from the house-warming party. When they pulled in to the curb she stared into the setting sun, face immobile below the sunglasses he'd given her.

"You don't have to do this," he said.

"See the icebergs?" she said.

"What?"

She nodded, and he turned to look. Light wisps of orange-tinged cirrus hung suspended above the sun. And it was true: three small, hard, glittering clouds had the appearance of icebergs floating in a patch of light blue sky. "How would that happen?" she said. "What are they?"

He shrugged. "I don't know."

She couldn't reach up far enough to open the front door and so she handed him the key. They walked through the downstairs, then checked upstairs, but he wasn't home. She didn't want him to wait.

"Not here," he said. "But I'm going to wait down the road. And when he comes home, I'm coming back in. Someone needs to tell him what's what."

"And what's that?" she said. They were standing in the hall, the front door ajar.

"This isn't about you," he said. "It's about him."

"It's about you," she said.

"He has to learn. I'm only going to warn him."

She bit her lip and looked down. "It wasn't Sean," she whispered.

He frowned. "Then who?"

"I don't know."

"You were jumped?"

"Jay," she pleaded, "trust me."

But he was adamant, insisting. She backed away into the corner behind the door and when he took a step towards her the words tumbled out as if they might fend him off. Job. Lost. Mortgage. Sean. Friend. Company.

"No fooling around, though," she said. She sounded dull, a sleepwalker. "That was the deal. Just company. For the races at Leopardstown. Just drinks and company."

And all he could think to say was, "You walked all the way in from fucking Leopardstown?"

"There was another girl," she said. "In the room. I think she was Thai." She reached up and removed the sunglasses, holding them out for him to take. Her right eye was closed behind a blackening bruise spreading from forehead to cheek. "They preferred her."

He swallowed dry. "Where is she now?"

"I don't know," she said.

"What room, though?"

"I don't fucking *know*," she whispered.

He didn't believe her.

HE DROVE TO THE FAR SIDE OF THE GREEN in the middle of the estate and reversed the car so that he was looking directly at the house. He opened the boot, found the wheel-brace, sat into the car again and lit a cigarette, huddling back in the seat to watch the house over the rim of the steering wheel.

Sean arrived walking, maybe an hour or so later. Smaller than James remembered, stick-thin even beneath the overcoat. He trudged to the driveway and stood outside looking up at the house with his hands buried deep in the pockets. Then his shoulders seemed to fall forward and he trudged up the driveway. He reached with the key, reconsidered, and rang the doorbell instead. He rang three times before the door opened, but when it did he stepped inside straight away.

Now Jay got out of the car and jogged across the green, sidling up the side of the driveway out of sight of the living room window. He gained the porch and stood with his back to the wall, half-crouched, the wheel-brace held rigid behind his thigh. Then he punched the doorbell with his forefinger and left it there, jammed down.

They didn't answer. Four times he pressed the doorbell, half-crouched against the wall, looking out at the quiet estate. Wondering if he could be seen from behind the lowered blinds that faced their house. He pounded on the door but no one came.

He looked out across the estate to where the sun was sinking behind the horizon. The icebergs were gone. The porchlights hummed, flickered, winked on. On the far side of the green his car seemed impossibly distant.

He wondered how long was reasonable to stay before walking away.

Word Games
Bryon Quertermous

"Fuck," Larry Pierce says to the guy in front of him.

"I don't get it," the guy says, with a mouth full of mall pretzel and lemonade. "Four letters and it's dirty just because it has to do with men and women and their dirty business?"

"What if your kid said it in front of you?"

"I don't have kids, but I know I talked a streak and a half with my buddies when I was younger."

"Your parents ever hear you?"

"My mom did once—and I got a mouth full of no-brand liquid soap for the effort. She didn't want to waste the good soap on me, I guess."

"Was it *that* word?"

"The F word?"

"Fuck," Larry said.

"No. Not that one."

"But you don't think that one is any worse than the others?"

"Four letters. Not like they ever killed anyone."

Larry clicks his tape recorder off and thanks the man for his time.

KERRI DADE HAS A CUSTOMER up her ass and is contemplating what
to give the kids for a snack when they came home from school. She's
thinking pizza bagels when the customer pumps too hard again and
she cramps.

"Fuck," she says. "Be careful."

"Mmmmm."

The customer finishes quick enough and falls face-first onto the
bed. Kerri hates anal, especially with the damn hemorrhoids that seem
to be getting more frequent, but it's good for more money when she
needs it and they always finish quick. After the customer leaves, she
takes a long shower and orders a steak sandwich from room service.
She eats the sandwich and watches Dr. Phil until it's time to go pick
up her son Dan and his friend from school.

The pizza bagels calm the boys down enough for her to concentrate on some school work. Most days she'll take a cock to the ass over
another stack of student sociology papers, but this class is one of her
favorites, featuring one of her favorite students. The stack in front of
her is proposals for the final field research project and his is on top.
She's pretty sure he only wrote it as an excuse to use the word "fuck"
in the classroom, but she likes the idea behind it and encouraged him
to explore it. Nothing else in the stack excites her and she's happy for
the distraction, when the doorbell rings.

"Uncle Mike," Dan yells.

Mike isn't Dan's uncle and Kerri knows what this is about. This
shit is getting old. The boys are harassing him for money when she
makes it out to the foyer but Mike is almost twice as tall as the boys
and has arms strong enough for them to hang on. He looks more like
a linebacker than a, well, than a pimp. He calls himself her business
manager, but a business manager would never give her a black eye if
a customer shortchanged her.

THE MIDDLE SCHOOL BASKETBALL GAME is in full swing when Larry
Pierce pulls into the lot. He'd talked to teenagers and middle-aged
adults at the mall, but he wants to see how they react to the word
around each other. Maybe he'll even be able to find a pervert to test.

At the mall he struck gold at the food court, so Larry decides to play the same card here and makes his way to the concession stand.

"I'm wondering how you feel about the word 'fuck,'" Larry says to a man and his daughter.

He expects a punch and is ready to dodge, but the man throws his nachos instead. When the nachos don't knock Larry over or send him running away screaming, the suburban father, obviously not used to this kind of confrontation, steps back and lets his daughter talk to Larry.

"Nasty," the girl says.

Larry figures she's about fourteen or fifteen. He holds out his tape recorder so the father can see he isn't a total nut job.

"The word itself is nasty, or what it represents?" Larry asks.

"You mean like sex or like swearing?"

"What are you asking my daughter about sex for? How the hell did you get in here?"

The girl says, "I say worse than that with my friends."

"Annie, shut the hell up, would you? I apologize for my daughter. She lives with her mother and her mother's degenerate tattoo artist boyfriend."

"You should have seen him at dinner last night," Annie says. "He was talking all about this chick he got to pierce in the clit and he was all excited and shit and mom was just looking at him like she was going to explode."

"Don't say clit. That's nasty."

"Have you ever washed your daughter's mouth out with soap?" Larry asks.

"We really need to be getting back to the game," the father says.

KERRI LEADS MIKE UPSTAIRS to the spare bedroom and sits down on the double bed.

"Always the spare bedroom," he says. "I thought we'd be closer than that after so many years."

"Why are you here?"

"You insulted my brother today."

"I didn't even know you had a brother. Nobody showed up and said—"

"You told him to be careful during anal. Guys don't pay whores to be careful. They look at porn to be careful. They fuck their *wives* to be careful. They pay whores to fuck in the ass, and they break the whore's fucking hips if they want."

"I'm sorry. I'll do whatever next time. But right now I've got to—"

"Right now you're going to prove you can handle what I send you."

"My kid and his friend are downstairs ..."

"Be a shame if either of them found out what really paid for this lifestyle."

Kerri bends over. Mike is a big guy everywhere but his cock. Taking him is embarrassing, but nothing she hasn't taken before. She pulls down her sweat pants and grabs the edge of the bed, bracing for penetration. Nothing happens. After a second she turns around to see Mike digging around in his backpack. He pulls out an enormous silver dildo that looks like a baseball bat from the future.

"Mike," she says, "I was—"

"I've got a reputation. I've got customers who can't just stick it anywhere. They need to be assured that—"

"It's not my regular trick, Mike."

He hits her with the dildo and splits her nose. She wants to punch him in the nuts, but that'll just piss him off and send him into a rage. It's hard enough explaining to people how she lives like this on a teacher's salary; it would be even harder if she's out of work with a broken body.

Jesus, can that thing even fit inside her?

Mike pushes her onto the bed and spreads her legs apart with the dildo.

"Scream and I start over again," he says.

She spreads her legs a little more and breathes like the bimbo down at the yoga center taught her. The dildo slides in easier than she expects. Mike is a gentle rapist but it still hurts. And it keeps going in until it feels like he's going to hit her spleen.

"Should I be careful?" Mike asks.

Kerri doesn't say anything.

THE FIRST DAY OF CLASS with Kerri Dade, Larry fell for her. The night she agreed to be his advisor for grad school, Larry followed her home just to see where she lived and keep her in his life a little bit longer. He didn't think he was creepy or anything, but he realized most perverts didn't know they were perverts.

Dr. Dade lives in the Palmer Woods section of the city, full of big old houses that used to belong to auto barons and other Detroit royalty. A nice Target superstore opened in the area a few months ago as part of renewed activity in the city, and every once in a while Larry pops in, hoping to run into her. Her car isn't in the parking lot when he pulls in tonight, but things can always change.

THERE'S NOTHING IN THE HOUSE more potent than aspirin so Kerri needs to pick up some extra strength pain reliever and a big ass jug of wine. The place around the corner from her house trends more toward the young and obnoxious than she cares for, but it's starting to rain and they'll have what she needs. She has her arms full of food when someone sneaks up behind her.

"Hey," Larry Pierce says, a little too loud.

Kerri twitches and drops the jug of wine and her bottle of pain killer. The jug explodes, spraying her and the floor.

"Oh fuck," she says. "God fucking damn it. Hi, Larry. I'm sorry."

"I didn't mean to sneak up on you, I mean I wasn't sure if it was you and I didn't want to look like a … oh wait, hey, let me help you. Oh, your nose. Are you OK?"

"Yes, just clumsy. Grab me another jug and let's get out of here before one of those weird kids comes over here to clean up."

"Are you going to, um, I mean should we go through the checkout first?"

"You think I'd steal wine? My job doesn't pay that bad."

"Oh no, that's not what I meant. You have a very nice house; I figured you probably made some decent change. I just figured with what you said about—"

"You've been to my house?"

Kerri is very careful not to let her students into her personal life.

Not since the last school. Not since the last one found out how she really paid for the big house.

"You must have talked about it in class or something. I shouldn't have said anything."

Kerri smiles. He looks cute when he backpedals. There's no maliciousness in his words, just charming desperation. He helps her through the checkout and neither of them say anything else until they're outside.

"I don't invite students back to my house."

"I didn't mean to say that I've been to your house or anything. I was just—"

"But you owe me a favor and I obviously shouldn't be carrying my own groceries. Since you already know where I live I guess I can let my guard down."

THE BOYS ARE IN THE TV ROOM with a loud video game sucking their attention. Larry carries the groceries in and tries to leave.

"How's the project coming?" Kerri asks.

"I've been thinking about the sex part of it more," he says.

"Tell me more."

Larry doesn't answer right away. His fingers tap nervously on the counter and Kerri can't help but think about other things those long, tender fingers could tap.

"The truth is, I'm more comfortable with the swearing part of the paper."

"You've got a nasty mouth on you, eh?"

"No, nothing like that really. I've just heard it more and … well, you know what I mean."

"Oh my god, are you still a virgin?"

"No, no way. It's not like that. I mean I'm not like a whore or anything. But yeah, I'm a little less … experienced in that area."

"So you say fuck more than you actually fuck?"

Larry smiles.

"Yeah."

"I've had a rough day," Kerri says, standing from the table.

"Oh jeez, I'm sorry, I shouldn't have stayed this long."

"That's not what I'm saying."

She takes his hand and drags him upstairs to her bedroom.

"No anal," she says. "My ass is like—"

Larry shuts her up with a sloppy, amateurish kiss full of saliva and teeth.

"Can I go down on you?"

Kerri tugs her sweat pants off and flops spread eagle onto her bed. She's hairier than normal, one of her regulars pays extra for it, but that doesn't seem to slow Larry down. With his lack of experience, Kerri expects him to go straight for the clit, but he surprises her by starting with her inner thigh.

"Jesus," she says.

He curls his fingers up inside her so they're pressing against the top of her vaginal wall. The pressure sends a throb of pleasure through her spine and he follows with a hard lick right under her clit that arches her back. The initial wave dissipates and Kerry thinks it's over, but then Larry starts moving his fingers in rhythm to his licking and it doesn't take long for him to send her over the edge. Before she has a chance to recover, Larry is on top of her, maneuvering his narrow cock inside her.

Under any other circumstances, Larry would be considered small and disappointing, but Kerri is still tender from her last encounter and Larry knows exactly where to hit her with his head. A few minutes into it, he rolls her on top of him and starts grinding into her hips.

"Jesus," she says again. "That needs to go in the paper."

LARRY STILL HAS AN ERECTION when he leaves the next morning because he can't stop thinking about the sex. Or what she told him afterward. It was a tender moment of intimacy and confession, but Larry keeps getting hung up on the visual of her with some other guy's dick up her ass and it makes him angry. Angry and hard. It's an awful feeling. Kerri sent him home with the jug of wine because she said she didn't like to keep alcohol in the house around her kid. She also said she wanted to see him again after class to talk about more physical aspects of his paper.

There's nobody home when Larry gets back to his house and he falls asleep to more dirty dreams. He takes a shower when he wakes up, mostly so he can masturbate without the mess, and wonders what to do to take his mind off of Kerri until it's time for class. Part of him wants to go over to her house or up to the school to see if he can run into her again. But their night together had been too amazing to jeopardize with something stupid like that.

KERRI GETS DAN OFF TO SCHOOL and damn near skips into the house with a smile on her face like she hasn't had since her last year of grad school before everything went screwy. She's changing into her baking clothes when Mike finds her. He's holding a brown lunch sack, standing in her bedroom door.

"I hope you gave the boy some money for lunch. Be a shame if he—"

"Get out of my house."

"Maybe your new boyfriend can protect you."

Kerri goes for the phone next to her bed, but Mike is faster and smacks it out of her hand.

"You pay for this house with the money you get from me. From the guys I send you. But that's not enough. You have to have a little something going on the side too?"

"He's one of my students."

"All of your students get to stick their head between your legs?"

"Fucking pervert. You were spying on me."

"There's no student discount. You fucked him and I want my money."

"I don't keep any money in the house."

"Let's go to the bank then."

Kerri has no intention of giving Mike any of her money. She's trying to think of ways to stall him when she hears the front door open downstairs. Dan. His lunch is still in Mike's hand.

"Mom?"

Mike leaves the bedroom and Kerri knows he's going to meet Dan. She's not going to let that happen. She grabs the gun from the top of her closet and makes sure it's loaded. Downstairs, Mike is holding Dan with one of Kerri's large kitchen knives near his neck.

"If you get to have something on the side, so do I," he says.

Kerri shoots Mike in the head without hesitation. Then she leaves a message on Larry's answering machine.

"YOU'VE GOT TO UNDERSTAND," Kerri says, "I did it for my boy."

"I know."

"That's why I was out last night, because of what this prick did to me. I was raw, in my ass and my emotions."

"That's why you slept with me?"

"It's something I've wanted to do for a long time. That was wonderful and beautiful and everything that Mike was not."

"You killed your pimp."

"My business manager."

"And you want me to help clean up?"

"I can't go to jail. Dan will have no one."

Everything she wants is implied in her face and body language, but she won't come right out and say it.

"I can do it," Larry finally says. "I can go to jail for you."

"It won't be a death penalty case because you can claim self-defense or something. And I heard on the news that they're giving guys who are wrongly imprisoned fifty grand for every year they're in jail."

Larry lights up at that.

"I could write with that money."

"Just a few years and I promise I'll come up with something. I'll get a lawyer to get you out. It shouldn't be hard because you didn't really kill him."

"You planned this?"

"Oh, no, baby, I wouldn't do this to you if it wasn't the only way."

"I'll be famous when I get out. If I don't get shanked in the yard first."

"About that," Kerri says. "I have an idea."

She takes Larry back upstairs and digs around in her closet until she finds an enormous black dildo with a veiny resemblance to an actual cock. Larry goes pasty white when she approaches him with it and holds his hand.

"You'll need to make a friend to stay safe," she says.

Larry starts to choke and tears catch in his eyes.

"I've learned a few things over the years," Kerri continues. "It doesn't have to be as bad as you think."

She kisses his ear as she unbuttons his pants and pushes them to his ankles.

"The first thing you'll need to learn is how to relax the muscles."

She spreads his legs apart with the dildo and tells him it's going to be okay.

The Biography of Stoop, the Thief

CHAPTER THREE: Stoop and Elizabeth

Steven Torres

Elizabeth Jones abandoned her son one day after he was born, the same day she named him Stupendous. For most of the fourteen years after that day, Stoop thought about her—where she might be, what type of person she was, whether she might love him if she ever got to know him well enough.

Once someone handed him a photo of her, or at least they thought it was her.

"If that ain't Lizzy Jones, then Lizzy ought to call the cops, 'cause someone done stole her face," the woman said.

"Can I keep this?" Stoop asked. He was about twelve at the time.

"Sure," the woman said, then she thought for a moment. "You got a dollar or something? Help a sister out?"

Stoop thought often of looking for his mother, but there wasn't time in the day—he maintained good grades, which kept social workers from looking in on him, and he had to go outside of the neighborhood several times a week to swipe the food and clothes he needed to keep body and soul together. Most days ended with his energy exhausted. When he dreamed, he dreamed of how his mother would hold his face and smile into his eyes when he found her.

Then one day he did.

He had traveled all the way to the Hunt's Point section of the Bronx—an area of factories and warehouses, wonder-filled hunting grounds for a person in his profession because there were always a hundred trucks being loaded and unloaded and not enough people keeping an open eye.

There were also drug dealers, addicts, and prostitutes enough to fill a dozen police vans. This day there were only two vans, two squad cars and eight police officers, one of them a lieutenant. They ignored Stoop with his box of men's fitted shirts. This day was for rounding up the addicts and dealers.

"Name," Stoop heard as he walked past an officer.

Stoop didn't turn to look; he knew the best thing was to keep walking.

"Elizabeth Jo…" the voice started. "Elizabeth George."

Stoop turned around to look at the woman as soon as he heard the stutter in the name. A glance told him he was looking at an older, worn version of the photo he had in his pocket. The word "mama" nearly escaped his lips.

He kept walking—no point in drawing attention to himself—and at the end of the block he dropped the box of shirts into a clump of tall grass. He searched the ground as he walked back to where his mother was now standing in a line, waiting to enter a van, her hands cuffed in front of her. He picked up a scrap of fencing wire.

There were three people ahead of Elizabeth Jones, filing into a police van, and two people behind her. One of the people behind her was a uniformed officer. Stoop tapped him on the shoulder.

"Two dealers just ran up that way," Stoop said. He pointed in the direction he just came from. "One of them had a gun out."

The officer looked back, then took a step over toward the lieutenant. Stoop moved to his mother's side, took the scrap metal to the handcuff locks, and had them off her in seconds. The cuffs and the wire fell to the ground, Stoop and Elizabeth started to walk off, and the man in line behind her moved up. It took him another minute to think he could have asked Stoop to do the same thing for him.

"Damn," he muttered to himself, but Stoop and Elizabeth had crossed the street and rounded the corner by then.

Looking over her shoulder a minute later, Elizabeth smiled broadly. She was rubbing her wrists though the cuffs hadn't been tight. She tapped Stoop on the sleeve.

"Who you?" she asked. They were still walking quickly.

"My name is Stupendous Jones," he answered.

"Stupendous," she repeated back. "That's a funny name if you don't mind me saying. Why I only knew one other person with that..."

Elizabeth stopped in her tracks.

"Stupendous JONES, you said?"

"It's not safe to stop here," Stoop answered. He took his mother gently by the upper arm and led her further from the cops and around another corner. After a few more steps with Elizabeth at his side, he pulled out the photograph of her and put it in her hands.

Elizabeth Jones stopped again for a moment.

"That's me?" she asked.

Stoop stopped just long enough to say, "I was hoping you'd tell me."

They walked on another block, made another turn, and Stoop led his mother, still looking at the picture intently, hardly believing her eyes, into a four-story apartment building. Inside, there was graffiti on the walls, household rubbish on the hallway floors, and a smell of rot in the air. Stoop jogged slowly up to the top floor, stopping at each landing to wait for his mother. She was still dazed.

Stoop unlocked the door to his apartment. His mother took a look around. There wasn't much to see—a torn couch, a milk crate with a board on it as a coffee table; the kitchen counter had a stack of Chef-Boy-Ardee cans. There was a bowl, a fork, a spoon and a pot.

"Want something to eat?" Stoop asked his mother, and she did.

The two talked long into the night. Elizabeth wanted to hear all about what Stoop had been doing with himself since the day after he was born. Stoop wanted to know all about what she did with herself, where she lived. He didn't ask why she had left him.

At three in the morning, Elizabeth got up and tried to sneak out of the apartment, but Stoop was sleeping too lightly. She smiled at him shyly.

"I need to …" She wasn't sure how to finish the sentence; she hadn't had enough practice talking to her son yet.

"What do you need, Mama?"

Elizabeth giggled a bit and looked down at her shoes.

"I need to go out for a little bit. You know … make myself right."

She rubbed her nose as though something were tickling her.

It took Stoop a minute to fully understand what she was telling him. By then, his mother had left the apartment. He sat until dawn, waiting for her to return, wondering.

"Stupendous," his mother said when she returned.

Her eyes rolled back in her head. They were glazed and red. The pause after saying her son's name was fully fifteen seconds.

"Stupendous," she repeated trying to focus on his face. She reached out and put a hand on each of his shoulders. "A woman like me … I wasn't meant to be no mother. Now. You're gonna have to forget about me."

Stoop tucked her into the only bed in the apartment. It was noon. The next night when she left the apartment, Stoop followed after her. First it was an abandoned building a block away. The city had closed off the windows and doors using cinder blocks, but dealers had broken through an entrance. They left most of the blocks covering the front door intact, using only a small hole to pass through product for those who had handed them cash. Elizabeth was one of those.

From there, Stoop's mother moved on to a bar that Stoop knew had been closed so many times for various violations that they kept plywood in the storage room to board up all their windows. Closing time was four in the morning, and Stoop was outside waiting, trying every once in a while to get a glimpse inside whenever a patron left or entered. When Elizabeth came out, she was on the arm of a man Stoop had never met and both were stumbling and slurring a song. The man was tall and weighed twice what Stoop did. He laughed at nothing in particular at the end of the verse, and Stoop moved in to do what he could.

"Hey, mister," Stoop said, one hand on the man's chest. "The bartender said you left your wallet inside."

"Wha?" the man said. He was having a hard time focusing on the boy.

"Your wallet. You left it inside. They have it for you."

"I got my wallet," the man said. A line of drool hung from his lower lip.

"Where?" Stoop asked.

The man patted himself, patted his pockets, found he did not, in fact, have his wallet.

"Sheee-it," the man drawled. He shook Elizabeth off his arm and stumbled back into the bar. Elizabeth laughed after him, but Stoop pulled her away. She let herself be pulled.

"Mama, there are programs," Stoop said the next afternoon as his mother was getting her hair in order.

"Programs?" she asked.

"Methadone," he said.

"Methadone?" she repeated. "Honey, I done tried the methadone."

"And?"

"And what?" Elizabeth asked, halting her grooming process. "I like smack better. Plain and simple."

"But, Mama, you don't need to get high like that. You don't need to go with men like Walter."

"Walter? Who in the hell is Walter?"

"Walter Crowe. The man you were with last night."

Elizabeth racked her brains but couldn't find a Walter.

"You mean that guy that lost his wallet last night?"

Stoop held the wallet up for her to see.

"Oh," his mother said. "You handy. Any cash money in that?"

She started brushing her hair again.

"Thirty-two dollars," Stoop answered.

"And you planning to keep all that for yourself?"

"You can have it, Mama. Take it all. Just promise me, no men. No strangers tonight."

She stepped away from the bathroom mirror and put the brush down. She moved in front of Stoop and took his face in both her hands. She looked into his eyes and moved the thumb of her right hand along his cheek. The touch was so delicious to him that he closed his eyes to receive it.

"Look at me Stupendous. You're a nice boy, a good boy to his mama. But you got to see me for what I am, not what you want me to be. You understand? I'm an addict, boy. I will do what I have to do to whoever I have to do it to in order to catch my high. Understand? Hell, I've been chasing highs since before you was born. Shoot," she said taking the wallet from Stoop's hand. "I was high on THE DAY you was born."

"You remember the day I was born?" Stoop asked.

"Of course I remember it, son. Well, I mean, parts of it anyway. I remember there was two doctors talking about how Stupendous you were. Two of them, and they ain't never seen anything like you."

She touched his cheek again, then turned away and left. Stoop followed her again a few seconds later, but this time she got into a gypsy cab, and her son had to be content with waiting for her in his apartment.

Three days later, Elizabeth was back, eyes raccooned, lip busted, nostrils rimmed with dry blood. Still, she was high and happy.

She touched his cheek and passed out on his couch without a word, and Stoop thought throughout the night of what he needed to do to save her life.

When she woke, Elizabeth first threw up then apologized to her son.

"I got to get me some medicine, you know, like you was telling me—something like methadone. Maybe morphine. Something I can control. You can help me. You know. Little by little, you can help me get off the morphine."

Stoop nodded though there was nothing about morphine that he knew about except how to steal it. His mother interrupted his thoughts.

"I most certainly am the saddest person," she said.

She looked at Stoop, and her face turned sad enough to match her description. She looked away a moment.

"I killed a man in Jersey last year," she said. "In HoHoKus. What kind of name for a place is that?" she asked, then she threw up again.

That same night, after Elizabeth had taken another taxi, Stoop walked a mile to a three-story hospital that he knew from experience had almost no security. He reported sharp stomach pains under a false name, and an hour later he was in a waiting area in the back, near the meds storage room. Fifteen minutes sitting there and he had seen three nurses punch in a code and use a swipe card. One accidental run in with a nurse later, Stoop was opening the door to the meds storage room himself.

It was another half hour before the nurse missed her swipe card. She searched for it frantically two minutes and found the card under some paperwork at the station she had been working. She breathed a sigh of relief just as Stoop was entering his apartment with a small white box with ten glass vials in it and a handful of syringes. He waited the night and into the morning for his mother to come home so she could start her regimen. "Treatment" was the word Stoop used.

Elizabeth woke her son in the morning by rustling the package on the makeshift coffee table. She was trying to read the package when he opened his eyes.

"That say morphine?" she asked him.

"Yes, Mama," he said. "We can start you off today."

Stoop padded into the bathroom. He was brushing his teeth when he heard the apartment door slam shut.

He tried to think of good things that could happen with his mother out on the streets with ten vials of morphine. Nothing really came to mind.

After a minute of bargaining, Elizabeth got the offer up to four speedballs, a nickel bag of marijuana, and a set of pills she couldn't identify. As soon as she took hold of the package and tried getting out of the car, smile still warm on her face, a gun was put to her head through her passenger side window.

"Get out of the car!" she was ordered. "Put your hands on your head!"

Elizabeth didn't return for hours. Near midnight, the police knocked at Stoop's door.

"Is it my mother?" he asked. It was an incautious word spoken to police, and you were never supposed to speak to the police at all.

The first police officer through the door had been about to force Stoop onto the floor, but he paused a moment, thought about saying something in reply.

They arrested Stoop. Showed him a warrant that allowed them to go through everything he had in the world. It didn't take them long. He was in the back of an unmarked car in five minutes.

"Guess what, kid?" a detective in jeans and a crewcut asked him as the car got moving. "We got a call last night about some missing morphine. You know what we said? We said there's not a chance in the world we can do anything about this in a city that, frankly, is drowning in drugs. Then guess who gets into my car this morning but a woman with a box of morphine. What do you think of that, kid?"

Stoop said nothing in return. He thought about how he would get his mother out of a precinct full of police once he'd had a chance to get out of the cuffs. Getting to her cell might be the hardest part. Would he have to set free an entire row of prisoners to make sure they didn't squeal? Or worse yet—what if his mother had already been transferred downtown for booking? How would he get to her then?

"This is our stop, kid."

The crewcut detective led Stoop up the stairs.

Inside the precinct, there was a slow moving mess. People crowded around the reception counter, some in handcuffs, some holding forms. The desk sergeant waved the crewcut detective forward with a look of exasperation on his face.

"Whaddaya got?" the sergeant asked.

"Morphine boy," the detective answered.

"Bee-u-tiful. Interrogation room three upstairs is supposed to be free if you need it. Let me know if it's not. Hate these crackdowns."

The sergeant was already waving forward another detective with another prisoner. Stoop and the detectives started up the stairs to the second floor. Through swinging doors, they entered an area with eight detectives' desks. At the far end of the open floor space there was a cage with several inmates. Stoop checked the cage with a glance. Elizabeth was in there, looking at her shoes.

The detective guided Stoop to a seat next to a desk.

"See, kid. That lady with the morphine started singing like a canary—told us all about you, your name, description, where you live, everything. Hell, she even said she knew you weighed three pounds and one ounce on the day you were born. If that's true, then, hell, who knows? Maybe you really are her son."

The detective sat back in his chair and studied Stoop's face a moment.

"Look, kid. You're young and you got no record. The lady says you swiped the morphine and gave it to her. She told us about you so she could walk out of here free, understand? Any chance you got something big on her? I'd just as soon keep her and cut you loose. See where I'm going with this?"

Stoop saw only too well that he was being asked to turn in his own mother. The trick was always to get the prisoners to point fingers at each other—everybody was guilty of something; there were enough charges for everyone.

Stoop said nothing; eventually the detective sighed deeply and pulled up to the computer keyboard on his desk. He called out to another detective.

"Hey, George. Bring the lady over, please? Thank you."

He turned to Stoop, held a picture up for comparison.

"Hospital sent us a video tape of you breaking into the medicine closet. This'll play great with the jury. Course, wouldn't have ever found you without the ID from the lady …"

The detective looked over Stoop's shoulder and stood up. Stoop turned and saw Elizabeth coming toward him. He rose from his chair.

"Mama?" Stoop said.

She avoided his eyes.

"Miss Jones, is this the young man that handed you the package?" the detective asked.

"That's him, Officer."

"Thank you. Now you just sign here and here and George will show you out."

Elizabeth Jones signed where the detective had indicated.

"Miss Jones, we thank you for your service."

Elizabeth turned to leave, but turned again and held Stoop's face a moment. She looked him full in the eyes.

"I'm sorry, baby. I am what I am. Best remember that," she whispered to him, then she kissed his forehead and turned from him. George led her away.

Stoop watched as Elizabeth walked out of the area through swinging doors to stairs that would set her free.

"That woman really your mother?" the crewcut detective asked, but Stoop wasn't listening to him at the moment. Instead, he watched the swinging doors and waited for his mother to return through them. It was a long time that he waited.

Roy
Brian Azzarello

She didn't come out from under the bed, even after the men were gone.

It wasn't because she was worried. Or that she was afraid of what she might find. She felt safe there, and she needed to feel safe. The house was quiet, like it was when she was alone. She wasn't alone though; Roy was there. But she stayed under the bed.

No fuckin' way, no fuckin' way … she heard it over and over in her head. Roy's words. He'd say it about … just about everything. While watching his games on TV, or talking to the radio. While she and Roy would look out the front window at the first snow in November. To his remaining friends, on the rare occasion that they'd show up for a visit. No fuckin' way. Like life was constantly surprising him, while he lived one without any.

Wake up.

Get out of bed.

Turn on the radio.

Make them breakfast.

Putter.

Have some lunch.

Take a nap.
Wake up.
Make them dinner.
Turn off the radio.
Turn on the TV.
Sit on the couch and eat.
Fall asleep.
Wake up.
Take the dishes to the kitchen.
Turn off the TV.
Get into bed.

The same every day. It was Roy's routine, and she was content to share it with him. But now, when the TV should be on, when they should be sleeping on the couch, she was under the bed. Because unlike Roy the TV wasn't there.

The men made a lot of noise while they were there. Tearing the place apart. Looking for anything valuable. They came in to the bedroom and pulled all the drawers out of the dresser. Throwing them on the bed. Looking. But never under the bed.

She was there, not making a sound. While the men made noise. While Roy moaned then gurgled no fuckin' way, no fuckin' way. The men were still making noise in the kitchen when Roy stopped making any. The men made more noise in the basement. Even more in the living room when they took the TV. From the sound of things, that was the only thing they took. The only thing they valued.

They left Roy. She crawled out from under the bed just before the sun came up. Roy was on the floor. She sat next to him, and said his name. Over and over. Roy Roy Roy. Loud, right in his face.

When he didn't move she went back under the bed. She needed to feel safe.

She pulled her legs close to her body, and fell asleep. She dreamt of Roy. She always dreamt of Roy.

She awoke when the phone rang. Then she heard Roy. He said I can't take your call right now, so please leave a message.

This made her sad.

Anxious.

Then she heard the salesman read the same bullshit thing he'd read last week. No fuckin' way. She started to cry.

She went down to the basement to go to the bathroom. Like the rest of the house, it was a mess. Roy kept everything, even after it was broken. Now everything was even more broken. From the men and their looking.

When she came upstairs she had a drink of water. She was hungry, but she couldn't eat—not with Roy the way he was. She went in the living room and paced back and forth next to his body. Roy Roy Roy she said. Roy Roy Roy she said again. She sat on the couch, then curled up on it. She looked at Roy. She looked where the TV wasn't. She fell asleep.

It was getting dark when she woke up.

She was hungry.

She couldn't eat, but drank some water.

She went down to the basement, stepped around the broken mess, and peed.

She came upstairs, looked at Roy, then went to the window. It was snowing. She watched the flakes dance in the wind. The radiator was warm. She fell asleep. It was all she could do.

It was dark when she woke up. The radiator was cold. She went to Roy, and laid down next to him. She kneaded him. He was cold like the radiator.

She dreamt of Roy, yelling at the TV, cursing at the radio, and laughing at something she did. She made Roy feel good, same as he did for her. It was love, because it was important and it defined their lives. It was love. The pure kind. One string, that connected them, attached.

She woke up on the couch alone to the knock knock knock of the radiator. It was the sound it made when it warmed. It was the sound that would get Roy to say no fuckin' way, gently push her off him, and get up and make breakfast. But that wasn't going to happen. For the second day in a row.

She tried to spend the day like she always did. But it was hard, because she was hungry, and she had drank all the water.

She walked around the house. Over the mess that the men had left. Over and over.

She looked at Roy.

She curled up on the couch.

She went to the window, and sat on the radiator.

She looked at Roy.

She went back under the bed.

It was dark again when she came out. She went everywhere that Roy wasn't.

On top of the bed.

The kitchen.

Down the basement. The smell was awful. Her smell.

But she found herself back next to Roy. He was the man she loved, and he was beginning to smell too.

One more time. Roy Roy Roy. He didn't move.

She reached out, and touched his face with her paw.

He didn't move.

She kept touching though. Over and over. Roy Roy Roy.

He didn't move. She didn't understand. She leaned in closer. He smelled.

And she took a bite.

Lie to me
(or yourself)

Back and Forth
Gregg Hurwitz

"Hello, sir. I, ah, I am here to see Don Carlo."

"Appointment?"

"No, I'm afraid not. But it's a matter of some importance. Please tell him Joe is here. Joe the Baker."

"The boxes?"

"Some, ah, some *dolce di fichi* I bring as a sign of respect."

"Fig cookies?"

"Yes, sir. Fig cookies. Here. You can look inside both boxes."

"Spread your arms."

"Apologies. I am ticklish."

"Come."

"Rocco! Rocco! Who is this?"

"Joe the Baker."

"He brings his own food into my restaurant? My food is not good enough?"

"I intend no disrespect, sir. They are, ah, they are a gift for Don Carlo."

"Don Carlo? I see. Apologies, *signori*. I did not realize. He is at his booth in the back room. Can I send something to the table? Another bottle of Brunello, perhaps?"

"No."

"Excuse me. Sorry. Excuse me. Back here? I, ah, I've never seen the private room. It's as nice as I've heard?"

"Quiet."

"Who's there?"

"Rocco."

"Open the door already, you *mook*."

"Sammy."

"Rocco."

"Pietro."

"Rocco."

"Don Carlo."

"Who is this?"

"Joe the Baker."

"Is that *dolce di fichi* I smell?"

"It is, Don Carlo, it is. Fresh batch. Just, ah, just baked them this morning for you."

"Why two boxes?"

"I thought perhaps you would bring a box home to Donacella."

"Let it not be said that you are not thoughtful, Joe the Baker. But I assume you did not drive all this way through Boston traffic to deliver me cookies."

"No, I—"

"You came a long way, Joe the Baker. What with Fenway traffic, the Big Dig, the *Americanas* taking up our precious few parking spaces here in the North End. I cannot imagine that you braved all that, driving from Quincy—it is Quincy—?"

"Yes, Don Carlo."

"—just to deliver these cookies."

"Well, ah, I—"

"You will be so kind as to sample one for me?"

"Of course."

"I will pick it from the box. How about that one? Is it good? It looks delicious."

"At risk of praising myself, it is, ah, quite good."

"I am eager to have one myself. Quincy is a long way from the North End, is it not, Joe the Baker?"

"It is."

"We mustn't forget where we come from."

"No, of course not."

"Take off your coat, stay awhile."

"Thank you, but I'm—"

"Rocco?"

"Your coat."

"Uh, thank you."

"I was saying, Joe the Baker, that we mustn't forget the traditions. Some men think they can move from here and it's a whole new life. A job trading derivatives at John Hancock, a splash of Ralph Lauren cologne, a *giuda* girlfriend. What would you think of a man like that?"

"I would not presume to judge."

"You are wise to hold your tongue, Joe the Baker. You know I speak of my son. You played in these streets together, a great big pack of you. You sat on these stoops and flipped trading cards. Rico Petrocelli was my son's prize card. In 1969—you boys were ten?"

"Eleven."

"Petrocelli set an American League record for the most home runs by a shortstop. And do you know what else he did that same season? He tied the record for fewest errors for a shortstop. He had pride, then, my son, in Petrocelli. He meant something different, Petrocelli, than Yastrzemski or Fisk. Do you understand that?"

"I do."

"I question that, Joe the Baker. Because still you moved away. Like my son, you moved away. And opened an Italian bakery in *Quincy.*"

"I have never forgotten the pride in my heritage my parents instilled in me."

"You're a Calegero, are you not, Joe the Baker?"

"Yes, Don Carlo."

"In the old country, your family had quite a reputation."

"I have heard the same, Don Carlo."

"They were proud and fierce. One crossed the Calegeros at great risk. They were fig farmers and bakers, were they not? The *dolce di fichi*—a family recipe?"

"My great-grandmother's."

"But they had a darker side in the old country, the Calegeros. I recall a tax collector drowned in a well near your family farm after the first world war."

"An old rumor, sir. My people were honest farmers and bakers."

"And fighters. When the Germans came, wasn't one of your forebears hung as a saboteur for destroying a panzer?"

"My great-uncle. Two panzers."

"And another Calegero was forced to work in a bread factory. And he poisoned the bread, killed two Nazi officers."

"I believe you speak of a myth, Don Carlo. A woman working in a factory with, ah, with my grandfather put broken glass in the dough. She was shot, along with two other women. My grandfather said it was, a-ahum, it was the worst thing he ever witnessed."

"I remember the story from my own father. About the poisoning."

"Then perhaps my grandfather was mistaken, Don Carlo."

"Perhaps he was. You come from proud, strong people, Joe Calegero—it is okay that I refer to you by your family name?"

"Of course."

"Your father, may he rest in peace, was not such a strong person. Once he got here, he didn't understand what it meant to honor the old ways. He and I had our disagreements."

"I recall you did, Don Carlo."

"And now here you come, bearing cookies for me. Your predecessors would never have come here, to my table. They were too proud. Your father was—*you* are—too lost in the new ways. You don't understand honor. Do you think this man is worthy of his predecessors, Rocco?"

"No."

"I do not claim to be the same as them, Don Carlo. I am a different type of man."

"And now we are back to the purpose behind the cookies. Why do you stare at me? I am not accustomed to being ignored. Am I accustomed to being ignored, Rocco?"

"No."

"I do not mean to ignore you, Don Carlo. I, ah … You are correct that I am different from my predecessors. I want only to live a quiet life, to be left alone. I have two girls, Don Carlo—"

"Picture?"

"I … excuse me?"

"Surely you carry a picture in your wallet? See, there you are. Beautiful angels. Has the oldest been confirmed?"

"Next year."

"*Che bella*. Here you are. I apologize. You were saying?"

"I am trying to set an example for my girls. I moved away from the North End because there are too many … entanglements for me here."

"Entanglements can be complicated."

"Yes, they can."

"That is why my son moved away as well. Entanglements. Please, continue."

"I was visited yesterday by one of your men."

"One of my men?"

"Yes, sir. Pietro here. He wanted me to provide the cake and *pizzelles* for your nephew's wedding."

"Pietro, is this true?"

"It is true, Don Carlo."

"It does not surprise me. My nephew, he loves *pizzelles*. And authentic *pizzelles*, you well know as a Calegero, are difficult to come by. Especially with so many of the fine bakers moving from the neighborhood."

"Yes, they are often, ah, often brittle. And many younger chefs use too much anise."

"But not you."

"No, Don Carlo."

"So Pietro came to see you. Did he attempt to take advantage of you, Joe Calegero? To not offer appropriate recompense for your services?"

"No, Don Carlo. He offered me a great deal of compensation. More compensation than is appropriate."

"So you are here to bargain yourself out of wages? Look at Pietro, how he laughs. Rocco I've known for twenty-five years. Rocco doesn't laugh. Is that why you're here, Joe Calegero? To argue that you are worth less than what Pietro offered you?"

"No, Don Carlo. As much as I am indebted to you for this generous offer, I would like to respectfully decline."

"Decline? Why would a baker decline such an offer? Why would a baker deny my nephew what he loves on his wedding day?"

"I ah, ah, ah—"

"Speak plainly, my son, and do not be afraid."

"I fear being indebted to you, Don Carlo. Like my father was, God rest his soul. With great respect to you, I hope you will permit me to simply run my little bakery away from the neighborhood in peace."

"I understand."

"You do?"

"Of course. I can understand perfectly why a *gentleman* such as yourself, a Calegero, wouldn't want to associate with a man like me."

"I fear you misunderstand me, Don Carlo."

"Pietro, check the alley, please."

"Don Carlo, I fear there has been, ah, a terrible misunderstanding."

"You can just set down the boxes of cookies on the table there."

"Alley's clear, boss."

"Come. You stand there? Perhaps you need a little help. Rocco, will you please provide our dear friend a little help?"

"No. *Nooo!*"

"Sammy, his other side."

"I have two beautiful daughters, Don Carlo."

"Beautiful, indeed. A cold night, is it not, Rocco?"

"Yes."

"Put him on his knees."

"God, please, no, Don Carlo. Have mercy on me. I am just a simple baker."

"Please stop sobbing."

"My daughters, Don Carlo."

"You were correct about one thing, Joe Calegero: You are nothing like your predecessors. They would be sickened by you."

"I am sorry for any affront I may have—"

"Rocco? Thank you. Do you see this, Joe Calegero?"

"Y-y-yes."

"Do you know what it is? Open your mouth. Open his mouth, please, Rocco. I'll ask you again. Do you know what this is?"

"*Nff!*"

"This is a .44 Magnum. A very powerful handgun. Did you ever see *Dirty Harry*?"

"Nnff! *Nfffrrff!*"

"I enjoyed it myself as well. As I was telling you, the .44 Magnum is a very powerful gun. Rocco has the weight to carry such a gun. The mass. His wife keeps him well fed, that he may carry a gun such as this. It is almost too powerful for an old man like me. You'll notice that I said *almost*, Joe Calegero?"

"Nmff hmm."

"My wife likes to shop for me, Joe Calegero. This makes you a very lucky man. Would you like to know why?"

"Mm hmm."

"This .44 will put your brain on the bricks there and backspray on my face. But I am wearing this beautiful camel-hair coat that Donacella bought for me. And Donacella will be quite upset with me if I return home with blood all over this elegant coat. It has happened before. And if you think that I am someone you don't want to see displeased, Joe Calegero, you should see my Donacella when she is cross. So you are lucky, because the moods of my bride and this camel-hair coat have given me pause. Now I am going to remove this gun from your mouth and I am going to ask you a question. I would be very appreciative if you would answer that question for me. Do you understand?"

"Nm hmm."

"Do you know what *fucked* means, Joe Calegero?"

"I, ah, ah, believe I do."

"I am not a man prone to using blue language, but there is really no replacement for the word *fucked*. It is unique in what it implies, in what it encompasses. Violation. Domination. Spilled fluids. So many uses, you see. A few that seem relevant right at this moment. Some old friends in an alley, a well-oiled .44, and a concern about spilled fluids upsetting one's wife back home. But sometimes, sometimes a good fucking is worth running a risk, even of upsetting one's wife. Is it not?"

"I think in this case—"

"Would it be alright with you, Joe Calegero, if I imposed upon you with another question?"

"Y-yes, Don Carlo. That would be fine."

"Does my Donacella have to be upset tonight?"

"N-no, Don Carlo. I would be h-h-happy to honor your request for your nephew's wedding."

"I am pleased that we reached this understanding."

"I am happy too, Don Carlo."

"Come, let's get up. Oops. Weak knees. Rocco? There you are. Let's get in from this cold. My nephew will be so pleased to have your delightful, authentic *pizzelles* on the day of his nuptials. And you will be well reimbursed. Your bakery will thrive. Your girls will be able to buy new uniforms for their private school out in Quincy. Here we are. Sammy, Pietro, sit. More wine. Rocco, will you please get our new friend his jacket?"

"P-please don't forget the cookies, Don Carlo."

"Now look what you have done with your trembling hands, Joe Calegero. One box of *dolce di fichi* on the floor."

"I'm, ah, ah, ah, I'm sorry, Don Carlo."

"They do smell delicious, don't they, Rocco?"

"Yes."

"Pass me that other box. Mmm. It is easy for me to see why my nephew so appreciates your baking. These are wondrous. Have a taste,

Pietro. Sammy? And of course, Rocco already chews away. He has a lot of weight to maintain. The only problem is, with that other box on the floor, what am I to bring home to my Donacella?"

"A clean camel-hair coat."

"Ha ha! See that? Joe Calegero has a sense of humor after all. This is a wonderful end to what could have been an unpleasant evening. Best of luck to you, son."

"Good-bye, Don Carlo. And thank you."

"What a *stunad*."

"Don't be ungenerous, Sammy. He's just a nervous fellow, like his father. Rocco? What's wrong?"

"*Kkgg!*"

"Quickly! Roll him over. Sammy, call a doctor! Sammy? You look pale. Are you—?"

"Ggrgl."

"Someone call for a doctor! Pietro!"

"The cookies, Don Carlo. The other box ..."

"Pietro? Pietro? *Madre di Dio! Madre d-drgrkle ...*"

Prisoner of Love

A Four Part Romance Told in Three Parts

Tim Maleeny

The nimrod in the Ford Taurus forgot to roll down his window before he started shooting at me. Maybe he got confused, saw me driving right next to him and forgot that I was the one in a convertible.

His side window exploded as sparks shot across my hood. Lucky for me, not so much for him. Shards of safety glass blew back into his face, one piece catching him in the left eye. He lurched to the right instinctively, dragging the wheel with him. The car swerved into a fire hydrant and the crumple-zones in the newly redesigned Taurus folded like origami gone bad.

He sailed through the windshield, bringing more safety glass with him but leaving his right arm behind. His gun hand wedged inside the steering wheel like one of those clubs designed to stop assholes from stealing your car. It was severed at the elbow, still holding his Beretta.

His name was Stu Maloney, small-time hood and half-assed trigger-man. Now he was an urban art exhibit, wrapped around the telephone pole on the corner of Mission and Twenty-first. Stu had taken something that didn't belong to him—my girlfriend Sarah.

I left my car idling in the middle of the street and popped the trunk on the Taurus.

"Hi honey."

She looked pissed. Can't say I blamed her, since she didn't even know I was in the life until Stu put a gun to her head and shoved her into his trunk. Fortunately for me, she had duct tape over her mouth.

She looked more scuffed than stunned. Stu had a surprisingly clean trunk—no tire irons or golf balls lying around, waiting to bash Sarah in the head whenever he took a hard left. She glared at me, which I took as a sign she hadn't suffered even a mild concussion. I smiled reassuringly and walked to the front of the car.

Stu had slid to the bottom of the pole. His head was jerking back and forth as he tried to locate his missing arm. The one that was still attached dragged him pathetically along the sidewalk. It looked like his legs might be broken. I stepped over a river of blood and bent down so he could see my eyes.

"Seatbelts save lives, Stu."

He spit safety glass before he managed to get his tongue working. "Blow me, Nat."

"Always so original." His left arm swung around and I shuffled back a step so he couldn't reach me. I had just gotten my slacks back from the dry cleaner. "Did the old man send you?"

Stu gargled and something rattled around deep in his throat. Maybe it was his voice, because it bubbled to the surface in a fountain of blood. "You stole ... our loot."

"*Our* loot?" I shook my head sadly. "You stole my girlfriend."

"She's hot." Stu actually managed to smile, his teeth broken and red.

"I'll tell her you said so. Who sent you?"

"I need an ambulance." Stu shook his head and banged his forehead on the sidewalk, leaving a red stain. I glanced at his side where his gun hand used to be. The river was flowing faster. When he looked at me again his eyes were milky. Somewhere in the distance I heard sirens.

"You don't."

"Yeah ... I fuckin' do."

I shook my head and pulled the Glock from my waistband, pressed the barrel against his forehead. Stu crossed his eyes for an instant as he tried to focus on the gun, then whipsawed back to me.

"Was it the old man, Stu?"

"I … need … an ambulance."

"No, you don't." I pulled the trigger.

I squatted on the sidewalk, watching Stu's brains mix with the blood from his arm, the whole mess flowing off the curb into the sewer drain. My pants were still clean but my shoes were a fucking mess.

I stepped to the trunk and got Sarah into a fireman's carry without giving her an opportunity to kick me in the balls. I thought about removing the tape but the sirens were louder now, only a few blocks away. I thumbed my remote and opened my trunk, then gently set her inside. Her eyes suggested my chances of getting laid that night were nil.

I smiled apologetically and closed the lid, then walked around to the driver's side and slid behind the wheel. Headed straight down Mission, keeping my speed low, passing two cop cars coming from the opposite direction. They didn't even give me a second glance.

I drove past a flower stand and thought about stopping, then changed my mind as I visualized the look on Sarah's face. Flowers weren't going to cut it this time.

WE'D MET LESS THAN A WEEK AGO, thanks to an Internet dating service. After years of fucking around, I finally took the plunge—online harmony, the promise of a virtual match, cyber-dating, whatever you want to call it. The last resort of a desperate man.

Kind of hard to meet a nice woman in my line of work. Not that strippers aren't nice, whores aren't perfectly pleasant, or madams don't have anything interesting to say. They just weren't the kind of girls I wanted to meet.

I knew plenty of guys smarter than me, but it didn't take an advanced degree in statistics to understand the state lottery offered better odds than trying to find my soul mate on the job. My clients were criminals and I worked alone.

I was a fixer. Something got broken, I patched it up.

That broken something might be a business deal—a little misunderstanding between associates—in which case money had to change hands. Cash carried by a neutral party, which would be me. Or maybe someone forgot to pay for something. A simple oversight with dire consequences. I'd get a call to fix that situation, perhaps by strongly encouraging the negligent buyer to pay up immediately, with interest.

Sometimes I delivered cash, other times equipment, and sometimes I delivered people. Sometimes the people were still breathing, other times they might be a little oxygen-challenged. Either way, the problem got fixed. I was damn good at my job.

Then a day before I met Sarah, something got so fucked up that even I couldn't fix it.

Simple heist, smash and grab job. Four guys chosen to hit a jewelry store after closing, right off Union Square. The old man managed to get blueprints and bribed a disgruntled security guard to cough up the alarm code. Then he blackmailed a clerk with a penchant for underage trim for the combination to the safe. The old man was thorough, had to give him that. Our guys would be wearing ski masks, so the surveillance cameras weren't a concern.

My job was to provide the gear and the car. I was also the driver. I bought the ski masks from three different outdoor stores, just in case somebody dropped theirs and the cops tried to trace the purchase. Flashlights, glass cutter, crowbar, a drawstring bag to hold the loot. No night vision or laser sights, no Austrian pistols, none of that shit. This was a robbery, not mission impossible.

The three other guys were Matt, Alan and Stu. Not the brightest beacons in the cosmos but perfect for this job. Matt was a bruiser weighing over three hundred pounds who could crack four walnuts simultaneously between his five fingers, a stunt good for getting people to buy him drinks but not much else. He liked hitting things, so he was on crowbar duty for any locked display cases or uncooperative inside doors. Alan was a ladies man with a geology degree and a gambling problem. He knew the right stones to snatch, an important qualification when time isn't your friend. Even with the alarm disabled we wanted to be in and out within minutes.

The job came off as planned, in that my three colleagues managed to clear the front door, break open the safe, and fill the velvet bag with shiny rocks and assorted jewelry. I had the engine running and the trunk open when they came around the corner into the alley.

Alan tossed me the bag and I locked it in the metal box bolted to the floor of my trunk, shut the lid without waking the neighbors and slid behind the wheel. I felt the shocks bounce as big Matt climbed into the backseat and shut his door, then I pulled away from the curb and drove straight to the old man's bar. As Alan so delicately summed up the job, we were in and out, as easy as a crack whore in heat.

Too bad the stones were fake.

Every single one was a lump of glass or finely-cast piece of plastic. Finding a cubic zirconium among the sack of shit we brought into the old man's office would have been cause for celebration. Given all the trouble he'd gone to—recruiting the jewelry store's employees to his cause—it's fair to say the old man was less than thrilled.

There were only two possibilities.

One, the store got tipped off and made the switch. Unlikely since the old man put the squeeze on the security guard and knew where he lived. The sales clerk was married with kids and couldn't afford the alimony, so the blackmail should have held tight. Besides, even a civilian knew the risks of crossing the old man.

Two, an inside job. Alan had tossed me the bag, but Matt had been holding it inside the store while the other guys filled it up, and Stu had handled it at one point when Matt was prying open the door to the office. Each man slipped out of the store separately so only one would get nabbed if a cop passed by—in other words, the guy who made the switch might have tossed the bag to an accomplice hiding outside. And any one of the three men who went inside could have stashed the bag of real gems near the building before I saw them come around the corner to the car.

We knew something was wrong the moment the old man looked through a loop, one of those little spyglass gadgets jewelers wear. His free eye went wide with disbelief over the magnified junk his other eye was seeing. He told us all to stay right where we were, not that anyone had made a move from the moment he muttered *Mother of Fucking Christ*. The old man got religious, you knew it was serious.

Bob the bouncer went outside and searched my car. I had given him the combination to my trunk safe, where he found my spare Glock and an extra magazine. But no gems. Never had I been so happy to be the driver, the outside man on an inside job.

We sat around the table, silent as monks as we waited for word to come back that a search of the street and sewer drains outside the store, conducted as discretely as possible, revealed nothing but litter. We were fucked.

The old man gave us each a hard stare, his black eyes boring a hole into your skull, his nostrils flaring like he could smell it if you were lying. I studied the other guys as he interrogated each in turn, knowing this was going to be my mess to clean up.

Matt was sweating like a pig, but he always did. No useful body language there. Alan smiled like a used car salesmen, but he owned a dealership on South Van Ness, so he really couldn't help himself. And Stu kept glancing from the old man to the door, as if he had to take a piss and might let loose at any moment. I took that as a sure sign of guilt until a sharp odor hit and I saw the trickle down the inside of his right pants leg. Guess he couldn't hold it any longer. After the excitement of the robbery, he should have gone as soon as we hit the bar. That's what I did.

I had trouble meeting the old man's eyes at first, then forced myself to swing my sockets around. I didn't want him thinking I felt guilty, so I held his black iron gaze. But I hated that disappointed look he got, that how-could-this-have-happened look. That fucking look that said I had better fix this before things got really fucking bad for everyone.

"How could this have happened, Nat?" His face drooped into sagging folds of dismay, like Walter Matthau in *The Taking Of Pelham 123,* or one of those sherpa-dogs.

"It's a mystery, sir." I always called the old man sir. He seemed to like it.

"A mystery." He nodded, then scanned the faces around the table. "You like mysteries, Nat?"

"I'm not much of a reader, sir."

"Check out Chercover, he's good. But I digress." The old man loved to use words like *digress*. Sometimes I thought he actually wanted things to go sideways, just so he could work a word like *ostracize* or *digress* into one of his lectures. Some wiseguys shot you in the kneecap, the old man beat you over the head with his vocabulary.

I nodded but didn't say anything.

"I want you to fix this, Nat."

Quel fucking surpise, if you'll pardon my French. But I kept the thought to myself and simply said, "Yes, sir."

He cut us loose and I felt the weight of his hand on my shoulder as I buttoned my jacket, the pressure of his eyes on my back as I stepped outside. I had to check the rearview mirror to make sure he wasn't sitting in the backseat, just waiting for the right moment to deliver a motivational speech.

I want you to fix this.

This never would have happened to me when I was thirty.

Middle age had hit me like a flagellant who suddenly realized it was a lot more rewarding to be a sadist than a masochist. I was on my knees, miserable and alone, with no chance of redemption. I needed a real woman to save my soul.

As if in answer to a prayer, the very next day I met Sarah.

The email caught me by surprise, because I had forgotten about my application. It had been more than two weeks since I sat at the bar next to Bob, who was taking a break from the door to help me with my profile.

"You want to meet the right girl, you have to tell her the truth." Bob gave me an earnest look. He'd been married fourteen years.

I gave him a look of my own. "After I meet the right girl, then *maybe* I'll tell her the truth. How many dates you think I'll get if my profile says I work for the mob?"

"Say you work in a family business."

"It asks how much money I make."

Bob raised an eyebrow. "How much does the old man pay you?"

"None of your business."

"Pick a number high enough to afford a nice car—that's important—but not so high you sound like a blue blood."

"Got it. What do I like to do more, walk on the beach barefoot or curl up on the couch with a blanket and a good book?"

"The fuck should I know?"

And so it went. Bob was a good sounding board, even if some of his suggestions lacked a certain romantic appeal. I did my best to paint a self-portrait that bore an uncanny resemblance to me, or a version of me that didn't break the law for a living.

Then I went back to work and forgot all about it.

Her email was short but witty. Plenty of attitude in very few words. I knew right away that I wanted to meet her. Must have edited my reply a dozen times before I hit Send.

We emailed back and forth the next day. It was a nice distraction from my troubles, especially since I'd decided to do nothing about them for at least twenty-four hours.

If it was an inside job, then one of our guys would be sitting at home waiting for the knock on the door, unless he was stupid enough to bolt. Whoever he was, I wanted him sleep-deprived, jumpy and scared, his confession written in the stains beneath his arms and the sweat on his upper lip. I wanted him to do something stupid and make my job easier.

I was, by nature, a lazy fuck.

The next day Sarah and I agreed to meet at a coffee shop. In person, she didn't disappoint. Like her emails, she could be described with very few words. Short, plenty of attitude, and beautifully put together.

Somehow I managed not to screw it up. I had memorized my profile before I left my apartment, and by the time we finished our coffee I almost believed I was the guy she was obviously attracted to— I felt like Bruce Wayne.

I invited her to dinner, then we exchanged numbers and said our good-byes, a lingering handshake that morphed into a tentative hug.

That night I got a call and answered before checking caller ID, hoping it was her, but the old man's voice was a golden shower of reality.

"Big Matt is no longer with us." The old man wasn't much for preamble.

"Where?"

"He's at home." The old man hung up. Guess he wasn't in the mood for one of his lectures.

But I digress.

The first question a professional asks isn't how someone got killed, it's where, because that tells you what kind of hit went down. Someone dies of natural causes you read about it in the paper, or the person calling you spells it out without fear of the Feds taping the conversation. But when someone dies of *unnatural* causes, the *where* can tell you a lot more than the *how*.

Kill a guy in public or dump his body where it will be easily found, then you're making a statement. Odds are a rival family or the competition—Mexicans, Jamaicans, Russians—are making some kind of move.

If a guy disappears, could be he ran. Witness protection, or maybe running from the Feds to avoid facing the horrible choice of turning State's or getting taken out by one of your own.

But if someone gets killed at home, where they live and sleep, then it's personal. Especially if they have a family. Then it's probably an inside job.

This tragic turn of events suggested big Matt may have been the culprit in our little caper, and he had a partner. As I dressed for dinner, I wondered if the partner was inside or outside our little circle of friends.

Sarah wore an LBD—little black dress—that was made from some test fabric developed by NASA to bond with every curve, slope and molecule of her body. I was in orbit by the time we ordered dessert, dizzy from lack of oxygen because I was holding my breath every time she leaned forward, touched her hair, or rested her hand on the table next to mine.

I was falling hard enough to ignore the gravity of my situation. I kissed her goodnight—a long, lingering kiss that promised our next dinner might turn into breakfast—and forgot all about stolen jewels, big Matt and my alter ego until I got home. My phone started ringing as I turned my key in the door.

"Alan is no longer with us."

"Where?"

The old man hung up without bothering to answer.

I bit my lower lip as I tried to think but tasted Sarah and got distracted. I poured myself a drink and breathed through my nose.

Alan had fit the profile. A gambling problem, soft touch for the ladies, fast fingers and loose moral fiber. He was also smarter than Matt, which meant he could have masterminded the scheme and then offered the big guy a cut. But with Alan out of the picture, things got complicated.

I wasn't just getting old, I was getting slow. Here I was sitting on my hands, supposedly waiting for the inside man to panic and run, but what if the double-cross was really a triple-cross? What if all three guys were in cahoots? Even though it was just a passing thought, using the word *cahoots* in a sentence gave me chills.

Maybe it was time to visit Stu.

The next morning I drank enough coffee to get my teeth vibrating, then drove over to Stu's place and waited outside. His car wasn't in the driveway and he didn't come outside to fetch the paper. By noon I was starving and antsy, so I drove to a nearby diner and ordered a club sandwich and a bowl of carrots. I liked eating carrots when I was trying to figure something out—it made me feel smart, like Bugs Bunny.

The bowl was almost empty when I realized what was up. Stu had a fuse shorter than an Irishman's pecker—he wasn't likely to wait around for someone to ring his doorbell and then shoot him in the face. If he thought one of the other guys stole the gems, he'd just take matters into his own hands and shoot the thieving bastard, score points with the old man. And if Stu thought one of us was going to do the same to him, he'd shoot first and not even bother to ask questions later.

Two days was an eternity to a guy like Stu. I had underestimated his instinct for survival, always a mistake with a sociopath. I finished my carrots and decided there was only one thing I could do. I called Sarah and invited her to dinner.

She agreed to meet me at the restaurant at six. By the time I slipped my phone into my pocket my pulse had quickened. I could hear my heart pounding in my ears, the drumbeat of love drowning out any voice of reason.

Dinner was perfect. Not rushed but not too drawn out, either. I forced myself to eat slowly, even though I was already thinking ahead to driving her home. I can't remember what we talked about, but I can still hear the sound of her voice. Then that cocksucker Stu interrupted dessert and ruined any shot I might have had at getting laid.

NOW I WAS LAYING HER GENTLY ON MY BED, her eyes shooting laser beams of anger at my face. I forced a smile and tore the duct tape off as decisively as I could.

As she spit fibers from her lips I yanked her clutch purse from my jacket pocket and tossed it onto the bed. It was surprisingly heavy. Her cell phone bounced out of the purse and landed a foot away near the headboard. I was impressed and vaguely horrified that she had managed to grab the purse while being abducted. If a woman had those kind of reflexes when it came to accessories, what was she like when it came to buying shoes?

I kept the thought to myself and squared my feet on the rug, bracing myself for the verbal onslaught that was sure to come once Sarah plucked the last strand of tape from her lower lip. She looked mad and sexy as hell.

"You lied to me." She sounded more hurt than pissed and I leaned forward to give her a hug, then caught myself when I met her gaze. Her measured tone belied the simmering anger lurking in her bottomless brown eyes. "You said you were a Claims Adjuster."

"Well …"

"Shut up." She shifted on the bed, got her legs underneath her. They looked great, no stockings, the only visible veins the ones pulsing on either side of her neck. I dragged my eyes away from her legs and tried to look contrite as she added, "Just shut up, Nat."

"OK"

"Why do I always attract the pathological liars?"

"Was that a rhetorical question, sweetie?"

"Did I just tell you to shut up?"

I didn't know how to answer that one.

"Fuck me." She sighed loudly. Before I could ask if that was an invitation to kiss and make up, she stood abruptly and grabbed her purse. Sarah pointed at the door. "Bathroom?"

I nodded, still waiting for permission to speak. Sarah gave me a hard look and then grabbed my hair with her free hand and pulled me forward to give me an even harder kiss.

"Asshole." The way she said it, I knew she was in love with me, too.

She disappeared down the hall and I heard the bathroom door close just as her cell phone started to ring. I ignored it at first and sat down heavily on the bed, the knot in my chest slowly unraveling.

The phone bounced against my thigh and I glanced down.

I recognized the number.

I stared at it for a minute, the little phone trilling like a baby bird, then I pulled my own phone from my pocket and quickly thumbed through my address book. The same number that was flashing on her caller ID appeared on the screen of my phone next to a name I had known for over twenty years.

It was a name I never used anymore because it was so much easier just to call him *the old man*.

I felt the knot in my chest being retied by a compulsive sailor and had to force myself to take a breath. Down the hall I heard the sound of a toilet flushing behind a closed door.

Bob the bouncer had helped me with my application. He didn't find the false bottom in my car safe, but the old man must have had his suspicions. I was always an outsider, and none of us was getting any younger. I was through fixing things for other people.

I just needed one last job that put everything in motion, distracted the old man long enough for things to fix themselves. Stu was the perfect wind-up toy, but I was the one who got distracted. I hadn't counted on Sarah.

I thought about the taste of her kiss, the adhesive from the tape pulling our lips apart with a painful tug. I thought about the weight of her purse and wondered what could be heavier than a cell phone. I pulled my Glock from my waistband and hefted it in my hand, already knowing the answer.

I was a prisoner of love and there were only two ways to escape. The only question now was which one of us held the key.

Paper Thin Hotel
Nick Stone

Miami was bad for marriages. That's what Max Mingus concluded, as he sat in Room 29 of the Zurich Hotel on the corner of Eleventh and Collins, waiting for the adulterers next door to get down to business so he could get along with his.

Of all the people he knew, only his best friend, Joe Liston, was still with his first wife. The rest were either on second or third marriages, divorce-stunted loners or, like him, widowers who hadn't quite got over, who lived with ghosts. This city wasn't a place for long-term commitments. Its nature was transient, its spirit restless. It was ever evolving, ever changing; shedding one glitzy layer of skin after another, like a rhinestone snake on speed. Miami was the midpoint between somewhere else and somewhere better, so hardly anyone was from here and hardly anyone ever stayed. People passed through, moved on and made way for more of the same. That was Max's theory at least, how he explained it whenever the subject came up. "Miami's a river rushing over quicksand", he'd say. "You can't stand up and you can't lie down. And you sure as shit can't build on it."

He wiped the sweat off his brow. He hadn't been in the room long, but his handkerchief was already soaked to the corners. It was the height of summer and the aircon was broken. The heat was damn near stifling and the place smelled of puke and food fights. He didn't want to open the window because the noise from the street would drown out the goings-on next door. Right now the two of them were talking. That's what they liked to do first. Talk. And laugh a little. Her mostly.

HE'D BEEN WATCHING THE COUPLE for three months. Fabiana Spenser and Rex Mendell. They were both married to other people. Rex, twenty-nine, was boss of a chauffered limo company called Island Limos. He lived out in Hallendale with his wife and two preschool kids. He was tall, blonde, gym-built and had the sort of safe, wholesome, all-American good looks models for banks and credit card companies had. Fabiana, twenty-five, was the fourth trophy wife of Emerson Spenser, Max's client. She was a Latin firecracker: long black hair, olive skin and big dark eyes set atop that kind of body whose curves were too perfect and generous to be real. She turned every straight man's head wherever she went.

Max really didn't blame either of them. Especially not Fabiana.

Emerson Spenser was a wealthy dentist who catered to an upscale clientele. He had offices in every major city in Florida. Max had met him once, in Tallahassee—where he lived with his wife—to talk about the job. He'd hated him on sight. Spenser was a small, sixty-something remnant of a man trying to cheat time with hairplugs, facelifts, botox and buy-a-brides like Fabiana. Of course, he took the job. He really had no choice, because he wasn't his own boss and, anyway, one look at Spenser and he'd figured it'd be quick.

Every Wednesday morning Fabiana would fly in to Miami. Rex would meet her at the airport with a blank expression and a sign with her name on it. They'd act like strangers when they met. He'd drive her towards South Beach on one of his fleet of Town Cars. On the way there, he'd pull over on a sidestreet or in an empty parking lot. He'd get in the backseat. A few minutes later the car would rock for a good ten to fifteen minutes, then Rex would get back in the driving seat and resume his professional duties, driving his client to The Shore Club, where she kept a suite.

In the evening he'd collect her, as formal as before, and drive her to the Zurich Hotel. She'd go in first and make her way straight to Room 30, which she'd block-booked for the rest of year. Rex would follow her in a few minutes later. When they were done he'd drive her back to the Shore Club. He'd return his car to the Island Limos garage and go home to his wife and kids. The next morning, he'd return to the Shore Club at around ten AM, collect Fabiana and drive her around town. She visited a doctor, an accountant, and then met a friend for lunch. Afterwards Rex drove her to the airport, stopping off along the way for a backseat farewell. By three PM she was on a plane back to Tallahassee.

Max had spent the regulation two weeks following Fabiana. He'd photographed everything from a distance, using a powerful zoom lens. He'd videoed the car rocking. He'd kept a record of the times of each assignation, as well as a description of what he'd seen. He was struck by how Fabiana and Rex had kept a professional distance, pretending, at first, that they didn't know each other, and then allowing only for the slightest thaw the following day, totally in keeping with surface appearances. When they'd met up the following week they'd started the charade from scratch. He guessed the role play was part of the whole thrill, the way they made it work. He decided to omit this last observation from the report he took to Emerson Spenser. It was none of the creep's business—even if he was paying for it to be.

Max was good at delivering bad news. It was all about expression and timing, something he'd learnt and perfected in his ten years as a Miami cop. He had a routine, an act. He let his clients know what was coming by wearing somber clothes and a matching look—profound disappointment with a strong hint of crushed optimism, as if he had somehow been expecting a different result. He didn't have to try too hard either. He wasn't one of life's smilers. His fifty-eight-year-old mien was lined and craggy, well suited to the dour seen-it-all, done-it-all, so-*please*-go-fuck-yourself expression he wore like a sentry uniform. It stopped people looking too hard, kept them moving on. That way they missed the heavy sadness about him, the trail littered with regret.

Once he'd set the scene, he got straight to the point. He didn't soften the blow. "Mr./Mrs. Cheated-On, you were right. Your husband/wife *is* having an affair." He talked for a minute to a minute and a half and covered the basic details. He handed them his report, complete with photographs. Then he let the client register and absorb. Once they had, he went into customer support mode. First he apologized. Then he empathized, or comforted, or listened to the poisonous and pained rant—or all three. When they were done, he told them they could call him whenever they wanted and said his goodbyes. A week later he mailed them his invoice.

That's the way it had always gone.

Until Emerson Spenser.

When Max walked into Spenser's offices with his game face on, he'd been completely thrown by his client's reaction. He'd read Max's look and smiled. And the smile had just gotten broader and broader—or as broad as his surgically stretched and botoxed skin would allow—his lips thinning out to near translucent pink slivers, like an elastic band pulled close to snapping point, displaying tens of thousands of dollars worth of perfect, white teeth, which made Max think of toilet bowls in a showroom.

Before he could finish his rundown of the details, Spenser asked him if he had any pictures. Max said he hadn't, only video of the car rocking back and forth. Spenser asked to see it. Max gave him a DVD of the footage he'd shot and watched his client view it on his computer. His client was unmistakably turned on.

Max didn't know what else to do but stay in character and finish off his routine. He'd got within of breath of the apology when Spenser waved him silent.

"This is a good start. A *very* good start," Spenser said.

"A good start?" Max queried.

"You're to get me more."

"More?"

"Proof."

"Proof?"

"Yes, proof, Mr. Mingus. Proof of *actual* penetration. You know—gonzo shit," Spenser said. When Max looked at him nonplussed he'd made himself perfectly clear. "Fuck pics. Lots and lots of fuck pics."

And that was how Max Mingus had found himself at the Zurich Hotel.

FIRST HE'D COME TO AN ARRANGEMENT WITH TEDDY, the night manager. Teddy was a red-haired guy with rimless pebble glasses who looked all of eightenen. He and a security guard were the only people on duty.

For one thousand dollars Teddy told him the couple stayed in Room 30 every Wednesday night, between seven and nine PM, and that Fabiana had booked the place until the end of the year. Max took the room next door for a month.

Rooms 29 and 30 were separated by an adjoining door. Teddy explained that the rooms used to be let out as suites, back when the Zurich catered to families and an older clientele. Max had Freddie unlock the door and leave it that way for another five hundred dollars. He oiled the squeaks and stiffness out of the hinges for free. Another thousand—with the promise of more later—bought Teddy's silence, discretion and vigilance.

Max checked out the love nest. It was identical to his room in every way—a round table with two bucket chairs and a lamp by the window, three small mirrors in the shape of flying geese going up the wall by the door, a TV and DVD player, a double bed with a framed vintage Miami Tourist Board poster. Teddy had explained that this was the hotel's only remarkable feature—each room had its unique historical poster. Max's was 1950—the year of his birth. Next door's was 1961. The only noticeable differences were that the air conditioning worked and it smelled much fresher.

The following Wednesday night he timed them.

7:07—7:23: Talking. Rex mostly, but he couldn't hear what he was saying because he spoke quietly, in a deep murmur. It must have been funny or Fabiana was in love, because she laughed a lot.

7:24—7:41: Quiet, mostly, then random moans.

7:43—8:17: Fucking. They were loud. She moaned, cried and yelped. He grunted and gasped. Then she started screaming and shouting. In Spanish. *"Más profuuuundo! Másss pro!-fundo! Si! Si! Mi amor! Si mi amor! Allí! Allí! Si! Siiii! Mi amor! Mi ángel."*

By then Max was sitting by the door with his fingers vainly stuck in his ears to block out the worst. He felt deeply embarrassed to be there, ashamed to be making money this way.

8:18-9:04: Deep, exhausted breathing—his and hers. Fabiana said, *"Su pene es una varita mágica,"* which made Rex laugh and reply, *"Call me Harry Fokker, mamacita."*

He heard the shower.

9:07: The door closed.

Max looked out of the window and saw Rex come out of the hotel and head for Collins Avenue.

9:17: The door closed again.

Fabiana left the hotel and headed in the same direction Rex had.

Max listened in on them for the next two weeks. They started slightly later than before, but the timings were near identical. The only difference from the first time was that he heard them talking a little more afterwards, although it was too quiet to hear what was said.

OVER THE NEXT FEW DAYS, he worked out how he'd sneak into the room and take pictures without being noticed.

It was easier than he thought. He wouldn't even have to step into Room 30, as he'd feared he'd have to.

The connecting door opened right to left. If he opened it a mere three inches, he could get a clear view of the bed and take as many pictures as he wanted without being seen.

7:56: MAX TURNED ON HIS CAMERA—a Canon SLR with a top grade Leica lens, two frames a second—and went and stood by the door. Fabiana hadn't quite started her screaming yet, but she was moaning louder and louder. He heard Rex's grunts and snorts too.

It was time.

He put his hand to the door handle, but suddenly pulled it back as a great greasy coil of nausea slithered across the pit of his stomach and made him gag.

In 1982, when he'd first thought of leaving the Miami PD and going private, he'd sworn he'd never work divorces. Not for him, that sleazy paparazzi shit. Sure, the money was good, the work plentiful, and, outside the corporate sector, it was the safest part of the profession to get into—the most you risked was a black eye or a split lip, if the adulterers managed to put their pants on quick enough to catch you—but he hadn't wanted to make a living that way. He'd wanted to do good, help people, not destroy marriages and make divorce lawyers rich.

Life had a way of poisoning your principles.

He let the feeling ebb and then opened the door a fraction. They'd left the lights on. Fabiana was screaming, "*Mi angel.*" Rex was alternately snorting and gasping. Max was sure everyone in the damn hotel could hear them.

He slid the door back a little more and got the image of the bed in his camera screen. He couldn't see anything. Just white. He zoomed in. Still nothing. Then he zoomed out. Now he had a clear view of the whole bed—white sheets, pillows, bluey shadows playing at the edge.

But there was no one on it.

The sounds coming from the room were getting even louder, the couple screaming in chorus. Maybe they were on the floor.

He peered through the gap in the door. He could see most of the room now. And what he couldn't see was too small an area for two people to be. He was deeply confused. He could still hear them. They were deafening. But the room was empty.

He opened the door all the way back and took a few tentative steps forward. Now he was in Room 30. He looked around. The room hadn't been disturbed at all. It was freshly made up.

He looked in the bathroom—but of course it was empty too.

He was baffled, asking himself a million questions.

Then he found himself looking at the TV.

A porno was playing—a dark haired woman on all fours, getting boned by a tall blonde white man, both arms sleeved in tattoos. That's where the sounds were coming from—the same sounds he'd been hearing for the last four weeks. The man wasn't Rex. And the woman wasn't Fabiana.

The film was coming off the DVD player.

He stood there, numbly watching but not seeing the TV screen, like someone trying to count his reflections in parallel mirrors, from one to the end of all light, to darkness itself. He tried to work out what had just happened, what had been happening, who was behind it and why. He suspected it was some twisted game Emerson Spenser was playing. But he couldn't be sure.

Something on the screen caught his eye. There was a poster above the bed the couple were on. It was identical to the one in the room. He kept watching. The film had been shot in the very room he was standing in.

8:23: Max went and hid in the bathroom, in case someone showed up in the room.

9:27: No one had turned up.

He opened the door of the room and looked out down the corridor. Empty and totally quiet. Weird for a Wednesday night, he thought. That's when the hardcore clubbers usually arrived.

He went back in and looked out of the window into the street, but he knew he wouldn't see them.

He turned off the TV and ejected the DVD.

The porno was called *One Nite in Havana.*

TEDDY WASN'T AT RECEPTION when Max went downstairs. It was some guy he hadn't seen before. An Asian man with a nametag that said George.

"Where's the manager?" Max asked.

"Me. I am. How can I help you?"

"No, the guy who was here earlier."

"I've been on duty since six PM," the man said.

Max thought back to when he'd walked into the hotel. He couldn't remember if Teddy had been at the desk or not.

"Teddy. The guy called Teddy."

"He quit last Sunday," the manager said.

"Last *Sunday*? Why?"

"I don't know. I didn't ask. I just got the job."

"When did you start?" Max asked. He felt anger flooding into him, creeping into his tone.

"Is there a problem with your room, sir?"

"Have you got an address for Teddy? Or a number?"

"We can't give out that information, sir," the manager said.

"How much?" Max sighed.

"Sir?"

"How much for his details? What's this going to cost?"

"Sir, I'm going to have to ask you to leave."

"*What?*"

"I'm *not* giving you his details," the manager insisted in a proud, self-righteous way he underlined by puffing out his small chest and squaring his coat-hanger-frame shoulders.

"Who put you up to this?" Max snapped.

The manager raised his hand and beckoned to someone over Max's shoulder.

"Sir. I'm going to have to ask you to leave the hotel with immediate effect," the manager said. "Security will escort you to back to your room to pack."

Max looked in the mirror behind the reception. He saw a fat, squat security guard in a black uniform and gunbelt standing at his back.

He caught a look at himself too. Bald. Snow white dome stubble mingling with small beads of sweat. Tired looking. Flush faced with anger lashing and humiliation, his eyes icy blue pinpricks. He still just about had his powerful build, but fat was starting to gain on the muscle. The guy in front of him was thirty years younger, so was the security guard. Back in the day he'd have hauled this little prick over the desk and threatened the information out of him. Back in the day he'd been a cop.

He looked at the manager. Was he in on it? Maybe not. He was just a guy working the shitty end of a shitty job in a shitty hotel. There were a lot of them around.

He walked out into the street. The hot blast of nocturnal Miami air hit him in the face. A whisp of a breeze carried smells of food, perfume, and the sea. There was music everywhere—from cars, restaurants, clubs, stores. He didn't know any of the tunes. They were alien sounds. Hip hop, R&B, robotic salsa, and something that sounded like an elephant's coronary. People passed him by, brushed against him, bumped him. Summer clothes, all young, smiling, talking excitedly. Heading down to Ocean Drive for dinner, or to Washington Avenue for clubs. Not a care in the world. Problems parked at the door. He envied each and every one of them.

He thought about what he'd do next. Go to the Shore Club, to see if Fabiana was there? Or should he call Monty, his boss, and fill him in? He wouldn't get far in The Shore Club, as far as getting information was concerned. Deluxe hotels guarded their customers well. He was curious about what had just happened, but a stronger part of him really didn't want to know, just wanted to walk away, forget it. Which left Monty. Only he really couldn't face talking to him right now. The sarcasm, the inquisition. Fuck that.

In the middle of his confusion and indecision, he saw a tall black man across the street, looking right at him. He was wearing a dark shirt with gold birds across it. Max recognised the birds immediately. They were the same as the ones on the Zurich Hotel room walls. He couldn't make his face out too clearly, the specifics blended in with the night and blurred with the neon, but he noticed his stare, level and insistent. He'd specifically picked Max out in the milling crowd, focused on him, targeted him. There were a lot of homeless in Miami. They migrated here for the climate and the guilty generosity of tourists. Max might have dismissed him as one of those, but his old cop instincts kicked in, the sense of a person not being right. And then there were the birds on his shirt. This wasn't a coincidence at all. This was related to what had just happened. Whatever it was. He knew it.

Someone somewhere was laughing at him.

Laughing hard.

Threat Management

Martyn Waites

I could see her from where I was crouching, behind the bushes. She was walking along the pavement, getting bigger as she came towards me, like all I could see was her. Only her. Wearing her usual stuff, business suit with a kind of belted mac thing over it, a short, beige one. Looked good in it, and all, her long black hair loose down the back. Umbrella up. Her heels made that crunchy clacking noise on the tarmac, the kind you only hear in films and think it must be made up till you hear it in real life. There were probably other people around, but I didn't see them. Cars going past made a wet whoosh in the drizzle but I hardly heard them. Saw only her. Heard only her heels clack clacking. Sounded louder than bombs.

I have to be honest, I wanted her then. Any man would.

By the way, this is a true story. I'm not making any of it up. I don't do that anymore. Which is something, which is progress. No, this is exactly how it happened. Exactly.

I've watched her every day this week. Know her routine better than mine. What time she gets up, what time she leaves the flat. Which bus she catches, tube station she gets off at, train she gets on. Which branch of Costa she gets her regular cappuccino, skimmed milk, at. What time she gets in to the office. In the city. Nice place. All steel and glass. Huge. Know what she does in there. Yeah, I've been in. Seen her.

She didn't see me, though.

A solicitor, she is. A legal mouthpiece.

Then lunch breaks, usually a Marks and Sparks sandwich at her desk, sometimes a trip down to one of those flash new places off Spitalfields Market with a couple of the girls from the office. Sometimes with Tony. Another solicitor. Met at some party. Her boyfriend, so she claims. They're an item. Not so sure he'd say the same thing.

And then coffee breaks—sometimes she'll come down to the Costa again, just for a walk, stretch her legs. But no fag breaks. Doesn't smoke. Too healthy. Know which branch of Holmes Place she goes to after work sometimes. And what times. Watched her work out.

Well, apart from that time when she had a broken arm. Just straight to work and back home, then. Alone.

That Tony, he's a cunt. Really, he is. He doesn't appreciate her, not nearly enough. Not an item. Cunt.

Then all again in reverse: tube, bus, home again. Unless she's been going out. Cinema, theatre, dinner. A bar. Usually uptown, nothing round here. Well not much. A couple of times she's been in my local. Once with a mate of hers. And once on her own. Sampling the local atmosphere, I heard her say to Mike behind the bar. But Mike behind the bar wasn't impressed. If he can't shag it or make money out of it, he doesn't want to know. And she wasn't about to become a regular. And she was way out of his league. So really, she knows no one round here.

Except me.

I unscrewed the small bottle, took a big swallow of whisky. Smacked my lips, savoring the aftertaste, feeling the burn. Good. Kept me warm. Helped me concentrate.

The rest of the pubs on the high road and the estate, she's too good for them. Wouldn't want her going in them again. I told her that. The men in there, they're animals. They'd tear her apart. And I might not be there to protect her. I mean, I try my best, but I can't be with her all the time.

I told her that the first time she came in the pub. She laughed then, asked what I did. I told her. Showed her the card. She said nothing.

The second time she came in the pub she said plenty, though. It was accidental, really. I just bumped into her in the street. Like I said, accidental. I hadn't been following her or anything like that.

Honest.

I asked her if she'd like to come for a drink with me. Couldn't believe it when she accepted. Took her to the pub, squired her round. All the other old bastards in there couldn't believe it. She was with me. Me.

We had a great time. Talked all night. She really listened, you know? To everything I had to say, no matter how stupid it sounded. She made me feel like the most important person alive. To have a pretty girl listen to you, and talk to you, it's the most beautiful thing in the world.

She made me feel special.

When she left, Mike from behind the bar said I should forget it. Get her out of my mind, she was too good for me. Whatever she had to say, she was just using me, stringing me along. I got angry with him. Told him just because she didn't like him or want to talk to him he was jealous. He just shook his head, walked off to restock his bottles.

I wasn't falling in love with her then. Honest.

It was dark now and cold. The fog made big patches of blackness between the streetlights. You could see your breath in front of you. I breathed out into my hand, up my sleeve. I didn't want her seeing mine. I watched.

She turned off the pavement like she usually did, made her way to the front of her block of flats. 1930s I think, lots of that type in this part of South London. Old, but still going strong. And worth more than where I lived.

I guessed what she would do next: put her head down, start rummaging through her handbag for her keys. I was right.

I'd been in that flat. Told them all in the pub that she'd invited me in. They didn't believe me. They never do. But she had done. Made me a cup of coffee, even. So yeah, I was really there, true. Let the others in the pub think what they like. Say what they like. I was there.

Honest.

It was comfortable. Really comfortable. That's the best way to describe it. The sofa looked like the kind you'd want to sink into after a hard day's work. The TV looked like the kind you would want to watch. On the shelves were books that looked interesting if you liked that kind of thing and CDs that I'm sure would have been good to listen to. There were other things around too, like candles and little ornaments and small lamps that gave off soft, warm glows. Rugs that reminded you of the expensive foreign holidays that you'd never be able to afford to take.

Not a bare bulb in the place. Not one piece of never never furniture from Crazy George's that'd given up on you before you'd finished paying for it. No mismatching knockoff carpet remnants, donated tables and chairs. Not like my place at all.

I told you I was there.

And in the middle was her. Sitting on the sofa, sipping some real coffee, not the instant shite I was brought up with. She was like the flat. Nice. Dark hair that was long and well cared for. Green eyes that made you want to smile just to look at them. And she had dress sense and style.

She was so sweet, so honest. So loveable.

Then she told me her troubles. Her problem. I listened, all sympathetic like. And when she'd finished, I knew. Knew I could help her. And I wanted to help her. Protect her. Because she was lovely. Really beautiful. And there's a lot of bad things, bad people, out there, just waiting to snatch that beauty away. Because they're cruel. It's what they do. She might live in this area of South London but she's not of it, if you know what I mean. So she needed me to look after her. Like her own guardian angel.

Of course, I didn't say any of this. Just drank my coffee, said I'd help her. But I think she knew. I could tell the way she was looking at me. She could tell what I was thinking.

She touched my hand. Told me how much it would mean to her if I would help. And I got that feeling, that little zing of electricity going up my arm like I'd just stuck my finger in a live socket. And I looked at her. Her eyes. Big enough to fall into.

I swallowed hard. Said I would do what I could. She could rely on me.

She smiled. And I felt my heart lift. Really lift. Like getting a blessing from an angel.

I smiled back. She just jumped like I'd hit her. I saw myself in the mirror over the fireplace when I did it. Don't blame her for jumping. Not a smile but a grimace. A blood lust one like apes do when they've just arse-fucked an outsider to the tribe and killed him by pulling his arms off. Once a squaddie always a fucking squaddie.

I stopped smiling. I was angry with myself, ashamed. She kept her hand there. Gave me another smile.

And that told me everything between us was still OK.

Now like I said, I wasn't falling in love. That would have been fucking stupid.

The hand in the bag was my cue. I'd planned the shortest route to her while I'd been waiting. I hadn't forgotten. The best view, the most camouflage, the quickest escape route. The bushes in the grounds of the flat. Obviously. Away from the road, the streetlight. Other people. Sarge would have been proud of me. Vicious old cunt.

I stood up, still hidden, breathing heavy, hand in front of my mouth, getting psyched, ready to run forward, ready for what was about to happen.

I thought about her all day long. All night. Even when I slept. Beautiful but vulnerable. I began to think things I'd never have considered a couple of months ago. Make little plans in my head. For the future. Thinking of her smile, the way she'd looked at me.

The future.

She stood on the front step, rummaging.

I waited.

But not for long.

They said at this charity that I go to that my problems go further back than just the shell shock. Go way, way back. Before the army. When I was a kid. To stuff that happened to me then. Bad stuff.

But I don't think about that now.

They said I needed an outlet. So I got one. When I told them in the pub what I was doing, when I showed them the cards, they just laughed. As usual. They never take anything I say or do seriously. Think I'm some mentalist, some nutter, spend all day at the library reading private eye novels. Thinking, like the counsellor at the charity said, like I'm the hero of my own fantasy. They think I'm away with the fairies. Delusional, they say.

Well, we'll see.

They say the drinking doesn't help either. I should stop it. Just feeds it.

We'll see.

They say that if I could just stop living out this fantasy life and get on with the real one then that would be something. That would be progress.

We'll see.

She got her key out, tried to put it in the lock, dropped it. She bent down.

And then he was on the doorstep with her. Tony. The cunt. Mouth open, hands going, talking to her, explaining something. Couldn't hear what, didn't matter. Didn't want to know.

And then his hands were on her. Grabbing her shoulders, his voice raised.

The cards I had printed. Threat Management. That's what they said. Got them done at a machine at Elephant and Castle shopping centre. Threat Management, that's what they say. Then my name. And a contact phone number. The pub's. Haven't got one of my own.

He grabbed her, pushed her up against the door. Her bag dropped on the ground. His arms were on her shoulders, holding hard. A blur of something dark and shiny flashed between them. Tony looked down, found the blade in his fist. Her body went towards his, his mouth was up against her ear. Saying something to her. Something unpleasant. They struggled, like two reluctant dancers. Locked together, they moved towards the side of the block of flats, like he was dragging her off.

That second night in the pub. On her own. Said she needed someone to take care of something for her. Someone she could trust.

Threat management.

Tony. The one who gave her the broken arm. Who thought women were there to do what he wanted. Who couldn't take no for an answer. Who claimed they were never an item in the first place but couldn't accept it when she dumped him. Who threatened to hurt her even more.

Hurt her bad.

Wanted someone to do that to him.

And once he was gone she would be grateful. Very grateful.

I was out of the bushes, adrenalin pumping the stiffness out of my legs, straight on him. My arm round his neck, his head in a tight lock, I pulled hard as I could, cutting off his air supply. He choked and gurgled. I pulled harder. Got my mouth close to his ear, said something unpleasant of my own.

He kept struggling.

With my other hand I grabbed for the knife, twisted him round. Saw fear in his eyes. Knew that feeling well. Had enough of that in the army. When you're up against something you don't know, something that could kill you. For me it was in Basra in Iraq. It was shell shock. It was anger. It was things I did there that I know will haunt me till I die. What I got thrown out of the army for. For him it was someone bigger and harder than him when he was only used to hurting girls.

He let her go. Now it was just him and me.

I heard her voice.

Take him . . . do it . . .

I twisted his hand, felt something snap. He dropped the knife. Gave a strangled gasp. I still had him round the throat, didn't want to let him get away. I pulled harder. Even in the darkness I could see him start to change color.

I started to pull him away. Just like we planned. Into to the bushes round the back of the flats, give him a talking to, get a bit heavy, teach him a lesson. Threat management. Dead easy. I started to drag him away.

Didn't get very far.

Because she was there, in front of him, on his chest. Calling him stuff that I would never have imagined she would ever say, stuff even I wouldn't say out loud.

Hissing at him, her voice low, like liquid hate pouring out of her mouth. I was stunned—she was like a whole different person. An angry, nasty, venomous one. I didn't know her.

The gurgling sound in his throat changed tone. I looked down. She had the knife in both hands and it was buried in his chest, right up to the hilt. Blood pooling round it, running down, staining through his clothes.

She stepped back, stared. Smiled. It wasn't pretty.

I didn't know what to do, I was too stunned to react. I let go of him, let him drop. He crumpled to the ground.

Ambulance . . . I said. Oh, Jesus Christ, call a fucking ambulance . . .

She gave me a look, shook her head with a look on her face like she was laughing at sadness, then ran inside the block of flats.

I looked at him. Felt helpless. No phone, like I said. Just stood there, with this bloke I didn't know but was supposed to hate because she had said so, watching the life drain out of him, his face wet with tears and rain.

He flopped and squirmed, like a fish hooked out of water and gasping, trying to get its gills to work properly and failing.

I don't know how long I stood there. But it didn't seem long before the sirens arrived. Police and ambulance. The works. Suppose I should have felt important.

She came out of the flat then. In tears. Looked like her old self, the one I had enjoyed being with so much. The pretty one, beautiful and vulnerable.

The one I absolutely, honestly, hadn't fallen in love with.

I heard her talking to the police. Picked out words.

Delusional.

Alcoholic.

Dangerous. Anger management issues.

Mental problems.

I said nothing. Just stared at her. Stood there in the rain with my parka hood up, face in shadow like some horror movie monk.

Threat management. I could have laughed.

She was a solicitor. A legal mouthpiece.

I forgot that.

She was clever.

They put me in the car. I let them. No sense in arguing. Drove me to the station, processed me, stuck me in an interview room. I told them everything. Everything I've said here.

Well, they listened, I'll give them that.

Then they went out. Left me.

And here I am. I don't know when they'll be back, but it doesn't matter. Because I know what they'll do with me. I know what's going to happen. And it's nothing like the future I was planning a few days ago.

The fantasy future. If anything was delusional, that was.

So what can I do now? Nothing.

But at least I've told the truth. I didn't make it up.

Honest.

I've told it exactly how it happened. Exactly.

So I suppose that's something. I suppose that's progress.

Players
J.D. Rhoades

"Winning was the worst thing that ever happened to me."

Some of the crowd seated in the rows of folding metal chairs nodded. Others spoke up: "Yeah." "You got that right." "Tell it."

I was barely listening. I was looking at Deanne, watching the curve of her neck, the way she brushed a stray lock of her long black hair back behind her ear, the way she jiggled her left foot. She glanced over at me. There was no welcome in that look, no promise, almost no recognition, but I felt myself getting hard at the sight of her. She looked away.

I tuned back in. The story went on in the same old groove. I knew the song by heart. After all, I'd lived it. Winning, then losing, then chasing—gambling more and more on increasingly risky games to make back the money you'd lost. Then the crash: thievery, bankruptcy, abandonment by everyone you ever loved or cared about because they'd just become sources of ready cash for you. Cash you lost and never paid back. Until finally, you tapped out, hit rock bottom, and ended up in a depressing place like this, a church basement on a Thursday night, telling the tale to a bunch of us other losers under the harsh, sputtering glare of fluorescent lights.

"I forgot one thing," the speaker said. I vaguely remembered that his name was Gary something or other. "The house always wins in the end. That's why there's a house."

"Thanks for sharing, Gary," the group leader said over the spatter of applause. "That's all the time we have for tonight. Don't forget there's the financial recovery and planning seminar next Tuesday at the community college ..." I tuned out again. I didn't look at Deanne but I could sense her, feel her presence in the room. We all joined hands, said the Serenity Prayer, and that was that.

I passed by the table with the coffeepot and the picked-over box of doughnuts. Some of the others were beginning to congregate there. One guy, a slim black dude named Theon, smiled at me and made like he was going to say something. I smiled back, but walked on past without pausing for small talk. I had somewhere I needed to be.

I only paused for a second when I passed the empty mug with cash stuck in it for the coffee fund. Time was, my fingers would have itched to reach out and snatch those crisp dollar bills, even the change at the bottom, to get me that much closer to scratching up another stake, another chance at winning. Not tonight, though. Like I said, somewhere to be.

Deanne's car was pulling out of the parking lot as I walked out. I jogged to my own car, fumbled for the keys. I peeled out of the lot, tires barking as I hit pavement. I tore after her, blowing through the yellow lights, my fingers tapping on the wheel. I felt the rush of blood in my ears, felt that old familiar tickle at the base of my skull.

Finally, I spotted her taillights.

My palms were sweaty.

It felt like being at the tables again.

It felt like home.

I saw her brake lights come on. She slowed abruptly and turned through the gate. I sped up to pass the driveway where she'd turned in, went down two more blocks, then did a fast three-point turn in the driveway of a darkened house and headed back. I found the driveway and turned in where Deanne had gone.

The cemetery was the city's oldest and largest, a garden of dirty gray and bone-white stone, stretching out over acres of gently rolling land. You came in through the older part, where the stones and statues were bigger and fancier. I took a right, then a left, until I saw the back end of Deanne's Mercedes, sticking out from one of the side paths. I pulled in.

She was leaning against the side of the car, waiting. Watching me as I got out. We stood there, looking at each other, not speaking. It was like a game we played, to see who broke first, who made the first move.

I won.

I moved first.

She straightened up off the hood and came into my arms, smiling. I kissed her hard, trying to wipe that smile off those gorgeous lips.

She kissed me back even harder, her hands in my hair, stroking, then grabbing a handful and pulling. I couldn't help it, I let out a little gasp, because it hurt.

She laughed at the sound, an edge of hysteria in it.

I dropped my lips to her neck and bit down, and then she wasn't laughing, she was gasping too. Her hands were at my belt, working frantically.

I knew what she wanted to hear. "Someone could see us," I whispered.

She let out a groan and yanked my pants down. I could feel the night air on my ass.

"Someone could see us," I said again, and she dropped to her knees.

"Someone could ..." I groaned as she took me in, "see us ..." I wrapped my hands in her hair, unable to speak anymore.

After a moment or two of that, she reached up and grabbed my wrists, pulling me down into the tall grass with her. She hiked her skirt up and pulled me to her.

I had a last brief conscious thought, wondering where her underwear had gone. Maybe she hadn't worn any.

Then it was fire and wetness and heat, and me grunting, "Some. One. Could ... See ...," and she was moaning in my ear as she came. That set me off, and I felt my back cracking with the intensity of it.

I rolled off her, still panting for breath. She was breathing hard as well. Then she laughed. "I wonder if someone's shivering right now."

I rose up on one elbow. "What?"

"You know how when you get a sudden chill, you say 'someone must be walking on my grave?'"

I never said that, but I nodded.

She giggled again. "I wonder what the feeling is when someone's fucking on your grave."

I didn't answer, but reached out and ran a shaky hand down her side. She was trembling, still wired.

I love you, I wanted to say, but didn't. There were some risks even I never took.

"Mmmm …" she said, and kissed me.

"I wish we could do this in a bed," I said.

"I don't know," she said. "I kinda like this."

"You like that we might get caught," I said. "But the damn mosquitoes are eating me alive." I pulled my pants up, but didn't fasten them.

She laughed. "Well, you know why we can't."

"Right." I tried to keep the bitterness out of my voice. "Your husband."

She kissed me again. "If I leave," she said, "I get nothing. After … everything that happened, he's got the right under that damn prenup to cut me loose without a dime. He does that, I'm out on the street. You going to take me in? You and your parents?"

That stung. The words came out automatically, stimulus and response. "It's just till I get back on my feet."

I'd lost everything when I crashed: job, home, spouse. She at least had kept some of her life. I didn't blame her for holding on to that. At least most of the time. "And what if he found out about this?" I said.

Her eyes grew clouded. "He'd kill me, Billy. I mean really kill me."

It hit me like a cold shock. I'd never met her old man, but I knew from what she'd hinted at that he'd been a real bastard to her. That was why she started gambling, she'd told the group. It was a way to get out of the house. Sometimes she saw it as a way to get back at him.

"Wait, you mean …"

She looked away. "When he found out about the gambling," she said, "he beat me so bad I thought he was going to kill me. He told me that was what I deserved for taking his money. He told me if I ever did it again, he'd beat me again. But he wouldn't kill me unless … unless I was with another man."

I felt cold again, but this time it was fury spreading through me.

"The son of a bitch." I sat up. "I can't … I can't stand to think of anyone hurting you."

She hugged me. "You're so sweet. I wish we'd met ten years ago."

"I wish we could be together now."

There were tears in her eyes. "I know, baby. I know."

"What if …" I trailed off. It was a half-formed idea at the back of my mind.

"What? What if what?"

I kept my voice as level as I could. "What happens if he dies?"

She shrugged. "If he dies, his kids from the first marriage get half of everything. I get the rest."

"Still a pretty good chunk of change."

"Yeah. But he's healthy as a horse."

I took a deep breath. "He doesn't have to be."

"Are you talking about …"

"I'm not talking about anything," I said. "Just thinking out loud."

But I was. I was thinking about something.

And we both knew what.

She looked at her watch. "It's getting late," she said. "I should get back." She started to get up. I grabbed her wrist. The words stuck in my throat at first, then came out in a rush.

"If he ever hurts you again," I said, "tell me."

She looked down at me. "And what'll you do then?" she said.

I felt the thrill go through me again. It was the top-of-the-roller-coaster feeling I got at the table. The feeling I had when I pulled into this deserted place, knowing she'd be waiting.

"I'll kill him, D. I swear it. I'll kill anyone who ever hurts you."
Her eyes were wide. "You mean it?"
I couldn't speak anymore. It was too intense. I could only nod.
She sank back down beside me. "I love you, Billy," she whispered.
My heart felt like it would explode. "I love you," I said.
She kissed me again, soft and slow, her tongue probing. "I can take a little more time," she murmured. She kissed my neck, opened my shirt to kiss my chest, then moved lower.
For the first time in months, I felt like a winner again.

SHE CALLED TWO DAYS LATER. "Billy?"
I put down the want ads. I'd been looking for a job for months, but after the debacle at my old job, no one would touch me. Hey, how eager are you to hire someone on probation for embezzlement?
"Hey," I said. "You okay?"
She never called me at home. He never left her alone long enough to do it, she'd told me, and she was sure he'd tapped her phone to make sure she wasn't calling a bookmaker.
"I thought about what you said. Did you mean it?"
"Has he ..."
"No," she said. "But ... I need to see you."
"Can you get away?"
"I'm at the farmer's market. Can you meet me?"
"Yeah. Yeah, I'll be there in five minutes."

WE SPOKE from opposite sides of one of the long wooden tables at the farmer's market, over a pallet of tomatoes. The green smell of fresh vegetables hung in the air and the place was crowded. We hadn't kissed. Too risky, she said. He might be having her followed.
"I can't get you out of my mind," she murmured. "After what you said you'd do for me ... god, Billy, I could fuck you right here on this table."
I moved closer to the table that held the pallets of tomatoes, hoping no one could see my erection.
"After the next meeting," I said. My mouth was dry.

"Waiting feels like torture," she said. Her murmur was almost a groan. "But," she went on, "what you said … you'd do that? You'd do it for me? So we could be together?"

"Yeah," I said. "If you want me to."

She paused for a long moment, then looked me in the eyes. "I do."

My hands were shaking as I picked up a tomato. I didn't look at it. "Give me a couple of days," I said. "I'll come up with a plan. You'll need to be away."

She smiled. "Just think," she said, "you'll finally get to fuck me in a real bed." She leaned over and whispered, "And you can do anything you want, baby. Anything."

THE NEXT DAY, I told my mom I was going out to look for jobs. Instead, I checked out the pawnshops, looking for guns. But I couldn't figure out how to get one that couldn't be traced.

I began to realize I was in over my head.

When I got back to the house, my dad was watering the rosebushes. I wasn't thinking and pulled into the driveway.

He turned, glared at me as if I'd run over his dog. I sighed and pulled back onto the street and parked at the curb.

"Sorry, Dad," I said as I got out.

"You get that oil leak fixed," he said, "you can park in the driveway."

"Okay, Dad," I said.

It was probably just as well I didn't have a gun then. I felt like blowing my own brains out.

THE SEX AFTER THE NEXT MEETING was the best we'd ever had. Deanne bent over the hood of the car for me and looked over her shoulder, brushing her hair back so I could see her face. "Don't be gentle," she begged.

When she came, she called out my name. She'd never called out my name before.

"When are you going to do it?" she asked afterwards.

"Soon."

"Look, if you're getting cold feet …"

"I'm not. But it's hard to kill someone without getting caught."

"You've got to take some risks, baby," she said.

Her eyes were bright, excited. I wondered if this was how she looked when she was a player.

"Deanne," I said. "This isn't a game. We screw this up, it's not just money we lose. We could die behind this."

The light faded from her eyes, leaving her looking sulky. "I know," she said. She looked at her watch. "Look, I've gotta go. He was suspicious last time."

"Yeah. Okay. We can't take the chance of him catching on."

"No," she said. "We can't take the chance."

I walked to the car and pulled the door handle. It didn't give. "Fuck," I said. I sighed and walked around to the back of the car. I started feeling up under the bumper.

"What's the matter?" she said.

"I locked my goddamn keys inside." I fumbled the little magnetic key safe out from under the bumper. I took my spare out and let myself in.

"You do that often?" she said.

"Often enough. Old piece of shit."

I used to drive a new car every year. They all had electronic locks. You got out, hit the button, and she locked right up, with the keys still in your hand. This old junker didn't have those, and it took some getting used to. After I'd had to open the lock a couple of times with a slim jim improvised from an old coat hanger, I'd gotten the key safe.

I looked over at her as I put the key back. She was looking at me with something that looked a lot like pity in her eyes. I hated her for that look. She still had the nice car, the nice house, the pool. She'd landed on her feet. I was still trying to claw my way back to a normal life with decent shit.

I wanted that life back. I wanted the life she had. And, I realized, all I had to do … all we had to do … was reach out and take it.

"I'm going to do it, D," I said. "I just need a plan."

She nodded, but she didn't look back at me as she got in her car and left.

"HE HAS A GUN," she said. We were back at the farmer's market, talking across a table of watermelons.

"What?"

"He has a gun. At the house. It's in his office."

"Okay …"

"Don't you see? This means you don't have to buy one from someone else."

It was the last piece of the puzzle. I'd been mulling a plan for the past couple of weeks. But I'd stuck on how to get hold of a gun. Under the terms of probation, I couldn't own a firearm legitimately, and buying one on the street would be nuts. It'd put my fate in the hands of a stranger. But now, she'd put a gun in our grasp.

"Okay," I said. "Here's what we do. Tomorrow night, you go out, someplace public. Leave a key under the mat. Make sure people see you. Make sure you get noticed. Cuss out a waiter or something. That way you have an alibi. I'll break in. I'll get the gun. Then I'll smash some shit up. It'll look like a robbery."

She shivered. "God, baby, this is really gonna happen."

"Yeah. You won't ever have to be afraid again."

"I love you."

"I love you."

"Make me yours, Billy," she whispered. "All yours. Forever."

AT DINNER THAT NIGHT, I didn't eat much. I pushed the food around on my plate for a while before excusing myself and going into the living room.

I turned on the TV and sat in the worn easy chair, not watching. I figured they'd turn in early, like they always did. Then I'd … it was hard for me to even put a name to it, even in my head.

My dad came in and sat down on the couch. He didn't say anything for a long time. Finally, he leaned forward, cleared his throat. He looked uncomfortable. My dad was never much of a talker.

"It's going to be okay, son," he said.

I looked at him. "What?"

"I know you're down. You're feeling bad about the mistakes you've made, and that ... I guess that's part of the recovery. But ..." and he hesitated, as if it embarrassed him to say it, "deep down, Billy, I know you're a good man. And you'll be okay."

I felt the tears welling up in my eyes. It was probably the longest speech he'd ever made to me. I stood up. "I'm going for a drive," I said. "I need some time to think."

He stood up as well. And then my Dad did another thing he never did. He hugged me.

I almost did lose it then. But he pulled away before I did and looked at me somberly.

"You say you're just going for a drive, Billy, and I'm going to believe you," he said. "But if you're thinking of going ... someplace else ... well, I hope you'll go to a meeting instead."

I looked away. I couldn't meet his eyes. "My meeting's not tonight."

"There's always a meeting. If not Gambler's, AA. Or NA. Just don't let yourself be alone with the disease."

"I won't, Dad," I said. "And I'm not going to gamble. I promise." He just nodded. This time it was me who hugged him.

"I'll be okay, Dad," I said, my voice choking on the words.

"I know you will, Billy," he said.

I walked out into the cool of the evening, out to my little piece-of-shit car.

I drove around for a couple of hours. Once or twice I even cruised by D's house. I slowed down to look at the big house with its big lawn and its big trees in the yard.

Finally, I realized that look was all I was going to do. I'd been fooling myself. I was no kind of killer.

I didn't know what I was going to tell Deanne. I'd have to figure it out tomorrow.

I drove home. The house was dark when I got there, my folks already asleep. I parked the car by the curb and let myself in as quietly as I could.

I went to bed. It was the first time in three years that I'd slept through the night.

The next morning dawned bright and cool. I got up, fixed some frozen waffles, and checked the want ads in the paper. I marked a few that looked promising, made some calls. One guy could see me, but only if I came right away. I put on my good suit, grabbed a resume, and walked out.

I noticed that my car wasn't where I'd parked it. It was in the drive, not on the street. It was leaking oil onto the nice, clean driveway.

I was standing there, wondering, when the police cars pulled in.

THEY BARELY TRIED DURING MY INTERROGATION. There were no verbal tricks, no good cop/bad cop, no sleep deprivation. As far as they were concerned, it was an open and shut case. The body was in my trunk. His gun was in my trunk. Case closed.

"Look," I said, "you need to be looking at her. She's the one who wanted him dead."

"Oh yeah?" It was the younger detective, Dunbar, the one who had the bushy mustache and sideburns that made him look like a 70s porn actor. "And why would that be?"

"He beat her, for one thing. He said he'd kill her."

"Kinda hard for him to do," said the older cop, whose name was Phelan. "Him bein' in a wheelchair and all."

I didn't think I'd heard right. "What?"

"Don't act like you don't know, Nolan," Dunbar said. "You shot the poor bastard in his wheelchair. He never had a chance. He could barely lift his arms."

"Besides," Phelan added, "we checked. At the time the neighbors heard the shots, she was having coffee with a friend of hers from your, ah, group. Guy named Gary Wilson."

"Gary ..." I saw it then. She had me in a box. I remembered her eyes when we were talking, how excited they looked when she talked about risks.

She'd found a new game to play. And she'd decided to hedge her bets.

I DIDN'T TESTIFY AT THE TRIAL. There was no point. The jury was out less than an hour in the guilt or innocence phase, and didn't take much longer sentencing me to death. Deanne was very moving on the stand, talking about how much she had loved her husband, and how I'd had this obsession with her that she'd tried to discourage. She had never known, she said tearfully, that I'd go so far. I told my lawyer not to ask her any questions. When the time came for the sentence, the judge asked me if I had any words to say before he pronounced sentence.

I looked back into the audience. She was sitting there, with Gary beside her. I wondered if anyone else could see the glitter in her eyes. I wondered if anyone else could see the way Theon, one row back, was looking at Deanne.

"You won this time," I said to her. "But you forgot two things. A player won't stop playing." I looked at Gary. "And the house always wins. Right? That's why there's a house."

They didn't answer, but Gary looked troubled. I smiled and turned back to the judge.

"Hit me," I said.

get Back at me

Robert Hayer's Dead
Simon Kernick

"I used to have a boy like you," the man said quietly. "A son. His name was Robert."

The kid didn't say anything, just kept his position, sitting on an upturned plastic bucket in the corner of the cellar. He was staring down at the bare stone floor, staring hard like it mattered. His naturally blonde hair was a mess—all bunched and greasy—and his clothes, which were the usual early teen uniform of baggy jeans, white trainers and white football shirt, had a crumpled, grimy look like he'd been sleeping in them, which he had.

"I'm going to tell you about my son," continued the man whose name was Charles Hayer. He was stood five feet away from the boy, watching him intently, his face tight and lined with the anguish he felt at recounting the story. "He was all I ever had. You know that? Everything. His mother and me, we were still together but things between us … well, y'know, it just wasn't right. Hadn't been for a long time. We'd been married getting on for twenty years, and the spark, the love, whatever you want to call it, it had just gone. You're too young to understand but that's sometimes the way it goes between a man and a wife. You'll find out one day."

"Will I?" asked the kid, still not looking up. No obvious fear in the voice. More resignation.

Charles Hayer gave the kid a paternal smile that the kid missed. "Sure you will," he said. "But you've got to listen to me first. The fact is, Robert was my life. He was a good kid, he never hurt anyone, and he was everything a father would ever want in a child.

"Then one day when he was thirteen years and two months old, they came and took him."

HE PAUSED. Waited. The kid said nothing. The kid *knew*.

Hayer continued. "There were three of them involved. The one driving the car was called Louis Belnay. He was forty-two and he had convictions going back to when he was in his mid-teens. Bad convictions. The kind that get you segregated when they put you behind bars. He should have been locked up for life because everyone knew he was going to remain a constant danger to young boys, because he always had been, and even one of his psychiatrists said he was untreatable, but I suppose that's not enough for some people. And Belnay was no fool. He knew how to pull the wool over peoples' eyes. That's why he'd only ever done time twice, just a couple of years on each count, which isn't a lot considering he'd been a child molester for more than a quarter of a century.

"He didn't look like a child molester, though, that was the thing. They often say they don't. He just looked like a normal guy. One of his tricks if he didn't have a kid he knew to hand, and he needed to get hold of one, was to impersonate a police officer, a plainclothes guy. Flash the badge, call them over, and bingo, he was away. That's how he did it with my son. Robert was walking home from his friend's place—and we're talking about a walk of a hundred yards here—one night last summer. It was about a quarter past nine, and it wasn't even fully dark. Somewhere on that hundred yards, Louis Belnay pulled up beside him, flashed that false badge of his, and called Robert over. Robert was a trusting kid. He had no reason not to be. His mother and me had warned him about talking to strangers plenty of times, but this guy was a cop, so of course it should have been no problem.

He did as he was told and approached the vehicle, and while Belnay spoke to Robert, his accomplice came round the other side of the car, had a quick check round to see that the coast was clear, then bundled him in the back, putting a cloth soaked in chloroform over his face to make sure he stayed nice and quiet. The accomplice's name was Patrick Dean."

HAYER COULDN'T ENTIRELY SUPPRESS A SHUDDER. Just repeating Dean's name aloud could do that to him. Always would now.

"Now some people say that child molesters can't help what they do, that they're diseased rather than wicked, and I don't know, maybe that's true for some of them. But not Dean. Dean was—is—just pure fucking evil. He just liked to hurt people, kids especially. It was a power trip to him, a way of showing how strong he was to the world, that nothing was sacred to him. If he was here with you now, he'd hurt you bad. Do things to you that you cannot even begin to imagine. Sexual things, painful ones. And he'd enjoy every minute of it too, right up to the moment he put his hands round your neck and squeezed, or put the knife across your throat."

The kid flinched. Hayer saw it. Like someone had threatened him with a slap. He still didn't look up. Hayer felt bad. He didn't like putting the kid through it, didn't like putting himself through it. But there was no other way. He had to *explain*.

"Dean was strong. Big too. Six three and fifteen stone. That's why they used him for the physical stuff. That, and the fact that he didn't scare easily. Ten years ago, while he was in Brixton prison, serving time for some assault and molestation charges, he made a formal complaint to the governor about the way he was being treated. The guards doing the mistreatment warned him that if he didn't drop the complaint, they'd stick him in with the general jail population and let him take his chances. He told them to go fuck themselves. They carried out their threat, he got the shit kicked out of him, but he still went through with the complaint. The guards ended up suspended, several of them lost their jobs, and he got released early even though he was what one detective called 'a walking time bomb.'"

"AND ON THAT NIGHT, the walking time bomb met my son and Robert never stood a chance. He must have seen Dean coming round the car but because he thought he was a cop he didn't run. Maybe if he'd been a couple of years older he would have done, and I guess they counted on that. It was all over in seconds. One minute he was walking down the street minding his own business, looking forward to the holiday the three of us were going to have in Spain the following week, the next he was unconscious in the back of a car, being driven away by two dangerous pedophiles who should never have been out on the streets in the first place. And no one saw a thing.

"I don't know how long he lived after that. I don't like to think about it, to tell you the truth. It's too much. Either way, they took him back to the home of the third guy, Thomas Barnes, and that's where they raped and killed him. Barnes said that the other two made him film it … everything … but the police never found the tape, so I don't know if he was telling the truth or not. But then, why would you lie about something like that?"

Hayer sighed. His throat was dry. He felt awkward standing there, looking down at a silent boy who was only a few months older than Robert had been on the night they'd taken him. Hayer wanted to cry again, to let his emotions do their work, if only because it would show the kid that he wasn't such a bad man—that he too felt pain—but no tears came out in the way they'd done on so many occasions before. It seemed like the well of sorrow and self-pity had finally run dry.

"After they'd finished with him, they cut up the body. Took off his legs, his arms, his head, and tried to burn the pieces separately. It didn't work properly—apparently the body fat melts and it acts to stifle the flames—so they ended up having to put everything in separate bin bags and dumping them at different sites. The bag containing one of his partially burned legs and a section of his torso was found washed up on a riverbank a couple of months later by a man walking his dog. Other parts turned up after that beside a railway line, and at a landfill site. But they never found his head. We had to bury him in pieces."

THIS TIME THE KID DID LOOK UP. His face was streaked with tears. "Listen, please. Why are you telling me all this? I don't want to hear it." His eyes were wide, imploring. Innocent.

Hayer's inner voice told him to be strong. "You have to hear it," he said firmly.

"But I don't—"

"Just listen," snapped Hayer.

The kid stopped speaking. His lower lip began to quiver and his face crinkled and sagged with emotion. Robert had pulled an expression like that once. It had been after he'd broken an expensive vase while he'd been fooling about in the family kitchen. The vase had been a birthday present from Hayer to his wife, and on discovering what Robert had done, Hayer had blown his top on the boy, shouting so loudly that he could have sworn his son's hair was standing on end by the time he'd finished. But when Robert had pulled that powerless, defeated face, all the anger had fallen away to be replaced by guilt at his own unnecessary outburst. God knows, he hadn't wanted to hurt him. His only child. His dead and gone son.

"They found DNA on the some of the body parts," he continued, his voice as dispassionate as he could manage under the circumstances. "The DNA belonged to Barnes, who was also a convicted child sex offender. Barnes was arrested, admitted his part in the death of my son, and expressed terrible regret. He also named Belnay and Dean as being involved.

"Belnay and Dean both went on the run but were caught quickly enough and charged with murder, as was Barnes. We buried what was left of our son and waited for some sort of closure with the trial. But of course we never got it. Because a man called Gabriel Mortish denied us that."

"Oh God," said the kid.

Hayer nodded. "Oh God, indeed. Gabriel Mortish QC, one of *the* best defense barristers in the country, well known for taking on the cases that no one else wants to touch. He's defended all sorts. Terrorists, serial killers, rapists. If you're one of the bad guys, he'll be there supporting your right to maim, torture and murder with everything he's got. If you've never done a thing wrong in your life, tried to treat others like you'd want to be treated yourself, then he's not interested in you. So, of course, it went without saying that Mortish took on the defense of Belnay and Dean. Not Barnes, because Barnes had shown some remorse for what he'd done, admitted that he'd played a part in it. That made him part human and Mortish is only interested in helping out subhumans.

"Belnay and Dean denied everything. Said it was nothing to do with them, but it came out that a neighbor remembered seeing the two of them leaving Barnes' house the day after Robert had disappeared, and when the police found the car used to abduct him, they found Belnay's DNA in that. But the two of them stuck to their story. Said that they knew Barnes, and had been round his house, but that that was the extent of their involvement. Instead they blamed him, claiming that he'd been acting very erratically when they were round there, and came close to admitting that he'd been the one responsible for the abduction. But Barnes said it was the other way round. According to him, it was Dean doing the killing with Belnay encouraging him, and it was Dean who did the chopping up of the body afterwards."

Hayer sighed. "Your dad did a good job, son. I had to give him that. I watched him every day in that courtroom. He sowed doubt like it was a breeding rabbit, put it everywhere. Sure, he said, Belnay and Dean were not nice guys, no question of that, but were they guilty of this heinous crime? He said the evidence suggested strongly that they weren't. He made the neighbor, the witness who'd seen them leave Barnes' place, sound all confused about whether it was actually them she'd seen. Then Barnes got put on the witness stand and your dad wound him up in knots. Did he see Dean or Belnay kill Robert? If so, why didn't he try to stop it? Wasn't he just blaming them to take the heat off himself?"

Hayer sighed, addressing the kid directly now. "You know what happened? Course you do. Barnes ended up admitting that he hadn't seen either of them actually kill him, that he'd been out of the room at the time, but he came across like a shifty witness—someone you weren't going to believe. Your dad made him look like that. Your dad discredited the evidence to such an extent that Barnes, who didn't have him as a lawyer, got life for murder, but Belnay got away with seven years as an accessory. And Dean ..." He spat the name this time. "The judge directed the jury to acquit him. Said the evidence against him just wasn't reliable. That was your dad's doing. He got one of them seven years, meaning the bastard'll be out in four, and the other—the one who was pure fucking evil, who cut my son into little pieces—he got him off. He walked free, and now he's living on the outside with police fucking protection, just to make sure that no one tries to take the law into their own hands and trample on his precious human rights, even though no one gave a shit about my son's human rights. He's even strode past this house a couple of times, just to fucking torment me. THAT IS NOT JUSTICE!" He shouted these last four words, shouted them at the non-existent heavens, his voice reverberating round the dull confines of the cellar.

The kid opened his mouth, started to say something, but Hayer was not to be interrupted. "That man ... your father destroyed me. He took away the last thing I had left: closure. A week after the trial, two months ago, Robert's mother and I split up. Neither of us could take any more. She's contacted a lawyer and the divorce'll be going through sometime soon. All I've got left is my job. Adding up numbers on one side of a page, taking them away on another."

"Please, I—"

"Shut up. Just shut up. Listen to me." He paused for a moment, tried to calm himself down, knew it wouldn't happen. Not until he'd said his piece. "I can't stand my job, I can't stand what my life has become. I can't ... I can't stand fucking any of it, and that's why you're here. You've got to understand that. What those men did to Robert, what they stole from me, that half put me in the grave. What your dad did, what he did on behalf of bastards who do not deserve to even be alive let alone walking free, well that pushed me the rest of the way. I've got nothing left to lose now. That's why I snatched you. That's why you're here. Because I've got to make him suffer like I've suffered.

It's the only way. Some people say two wrongs don't make a right, some people say that you can't stoop down to a bad man's level, but it's bullshit. It's all fucking bullshit propagated by people who haven't been torn apart by suffering, by injustice."

"But you don't understand."

"Don't understand what?" he yelled. "Don't understand what? I understand fucking everything, that's the problem!"

The kid shook his head. Fast. "No you don't. Honestly. The man you're talking about ...," the voice quietened, almost to a whisper. "He's not my dad."

"What?"

"This man, Mortish, he's not my dad. My name's Blake. Daniel Blake. Lucas Mortish goes to my school. We've got the same color hair, but my dad's an IT director. Please, I promise you."

The tension in Hayer collapsed, replaced by a thick black wave of despair. He looked closely at the boy. Was he wrong? What if he was?

"Oh shit. Oh no."

The cellar seemed to shrink until it was only inches square. A heavy silence squatted in the damp air. The kid snivelled. Hayer just stood there, defeat etched deep on a face that had seen far too much of it during the previous year.

Ten seconds passed. The kid snivelled again. Hayer didn't know what else to say.

It was the kid who finally broke the silence. "I'm sorry about your son," he said, trying to look like he understood, "but it was nothing to do with me."

This time it was Hayer who couldn't bear to look the kid in the eye. Instead the whole world finally fell apart for him, and with a hand that was shaking with emotion, he reached into the pocket of his jacket and pulled out the .22 caliber handgun he'd bought illegally three weeks ago in a pub (for either a murder or a suicide, he hadn't known which), fumbled and released the safety, then placed the cold barrel hard against his temple, and pulled the trigger.

He died instantly.

LUCAS MORTISH SIGHED WITH RELIEF, then stood up, staring down impassively at the body of the deranged lunatic who'd abducted him from the street the previous afternoon, chloroforming him in the process. He was hungry. And thirsty. The lunatic's head was pouring out blood onto the uneven concrete floor and already the corpse was beginning to smell. Lucas Mortish wrinkled his nose and stepped over it, making for the steps that would take him to freedom.

It had been an uncomfortable experience and one in which he'd had to use all his natural cunning to survive, but it had also been a very interesting one. He couldn't wait to tell his friends about it. And his father. His father especially would be proud of the way he'd thought on his feet, catching his kidnapper out so smartly.

His father had taught him so many good lessons. That words can tear an opponent to pieces far more effectively than even the strongest blade.

And of course, that in law, as in life, there is no place for sentiment.

So what if the lunatic's son had died? His death had had nothing to do with Lucas, nor with his father. His father had simply done his job. Why then should they be made to pay for this other man's misery?

He mounted the steps, opened the door and walked out into Hayer's hallway. Ignoring the photographs on the wall, quite oblivious to them, he went over to the phone, even allowing himself a tiny triumphant smirk as he dialed the police.

Didn't hear the footsteps behind him. Only knew that something was wrong when the phone suddenly went dead before it was picked up at the other end. As if it had been unplugged.

He turned round slowly, the hairs prickling on the back of his neck. Saw the man.

Stocky, with close-cropped hair and narrow, interested eyes. Dressed in an ill-fitting blue boiler suit. Stained. An unpleasant familiarity about him.

Found his eyes moving almost magnetically towards the huge, gleaming blade of the carving knife in the man's huge paw-like hand.

The fear came in a quivering rush.

Now it was Patrick Dean's turn to smirk.

Welcome to Wal-Mart, Motherfucker
Patrick Shawn Bagley

I moved in with my uncle Alton Rowell when I was sixteen. My mom had given up on trying to keep me home by then. When you've already run away five times, moving out is no big deal.

"Least this way, I'll know where you are," she said. There was something else in her eyes, the unsaid thing that we both understood: Alton would never try to get into my pants.

I stood in the kitchen with a garbage bag full of my clothes at my feet and my stuffed dog, Scooter, in my hand. Mom sat at the table, smoking a menthol cigarette and sipping at coffee. Her robe hung partway open, and I saw a blue vein running down into her cleavage.

"I can call sometimes if you want me to," I said. It was mid-July, the morning already hot and made worse because Mom never opened her windows. Sweat ran down the small of my back. I wanted to run out the door, jump into Alton's car and never look back, but it felt like there was something else I should say. What, I didn't know. Just something. "I'll call," I said again.

Mom shook her head. "You better not. Kevin won't like it if you call."

"'Cause I'm a slut."

"You know that ain't true, Tina." Mom flicked ash from her cigarette. The ashtray was still full of last night's butts.

"Whatever," I said. "I got to go. Alton's waiting." I picked up my stuff and headed for the door.

Mom got out of her chair and cut me off. She grabbed me tight above the elbow and yanked me close to her. "Kevin's a good Christian," she said. "The first decent man I've had in a long time."

I did not try to break away. I got right up in her face and said, "Yeah, he's a real good Christian. Said he didn't want to spoil me for marriage. That's why he tried to fuck me in the ass instead. Kevin's just like all the rest, Mom. Except he goes to church every Sunday and gets forgiven."

She shoved me away then. I ran outside, letting the screen door bang shut behind me. Alton had kept the car running, the windows all rolled up and the AC cranked. I got in, shoved the trash bag on the floor between my feet, sat back and closed my eyes. Maybe that would keep me from crying.

Alton backed the car out of the driveway. "Went well, did it?"

ALTON HAD A TRAILER out on Cornville Road. There was a little bit of a yard, with trees crowded right up close on three sides. There was a trail through the woods that led to an old sugar shack, but Alton never used it. He had built a deck on the front of the trailer and an addition in the back. That addition was the biggest room in the place. Alton used it for storage, but he turned it into my bedroom when I moved in. Everything I owned fit into one garbage bag, so even with the bed and bureau Alton bought me the room looked pretty empty.

"You'll fill it up with posters and junk soon enough," Alton said. He was a big man, about six-one and probably two hundred and fifty pounds, so broad he had to turn sideways to get through the doorways in that trailer. Alton had been a marine for twenty-four years, and still kept his gray hair done in a flat-top. His goatee was short and neat, too. Mom always said it was too bad a guy that good looking had to be queer.

My first night at his house, we sat out on the deck, watching fire-flies and listening to the peepers in the bog across the road. That was our entertainment because my uncle didn't own a TV, or even a radio. No phone, either. Alton said the world wasn't interested in him and he wasn't interested in the world. So we sat there, him drinking Bud Lite and me with a Diet Coke.

"You can stay here as long as you want," Alton said. "The only thing I expect of you is to do a few chores, and stay in school and get decent grades."

"School sucks."

Alton gave a little chuckle. It was too dark to see his face. He said, "Yeah, it does. It sucks big time, but doing good in school is the only way you're going to get away from this place."

"If Wesserunsett's so bad, how come you came back?"

"You just worry about you, Tina." There was a pop and hiss as Alton opened another can. I slouched down in my chair, listening to my uncle gulp down his beer.

THE THING I HAVEN'T SAID about Alton is that he got shot over in Iraq. He told me the name of the place once, but I'd never heard of it and now I don't remember it. I Googled the village at my high school li-brary, and the map showed it as a dot in the middle of some desert. Much as I hated Wesserunsett, I could never figure why anybody would want to live in a fucking desert. Anyway, Alton got his right leg all chewed up by machine-gun fire. A bullet shattered his knee, so the doctors put in a replacement. Alton walked with a cane when he first came home. The cane was gone by the time I moved in with him, but he still limped. The one time I saw him in shorts, I almost puked from looking at his leg.

When Alton came home, not long after my fifteenth birthday, it was the first time I'd seen him since I was a little kid. He got hired as a greeter at the Wal-Mart in town. It wasn't the job he wanted, but it was all he could find. He bought his trailer and eight acres on the Cornville Road with some money he had saved. Mom told me that, being queer, Alton saved a lot of money because he didn't have to spend it on a wife or kids or taking out girlfriends. That sounded like bullshit to me, but you can't tell my mother anything.

ONE OF MY CHORES WAS LAUNDRY. We ran up a clothesline from a pole by the deck to a maple tree on the edge of the yard. It was on a couple of pulleys, so I didn't have to lug the basket far. Dave Dunphy drove in Friday morning while I was hanging out a load of whites.

He leaned out the window of his pick-up. "Hey, Tina. Your uncle home?"

I pinned one of my bras to the line, wishing it was a pair of jeans instead. Dave stared at me the same way all Mom's boyfriends did. His dirty thoughts stuck to me, made me want to go wash myself all over. I said, "He's at work." Like Dave didn't know that already.

Dave grinned and got out of the truck. He puffed out his scrawny chest and said, "Wal-Mart greeter. Jesus Christ, that's a shitty job for a man." Dave and Alton had run together back in high school. I had no idea what he did for work, but he hung around the trailer a lot. At first I thought maybe he was my uncle's boyfriend, but Dave was married with three kids. Yeah, I knew that didn't mean much. But I also knew that no gay man would ever look at me the way Dave did.

I shrugged and hung up a pair of socks. "Alton says a paycheck's a paycheck."

Dave walked over to the deck and stopped at the bottom step. "He always was a philosopher. Listen, Tina, I'm thirsty as hell. Alton got any beers in the fridge?"

"You can't drink and drive." I didn't care if he got shitfaced and wrapped his truck around a telephone pole, so long as he did it far away from me.

"I ain't gonna. I figured I'd sit with you a while, drink a few. You can have some, too. I won't tell on you." He took a pack of cigarettes from his t-shirt pocket and tapped it against the heel of his other hand. "Want a smoke?"

I shook my head. The load was all up on line, so I walked to the door, keeping the empty basket between me and Dave. He lit a cigarette, then came up the steps and tried to take the basket from me.

"Let me get that for you," he said.

I pushed him away. "Alton keeps a loaded twelve-gauge behind door." I didn't wait for him to say or do anything, just went in and dropped the laundry basket on the floor. I locked the door and picked up the shotgun. I wanted to look out the window and see what Dave did, but then he might see the fear in my eyes and, the next time he tried something, my tough talk wouldn't mean shit. His truck started up and I heard it back down the driveway. I went to my bedroom, taking the twelve-gauge with me. It was just one of those single-shot things, but I figured one shot from a twelve-gauge ought to be enough for anybody. I laid there with Scooter in one hand and the gun in the other.

A CAR DOOR SLAMMED and woke me up. The brass alarm clock next to my bed read half past four. Alton worked from eight in the morning until two in the afternoon, and he'd never come home so late in the week since I'd moved in. I got out of bed, grinding my knee into the shotgun because it had been lying there next to me. I picked it up and ran down the hall, rubbing my knee. Alton was coming up the deck steps. I propped the twelve-gauge in the corner and unlocked the door.

Alton came in and tossed his necktie on the kitchen table. He looked around for a second, then opened the fridge and grabbed a beer. He opened it, but didn't drink right away. "How come the breakfast dishes are still sitting in the sink?"

I said, "I didn't feel good after doing the laundry, so I went back to bed for a while. Guess I fell asleep."

"Oh." He took his beer into the living room and turned on the ceiling fan before sitting down in his recliner. I watched him, and then I really didn't feel good. Because Alton always had at least one funny story to tell about some weird customer or the goofy-ass people he worked with at Wal-Mart. But that day, my uncle just sat in his chair staring out the window.

I got myself a Diet Coke and sat cross-legged on the floor in front of Alton. "What's the matter?"

He looked down at me and shook his head. He drank some beer. I untied his work boots and took them off. "Something's bothering you. It ain't like you to mope around."

"You ever wish you didn't have a fag for an uncle?"

"That's stupid. You're you. I love you the way you are."

"Your mother hates that I'm gay. It shames her."

"My mother fucks every guy she meets."

Alton scowled and pointed a thick, callused finger at me. "Whatever you think about her, Jeanie is still your mom. When my mother died, I hadn't spoken to her for fifteen years. I don't want it to be that way for you two."

I drew a line through the sweat on my soda can. "So what's this have to do with whatever's bothering you?"

"I saw Kevin at the store today. He came in with a couple of his church buddies."

My stomach felt cold, down at the bottom. "He give you a hard time?"

Alton sipped his beer and wiped his lips with the back of his hand. He said, "Nothing I haven't heard before. Just the usual fagbashing, you know?"

I nodded even though it was hard to imagine anyone ballsy enough to start something with my uncle.

Alton said, "But after they'd had their say and laughed about it, Kevin looked at me and asked why I didn't say "Welcome to Wal-Mart." I ignored him because other customers were coming in. Kevin went over to the service desk and complained that I was rude to him. Said he wanted to see the manager.

"Well, Billy True came out of the office and heard what Kevin had to say. He asked me why I hadn't greeted Kevin. What the fuck was I supposed to tell my boss? That I got offended because Kevin and his buddies called me a cocksucker and a fudgepacker? No. I already knew how that would go over. So I said I just forgot. Billy said I had to apologize to Kevin, right there in front of everyone."

"You didn't, did you?" I got up and paced around the living room. "Why the fuck should you apologize to that asshole?"

"Calm down," Alton said. "I'm telling you what happened. Like I said, Billy wanted me to apologize, but there were Kevin and those two other guys, grinning at me. One was trying so hard not to laugh that he had to turn away. Other customers watched, plus Bea at the service desk and the girl from kids' clothes. I couldn't take it, Tina. I said … well, I said "Welcome to Wal-Mart, motherfucker." And then I quit before Billy could fire me."

"I'm surprised you didn't deck him."

"Kevin Dore's not worth going to jail for."

"You should have decked him."

I FIXED US A MACARONI SALAD FOR SUPPER. I made it like Mom always did: elbow macaroni, sliced hard-boiled egg, chopped tomato and cukes, plenty of mayo and a little mustard. I wanted to sprinkle paprika over the top, too, but Alton didn't have much in the way of spices. Alton lit the gas grill and threw on a couple of hamburgers for each of us. He asked me to mix up some Kool-Aid.

"No beer tonight? On a Friday?"

He said, "Not when I'm bummed out."

We sat at the little round table on the deck. Alton lit a citronella candle to keep the bugs away. I took a big bite out of my burger, and just about choked when Dave Dunphy's truck came down the road and pulled into the driveway.

Alton patted me between the shoulder blades. "Smaller bites, Tina," he said. "Your food's not going to get away."

I nodded and drank some Kool-Aid.

Dunphy came up on the porch. He gave me a quick look and sat down near Alton. "Hear you got fired this morning," he said.

"Guess you heard wrong," Alton said. "I quit."

They laughed about that. Alton offered Dave a beer.

"Nah. I'm only stopping for a minute. Want to talk business with you."

Alton pushed his plate away and sat up straighter. "Is this the same thing you asked me before?"

Dave nodded. He watched me out of the corners of his eyes. I went back to eating and pretended not to be interested.

Alton said, "Then the answer's still the same."

"Jesus Christ, Al. It ain't like you're rolling in money here, and now you've quit your job. I'm trying to help you out a little. You don't even have to do nothing, you know. Just rent me the fucking shack."

"There's a house not even half a mile through the woods from that shack. They'll see."

"No problem," Dave said. He waved his hands in the air while he talked. "I checked the place out already. Some old couple lives there. They hardly ever go into their backyard, and there's no way they could see the shack through the trees. It's a perfect setup."

"I'm not getting caught up in this shit," Alton said. "Especially now that Tina's here."

Dave turned to me. "Tina, why don't you go play in your room or something? Me and your uncle need to talk."

I said, "I'm eating my supper."

He wanted to smack me. Or fuck me. Or both at once. I saw that in his eyes, that same look Kevin always gave me. I smiled through a mouthful of macaroni salad.

Alton said, "She doesn't need to leave because there's nothing to discuss. I told you no."

"You give me that look, that high-and-mighty look like you always used to," Dave said. He got up from his chair and loomed over my uncle. "Did I ever judge you, Al? Ever? And now you look at me like I'm garbage. Well, fuck that. I'm offering you a straight-up business deal that you're tossing away because of that little cunt there."

Now Alton stood up, too. Dave looked tiny next to my uncle. Alton said, "Time to go."

Dave turned and walked off, head down and muttering all the way to his truck.

IT TOOK ME UNTIL THE NEXT MORNING to get up the guts to ask Alton what kind of business Dave was talking about.

Alton had his nose in a book, a weird old sci-fi looking thing by some guy named LaSalle. He looked up and reached for his coffee. He said, "Dave wants to rent that old sugar shack of mine, back in the woods."

"Why? You can't make maple syrup in the middle of July. Even I know that." I poured Cheerios into my bowl, poured in some milk and scattered two spoons full of sugar over the top.

Alton put down his book. "I want you to tell me if he comes around here when I'm out. He might think he can put something over on me, but that's not happening."

I said, "Dave's an asshole."

"Uh huh, but he's still my friend."

"So why's he want the sugar shack?"

"His meth lab burned down. He needs a new one."

ALTON TOOK A SHOWER AND SHAVED. He put on his khakis and a dress shirt. He said, "I'm going into to town to fill out applications at some places. I'll be back in time for lunch."

"Let me go with you."

"No, that's okay."

I said, "I can drive you around, be like your chauffeur. I've hardly had any practice at all since I got my permit."

"You'll get bored, Tina. Besides, it doesn't look good when you go dragging kids with you to apply for a job."

"Yeah, right," I said. "You embarrassed of me? Or maybe you're meeting your boyfriend."

He shook his head and left. I cleaned up the breakfast mess. Alton had an old mountain bike in his shed, and I wanted to go for a ride just to get out of the house. But I didn't want to be out on the road by myself if Dunphy came along.

So I hopped in the shower after locking the doors and looking out the windows, too, just to make sure Dave Dunphy wasn't hiding in the woods, waiting to get me. The whole time I was in the shower, I kept opening the curtain a crack and peeking out. I wondered if I should have brought the shotgun into the bathroom with me. All I had in there was my little pink razor.

Nothing happened. I dried off and put on a pair of shorts and a black tank top. I figured on doing my nails and then goofing off the rest of the morning. The nail polish had barely dried when I heard someone drive up and get out of a vehicle. I stood at the front door, looking out through the screen.

Dave Dunphy waved to me as he came up the steps.

I said, "Get the fuck out of here." Then I slammed the door and locked it.

Dave walked over to the living room window and looked inside. He ran his fingertips over the screen. "I know Alton ain't here 'cause I followed him into town just to see what the old cocksucker was up to. You ain't going to keep me out of this flimsy fucking trailer if I want to get in, so either unlock that door for me to come in, or you come on out here. We'll have a nice talk."

"I got nothing to say to you."

"The fuck you don't," Dave said. He walked back to the door.

I grabbed Alton's twelve-gauge and stood back from the door, waiting for Dave to kick it in. The doors on old trailers aren't good for much; even I could knock one off the frame if I wanted to bad enough. I imagined Dunphy's hard-on could do the job.

He only hit the door twice before the jamb splintered. Then he pushed it open and came in, grinning. I raised the shotgun and cocked the hammer.

Dave stopped, but he kept grinning. "You ain't ever fired a gun in your life," he said. "The way you're holding that thing, it's going to knock your arm right out of the socket when you pull the trigger."

I kind of tightened up all the muscles in my shoulders and it felt like I was squeezing the trigger with the whole upper part of my body. There was a dry snap and that was all.

"Should've made sure it was loaded, retard," Dave said. He started across the room.

I jabbed the shotgun straight out from me, hard as I could, and nailed him in chest with the muzzle. Dave grunted and stopped, holding his hand over his heart like he was going to say the Pledge of Allegiance. Instead, he said called me a cunt again and said, "You think that's funny, we'll see how you laugh when I pinch your nipples. We'll put some clothespins on those little titties."

I brought the shotgun back like it was a baseball bat and whipped him across the face. I felt the impact in my hands and wrists. Dave fell over sideways into Alton's recliner. He held up his arm to protect his head, but that didn't slow me down. I said, "Welcome to Wal-Mart, motherfucker." Then I swung the twelve-gauge down across Dave's arm.

He howled and let the arm drop, so I hit him again. I got his head that time. Doing it felt good. I was hot and shaking, and I kept on hitting him and yelling that same shit about Wal-Mart.

After a while, I stopped shouting.

Some time after that, I stopped hitting Dave.

I dropped the gun. My arms were too tired to hold it. Dave didn't move. He didn't make any noise. He didn't look like Dave anymore. Pools and spatters of blood covered Alton's chair and the end table next to it. The carpet was squishy with the stuff. There was blood on my arms, on my clothes and my legs. My face felt wet. Some of that was from tears, but the rest was blood. When I took a breath, that blood was all I smelled.

I didn't what to do next, so I took another shower. As I stood there under the spray, I scrubbed myself longer than I had to. It felt good. Tingly. I rubbed the rough washcloth over my nipples and down between my legs. It wasn't enough to get off, because that would be sick, but to keep that good feeling going just a little bit longer.

IT WAS STILL A COUPLE HOURS before Alton was supposed to come home. I put on clean clothes and threw a blanket over Dave because I didn't want to look at him anymore. But I knew other people would want to see the son of a bitch. Dave had a wife and kids, and they'd be looking for him. There were plenty of places to hide the body, but his truck was right out there in the dooryard where anybody going by could have seen it. It wouldn't take the cops long to find out Dave Dunphy had been here. They would probably think Alton had something to do with it, or that he'd done the killing. Fuck that. I'd make sure they knew it was me.

I wiped as much blood as I could off the shotgun. It took me a while to find where Alton kept the shells. There were two boxes of double-ought buckshot in the kitchen junk drawer. The boxes were skinny, and only held eight shells between them. I took the shotgun and the full box of shells out to the truck, hoping that Dave had left the keys in it. I didn't want to fish through his pockets to find them. But if the truck had a standard tranny, the keys wouldn't make a difference anyway because I didn't have a clue how to drive a stick.

That's how I knew I was doing the right thing; the keys were in the ignition and the truck was an automatic. I laid the gun across the seat and climbed in, frigged around with the mirrors until they were how I wanted them. Dave had left the windows down, but it was still hot in there. No AC, either. I backed out into the road and headed for my mother's house; Kevin would probably be rolling out of bed by the time I got there. If not, I'd wake him up.

The air blowing in through the windows cooled the sweat on my forehead and at the back of my neck. There was the hot sun and the cool breeze. The faster I went, the more the truck shimmied and that felt good, too. Every time I passed a house or another vehicle, I shouted out the window, "Welcome to Wal-Mart, motherfucker!"

Fire Girl
Victor Gischler

I'd just shaved my legs that morning, so I wasn't surprised the man leered. I had on a pretty sundress, short, a light and wonderful flower pattern that brought out my eyes. I was pretty. But he shouldn't leer.

I hated him.

But I didn't want him to stop looking. I liked that he knew I was pretty. But he was rude.

Whoever he was, I hated him. I hated the leer. I'd painted my toenails bright, and the toes poked out delicate and pink from my sandals. I had a good shape. You could see it through the thin fabric if the sun came at it just right. But he didn't look with appreciation. The raw desire in his eyes was terrible.

I glanced over my shoulder as I moved up the sidewalk, made sure he was still watching. I swayed my hips as I walked to keep his eyes down, keep him from looking at my face. Never the face.

I was pretty. I knew I was because he looked, but never the face.

Oh, how I hated him.

Not just for looking, but also because he was in the way.

I glanced again, made sure he saw me looking at him. He did. He smiled, and I shivered. Not a friendly smile. It's never friendly. Men never smile the right way. The smile always made me feel pretty, but always with the oily coating. Like ash. Like cold soot that rubbed off on your hands. Fire was warm and beautiful, but it always left the soot. Always a mess.

He followed now.

Good, move away from the building, Mr. Leer. King Leer, leerman. Another glance kept him coming. Just a glance. I never turned fully or he'd see the face, the other side. He'd see where—

He walked a little faster, trying to catch up. But he was away from the building. That was all I needed. I could go now, leave him to leer at some other woman.

But I glanced back just once more.

He caught me, tapped me on the shoulder. I stopped, half turned with my head down, blond hair falling over my face. I looked up at him through the strands.

"Hi." His oily smile again, rubbing off on me. "I saw you looking and thought I'd say hi."

"I wasn't looking." In my head it sounded confident, defiant. It crept from my lips, a shy whisper.

"No, it's okay. I noticed you too," he said.

I turned fully to face him, tucked my hair behind my ears.

His next comment withered in his throat. His eyes grew large before looking past me. "Uh . . . sorry."

"What's the matter?" My voice louder now.

"Nothing. My mistake. I thought you were someone I knew—"

"You're a liar." My hand flew up to touch the scar on my left cheek. The vaguely oval patch of marred flesh from my eye to my chin. I remembered the flames and the heat and jerked my hand away. I'd touched the scar again. I hated myself for touching it.

Mr. Leer started to lie again. He opened his mouth to offer slick apologies, but he never got them out.

The ground shook when the flash charges went off. The blast blew out the windows of the three-story building behind us where he'd been standing. Glass rained, flew across the street, *tinkled* and *clinked* on the sidewalk in a glittering shower.

Leer went to his knees, arms over his head.

I watched.

After the initial flash, the flames burned white hot in the windows. The flash explosions were small; the brick structure would survive. I'd been paid for a gut-job. No danger to anybody unless they went inside. The structure would stand. Hollow and scorched, but it would stand.

I realized Leer was tugging at my arm.

"Come on. The fire could spread. Get back."

Fool.

I shook him off. He gave up and ran.

The flames licked and danced in the windows like burning eyes. Beautiful. Hypnotic. My hands rubbed my thighs. I closed my eyes, felt the wave of heat roll over me. One hand drifted to my seam, rubbed lightly. I stood with legs spread.

It was beautiful and warm, and I was beautiful too.

Sirens.

I opened my eyes. People spilled from other buildings to watch. I turned. Time to go. The fire engines would come. Men and their hoses. They would be too late. The chemicals burned quickly and completely with little oxygen. It had been a good job. Professional. Time to go get paid.

WADE AVENUE PAWN was right next door to the filthy adult video store. I would have burned it for free except Gene owned the pawnshop and video store both. Gene kept me in business, found my jobs for me. I loved Gene, and Gene loved me.

He buzzed me into the shop, and told Fat Rico to watch the counter while we went back to his office. In his office, we sat. He unlocked a strong box and took out a wad of cash that was for me.

"That's five thousand, and 20 percent for me." He scribbled in a spiral-bound notebook as he spoke. He counted out four thousand and pushed it across the desk. I took it, rubbed the money between my fingers. It felt good. I folded it, put it in my purse.

Gene was what people called a midget, but when he sat across from me at the desk, he looked totally normal. Maybe he was sitting on phone books or something, but I never asked, and I never looked. I was polite. His dark, slicked back hair and pointed beard made him look like Don Juan.

"What about expenses?" he asked.

"No expenses."

"None? What did you use?"

"I had stuff left over from the last job."

"You should charge expenses anyway. It's more professional."

"You're right, Gene. I will next time."

He put away the notebook and the lock box. He took an envelope out of his top desk drawer and handed it to me. "I've got another job for you."

"Already?"

He raised his eyebrows. "Maybe it's the busy season. What do I know? But you're in demand. I might have another one after this too."

"I-I can't rush these jobs, Gene. If I do I could get caught or botch the job or—"

"Hush, honey, now take it easy." Gene smiled, warm not oily. "I told the lady to check back because you were all booked up."

"The lady?"

"More like a girl really," said Gene. "She said she needed somebody talented for something special. I said I knew who was the best, but she's expensive and there might be a wait. No hurry, okay? Take it easy. If she can't wait, she'll just have to find somebody else. Okay?"

I didn't say anything.

"Cassandra?"

I warmed, eyes brightened. I loved the sound of my name in his mouth.

"Just take it easy."

"Okay." I fingered the envelope. "What about this one?"

"It's all written down."

"What kind of job?" I didn't want to leave yet, wanted to talk. I wanted to be with Gene.

"You know I don't like to discuss details. Okay? It's all written down."

"I'm sorry."

"It's okay. Now run along."

"I love you, Gene."

"Huh?"

"I love you."

"Oh, yeah. I love you too, honey."

I loved Gene, and Gene loved me.

THE OLD FIRE STATION on Branson Street had been built back in the thirties when fire engines were smaller. Now it was an auto mechanic's shop downstairs and an apartment up top. My apartment. I always took the back stairs home to avoid the roaming eyes of the greasy mechanics.

I wrapped the four thousand dollars in aluminum foil and put it in the freezer with the rest. I wondered how much I had. I hadn't counted it in a long time.

In my bedroom, I lit the circle of candles around the mattress on the floor. The sheets were new and clean and cool. Satin and red. I lifted the sundress over my head, lay back against the sheets in just my panties. Writhed against the satin.

I was tired. Maybe a nap.

But first I wanted to know what my next job was. I ripped the end off the envelope and dumped the contents on my flat belly. Blueprints, directions, all the pertinent information. Gene always gave me a wonderful scouting report.

It was a home. A family home. I almost never did homes. Sometimes divorcing couples or vengeful spouses would ask for a house burning, but usually I did commercial property. This home housed a family of five. It was a big two-story on St. Mary's. They wanted it totally razed. A tough order if it were brick, and most of the houses around there were. But it was old and wooden. I could reduce it to ashes with little trouble.

A note with a special order: the client wanted forty-eight hours notice to get family and a few personal possessions out. Good. I burned buildings, not people.

I put the instructions aside and drifted off. Sleep was good at first. It always was. But sometimes it twisted into nightmares. The flames again, the heat, the suffocating smoke. I was just thirteen when it happened. He had me in his arms fending off the flames, the sleeves of his shirt sparking and smoking. He carried me out, then went back in.

No.

Went back in, mother and I screaming at him, begging, but he went back in.

No.

He went back for my sister, didn't come out, neither did she.

The roof caved, spinning pillars of spark and ash twirling and reaching into the night sky, disappearing toward the moon. *Daddy.* In a dream you try to scream something, to shout. You know how it is. You can't make your mouth work. *Daddy.*

I awoke grunting, trying to shout. I was matted with sweat, slick and wrung out.

It would be okay. The dream wouldn't come again for a few nights.

I got up early the next morning, picked the sundress off the floor and slipped it back on, stepped into my sandals. I went downstairs, yawning, rubbing my eyes. It was just after seven AM I wanted to scout the house, but I needed a little wake-me-up.

I squinted at the sky, and decided it was going to be a nice day. I almost never turned on the television to check the weather. I had a very good sense about these things, and I could usually tell the weather by the morning sky.

I put down the top on my convertible Volkswagen Rabbit and headed for McDonald's. I bought a coffee and Egg McMuffin through the drive-thru and headed for St. Mary's.

The house was on the corner of St. Mary's and Fairview Road. It was gloriously white and large with a picket fence and a basketball court at the end of the circular driveway. Neat hedges, probably well-trimmed by an obedient housewife. Rosebushes. It looked like upper-middle class Heaven, and I burned to know why anyone would want it turned to charcoal.

But I never got to know those things.

But who'd asked for the fire-job? The wife? The husband? If it was the husband, did the wife know? The poor kids. How old were they, I wondered.

No, no, no. Forget it. Just case the place.

I drove past the house three times making a mental list, what I needed to do the job completely but without waste. I'd received no special instructions to make it look like an accident, but I'd make it hard for the inspectors if I could. I didn't want to leave trace chemicals all over the place. A perfect fire-job will burn the evidence along with the building.

As I drove past the fourth time, I decided I needed to see the back. I parked the car on the street two blocks up and took my coffee with me. It was starting to cool, but I never minded cold coffee. There were no cars in the driveway, and it was a school day, so I walked right around back without hesitating. It was easy enough to make up a lie if I were caught, and nobody ever expected anything sinister from a young girl in a pretty sundress.

The backyard. No pool. Good. Soot and ash would gather in a pool, make it easier to gather samples. The chlorine wouldn't hide much. But there wasn't a pool. There was a large wooden swing-set, slide, a teeter-totter. A dog house.

I froze, waited. No dog. Good. But I'd have to double-check. He might be at the vet's. I checked a set of low windows, squatted and peeked inside. A basement. Perfect. I'd start it in the basement and it would burn straight up, fall in on itself. One-two-three, A-B-C.

It was settled. I'd tell Gene to pass the word that I'd do it Thursday afternoon. A weekday. Not so many neighbors home.

I walked back to the car.

Someone was waiting for me. A woman.

"Hello," she said.

I stepped back, eyes darting side to side before settling on her. "That's my car."

"I know. I'm waiting for you. Cassandra, yes?"

I tensed, ready to run. "Who are you?"

"I just wanted to talk. Can we go someplace? I can refill that coffee."

"I-I'm in a hurry. I have to go someplace. That's my car, and I have to go—"

She smiled slow, spoke softly. "Cassandra, my name is Brenda. I need your help. I need something burned."

"Y-you're—" I shook my head. "You have to talk to Gene. I don't—Gene handles—"

"It's okay. I'm not going to harm you. That's a pretty sundress you're wearing. I was thinking of doing some shopping myself. Maybe you can help me pick out something like that."

I hesitated.

"It's getting hot," she said. She wore a dark green spandex outfit for running. Shorts and a scoop neck tank-top. She wiped between her breasts, the hand glistening sweat. "I need some lighter clothes." Casual talk, like old high school friends. Black hair, bright eyes. Striking.

"You . . . run?"

She nodded, smile growing wider. "I have to if I want to be this thin. It's not as easy for me as it is for you. What a nice figure. You must never eat at all."

My cheeks grew warm. My hand moved toward my scar but I caught it in time, turned the motion to a casual gesture. "I just . . . I've always been thin."

She nodded. "Lucky. Men must love you. I have to run and run and run or I get these terrible hippo-hips."

I nodded, stepped toward her carefully. "You're pretty," I said. Now me. Tell me.

"Thanks, Cassandra, sometimes we need to hear that. And so are you. I didn't expect you to be so beautiful."

"You said—" I cleared my throat. "You said you needed help. My help."

"Yes, I do. Very much. Can we talk about it?"

I frowned, thinking.

"I know this isn't how you usually do business, and I'm just so sorry. It must be a surprise. But Gene said it might be a while before you could help me and it's just so important."

"I couldn't go behind Gene's back."

"We can tell him all about it afterwards. You can even make sure he gets his cut, so he doesn't feel left out. How does that sound?"

"I guess that's okay."

"Let's have that coffee. I'll tell you what I need, and you can give me your expert advice."

"Okay."

We got into the Volkswagen, and I drove us to a little place at Five Points.

"I feel good about this," she said as I parked. She gave my arm a little squeeze, only an instant. "I'm sure you're the one to help me."

"I'm sorry," I said. "I've forgotten your name."

"It's okay. Brenda Mason. But please call me Little Miss. My friends do."

My arm pulsed with heat where she'd touched me.

She bought us mocha lattes. They were warm, sweet, thick. She moved like a ballet dancer, gestures fluid and graceful, back straight and tall as she walked. Eyes bright, chin lifted when speaking.

The coffee shop was called The Third Place. I didn't know why, but I liked it. We sat at a dark table near the back and nobody looked at me. The other patrons were young. Colored hair, nose rings—all very bohemian. Art on the walls. Some of it good.

We talked and laughed. Little Miss was nice. I waited for her to look at my scar, watched her eyes. But they never once moved from mine, flitted to the side, lingered over the destroyed flesh. It was as if she didn't see it at all. I'd met a few people like that. Gene was like that. I always thought it was because we had a deal. I didn't notice he was small, and he didn't look at my scar.

But I had no such deal with Little Miss. How could I? She was perfect, nothing for me to overlook. I had nothing to offer her in the way of acceptance. I'd found that love was based on trading acceptances. There must've been more to it.

But she'd said she needed my help. I asked her how.

"Don't worry about that now," she said. "When you finish your current project, we'll discuss it in depth. I just want us to be friends first. It's so much nicer to work with someone you like and trust."

Yes, yes. I know exactly what you mean.

"I'll see you again," she assured me.

"How will—do you want to know where to find me, where I live?"

"I know."

She said good-bye, touched me lightly on the hand before leaving.

Sitting in the coffee shop without her felt strange. I looked up quickly to see who was staring at me, but nobody was. I finished my mocha quickly and left.

BACK AT THE FIRE STATION, I flopped onto my mattress. Even though it was early in the day, I felt tired, mentally exhausted. I closed my eyes, drifted off.

I stood in a rainforest. Everything looked blue, as if viewed through a filter. Cool. Wet. I was naked. I followed a path to a river. Followed the river to a pool. It glowed blue. Across the pool was a waterfall. It flowed smoothly, like glass, a single curtain of clear water.

Little Miss stood on the other side. She looked blurry behind the shimmering flow of water, but I knew it was her. She reached a hand through the water, beckoned. I wanted to go.

But I stopped first. Looked at my reflection in the glowing pool. I looked for my scar, but I couldn't see it. I wondered if it were a trick of the pool, which made an unclear mirror because of the lapping water, the waterfall stirring and churning.

I almost reached for the scar to touch it, see if it were really gone, but I stopped. I didn't want to know, wanted instead to believe the re-flection. I wanted—

Ringing.

I sat up, rubbed my eyes. The phone rang again and I answered.

"Y-yes. Hello?"

"The client wants to know when on the St. Mary's house." Gene.

"I'm so sorry Gene, I was going to call you. I just took a little nap."

"No sweat. What's the word?"

"Thursday afternoon, unless that's too soon."

"I'll tell him. If it's bad, I'll call back. Later, honey."

"Gene?"

"Yeah?"

"How are you?"

"Can't complain, but I got to get back to work."

"Sure. Bye."

"Bye, honey." He hung up.

I AWOKE VERY EARLY IN THE MORNING, dawn just peeking over the treetops. I brushed my hair, slipped into denim shorts and a red halter top. My legs looked long and good in shorts. Sandals. I took a toe ring out of my cedar jewelry box and put it on the next to smallest toe of my left foot. It was cute and silver, highly polished, and glittered when it caught the sun. It drew eyes to my legs and feet.

I made the rounds around town, buying wires here, detonators there. Harder to trace when you spread around the purchases. A long-time contact would provide the explosives and special chemicals.

I went home to rest.

My apartment was unbearably quiet, still. I turned on the TV for noise. I flopped onto my mattress.

Soon the dream came. I knew it was a dream, but I couldn't stop it. That's how it was sometimes. But this wasn't the same one. I hardly ever had this dream.

The box of wooded matches in my hands. I lit them one by one and shook them out because I liked the smell. Light, shake out, smell, drop the blackened matchstick on the floor. A hypnotic routine. I knew what was coming, tried to will my dream self to put down the matches, go upstairs and wake Mommy from her nap. I shook out another match and dropped it.

But it wasn't out.

It burned an ever-widening circle. Left the carpet black where the flames had marched. I stood dumb, fascinated. I jerked from my trance. Daddy would be furious. I tried to blow out the circle, but it had spread too big. I threw a blanket on it. The flames clawed through, caught the blanket.

Then the dream sped up, and the room was afire nightmarishly fast. I shrunk from the heat burning my eyes, the smoke scorching my throat. The flames on me on me on—

I awoke. Screamed, drew breath, screamed. Tears rolling fat and salty down my cheeks.

I cried hard, buried my face in the pillow, knuckles digging in, clenching. At last I sat up, wiped my face with the palms of my hands. Light headed. This had been the worst in a long time. I forced my breathing to slow. My heart calmed.

I crawled to the phone, sat cross-legged on the floor and held it in my lap. I dialed Gene's number at the pawnshop. It rang. I'd ask Gene to come over. I needed to be with him, see him. I didn't want to be alone.

It rang several more times, and I neared panic, thinking he wasn't there.

"Hello, hello." Gene, out of breath.

"Gene."

"Cass, what is it? You sound bad."

"I—can I come over there where you are?"

"Honey, what is it? A problem with the job?"

"No, I just . . . I'm scared."

"Jesus, what is it? Are you hurt?"

"I had a bad dream."

Gene blew air, huffed into the phone. "For Christ's sake, honey, you scared the shit out of me."

"Can I come over?"

"It's just a dream. Have a glass of wine. Take a hot bath. Whatever you girls do."

"Please, I just want to see you."

"I'm busy as hell here, honey. It's just a dream. You're okay."

I swallowed. "Okay."

"I love you, Gene."

"I got to go, Cass. You take it easy. Bye."

Bye.

LITTLE MISS WAS WAITING FOR ME in the passenger seat of my Volkswagen. I spotted her on the way out of the guy's house who builds my timers for me. I paused but then climbed in behind the wheel.

"How did you know I was here?" I wasn't mad, but I was worried.

"I know all about you, Cassandra."

I didn't know what to say, so I waited for her to talk.

"Cassandra, I have a number of people who work for me. We work together. Like a team. Some can open locks and safes. Others know about weapons or mechanical things. All these people are the best at what they do. Just like you. I want you to work for me."

"I can't." Anxiety welling in my chest. "I work for Gene."

"I know," Little Miss said. "I also know you need to find out for yourself that Gene isn't right for you."

I felt squirmy. "What do you mean?"

"I offered Gene twenty thousand dollars for you to do an arson job for me."

"Why are you telling me that?" I asked.

"You know why."

"No." I couldn't look at her. My stomach felt funny.

"I feel confident you know what to do with that information." Little Miss got out of my car, paused to wink at me and then started walking.

I watched her walk around the corner in my rearview mirror.

I WENT INTO THE PAWNSHOP FIRST, and Fat Rico told me Gene was next door at the porn store. I never went in there, but I didn't want to wait. Down an aisle of dildos and rubber vaginas, I found him talking to an employee, checking off items on a clipboard.

He saw me, his whole face scrunching in a grimace. "What are you doing here, Cass?"

"I-I need you, Gene. Please."

"This isn't about some bad dream, is it?"

"No."

"Go wait."

"Gene."

"Wait next door dammit, right now."

I went back the way I'd come, eyes straight ahead, not looking at the vulgar items that lined the shelves.

Fat Rico let me into Gene's office. I waited. It seemed like a long time, and it was cold in the office. I huddled in the chair across Gene's desk, hugging myself tight. Finally he came. He waited until he was in his seat before speaking.

"Now what is it, honey? Tell Gene."

And I did. How Little Miss approached me and said she had a job for me.

"How much did she offer to pay?" I asked.

"Same as always. Five Thousand."

"She said twenty."

He bounded out of his chair, leapt atop the desk. He looked like a chubby lawn jockey, small and grotesquely terrifying. His eyes were fire, pudgy hands balled into fists. "You calling me a liar?"

"G-Gene, p-please, I—It's not—"

The smack was like a little *pop*, his open hand stinging my check. The flesh under my eye prickled hot. A hundred tiny stickpins.

"What the hell made you think to take a job behind my back? You don't even know anything about this woman."

"I-I wasn't going to cut you out. You'd get your percentage."

"Fuck that. My percentage ain't the point. Don't you ever use your brain? Bitch is full of shit."

"Gene, I won't—I'd never do anything to hurt you."

"You stay away from her."

"Okay."

"And don't come around here for a while. Not for a week."

I choked. "Gene, please."

"Stay away for a week. Let things cool down. If that bitch was a cop, I don't want you leading her to me, you understand?"

I left, numb, climbed into the Volkswagen, drove in a trance. I wanted to cry, but maybe I was all out of tears. I only felt heavy, moaned low to myself from the throat.

THE ALARM SCREAMED SIX AM I rolled over and smacked it quiet.

It had been a dreadful night, tossing and turning, sliding in and out of dreams, faces swirling before me. Gene angry. I couldn't shake the heavy, queasy feeling, the cloying misery.

I rolled around, looked at the clock again. An hour had slipped by. I sat up on my mattress, barely able to keep my head up. Oh, Gene.

It was burn day, the house on St. Mary's.

Did Gene still want me to do it or had it been called off? I could call him! Yes, perfectly reasonable. I'd need to know, wouldn't I? A valid reason to call. I stretched across the bed, grabbed the phone and pulled it into my lap, dialed the first three numbers.

I slammed it down quick, the clang of the bell hanging in the apartment for a long time.

No calling. Did stay away mean no calling? I didn't know. Maybe Gene would be mad if I called. Might tell me to stay away for *two* weeks. I pushed the phone off my lap, curled into a ball trying to think what to do.

I got up, pulled another sundress from the closet. The flower pattern on this one was a dark blue. Thong panties. Sandals. I loaded the stuff into the Volkswagen.

I'd do the burn. Nobody had called it off. Gene just said to stay away.

I'd do the burn.

I'D SPRAYED THE WHOLE HOUSE starting at the attic and working my way to the basement. I had a big silver exterminator's sprayer I'd filled with a highly flammable chemical mix that soaked quickly into the old house's wooded beams.

I lucked out in the basement. They had a weed-eater with a little tank of gas on the side. I'd begin there. I grabbed a stack of towels and sheets from upstairs and made a pile of old rags. The basement stairs were wooden. More luck. I sprayed a chemical trail up the stairs and rigged the kitchen drapes to catch.

There was plenty of old, wooden furniture throughout the house, much of it quite nice. A shame. The rosewood table would look nice in my apartment. No. No souvenirs. I soaked it all down with the spray, also anything cloth or upholstered.

Back in the basement, I soaked the rag pile. I put an incense stick on top of the rags, situated it to point straight up. It would take a few minutes to burn down, more than enough time for me to get upstairs and outside and better than one of the timers.

I looked around to make sure I hadn't left anything, grabbed the spray can and left the house.

I put the can back in the trunk of my car, looked around. Nobody watched. I went back down to the basement, lit the stick of incense and ran.

There was no danger, not really, but I was always extra careful. It would take awhile for the burn to really get going.

At the far end of the backyard, a row of high hedges hid me pretty well, let me watch to see if the burn would take. I didn't want to have to go in and relight the thing, but I had to make sure it went off okay. I'd only had to go back to a place twice in my whole career. I was pretty confident it would go.

And I would have watched anyway. I already felt the spine-tickle of anticipation. For the first time today, I hadn't been dwelling on Gene. Maybe that's why I'd decided to go ahead with the job. I knew how it would make me feel the thrill of the heat washing over me. The hypnotic dance of the flames in the windows, like passion burning behind clear eyes.

Yes, I was ready, yearning. I needed to see the house resist the flames before finally toppling in on itself, collapsing into ash, consumed by the heat. I ran a hand along my bare thigh. How long? Where was the smoke?

I smelled it a long time before I saw anything. The odor of burning wood, plaster and cloth, only a faint tinge of the chemical. People don't recognize the smell. Oh, firemen perhaps or other firebugs. But ask most people. They think it's like a charcoal barbecue or a fireplace. No. There was a texture to a house burning, phases of odor released in a certain order, like rings in an old tree. You could smell a family's life in a house fire, clothes, furniture, photo albums, even this morning's newspaper. The flames ate them all one by one, excreted them as uniform gray ash.

All burned clean with exquisite finality.

The flames were clearly visible in the windows now, and I found that my hand had dipped under the hem of the sundress, caressed my mound through the panties' thin fabric.

Vanguards of smoke wormed their way into the creases of the house, burrowing for escape. Against the deep blue of the sky, I saw the fingers of smoke reaching upward. They were always thin at first and would soon billow into angry black clouds when the windows burst.

Fingers inside the panties. Moist.

I heard the first windows burst and rubbed myself faster. I strained to see but couldn't, stayed squatting in the hedges. Then the kitchen window in the back cracked, glass showering. The flames licked out and along the white wood. A wave of heat. A heavy belch of black smoke floated around and up. It was louder now too, the wood snapping, beams straining.

My orgasm started from a long way off. I circled my clit slowly, two middle fingers demanding but disciplined. *Don't hurry.*

I thought I saw movement to my left, the hedges parting. But I was lost, hypnotized. The flames writhed in all the windows now, heat nearly overwhelming, smoke pumping constant and hard.

Someone behind me, a hand on my back.

My eyes popped, mouth dropped open to scream.

But a soft hand clamped over my lips. I tensed to rise, but the person moved in behind me, the other hand covering mine where I touched myself.

"Keep going." A whisper in my ear, a woman's voice. And I knew it. Little Miss.

"Keep touching. I want to watch."

She knelt behind me, pressed close to my back. Sweat ran between my breasts, behind my ears. The pressure of her hand on mine was light but insistent. I began the slow circles again, her hand keeping the rhythm, her heartbeat matching mine.

I fixed my eyes on the house again. The symphony of flame had built to a magnificent roar, the fire coming through the roof now. My eyes stung with smoke and heat, and my fingers circled faster.

"You're beautiful," whispered Little Miss.

Yes, I was. The trembling started, worked down my legs, spread warm through my body. Little Miss held me tight, held me up, her hot breath on my neck. I shuddered, legs turning jelly, the hot electricity spiraling out from the center.

Tears streamed from the corners of my eyes, and a strangled, hoarse cry caught in my throat. And then—I—it was—

The heat—fingers circling, digging—

—Little Miss, her hand—

—and I was beautiful—

I reached my other hand toward the burning house, felt the heat, the taste of buzzing blackness, the crowding rush of pleasure, the world spinning—

I am beautiful.

MY EYES POPPED OPEN. I rocked gently in the passenger seat of my Volkswagen.

Little Miss drove. She smiled down at me.

I asked, "What happened?"

"The fire trucks were coming, so I had to take you out of there," said Little Miss. "You passed out, but I carried you."

"Thank you."

I frowned.

"What's wrong?"

I told her about Gene, how I'd made him angry.

She didn't look mad, but her smile withered. "Let's go see him."

"No, I—he said to stay away."

She shook her head. "No. I'll fix it."

I didn't protest.

We parked in front of the pawnshop, and I followed her in.

She already knew where the office was and made for it.

Fat Rico was on the counter. He held up a hand. "Stop right there, lady. You want to see Gene? I got to buzz you back before—"

Little Miss leapt atop the counter, kicked Rico in the chin. He bit his tongue, flopped back and spit blood. He was quick for a fat guy, pulled a little pistol from someplace and tried to bring it around.

Little Miss stamped it with her heel, smashed it against the glass countertop, which shattered. She jumped down on Rico's side and chopped him in the throat. She punched once, twice. He went down, crashed into a heap behind the counter.

She unloaded the pistol, threw the bullets over her shoulder and tossed the pistol away. She thumbed the buzzer and kicked open Gene's office door. I followed her in.

He sat behind the desk, looked surprised, alarmed, frightened, angry.

"Shit motherfucker." He jabbed a stubby finger at Little Miss. "What the fuck are you doing here?"

"I want to talk to you."

"Kiss my ass." He reached into his desk drawer. Another pistol.

Little Miss was like a cat. She launched across the desk and grabbed his wrist in one smooth motion. Gene had a little automatic in his tiny fist. She twisted and he winced, dropped the gun.

She grabbed him by the shirt, pulled him across the desk, scattered paper, knocked a calculator on the floor. His stumpy legs kicked behind him, and he squealed.

"Goddamn, you crazy bitch. What are you doing?"

She lifted him up, tossed him across the room. His head banged against a filing cabinet and he hit the floor. He tried to get up, but she had him by the hair, kicked him in the stomach.

He moaned, sucked air.

Little Miss yanked the phone cord out of the wall and used it to tie Gene up.

"Do I have your attention?" she asked.

"Jesus, what the hell you want?"

"Cassandra."

"That crazy—"

She backhanded him across the lip. Blood.

"She's mine now," said Little Miss. "Don't talk to her or see her or touch her."

"Fucking shit, fine, whatever."

Little Miss walked out into the pawnshop and returned a second later. She had a big black case with her. She opened it and took out the cello inside. She stuffed Gene into the case and clamped it shut.

"Holy shit." Gene's voice was muffled. "I'm going to fucking suffocate in here."

"Do you get what I said?" Little Miss kicked the case.

"Let me out!"

"Do you understand or not? Lay off Cassandra, or I'll come back and kill you."

"Okay, okay." Gene's voice was more desperate. "Just let me out."

Little Miss touched my arm. "I've fixed it. Let's go." She walked out.

I hesitated a moment, looked back at the cello case, Gene throwing a tantrum inside. I felt sort of bad for him. Not because Little Miss had hurt him. Because she'd reminded him he was small. A little man.

But it would be okay. Everything was fine.

Because I loved Little Miss. And Little Miss loved me.

Hotshot 52
Greg Bardsley

His problem is, he's just there...

The young man is just there, on the other side of the nearly empty noodle house, hunched over his bowl, trying to suck up the long dripping noodles, and I am on the opposite end, feeling as if I'm about to dissolve into a mound of lifeless flesh, my shoulders slumping, my vision blurring and refocusing, the oozing lump of darkness at the base of my chest making me want to moan until I run out of air and breathe nevermore.

I look at my own noodle bowl—hot and spicy soup—and moan so loud that the couple huddled across from me shuts up. *Are they trying to ignore me?* When they don't look up, I sigh long and hard and refocus on the young man across the room.

What the hell is happening to me?

He makes me mad. I'm not sure why, and I'm not sure I care. All I know is, this is the first droplet of passion I've experienced all day, maybe all week, and right now, anger feels so much better than that slow-moving block of sticky nothing I've housed inside my chest the past four weeks. Or has it been months?

I'm sick of feeling nothing.

Sick.

Sick of my long commute. Sick of my IT job. Sick of working on protocols and network proxies and scripts. Sick of spending hour upon hour in my cube, each day adding to my own IT toothpick sculpture—a monstrous, complicated mound of throbbing, tangled manure that works now but surely will decay into nothing within the decade. Sick of being so bored, only to come home each night to the blank stares of my two teenagers.

And I was going to be a teacher.

I was going to help kids.

Touch their lives in ways that would last lifetimes.

The irony makes me laugh, and now I catch the couple glancing at me, exchanging whispers. I look away and roll my eyes. *I've seen your types a million times, kiddos.*

Sick.

Sick of the same lunch locations—this pathetic, empty noodle house, a Subway Sandwich shop around the corner, a tiny park with twigs for trees. Sick of returning to the same office to hear the same comments about the same incompetent managers in the same cubes. Sick of watching my life-force drain away, like a babbling brook drying up a little more each day, blistering heat taking over, the surrounding grass turning brittle and brown, a rabbit carcass imploding on the bank, the water going stagnant, turning green, seconds from going brown.

I was going to touch lives. Young lives.

For decades, I've pushed that thought to the recesses of my consciousness. But today, out of nowhere, it makes me moan.

The couple huddles closer, giggling, insisting on having their great time no matter how miserable I might be. *Scum.*

Me?

Well, for me, nothingness seeps over everything. Banality reigns in my daily rituals, and nothing is new. Nothing is interesting. Headline news, natural disasters and reports of calamity sail right through my soul. I feel nothing when my wife says, "I love you."

But now, this man. This man across the restaurant, slurping noodles, making that sucking sound as he tries to capture the broth before it drips out, looking like a fool. This man. This man annoys me, and I'm sick of him. Never met the man in my life, but I'm sick of him already. And this is a relief.

And so I get up.

And I stare at him, thinking about it.

Preparing myself.

And finally—it feels so good—my heart is pounding.

Life. I'm feeling life, as I fold my *New York Times* and place it atop my first-edition hardcover of *Les Dijon*, straighten my blue collar shirt, look down at my polished wingtips and draw in a deep breath. I can feel the blood coursing through my body, my heart thumping, my eyeballs twitching, and I close my lids, trying to inhale the mealy texture of this moment, trying to make it last.

I whisper to myself, "What if?"

I look at the guy, that guy still sucking in the noodles over there. Entirely oblivious.

I walk toward him, my mind faint, my knees weak, and I realize he's at least twenty years younger than me—maybe thirty. He's one of those young men with the flimsy t-shirts and styled hair that looks disheveled but isn't, and I notice his arms are big and hairless. I never had arms like that, even when I was young and I could do anything I wanted.

This time, when I'm close, my breathing gets shallow from the fear, the taste in my mouth goes metallic, and I say it louder.

"What if ..."

He looks up, more curious than surprised, noodles hanging out of his mouth, broth dripping back into the bowl.

"... I told you that ..."

I stop in front of him, grip the ends of his little table, lower my head and stare right into his brown eyes. My ribcage spasms.

" ...I don't like your face?"

He's frozen, noodles still hanging but no longer dripping, and he's looking at me, waiting, I'm sure, for some type of social cue.

"In fact, what if I told you …" I pause, looking at his large jaw, then his heavy brows, and finally his giant mouth. "… that I *hate* your face?"

BACK AT HEADQUARTERS, I'm standing in the men's restroom, my back so damp from the sweat that it sticks to my shirt, and I'm staring into the mirror, admiring my face—the wrinkles turned up, the experienced gray eyes, the jawline that that suddenly seems to have defied sixty-five years of gravity. In the past four years, has this face ever looked so alive? Has it ever felt this flush? Have my eyes ever sparkled like this?

I try to replay the moment in my mind. *What did he say? Something like, "Come back and say that again, Grandpa."*

Thinking about it, I laugh loud and hard.

AS I SAID, FOUR YEARS AGO.

That was the last time I had a rush like this, the last time I felt so alive. Four years ago, I had been trying to ignore the same emptiness until it was unbearable, until I knew I had to do something to shake it off. Back then, I figured it was either *that* or a trip to the psyche ward. And sure, I could have jumped off an airplane or trained for a marathon or tried cliff diving, but I was looking for something far more polarizing, something that would shock my psyche out of paralysis, something that would give my moral equilibrium a jolt, something that would be brazen and confrontational. Something delinquent. So I got my wife's sister drunk, led her upstairs in the middle of a barbecue, leaving the others on the patio, pulled her into the hallway closet and forced myself on her, giving her what I'd wanted to give her for twenty-two years. She sobbed the entire time, whispering, "You'll destroy this family." But she never said "Stop." In fact, she opened her legs and moaned. But that didn't matter so much; what mattered was, I was being a bad man, and it made me feel so good.

So bad. So alive.

So alive, in fact, that the next day, after the sister-in-law, I wanted more—more juice, in whatever form. I needed that feeling again, that alive feeling, that feeling of dance-walking across a high-wire, drunk and blindfolded, a glass of whiskey in my hand, yelling "Piss off" to the jagged rocks far below.

So I drove the Lexus two towns down the interstate, walked up to the counter of a crowded movie theatre and stared at the young clerk, this red-head in a little vest and bow-tie. Another one-on-one scenario, just the way I like them.

"You want my money?" I said, reaching into the pockets of my blue blazer. "You can have my money." I threw two handfuls of pennies onto the Formica counter, right in front of him, and they shot everywhere, like an explosion.

The place went silent.

The kid looked at me like I was an alien.

I turned and walked out, my posture perfect, my heart beating so hard, my mind so sharp, my jaws twitching, my stomach going cold, and I loved every second of it.

Returning to my car, I realized I had to cut this thing off—right then, right there, for as long as I would last—because I could feel it in my bones, I could feel more to come if I didn't stop.

And I knew it would be far darker.

LOOKING IN THE MIRROR NOW, I marvel at how I had lasted four years, how I had suppressed so much for so long.

Had I been on autopilot all those years?

Coming out of the restroom, so happy about the noodle-house adventure, so alive, I run into Tommy Baker and his family—a pretty little wife chasing after an adorable three-year-old boy who's hopping around in a store-bought basketball costume.

I bend down, getting at his level, smiling at him.

"And who are you?"

He pushes his chest out and points to the slogan on his jersey—*Hotshot 52.*

"I'm Hotshot…" He throws his hands into the air and adds, sing-songy, "Fifty-Two."

His parents laugh.

I poke in him the tummy, and he squeals.

"Yeah?" I say. "Hotshot Fifty-Two?"

He giggles, his eyes turning to slits.

"You know what, kiddo?"

He stops and looks at me, waiting.

"I think I'm one, too." I straighten and puff out my chest, beaming. "I'm a Hotshot Fifty-Two."

Tommy Baker laughs, but his wife can barely force a weak smile. I can tell I give her the creeps.

I'M IN MY CUBE, still giggling from the high, thinking about Tommy Baker's little kid.

Hotshot 52.

The kid was so happy with himself. So free and open about it all. The kid was Hotshot 52, and he wasn't hiding it. And here I am, worrying about being a freak, worrying about what everyone else thinks, trying to tell myself I don't deserve "the juice," trying to suppress the Hotshot 52 inside of me.

Well, not anymore. If Tommy Baker's kid can be Hotshot 52, so can I.

TWO DAYS LATER I am outside the noodle house, leaning against the front fender of the Lexus, legs crossed, toothpick in my mouth. I gaze at the building as I recite with a whisper that line from Spinoza, his string of seventeenth-century reason nourishing my conscience, releasing my inhibitions: "One and the same thing can at the same time be good, bad, and indifferent. Music is good to the melancholy, bad to mourners, and indifferent to the dead."

I am here to create music.

I know he's in there. Pretty boy with the big arms, getting ready to leave, expecting, no doubt, to return to his own cube someplace nearby. Certainly not expecting "Grandpa" out here waiting for him in the parking lot, ready to have a little discussion.

My throat is so tight, I can barely swallow. I love it.

Finally, he steps out into the sunshine, squinting, heading toward me. In fact, he walks right past me, not even looking, staring at his Treo, some meaningless message flashing on his screen. So I have to say, "Remember me?"

He turns, startled.

"It's me," I say. "Grandpa."

Then it clicks, and his face registers pure joy. He slides the Treo into his front pocket and starts toward me, preparing to push the issue, to finish our noodle-house business in some kind of way.

"And I still don't like your face."

He chuckles. "Oh, yeah?"

"Your stupid ... dull ... face."

He's tries to stare me down, and comes closer, just where I want him.

THE KNIFE GOES IN EASIER than I had expected.

He falls to his knees, looking up at me, and I'm wondering how many people can see us.

"Do you know who I am?"

He coughs up blood, but keeps staring.

"Well, I'm not Grandpa."

He begins to cry, I think, as I squat, getting down to his level, poking him in the tummy, the bloody tummy, my eyes twinkling.

"No, I'm not Grandpa," I whisper. "I'm Hotshot 52."

I pull the dagger out and plunge it into his chest, pushing it hard. "Hotshot 52."

He falls over, forehead hitting the pavement.

I hear the sirens.

"And Hotshot 52?" I release a long, that's-too-bad sigh. "Well, I'm afraid he just doesn't like your face."

And I close my eyes and smile, because now I can see. The stagnant water is gone. The dried weeds have softened and greened. Fluffy bunnies hop about. My brook babbles with crystal clear water, and I can see the butterflies bobbing overhead.

I am Hotshot 52.

School Daze

A Harry McGlade Mystery
J.A. Konrath

"Cute kid," I said.

The kid looked like a large pink watermelon with buck teeth and bug eyes. If I hadn't already known it was a girl, I couldn't have guessed from the picture. What was that medical name for children with overdeveloped heads? Balloonheadism? Bigheaditis? Melonoma? Freak?

"She takes after her mother."

Yeeech. My fertile mind produced an image of a naked Mrs. Potatohead, unhooking her bra. I shook away the thought and handed the picture back to the proud papa.

"Where is Mom, by the way?"

Mr. Morribund leaned close enough for me to smell his lunch—tuna fish on rye with a side order of whiskey. He was a thin guy with big eyes who wore an off-the-rack suit with a gold "Save The Dolphins" tie tack.

"Emily doesn't know I'm here, Mr. McGlade. She's at home with little Rosemary. Since we received the news she's been … upset."

"I sympathize. Getting into the right preschool can mean the difference between summa cum laude at Harvard and offering mouth sex in back alley dumpsters for crack money. I should know. I've seen it."

"You've seen mouth sex in back alley dumpsters?"

I nodded my head in what I hoped what looked like a sad way. "It isn't pretty, Mr. Morribund. Not to look at, or to smell. But I don't understand how you expect me to get little Rotisserie—"

"It's Rosemary."

"—little Rosemary into this school if they already turned down your application. Are you looking for strong-arm work?"

"No, nothing like that."

I frowned. I liked strong-arm work. It was one of the perks of being a private eye. That and breaking and entering.

"What then? Breaking and entering? Some stealing, maybe?"

I liked stealing.

Morribund swallowed, his Adam's apple wiggling in his thin neck. If he were any skinnier he wouldn't have a profile.

"The Salieri Academy is the premier preschool in the nation, Mr. McGlade. They have a waiting list of thousands, and to even have a chance at attending you have to fill out the application five years before your child is conceived."

"That's a long time to wait for nookie." But then, if I were married to Mrs. Potatohead, I wouldn't mind the wait.

"It's the reason we took so long to have Rosemary. We paid the application fee, and were all but assured entrance. But three days after Rosemary was born, our application was denied."

"Did they give a reason?" *Other than the fact that your kid looks like an albino warthog who has been snacking on an air compressor?*

"No. The application says they reserve the right to deny admittance at their discretion, and still keep the fee."

"How much was the fee?"

"Ten thousand dollars."

Ouch. You could rent a lot of naughty videos for that kind of money. And you'd need to, because those things get boring after the third or fourth viewing.

"So what's the deal? You want me to shake the guy down for the money?"

He shook his head. "Nothing of the sort. I'm not a violent man."

"Spell it out, Mr. Morribund. What exactly do you want me to do? Burn down the school?"

I liked arson.

"Goodness, no. The Salieri school is run by a man named Michael Sousse."

"And you want me to kidnap his pet dog and take pictures of me throwing it off a tall building, using my zoom lens to capture its final barks of terror as it takes the express lane to Pancakeville? Because that's where I draw the line, Mr. Morribund. I may be a thug, a thief, and an arsonist, but I won't harm any innocent animals unless there's a bonus involved."

Morribund raised an eyebrow. "You'd do that to a dog? The Internet said you love animals."

"I do love animals. Grilled, fried, and broiled. Or stuffed with cheese. I'd eat any animal if it had enough cheese on top. It wouldn't even have to be dead first."

"Oh."

Morribund made a face, and I could tell he was thinking through things. I glanced again at his "Save the Dolphins" tie tack and realized I might have been a little hasty with my meat-lovers rant.

"I had a dog once," I said.

"Really?"

"Never tried to eat him. Not once."

I mimed crossing my heart. Morribund stared at me. When he spoke again, his voice was lower, softer.

"Headmaster Sousse, he's a terrible man. A hunter. Gets his jollies shooting poor little innocent animals. His office is strewn with so-called hunting trophies. It's disgusting."

"Sounds awful," I said, stifling a yawn.

"Mr. McGlade," he leaned in closer, giving me more tuna and bourbon, "I want you to find out something about Sousse. Something that I could use to convince him to accept our application."

I scratched my unshaven chin. Or maybe it was my unshaved chin. I get those words confused.

"I understand. You want me to dig up some dirt. Something you can use to blackmail Sousse and get Rheumatism—"

"Rosemary."

"—into his school. Well, you're in luck, Mr. Morribund, because I'm very good at this kind of thing. And even if I don't find anything incriminating in his past, I can make stuff up."

"What do you mean?"

"I can take pictures of him in the shower, and then Photoshop in the Vienna Boy's Choir washing his back. Or I can make it look like he's pooping on the floor of the White House. Or being intimate with a camel. Or eating a nun. Or—"

"I don't want the sordid details, Mr. McGlade. I simply want some kind of leverage. How much will something like that cost?"

I leaned back in my chair and put my hands behind my head, showing off my shoulder holster beneath my jacket. I always let them see the gun before I discussed my fees. It dissuaded haggling.

"I get four hundred a day. Three days minimum, in advance. Plus expenses. I may need to bring in a computer expert to do the Photoshop stuff. He's really good."

I took a pic out of my desk drawer and tossed it to him. Morribund flinched. I smiled at his reaction.

"Looks real, doesn't it?"

"This is fake?"

"Not a single baby harp seal was harmed."

"Really?"

"Well actually, they were all clubbed to death and skinned. But the laughing guy in the parka wasn't really there. We Photoshopped him into the scene. That's the beauty and magic of jpeg manipulation. Look at this one." I threw another photo onto his lap. "Check out that bloody discharge. And those pustules. Don't they look real? It's like they're going to burst all over your hands."

Morribund frowned. "I've seen enough."

"Want to see one with my head on Brad Pitt's body with Ron Jeremy's junk?"

"I really don't."

"How about one of a raccoon driving a motorcycle? He's wearing sunglasses and flipping the bird."

Morribund stood up.

"I'm sure you'll come up with something satisfactory. When can you get started?"

I fished an appointment book out of my top drawer. It was from 1996, and only contained doodles of naked butts. I pretended to scrutinize it.

"You're in luck," I said, pulling out a pen. I drew another butt. A big one, that took up the entire third week of September. "I can start as soon as your check clears."

"I don't trust checks."

"Credit card?"

"I dislike the high interest rates. How about cash?"

"Cash works for me."

After he handed it over I got his phone number, he found his own way to the door, and I did the Money Dance around my office, making happy noises and shaking my booty.

Things had been slow around the agency lately, due to my lack of renewing my Yellow Pages ad. I didn't get many referrals, because I charged too much and wasn't good at my job. Luckily, Morribund had found me through my Internet site. The same computer geek who did my Photoshop work was also the webmaster of my homepage. Google "Chicago cheating spouse sex pictures" and I was the fourth listing. If you Google "naked rhino makeover" I was number two. I still didn't understand the whole keyword thing. That's probably why Morribund thought I was an animal lover.

A quick check of my watch told me I wasn't wearing one, so I looked at the display on my cell phone. Almost two in the afternoon. Time to get started.

I booted up the computer to search for the Salieri school and

Christopher Sousse. But instead, I wound up on YouTube, and watched videos of a monkey in a funny hat, a fat woman falling down the stairs, and a Charlie Brown cartoon that someone dubbed over with the voice track to *Goodfellas*.

After wasting almost an hour, I went to MySpace and read all of my messages from all of my friends, all of whom seemed to work in the paid escort industry.

After that, I checked my eBay bids, my Hotmail account, and added a new entry to my blog about the high cost of parking in the city.

After that, porn.

Finally, I located the Salieri school's website, found their phone number, and dialed.

"Salieri Academy for Exceptionally Gifted Four-Year-Olds, where children are our future and should be heavily invested in, this is Miss Janice, may I help you?"

Miss Janice had a voice like a hot oil massage, deep and sensual and full of petroleum.

"My name is McGlade. Harrison Harold McGlade. I'd like to enroll my son Stimey into your school."

"I'm sorry sir, there's a minimum five-year waiting period to get accepted into the Salieri Academy. How old is your son now?"

"He's seven."

"We only accept four-year-olds."

"He's got the mind of a four-year-old. Retard. Mom dropped him down an escalator, he fell for forty minutes. Very sad. All someone had to do was hit the Off switch."

"I don't understand."

"Why? You a retard too?"

"Mr. McGlade—"

"I'm willing to pay money, Miss Janice. Big money. I'll triple your enrollment fee."

"I'm sorry."

"Okay, I'll double it."

"I don't think that—"

"Look, honey, is Mikey there? He assured me I'd be treated better than this."

"You know Mr. Sousse?"

"Yeah. We played water polo together in college. I saved his horse from drowning."

"Perhaps I should put you through to him."

"Don't bother. I'll be there in an hour with a suitcase full of cash. I won't bring Stimey, because he's with his tutor tonight, learning how to chew. Keep the light on for me."

I hung up, feeling smug. I hadn't shared this with Morribung, but this case really hit home for me. Years ago, when I was a toddler, I'd been forced to drop out of preschool because I kept biting and hitting the other children. The unfairness of it, being discriminated against because I was a bully, still haunted me to this day.

I hit the computer again and prowled the Internet for dirt on Sousse. Nothing jumped out at me, other than a minor news article a few weeks back about one of his teachers being dismissed for reasons unknown. According to the story, Sousse was deeply embarrassed by the incident and refused to comment.

Then I surfed for Morribund and his wife and kid, and found zilch.

Then I surfed for naked pictures of Catherine Zeta Jones until it was time for me to keep my appointment.

But first, I needed to gear up.

I wound my spy tie around my neck, careful with the wires. Concealed in the tie clip was a digital camera, a unidirectional microphone, and a twenty-gigabyte mp3 player loaded with bootleg *Tori Amos* concerts. It weighed about two pounds, and hurt my back to wear. But it would be my best chance at clandestinely snapping a few photos of Mr. Sousse during our meeting—photos I could later retouch so it looked like he was molesting a pile of dirty laundry.

People would pay a lot of money to keep their dirty laundry out of the news.

Forty minutes later I was pulling into a handicapped parking spot in front of the Salieri Academy on Irving Park Road. Last year I'd bought a handicapped parking sticker from a one-legged man in line at the DMV. It only cost me ten dollars. He had demanded five hundred, but I simply grabbed the sticker and strolled away at a leisurely pace. Guy shouldn't be driving with only one leg anyway.

The Academy was a large, ivy-covered brick building, four stories high, in the middle of a residential area. As I was reaching for the front door it began to open. A woman exited, holding the hand of a small boy. She was smartly dressed in a skirt and blazer, high heels, long brown hair. Maybe in her midthirties. The boy looked like a honey-baked ham stuffed into a school uniform, right down to the bright pink face and greasy complexion. When God was dishing out the ugly, this kid got seconds.

I played it smooth. "Wouldn't let you in, huh?"

"Excuse me?"

I pointed my chin at the child.

"Wilbur, here. All he's missing is the curly tail. The Academy won't take fatties, right?"

The boy squinted up at me.

"Mother, is this stupid man insinuating that I have piggish attributes?"

I made a face. "Who are you calling stupid? And what does 'insinuating' mean?"

"Just ignore him, Jasper. We can't be bothered by plebeians."

"Hey lady, I'm 100 percent American."

"You're 100 percent ignoramus."

"What do dinosaurs have to do with this?"

She ushered the little porker past me—no doubt off to build a house of straw—and I slipped through the doorway and into the lobby. There were busts of dead white guys on marble pedestals all around the room, and the artwork adorning the walls was so ugly it had to be expensive. I crossed the carpeted floor to the welcoming desk, set on a riser so the secretary looked down on everyone. This particular secretary was smoking hot, with big sensuous lips and a top drawer pulled all the way out. Also, large breasts.

"May I help you, sir?"

Her voice was sultry, but her smile hinted that help was the last thing she wanted to give me. I got that look a lot, from people who thought they were superior somehow due to their looks, education, wealth, or upbringing. It never failed to unimpress me.

"I called earlier, Miss Janice. I'm here to see Mikey."

Her smile dropped a fraction. "I informed Mr. Sousse that you were coming, and he regrets to inform you that—"

"Cork up that gas leak, sweetheart. I'm really a private detective. I'd like a chance to talk with Mr. Sousse about some embarrassing facts I've uncovered about one of your teachers here," I said, referring to that incident I'd Googled. "Of course, if he doesn't want to talk with me, he can hear about it on the ten o'clock news. But I doubt it will do much for enrollment, especially after that last unfortunate episode."

Miss Janice played it coy. "Whom on our staff are you referring to?"

"Are you Mr. Sousse? I can avert my eyes if you want to lift your skirt and check."

She blushed, then picked up the phone. I gave her a placating smile similar to the one she greeted me with.

"Do you have ID?" she asked, still holding the receiver.

I flashed my PI license. She did some whispering, then hung up.

"Mr. Sousse will see you now."

"How lucky for me."

She stared. I stared back.

"You gonna tell me where his office is, or should I just wander around, yelling his name?"

She frowned. "Room 315. The elevator is down the hall, on the left."

I hated to leave with an attractive woman annoyed with me, so I decided to disarm her with wit.

"You know, my father was an elevator operator. His career had a lot of ups and downs."

Miss Janice kept frowning.

"He hated how people used to push his buttons," I said.

No response at all.

"Then, one day, he got the shaft."

She crossed her arms. "That's not funny."

"You're telling me. He fell six floors to his death."

Her frown deepened.

"Tell me, do they have heat on your planet?" I asked.

"Mr. Sousse is expecting you."

I nodded, my work here done. Then it was into the elevator and up to the third floor.

Sousse's office was decorated in 1960's Norman Bates, with low lighting that threw shadows on the stuffed owls and bear heads and antlers hanging on the walls. Sousse, a stern-looking man with glasses and a bald head, sat behind a desk the size of a small car shaped like a desk, and he was sneering at me when I entered.

"Miss Janice said you're a private investigator." His nostrils flared. "I don't care for that profession."

"Don't take it literally. I'm not here to investigate your privates. I just need to ask you a few questions."

A stuffed duck—of all things—was propped on his desktop, making it impossible for me to get a clear shot of his face with my cleverly concealed camera tie. I moved a few steps to the left.

"Which of my staff are you inquiring about?"

"That's confidential."

"If you can't tell me who we're discussing, why is it you wanted to see me?"

"That's confidential too."

I shifted right, touched the tie bar, heard the shutter click. But the lighting was pretty low.

"I don't understand how I'm supposed to—"

"Does this office have better lights?" I interrupted. "I'm having trouble seeing you. I'm getting older, and got cadillacs in my eyes."

"Cadillacs?"

I squinted. "Who said that?"

"Do you mean cataracts?"

"I don't like your tone," I said, intentionally pointing at a moose head.

Sousse sighed, all drama queen, and switched on the overhead track lighting.

Click click went my little camera.

"Did you hear something?" he asked.

I snapped a few more pics, getting him with his mouth open. My tech geek should be able to Photoshop that into something particularly rude.

"Does your tie have a camera in it?" he asked.

I reflexively covered up the tie and hit the button for the mp3 player. Tori Amos began to sing about her mother being a cornflake girl in that whiney, petulant way that made her a superstar. I fussed with the controls, and only succeeded in turning up the volume.

Sousse folded his arms.

"I think this interview is over."

"Fine," I said, loud to be heard over Tori. "But you'll be hearing from me and Morribund again."

"Who?"

"Don't play coy. People like you disgust me, Mr. Sousse. Sure, I'm a carnivore. But I don't get my jollies hunting down ducks and mooses and deers and squirrels." I pointed to a squirrel hanging on the wall, dressed up in a little cowboy outfit. "What kind of maniac hunts squirrels?"

"I'm not a hunter, you idiot. I abhor hunting. I'm a taxidermist."

"Well, then I'm sure the IRS would love to hear about your little operation. You better hope you have a good accountant and that your taxidermist is in perfect order."

I spun on my heels and got out of there.

Mission accomplished. I should have felt happy, but something was nagging at me. Several somethings, in fact.

On my way through the lobby, I stopped by Miss Janice's desk again.

"When Sousse fired that teacher a few weeks ago, what was the reason?"

"That's none of your business, Mr. McGlade."

"Some sex thing?"

"Certainly not!"

"Inappropriate behavior?"

"I won't say another word."

"Fine. If you want me to pick you up later and take you to dinner, stay silent."

"I'd rather be burned alive."

"We can do that after we've eaten."

"No. I think you're annoying and repulsive."

"How about a few drinks? The more you drink, the less repulsive I get."

She folded her arms and her voice went from sultry to frosty. "Employees of the Salieri Academy don't drink, Mr. McGlade."

"I understand. How about we take a handful of pills and smoke a bowl?"

"I'm calling security."

"No need. I'm outtie. Catch you later, sweetheart."

I winked, then headed back to my office. When I arrived, I spent a good half hour on the Internet, digging deeper into the Salieri story, using a reverse phone directory to track a number, and looking up the words "insinuating," "plebian," "ignoramous," and "taxidermist." Then I gave Morribund a call and told him I had something for him.

An hour later he showed up, looking expectant to the point of jubilation. "Jubilation" is another word I looked up.

"Did you get the pictures, Mr. McGlade?"

"I got them."

"You're fast."

"I know. Ask my last girlfriend."

We stared at each other for a few seconds.

"So, are you going to give them to me?"

"No, Mr. Morribund. I'm not."

He leaned in closer, the whiskey coming off him like cologne. "Why? You want more money?"

"I'll take all the money you give me, but I'm not going to give you the photos."

"Why not?"

I smiled. It was time for the big, revealing expositional moment. "There are a lot of things I hate, Mr. Morribund. Like public toilets. And the Red Sox. And massage girls who make you pay extra for happy endings. But the thing I hate the most is being lied to by a client."

"Me? Lie to you? What are you talking about?"

"You don't want to get your daughter into the Salieri Academy. You don't even have a daughter."

His eyes narrowed.

"You're insane. Why would you think such a thing?"

"When I went to the Academy, I ran into some kid in a Salieri uniform, and he was uglier than a hatful of dingle-berries with hair on them. If he got in, then the school had no restrictions according to looks. Isn't that right, Mr. Morribund? Or should I use your real name … Nathan Tribble?"

He sighed, knowing he was beaten. "How did you figure it out?"

"You didn't pay me with a check or credit card, because you didn't have any in the name you gave me. But you did give me your real phone number, and I looked it up on the Internet. I also found out you once worked at the Salieri Academy. Fired a few weeks ago. For drinking, I assume."

"It never affected my job! I was the best instructor that stupid school ever had!"

I didn't care about debating him, because I wasn't done with my brilliant explanation yet.

"You came to me because you found me on the Internet and thought I liked dogs. That's why you wore that "Save the Dolphins" tie tack. You said Sousse was a hunter, to make me dislike him so I'd go along with your blackmail scheme."

"Enough. We've established I was lying."

But I still had more exposing to expose, so I went on.

"Sousse isn't a hunter, Tribble. He's a taxidermist. And you're no animal lover either. You can't be pro-dolphin and also eat tuna. Tuna fishermen catch and kill dolphins all the time. But your breath smelled of tuna during our last meeting."

"Why are you telling me things I already know?"

"Because that's what I do, Tribble. I figure out puzzles by putting together all the little pieces until they all fit together and form a full picture, made of the little puzzle pieces I've fit together. Or something."

"You're a low-life, McGlade. All you do is take dirty pictures of people. Or you make up dirty pictures when there are none to take."

"I may be a low-life. And a thief. And a voyeur. And an arsonist. And a leg-breaker. But I'm not a liar. You're the liar, Tribble. And you made a big mistake. You lied to me."

Tribble snorted. "So? Big deal. I got fired, and I wanted to take revenge. I figured you wouldn't do it if I asked, so I made up the story about the daughter, and added the pro-animal garbage to get you hooked. What does it matter? Just give me the damn pictures and you can go play Agatha Christie by yourself in the shower."

I stood up.

"Get out of my office, Tribble. I'm going to make two calls. The first, to Sousse, to tell him what you've got planned. I bet he can make sure you'll never get a teaching job in this town again. The second call will be to a buddy of mine at the Chicago Police Department. She'll love to learn about your little blackmail scheme."

Tribble looked like I just peed in his oatmeal.

"What about the money I gave you?"

"No give-backsies."

He balled his fists, made a face, then stormed out of my office.

I grinned. It had been a productive day. I'd made a cool twelve hundred bucks for only a few hours of work, and that was only the beginning of the money train.

I got on the phone to my tech geek, and told him I was forwarding a photo I needed him to doctor. I think Sousse would look perfect Photshopped into a KKK rally, wearing a Nazi armband and goose-stepping.

Sure, I wasn't a liar. But I was a sucker for a good blackmail scheme.

Not bad for a preschool drop-out.

Like That Japanese Chick
What Broke Up Van Halen
Stephen Blackmoore

The best part is the blowjobs.

Screw the music. It's the pussy Johnnie gets that keeps him play-ing bass. Sam, Paint Huffer's drummer, calls them groupies. Bunch of drunk girls who think it'd be cool to fuck a rocker in a garage band.

That was before Vicki.

Johnnie takes a pull on his Budweiser, a drag on his Marlboro. Sam lying there in a pool of his own piss and blood, Vicki's KA-BAR so far through his left eye it pops a little out the back of his skull.

Say good-bye to the blowjobs, Johnnie. The band's done gone broke up.

JOHNNIE DOESN'T NOTICE HER IN THE CROWD. Too busy remember-ing chords through all the ecstasy and blotter he took after that last song. He isn't even peaking and it's like he's wearing Mickey Mouse gloves. Everything's too goddamn big. Too far away. Barely keep his cigarette in his mouth.

Sam's hammering away at his drums. Nathan on his guitar, wail-ing his way through "Dirty Deeds."

She slides up to him at the bar afterward. Short, brown, buzz-cut hair. Lean muscle. No boobs. Nothing like the soft, big-titted girls in pleather grinding their asses against Nathan in the back of the bar.

Maybe it's the acid, maybe it's the X. Maybe it's her eyes. Bright green like cut emeralds, or jade or beer bottles the way sunlight burns through them on a hot afternoon, temps crawling to 120.

Maybe it's just the baggie she waves in front of him when she says, "Got some blow. Wanna party?"

They do a couple rails off the sink in the bathroom. In the greenish white of the fluorescent, she looks lean and hungry, tribal tats dancing up her neck from underneath her black t-shirt.

She wipes the excess from her nose, runs it along her gums. Looks him over like she's picking out beef.

"Wanna fuck?"

Please. He's nineteen years old with a nose full of blow and a dick so hard a cat couldn't scratch it.

She takes him out to her beat up Econoline, rides him like she's running a jackhammer. Doesn't even take off his pants. Just slides him in and grinds him down into the pile of Army blankets in the back.

She runs him through his haze of X, coke and acid. He's peaking but the knowledge is so far away he couldn't hear it if he tried. Takes him forever, but when the dam finally blows open he's come three times and fallen in love with her.

He doesn't even know her name.

"THE FUCK SHE ALWAYS HANGIN' AROUND FOR?" Sam's twirling his sticks one-handed. Every third try they clatter to the floor.

"She's my girlfriend," Johnnie says, tuning his bass, wondering if it's true.

Didn't learn her name was Vicki for almost a week. Kicked his ass out of the van when she was done with him. Popped up later at a gig at O'Connor's. Sucked him off in a bathroom stall.

Johnnie hits a sour chord that bounces off the cinderblock walls of Nathan's parents' garage. Nathan keeps saying they'll cut an album one of these days, make some real money. Not fucking likely if Sam keeps dropping those goddamn sticks.

"Fuckin' creepy is what she is. What the hell is with that combat knife?"

"She likes knives, what of it?" Likes knives a little too much, actually. Keeps a massive KA-BAR tucked in her boot. Likes to play with it while they're fucking.

First time she put the flat of that cold steel up by his nutsack he lost his shit. She laughed and called him a pussy.

"She cut me." Sam says.

"Shouldn't have given her any shit, then."

"She said my drumming sucks."

"It does."

Sam glares, twirls his sticks. Drops them when Vicki walks in through the side door.

"Got you a gig at Cozy's," she says.

Sam and Johnnie stare at her.

"Well, don't fucking thank me all at once."

"We gotta talk to Nathan," Sam says, voice quiet. Johnnie's pretty sure that if she said boo he'd shit himself.

"What, you can't make a decision without your mama? I s'pose you don't wipe your ass unless he tells ya?"

"No," Sam says. "It's his gear."

She's got that look on her face Johnnie knows means she's thinking. "I'll handle it." She turns around and walks out. Hasn't looked at Johnnie once.

"Dude, she's gonna fuck him."

"What? Shut up. She is not."

"How else you think she's gonna get him to go out there." Cozy's is out off the 40 near Ludlow. They played there about a year ago. Mean drunks. Nathan had a chair over his head before they'd started the second set and somebody stuck a knife in Johnnie's amp.

Johnnie watches as she heads into the house. "She's not his type."

"Wasn't yours, either."

THEY PILE THE GEAR IN VICKI'S ECONOLINE, Nathan riding shotgun. Vicki's done her hair purple, taken out her piercings. Almost like she's somebody else.

Johnnie sits in the back with Sam. Bastard's mouthing the words "fucked him" over and over until Johnnie hits him.

Nathan lights up in the front seat and hands the spliff back to Johnnie. He's not sure, but it looks almost like a peace offering. He takes a big toke, hands it to Sam.

Nobody talks most of the trip, giving Johnnie lots of time to buzz on Vicki and Nathan. Thought they had something. Seeing Nathan up front there with her, he's not so sure.

Vicki breaks the silence as they pull into the empty gravel lot. "You guys just play your set. Do some Scorpions or Ratt, or whatever headbanger shit you do."

That's a bad idea and Johnnie knows it. Sam and he talked about it. Country western or nothing. Even practiced some Waylon Jennings just to be on the safe side. No goddamn way is Johnnie getting another bottle upside his head for doing some Def Leppard.

But Nathan's nodding his head like it's the plan. Already decided.

Johnnie tokes up some more, but he's still worried. Tries to get the edge off, but it keeps crawling back. Gets worse after they head in to the parking lot and he sees Nathan pulling a gun out of his gym bag and stuffing it in his waistband.

"The fuck you lookin' at?" Nathan pulls his shirt down to hide the piece, giving Johnnie his best don't-fuck-with-me glare.

"Nothing. Just unloading the van."

"Yeah. Nothing. Now shut up and go do your fucking job." He heads after Vicki where she's talking to the owner like she's their manager or something, Johnnie wondering when this all turned into a job.

THE PLACE IS IN AN UGLY MOOD even before they hit their first notes. This is not a music crowd. This is a get drunk and beat the shit out of your neighbor crowd. At least with the headbangers they'll slow down long enough to appreciate a good guitar riff.

Nathan starts them off with some Black Sabbath, takes them into a couple of Dio covers. Sam's this close to freaking the fuck out and he keeps missing beats. A little too fast on "Crazy Train," a little too slow on "Master of Puppets."

Watching the crowd, Johnnie realizes, is kind of like watching porn. There's that steady beat, the thudding bass. The whole time it's moving faster and faster toward the inevitable. And you just know, with all that noise, sweat and ass slapping, that when it goes it's gonna go big.

Takes almost an hour for the shit to hit the fan. Johnnie was beginning to think that maybe it wouldn't get too bad. But the minute the first bottle comes sailing over the crowd, he knows it's already too late.

One thing about bar fights Johnnie learned a long time ago: everything's fine until somebody grabs a pool cue. Well, the pool cues run out in the first twenty seconds and now it's chairs, billiard balls, broken bottles.

The chickenwire around the stage bounces it all back into the crowd. It just pisses them off more. Somebody gets to the screen door on the side, yanks it open. Some shitkicker with a mustache you could mop a floor with. Eyes wild from too much Southern Comfort.

"Fuck this," Johnnie says, pulling off the bass. The strings shriek in a pig squeal as he grabs the neck like a baseball bat. Piece of shit he picked up in Barstow. Won't be sorry to see it go.

He takes a swing at the middle of the mustache, shattering the guy's nose and whipping his head back in a spray of blood and busted teeth. The guy behind is scrambling over his buddy to take his place. Not even paying attention to the freaked out teenager with a bloody bass coming at his head.

Two down. Then the room splits with the hammer of gunfire. At first, Johnnie thinks it's Nathan, but he hasn't pulled his piece. Too deaf to know where it came from.

Nobody's paying any attention to them anymore. Eating each other like fucking wolverines.

Sam's kicking the door at the back. Locked with a deadbolt and he's crying and pissing his pants. Nathan shoves him aside. Blows the lock through with his pistol.

Outside, Vicki's peeling the van across the lot, rooster tail of gravel behind her. Nathan throws Sam through the open side door, jumps in after. Johnnie barely makes it, legs scraping the ground.

Sam's screaming. Nathan's laughing. Vicki's got this cold-eyed, dead stare through the windshield. Hits the freeway doing eighty, that nasty looking KA-BAR stuck into the dashboard. Blood running off it like the car's bleeding.

THEY HOLE UP IN A MOTEL. Double queen beds, hotel art. Nathan already had a reservation.

Sam's in the bathroom cleaning himself up. Johnnie can hear the sobbing through the hollow wooden door.

Nathan's got a pile of cash he pulled from a duffel bag, counting out neat little piles, drinking a beer. Three thousand so far and he's got another duffel to go.

"Don't you fucking look at me like that," Vicki says, staring Johnnie down. She's sitting across from him at a small table wiping down the KA-BAR with an oiled cloth.

Johnnie hadn't realized he was looking at her at all. Probably because he can't recognize her. Or maybe he does. For the first time sees what she really is.

"The hell was that all about back there?"

"Oh, give her a break," Nathan says. His stacks are getting larger. "She just made you a shitload of money. All you had to do was keep the crowd busy."

"Yeah? That why you two fuckin' each other? You fuck him to get him to do this? Huh? Did you fuck me to get to him?"

Nathan laughs. "Christ, Johnnie, I wouldn't fuck her with your dick. Bitch has a face like a mule's ass."

Vicki grips the knife, slams it into the Formica of the small circular table where it quivers. "You wanna be careful there, faggot."

Johnnie can feel the tension ratchet. The sound of a slide being racked shuts them all up.

"This is her fault." Sam standing in the bathroom door. Towel around his waist, Nathan's gun in shaking hands.

"Sam—" Johnnie starts.

"Shut up. We had a good thing going. We were gonna go someplace. She fucked it all up. She's like that Japanese chick what broke up Van Halen."

It takes a second for Johnnie to figure out what he's talking about. "Yoko Ono," he says. "You're thinking the Beatles, dumbass."

"You want to put that gun down," Vicki says, ice and razor blades in her voice.

Nathan grabs the telephone from the bedside table, hurls it at Sam's head. The gun goes off.

JOHNNIE FIGURES HE'S GOT TIME for another beer before the cops show.

Nathan's between the two beds, legs stuck in the air like a bug. Missing a big chunk out of his neck. Thick pool of blood soaking into the carpet.

Vicki managed to get across the room and shove the KA-BAR into Sam's head before he shot her. Blew a hole right through her gut. Now she's lying there, going in and out of consciousness, eyes barely focusing.

"Hey." Voice weak, full of gravel. "Gotta get us out of here, lover. Go get the van."

Lover. First time she's ever called him that. Wonders if that's what she called Nathan. Figures it doesn't really matter now.

He walks over to her, careful to step around the puddles. Takes a drag on his cigarette. "You oughtta see yourself in a mirror."

"No, sugar. I'm fine."

He thought about running. Grab the cash. Get the hell out. But where? Vegas? Texas? They'd just track his ass down. Way he figures, sticking around is his best bet. Halfway decent lawyer, white kid, no priors. He'll be fine.

Vicki's breathing's tighter. Rapid gasps. Body starts to shake. Johnnie smokes. Watches her bleed out. Watches her die.

In the distance he can hear sirens.

Fetishize me

The Ballad of Manky Milne
Stuart MacBride

A nd that was why, on a cold night in February, Duncan Milne was ... up to his neck in shite. Literally. There was a small stunned pause, and then the swearing started. "FUCK, Jesus, fuck! Aaaaaaargh!" Then some spitting, then more swearing.

A silhouette blocked out the handful of stars visible through the septic tank's inspection hatch. "You OK?"

"No I'm not fucking OK!" More spitting. "Argh! Jesus—that tastes horrible!"

"Aye, well … it is shite."

Duncan "Manky" Milne wiped his eyes and flicked the scummy liquid away. The smell was appalling. "Don't tell me it's shite, OK? I know it's fucking shite! I'm bloody swimming in it!" He screwed his face up and spat some more. Breaking into Neil McRitchie's septic tank had seemed like such a good idea at the time—smacked out of their tits and jacked up on shoplifted vodka—but treading "water" in a subterranean vat of raw sewage, Milne had to admit it was loosing its appeal.

"Can you see it?"

He scowled up at the dark shape. "Help me out!"

A pause, then, "But—"

"Josie, I swear: if you don't help me out of here I'm gonna stab you in the fucking eye!"

"But you're down there anyway ..." Wheedling, putting on her "little girl" voice, because she thinks it makes men squirm.

"It's pitch black down here. I can't—"

"So feel about for it! It'll be easy enough to find. I'll bet it floats."

Milne spat again, trying to get rid of the aftertaste. "Why the hell would it float?"

Pause. "Well, it's powder, it should—"

"Oh for God's sake. If it was bloody powder it'd be dissolved in all this crap! It'll be wrapped in polythene. And parcel tape. Like in the movies." A kilo of heroin for their very own.

"OK, so it'll sink. You just have to feel about for it."

"You fucking 'feel about for it'! Jump down here and see how you like it!"

"Come on Duncan, pwease?" She was bringing out the big guns now—the fake lisp. Silly cow. It hurt to admit it, but she was probably right—he might as well look while he was down here. Wasn't as if he was going to get any mankier than he already was.

Grumbling and swearing, he started groping about in the lukewarm liquid. Trying not to think about what was bobbing about his throat. Thank God he was six feet tall—four inches shorter and his mouth and nose would be submerged. The scum layer was warm, steaming gently all around him. Further down it got colder—between the putrid froth and the knee-deep sludge at the bottom of the tank. That was slightly warm too, soaking through his nylon tracksuit and socks, seeping into his trainers.

Milne cursed again. A kilo of heroin would sink. And that meant he'd have to duck under the surface to get it. Not that he hadn't already been there, having fallen head-first through the inspection hatch. Gritting his teeth he waded forward, feeling for the parcel in the sludge with his feet. Nothing. "It's not—" was as far as he got before Josie hissed, "Shut up! Someone's coming!"

He froze.

Thin light swept past the access hatch, caught in the steam rising from the rotting sewage, and then voices: "What the hell do you think you're doing?" A man. Angry. Very, very angry.

"I … I was looking for someone." Josie trying her "little girl" voice again. Only this time there were no takers.

"You think I don't know what you are? Eh? Think I'm stupid?"

"I don't think you're—"

"We've had ENOUGH! Whores and drug addicts coming round here all hours!"

"But—"

"ENOUGH!"

"You know what: *fuck you* granddad—" A muffled *thunk* and the sound of something hitting the ground. Something undernourished and three months shy of her nineteenth birthday. *Thunk. Thunk. Thunk.*

"Enough …" And then it went quiet for a bit. And then there was some crying. And then some grunting. And then scraping, like someone was being dragged—the stars were blotted out again. Milne backed away quietly until he was against the far wall of the septic tank.

Click and a beam of cold white light leapt through the access hatch, making the milky-brown liquid glow. More grunting and then an almighty splash as something was unceremoniously dumped in. Making a tidal wave of human waste. Milne closed his mouth and his eyes and prayed for the best.

When it was over he wiped his face, and stared at the thing floating face-up in front of him.

Some fumbling and a curse and then the torch was hurled in after her, bouncing off Josie's cheek and spinning away into the scum. It stayed lit, sinking through the layers of liquid, glowing like a firefly. Flickering. Then dying. Leaving the tank in darkness once more.

The sound of heavy lifting came from above and slowly the patch of stars disappeared. *Clunk!* And they were gone. Milne and Josie were entombed.

TWO DAYS WAS A LONG TIME to spend trapped in a septic tank. Especially when the shakes started to set in. Coming down from a heroin buzz to the depths of cold turkey. Making him sweat and shiver, even though the liquid waste was just warm enough to steam. To start with he'd held Josie close, like a child would its teddy bear, but then she started to smell worse than the sewage and he'd been forced to push her to the far side of the tank. Wedging her under the inlet valve so she stayed beneath the surface.

Now it was just smells and darkness. He knew it was two days because the watch he'd taken from Josie's dead wrist glowed in the dark. Two days shivering and sweating. Feeling terrible. Scratching at the holes in his arms, unable to stop, even though he knew they'd get infected. Didn't matter now anyway. He was dead.

He'd spent hours trying to get the tank's thick concrete lid to move, but it was too heavy and too high above his head. He was well and truly trapped.

Two days without a hit and the hallucinations were in full swing, following him in and out of consciousness as he floated on the surface with the frothy scum. Where it was warmest. Trying to stay beneath the ventilation pipe, hoping enough air would be drawn down by the internal/external temperature difference to keep him from suffocation as he slowly died of dehydration.

Drifting on a sea of warm shite and cold turkey ...

WITHIN EIGHTEEN MONTHS of meeting Duncan "Manky" Milne, Josie has turned into a straggly scarecrow with sunken eyes and track marks down both arms. Red and angry like hornet stings around the crook of her elbow.

And Duncan hasn't fared much better—his boyish good looks are gone; now he's just skin and bone with a drug habit. And it's all about where the next fix is coming from. Which is why they're standing at the bar of the Dunstane Arms on George Street, trying to scrape together enough change for two pints of cider. Prior to a trip down the docks to see if anyone wants to rent Josie for a quick blowjob.

Of course, in the old days they both tried it, but no one wants to screw Manky Milne for cash anymore. So these days he's her Pimp Daddy. Even if he can only come up with enough cash for a pint and a half. Being a gentleman, Milne lets her take the pint—after all, she'll be the one doing all the work tonight—and they settle back into a booth, out of sight of the barman who's been giving them the evil eye since they slouched in five minutes ago, looking like shit.

And that's when they hear about Neil McRitchie.

Two blokes standing by the bandit—poking the buttons, making the wheels spin, the light flash and the music ding—laughing about how Neil McRitchie just got this big consignment in from Amsterdam: a kilo of uncut heroin. How Grampian Police decide to raid his house, but McRitchie flushes the whole parcel down the toilet before they break down the door. A kilo of smack, right down the drain. And then they drag him off to the station.

Milne sits back in his seat, face creased in thought, trying to get his drug-addled mind to work. Neil McRitchie … A small time dealer on the south side of the city—Kincorth, Nigg and Altens. Milne's bought from him before: blow, smack and a bit of speed. All from the guy's house.

A smile creeps onto Milne's dirty face. McRitchie's house is on the back road between Nigg and Charlestown, the end cottage in a row of four. Not so far off the beaten track that you can't walk there, but far enough to need private drainage. And private drainage means a septic tank.

The police won't have a bloody clue. They'll think it's gone for good, but McRitchie's kilo of heroin isn't wheeching its way out to the North Sea—it's bobbing about in a vat of shite, buried at the bottom of the garden. That's one good thing about being the son of a plumber: Milne knows his drainage. And that's when the plan—

HE'S HIDING BEHIND THE CHRISTMAS TREE, cowering down behind the sharp, dry needles, trying not to breathe, because he knows they'll fall and spatter against the bare floorboards. And then his father will find him. A scream from the corridor and a thump—his mother hitting the floor, then a thud—his father hitting her. Other kids want Giga-Pets and Furbies for Christmas. He wants his father to die. Six years old and all he wants—

MILNE SPLUTTERED, dragging his head back above the surface. Coughing. Shivering. He was burning up—cold, aching, feverish. It wasn't just the DTs: it was the sewage. Oozing in through the open sores on his arms and legs. Spreading tendrils of septicaemia through his already battered system.

And it was all for nothing. He'd searched the tank from top to bottom and there was no heroin. No kilo of smack wrapped up in a nice plastic package, sealed off with parcel tape. They'd been stupid to ever think there was: how was it going to get through the pipes? The package wouldn't have got round the toilet U-bend. They'd been stupid and now—

HALF PAST TEN AND JOSIE'S ON HER KNEES, earning them enough cash for three wrappers of heroin and a Big Mac with fries. The guy's something in accounting from the look of him, dressed in a Barbour jacket and checked shirt with his chinos round his ankles. Leaning against the wall and grunting as Josie's mouth works its magic.

Hiding in the shadows, Milne gives the guy's car a once over. It's an anonymous Renault with all the panache of a bottle of brown sauce. Perfect. Milne fingers the lump of brick in his pocket and crosses the road. He doesn't even let the guy finish before smashing him over the back of the head.

Josie sits back on the doorstep, giggling as Milne pops the Renault's boot and tries to manhandle the guy inside. He's still breathing, but the bastard weighs a ton! A quick search of his pockets turns up car keys, house keys, credit cards, a wallet with a hundred quid in it—result—and half a packet of cigarettes. Milne strips him naked and ties him up with his own clothes. The man just lies there, pale, curled up like a fetus, bleeding into the dark blue carpet. Not moving. Milne slams the boot shut, then he and Josie smoke the guy's cigarettes. Telling jokes about—

IT'S COLD, BARELY PAST DAWN, but he's running for all he's worth, chasing down the blond kid from Robert Gordon's private school, diving at him, dragging him to the ground. The rugby ball flies off to one of the other wee boys on the opposite team, but Milne doesn't care, just starts punching and kicking the blond kid. Hammering away until the teacher acting as a referee drags him off. Shouting and swearing.

The wee blond kid lies on the frosty grass, curled up in a ball, bleeding and crying. And Milne has no idea why he did it. But he's crying too. And the teacher hauls him round and screams in his face—

IT'S AFTER MIDNIGHT, but they're nowhere near sleepy. A hundred quid goes a long way if you know what you're doing. A woman Josie knows sells them a couple of wrappers of heroin each and a liter bottle of Asda's own-label vodka—shoplifted fresh that afternoon by a gang of eight-year-old girls. And then Josie and Milne are driving off to McRitchie's house in the guy's stolen car, pausing to shoot-up in a lay-by off the A90. Taking the long way round.

Milne parks down the road a bit, where they've got a good view of the cottages, but far enough away not to draw any attention. This is the difficult bit, figuring out where the septic tank is. Sometimes it's right up close to the house, sometimes it's more than a field away. But it always—

HE COULDN'T TELL if the noise was coming from inside his head or not. A dull rasping, grinding sound, like two stones being dragged apart. And then the air burst into fiery light. He opened his mouth to cry for help, but nothing came out. Not even a dry croak.

"Bloody hell …" A man's voice. It took a minute for Milne's brain to catch up, but he knew it was the same one who'd shouted at Josie. Who'd battered her head in with the heavy, metal torch. Milne had found it when he was searching the tank—lying buried in the bottom layer of sludge—the casing all battered and dented round the bulb end. Like someone had used it as a club.

The sound of gagging from above and the light drifted away, then swung back in through the inspection hatch. Milne pulled back against the wall, screwing his eyes shut, unaccustomed to the change from perpetual darkness—

Standing at the side of the grave, looking down at the shiny brown coffin. Holding his mothers hand. Pretending not to see the woman in the dark blue uniform cuffed to her other wrist—

A long pole reached in through the hatch, bringing the sound of muttered swearing with it. Something about backed-up plumbing and blocked pipes and people starting to notice ... The pole slipped into the layer of frothy scum, leaving a trail behind it as the man above swept it through the sewage. Looking for something.

Prod, prod, prod. And then Josie's bloated corpse floated to the surface, bringing with it a smell even worse than before. Her face appeared above the froth for a moment, then slipped sideways. Eyes open, looking at Milne one last time, before sliding over onto her front.

The pole clattered down into the tank as the sound of retching erupted from above. The light disappeared again. Then more retching. Spattering. Swearing. Coughing. And finally the light returned.

The Angry Man's voice: "Come on, you can do this ..." The pole, poking away at Josie's shoulder, trying to hook onto the tatty lumberjack shirt. Failing. More swearing.

Milne shook his head, trying to make things settle down. Trying to think clearly for the first time in a year and a half.

A bright-yellow Marigold rubber glove appeared in the opening, and then another one, attached to a disgusted-looking man in his late forties with a plastic torch clenched between his teeth. His greying hair just visible in the torchlight as it bounces back from the layer of sewage-froth. He stretched out, reaching for Josie's body ... And that was when Milne grabbed him—

Sitting crossed-legged in Colin's bedroom, ignoring the blaring of his parent's television, sinking the needle into his virgin arm. Biting his lip at the bee-sting pain. Pressing the plunger—

There was a high-pitched scream and the man toppled forward, dropping the torch as he pitched head-first into the tank. Arms flailing—

Standing down the docks, selling himself for the price of a hamburger. Enough to pay for a single wrapper. Feeling disgusted as he goes down on a man old enough to be his own father—

Milne curled a bony hand into a fist and slammed it into the screaming man. Over and over again, splashing and hitting and punching and biting in the dark. And all the time Josie's body bumps against them. Like she's trying to intervene. Trying to break them up. Make them—

Breaking into an old lady's house in the dead of night. Rifling through her things as she sleeps in the next room. Stealing anything he can sell down at the pub for a couple of quid. Passing them out through the window to Josie, who's standing watch. Punching the old lady in the face when she wakes up to see what all the noise is about. Watching as she lies there on the floor, not moving, too scared to check if she's still alive—

The man gurgled, struggling as Milne grabbed him by the lapels and forced his head under the surface. Holding him there. An arm swept up from the stinking water, catching Milne on the side of the head, but he didn't let go. Grunting, teeth gritted, feeling the man start to go limp. Keeping him submerged. Drowning him in piss and shit—

There's no one in the cemetery at this time of night. No one to watch him drop his trousers and squat over his father's grave—

The struggling stopped after a couple of minutes, but Milne didn't let go. Just in case. A long, slow count to five hundred and he figured that was enough. The bastard deserved what he got. He released his grip and the body bobbed to the surface.

Milne rummaged through the guy's pockets, taking everything he could find—keys, wallet, spare change, handkerchief—before releasing the body to sink into the sludge. And then he reached up and clambered out of the tank, back into the real world.

He lay on his back, staring up at the night sky. Shivering. Steaming gently. According to Josie's glow-in-the-dark watch it was half past eleven. Wednesday. Two days without food or water. He was lucky to be alive at all. And that thought set off a fit of the giggles. And then some coughing. And finally some sort of seizure. He was pouring with sweat, juddering away, teeth clamped shut from fear of biting his tongue in half. Not healthy. Not healthy at all.

Milne rolled over onto his front and levered himself up onto his knees. Trembling all the time. Knowing that without something to drink soon, he was going to die. The world tangoed round his head as he stood upright, the night sky swirling and pulsing as he took a deep breath and lurched towards the darkened row of cottages.

A security light blared into life, catching him halfway down the first path, but he staggered on to the front door. Locked. Milne dragged out the keys he'd taken from the bastard who'd killed Josie and tried them in the lock, one by one. None of them worked.

He lurched across the garden and nearly fell over the waist-high fence, clambering into next door. The keys still didn't fit. But another dose of the tremors grabbed him, shaking him to his knees. Leaving him gasping and wracked with a cramp on the top step. The third house was the same, only this time he had to crawl through the garden to get to the front door. The keys were useless. Milne almost gave up. Just curled up on the path to die: get it over with.

But there was one more house left—the one on the end. Where McRitchie lived. McRitchie would still be banged up in Craiginches; Milne could break in without having to worry about an irate householder coming after him with a shotgun.

It was pitch-dark round the back of the cottages and Milne felt his way along the wall, stumbling over a pile of something that rattled and clattered, before finding McRitchie's back door. It was one of the part-glazed kind beloved of housebreakers everywhere. Smiling, Milne tried to smash one of the panes with his elbow. It bounced, sending shooting pains racing round his body, making his whole arm feel like it was on fire. Biting his tongue he sank to his knees and nearly passed out.

Deep breaths. Deeeeeeep breaths … Oh God, he was going to be sick. But there was nothing to be sick with, just a thin string of bile, spiralling bitterly down the front of his soaking, stained clothes. He grabbed a rock from the garden and did the window properly, send-

ing shards of glass shattering into the kitchen. Fumbled with the lock
and doorknob. And he was in. Oh thank God.

He slumped against the worktop and tried not to pass out. And
tried—

IT'S HIS BIRTHDAY AND HE'LL CRY IF HE WANTS TO. Nineteen years old
and his present is getting the crap beaten out of him by Colin McLeod
over a small matter of an unpaid debt. Fifteen pounds. That's all it
takes for Colin McLeod to give him two weeks in hospital. Happy
birthday.

The doctors come past and the counselors and the police too, but
he doesn't say anything. Just lies there and tries to move his toes again.
They give him methadone and group therapy, but as soon as he gets
out he's back on heroin again. Borrowing money and—

BANG! And his head hit the linoleum floor. Milne lay flat on his back,
staring up at McRitchie's kitchen ceiling, wondering how he got there.
He was in the hospital and the next thing … He closed his eyes and
shivered. He needed a drink.

There was a bottle of whisky on the kitchen table—illuminated
by the faint green light from the clock on the microwave. He picked
it up with trembling hands and fumbled the lid off, swallowing
mouthful after mouthful, not caring that it burnt all the way down.
Until it hit his stomach and bounced, spewing out through his mouth
and nose, making a slick of alcohol on the kitchen floor.

Water, he needs water, not whisky. Lurch to the sink, turn on the
tap and stick his mouth against it. Sucking it down. This time he was
bright enough to stop after a couple of mouthfuls, feeling his stomach rebel after two days on "nil by mouth." Two mouthfuls and then
a break, then another couple. Slowly building up until he wasn't
thirsty anymore. He was ravenous.

McRitchie's fridge wasn't exactly packed with tasty goodies, but
Milne didn't care. He grabbed things at random, stuffing them in his
mouth, barely chewing. Eating by the cold-white glow of the fridge
light. Cheese, cold mince, raw bacon. For a moment he thought he

was going to bring it all up again, but it stayed down. Now all he had to worry about was the—

Click. Light blossomed in the kitchen and someone said, "What the FUCK?"

Milne spun round, eyes wide, cold beans falling from his open mouth. It was McRitchie, looking very pissed off. The man was easily as tall as Milne, but a hell of a lot broader. Muscled, not junky stick-thin. Someone that didn't sample his own product.

Milne raised his hands, dropping the tin of beans. It bounced off the linoleum, exploding red sauce and pale beans everywhere, joining the whisky vomit. He tried to explain what he was doing there, but his throat wouldn't work.

McRitchie yanked a drawer open and dragged out a long-bladed kitchen knife. "Break into *my* house? You stupid smack-head bastard!" He charged forward. "I'll fucking—" And stepped right in the slick of spilled beans and whisky. His left leg shot out from underneath him and for a brief second everything went into slow motion: the knife sailing through the air, his head sweeping downward and catching the edge of the kitchen table. The loud *thunk!* as it hit. The knife skittering away across the working surface, clattering into the sink. Another thump as McRitchie hit the floor hard. Eyes shut, mouth open wide. Not moving.

Milne grabbed the knife from the sink and crept forward. Trembling. McRitchie was still breathing. But it didn't take long to fix that.

THE GUY'S CAR was in exactly the same place he and Josie had left it two days ago. It even started first time. Milne sat behind the wheel, shivering and shaking, coughing until the world slipped into shades of black and yellow then disappeared.

He came to with his head resting against the wheel and the car's horn braying in his ear. Snatched himself back upright, felt the car whooooosh around him. And closed his eyes. Forcing everything back down. Turning the key in the ignition.

It had taken every last ounce of strength to drag McRitchie's heavy arse round to the septic tank, tumbling him in with Josie and her killer. Then a considerable breather before levering the inspection hatch cover back into place. Good job McRitchie had a HUGE stash of speed hidden in his bedroom or there was no way Milne would have managed it. In fact all of McRitchie's stash was now stuffed into the glove compartment, Milne's pockets and under the driver's seat. He had enough to last a couple of months, if he was careful and didn't go mad in the first week.

All he had to do now was get back to the squat and he'd be fine. Sell the car, get some spare cash and live on drugs and delivery pizza until April. Every junky's dream.

The A90 was quiet as he pulled onto it, face screwed up in concentration, keeping the car at a steady thirty, trying to stay between the white lines. And doing a pretty good job of it too. Three tablets of speed and he was back in form. No more shakes and shivers. No, he was feeling—Oh shit.

A flash of blue light in the rearview mirror. Oh SHIT!

Eyes front. Maybe it wasn't for him? Maybe the police wanted to pull someone else over and they were just … No. It was him. And he was too wasted to make a run for it. He pulled over.

The traffic policeman was a woman. She rapped on the driver's window and Milne fumbled with the electric button thing until it slid down. She recoiled back, one hand covering her mouth, gagging. "Holy shit!" she said at last, spluttering. "What the hell is that *stink*?"

Milne shrugged. After two days in the tank he couldn't smell himself anymore. "I fell in some shite." He said, trying not to twitch, or shiver, or sound like he was out of his face on stolen drugs.

"You OK, sir?" she asked, shining a torch into the car, spotlighting him in all his manky glory. "You look ill."

Milne nodded, she had him there, he could see himself in the rearview mirror: pale grey, sweaty, dark purple bags under his eyes, threads of fiery red spreading through his skin. "I fell in some shite."

She turned and shouted back at the traffic car, "Norm, get an ambulance up here sharpish!" then knelt down, breathing through her mouth, like she didn't want to smell him anymore. "You're going to be OK, we're going to get you to the hospital."

He opened his mouth to tell her he just wanted to go home, but couldn't. All that came out was, "I fell in some shite ..." again. Sitting there, watching the policewoman fading away until there was nothing left but darkness and—

HEADACHE. Killer, bastard headache. Like a chisel driven between the eyes. Milne cracked open an eye to see a pretty nurse hovering over him with a syringe.

"Where am I?" was what he tried to say, but all that came out was a dry croaking sound. The nurse didn't smile at him, just held a squeezy bottle to his lips and let him take a small sip. "Thank you ..." Weak, but almost sounding human again.

The nurse nodded, then said, "There's someone here to see you." Brisk, matter of fact, beckoning over a uniformed constable and a big, fat bald bloke with a tight suit and a constipated expression.

"Mr. Milne," said the fat one, looming over the bed, "we'd like to talk to you about the car you were driving when you were brought here."

Milne frowned. "I ..." Shit—they'd found the drugs. All of McRitchie's lovely drugs and he'd barely had a chance to sample any of them.

"Specifically, we'd like to talk to you about the car's original owner. And how his dead body wound up in the boot covered in your fingerprints."

And that was it: Duncan "Manky" Milne was up to his neck in shit again.

The Turnip Farm
Allan Guthrie

Lester closed the gate, stepped into the field, wiped his brow with the back of his hand. Sweat glistened in the creases of his skin. He wiped his hands, front and back, on the legs of his dungarees.

It was only five o'clock, but already Lester could tell it was going to be a hot one. Yep, by doodly, he'd better do it now rather than chance it later during the heat of the day.

Decision made, he felt his dangle stir. He gazed at the dozens of rows of turnips poking through the soil like a field of breasts, round and firm and ripe, and his dangle stirred some more.

He glanced around. Nothing moved, apart from a couple of crows gliding in the thermals above the barn. Back in the cottage, everyone was still asleep.

Lester dropped to his knees, reached down, brushed surface dirt off a pair of fine wee beauties and placed them in the palms of his hands. He grasped them tightly, pressed against their fullness, and relaxed. Pressed and relaxed. As he kneaded the turnips, his breathing grew faster. He shifted, leaned forward, squeezed and stroked and tugged and nipped. He drew circles with his thumbs on the skin of the turnips, whispering, "Like this? Oh, yeah." He squeezed and stroked again until his fingers were tired and the muscles in his thighs burned.

"Use my mouth? Okay."

He lay on his stomach and wrapped his lips around the sweet, bare turnip flesh, and sucked and licked and nibbled, first one turnip and then the other, until the earth beneath him moaned.

"You want me to touch you there? In a minute." He liked to tease.

When his lips were numb and his tongue was raw, he gently placed his fingers between the turnips and traced a line in the soil towards his belly, stopping only when he felt the earth under his fingers part. He prodded and pushed until his fingers sank inside a delicious softness, the soil still moist from yesterday's spurts of rain. His fingers stiffened and he thrust them deep into the welcoming shaft that wrapped around his skin, clinging to him as he probed deeper and deeper, his fingers throbbing like over-excited hearts about to explode.

He was about to unzip himself when something caught his eye. He squinted. It was Sheena, his tractor, the shiny jealous ring of her exhaust pipe glinting in the sun. This is where his fumble with the turnips ended. Sheena wanted him inside her. She wanted him to ride her hard and fast, up and down the field, in and out of the turnips, harder and faster, engine roaring and screaming, until she shuddered, finally, to a furious climax, and came to rest by the gate, spent.

That's what he did most mornings and he'd have done it again today if his oldest brother, Anne, hadn't shouted at him from Mum's bedroom window, "Lester, come up here. We've got a problem."

IT WAS STILL EARLY, and Lester was surprised that Anne was up, but he saw right away when he stepped into Mum's bedroom that she hadn't budged from her usual position. Lester couldn't remember the last time he'd seen her out of bed. When their dad had got ill, she'd watched them move him into the barn, and then she'd sunk between the covers and stayed there.

Lester supposed she must have got up to go to the bathroom now and then, but he'd never seen her do it. And she didn't have to get up to eat cause Lester's youngest brother, Bamber, brought her food that he'd caught himself in his traps and prepared in the kitchen. He wasn't a bad cook, but all he'd cook was meat. Lester liked to prepare the vegetables, but the rest of the family were often reluctant to let him. They'd seen what he'd done with a carrot once, a long thick one. Walked in on him on his back on the table with his pants down and his legs in the air. Wasn't his fault. He was only human, with human desires.

Mum was in bed but she was awake. Sitting up, propped up against the pillows. Petey, one of Lester's other brothers, had his back to her, facing the wall, and his body shook under the covers. Made a change that the pair of them weren't curled up together. They were always giggling. Lester used to giggle too, but not for a while.

Dad would have been mad if he'd seen them, Mum and Petey. He was mad when he saw his friend, Alf, between the sheets with Mum. He'd shot Alf and then fed him to the pigs. Course, they didn't have the pigs any longer, not since animal welfare had visited. Lester missed the pigs. He liked how they snuffled and squealed and how sometimes they looked like they were smiling.

Anne stroked his beard and looked round the room.

"What's going on?" Lester said.

Petey snuffled.

"Waiting on Bamber," Anne said.

"Want me to fetch him?" Lester said.

Anne shook his head. "He knows we're meeting here. We'll wait."

They waited, fidgeting, listening to Petey's slavering sobbing noises.

When Bamber finally appeared an hour or so later, he was carrying a tray with steaming plates of food on it. "Sorry I'm late," he said. "But I thought you might be hungry."

They all tucked in, except for Petey, who ignored everybody and groaned now and then. Mum had Petey's, along with her own.

"Very good," Lester said to Bamber. Rabbit. Would have been better with potatoes, though. Potatoes in their skins. Lester enjoyed peeling the skin back and nuzzling the exposed potato underneath.

After Lester had finished licking his plate, he turned to Anne. "What did you want us all here for?" he asked.

Anne rose to his full height of six foot eight and bit his lip. "Mum," he said. "You better tell Lester and Bamber the news."

Mum looked a little worried. Her hair looked even wispier than usual and her bald patch seemed larger. She looked more worried when the bed began to shake with Petey's sobs. She slid down the bed and out of sight under the covers.

Anne sighed. "It's Dunlop." Dunlop was their nearest neighbor. He lived four miles away, called himself a farmer but he just rented out his land and lived off the proceeds. Didn't even own his own tractor. "He's asked her to marry him."

Lester felt the undigested meat in his stomach come alive. He looked at Bamber and Bamber shook his head sadly. "No," Lester said. "She can't, by doodly. Dunlop's not right in the head." He'd never been the same since Ruby, his daughter, got her tongue pierced. After the accident, Dunlop had started to talk to himself, not like normal folk, but whole conversations. And not just one side either as if he was talking to an imaginary friend. With Dunlop, you got both sides.

"Mum," Anne said. He walked over to the bed, prodded the figure huddled under the covers where her head might be. "Mum. Tell them."

"I'll tell them," Petey yelled, throwing off the bedclothes, and rolling out of bed with his fencepost that hadn't left his side for nigh on four years now. "I'll tell them," he repeated, his dangle waggling as he shook the post. "She only went and said yes."

"But she can't," Lester said. "Mum, you can't. What about Dad?"

"Why don't we go ask him?" Bamber suggested.

DAD LIVED IN THE BARN. Well, most of him did. When he'd taken ill a while back, he'd cut off one of his arms and a foot with a machete. Anne had said measles could do that to you, but Lester wasn't convinced it was measles.

Anne had patched him up pretty good, anyway, and you could hardly tell the arm had been sewn on again. Pup, the dog, had got to the foot, though, and eaten most of it. Bamber had given what was left to the girl who lived in the cupboard under the stairs to play with, and Pup ran away soon afterwards and hadn't been seen since.

Dad hardly spoke these days. All a bit of a trauma for him. He just sat in his chair in the middle of the barn, head slumped to the

side, jaw hanging open. They'd tied him to the chair for his own protection. Didn't want him trying to hurt himself again.

"I think he might be dead," Bamber said.

Anne smacked Bamber with the back of his hand.

"Ow," Bamber said. "I'm just saying."

"Well, don't," Anne said. "He's clearly not dead."

"He looks dead, that's all I'm saying."

"What happens to dead people, Bamber?"

"I don't know," Bamber said. "They stop moving?"

"And?"

"They stop breathing?"

"And?"

"I don't know."

"They go to Heaven," Lester said.

"Exactly," Anne said. "And where's Dad? Right here."

"So he can't be dead," Lester said. "Right?"

"But when we had the pigs," Bamber said, "they didn't go anywhere when they died."

"Cause they're pigs," Anne said. "Pigs don't go to Heaven, stupid."

Petey rubbed his eyes. "Mum can't marry Dunlop if Dad's not
dead."

"That's right."

Petey smiled. "So that means everything's okay."

"Far from it," Anne said. "If Dunlop and Mum are planning on
getting married, it can only mean one thing."

They all looked at him, waiting.

He coughed, stretched, coughed again. "They're planning on
killing Dad."

"Wow," Lester said.

"Mum wouldn't do that," Petey said, clutching his fence post to
his chest.

"No," Lester said. "But Dunlop would. Lightning strikes your
daughter's tongue stud and kills her, it's sure to drive you batty. And
batty people get up to all sorts of evil."

"So what are we going to do?" Anne said.

They were silent for a moment. Then Bamber spoke up. "I have an idea," he said. "How about we hire a hitman?"

"Brilliant," Anne said. "Anybody know any hitmen?"

ANNE AND LESTER WENT INTO THE VILLAGE the next day and asked around. Bit of a wasted journey, since nobody at the post office or the shop was able to help. Lester suggested they try the pub.

There were six people inside, not including them or Domenic, the barman, who'd left home a few years ago when he was still called Susan. He asked how Mum and Dad were and Lester asked if he could see Domenic's Teflon rod again that he slipped inside his dangle to make it stiff, and Domenic showed him, and then they ran out of conversation. So Anne and Lester played some darts while they knocked back a few pints.

After an hour or so, one of the blokes at the table nearest them challenged Anne to a game.

Lester let them get on with it, went to empty his bladder.

There was a guy in the toilet with a monkey. "Hello," the guy said.

"Hello," Lester said.

"I hear you're looking for a hitman."

"Hang on," Lester said. "I'll go fetch my brother."

THE HITMAN followed them back to the farm in his Mini.

"Nice guy," Lester said.

Anne grunted.

"Don't you think he looks like Mum with a moustache?" Lester said.

Anne grunted again.

"What's the matter?" Lester asked.

"That monkey," Anne said. "Don't trust it."

LESTER GRABBED BAMBER out of the kitchen, dragged Petey out of Mum's bed, and led them to the barn where the hitman was pointing at the monkey who'd jumped onto Dad's lap.

"I've killed over a thousand people," the hitman was saying. "I should know when someone's dead."

"You would think so," Anne said. "Makes me doubt your thingummybobs."

"My what?"

"You know. Makes me doubt you can do what you say you can do."

"I've never been doubted," the hitman said. "I take great exception to that comment. Your father's definitely dead."

Anne smacked him with the back of his hand.

"Ow," he said.

"Watch your monkey," Lester said.

The monkey had been playing with Dad's fly. Pulling the zip down, and chattering, pulling it back up, chattering. He'd pulled it down again, grinned and stuck his little fist inside.

Lester said, "He's going too far."

The hitman rubbed his cheek, looked at the monkey and yelled at it. It yanked its hand out of Dad's pants and leapt onto the floor and scurried away into the corner, out of sight behind the large freezer that Dad used to climb inside when the weather was too warm.

"He's not dead," Anne said.

"Right," the hitman said, still rubbing his cheek. "I want ten grand. Half now, half later."

"I don't know," Anne said. "We're a bit strapped."

"Eight, then."

"Well …"

"Six."

"I don't know …"

"Five?"

"Okay," Anne said. "How about we give you a hundred and fifty quid now and the rest when it's done."

"What do you think?" the hitman said, looking over to the monkey.

The monkey jumped on top of the freezer, screeched, then chattered its way over to the hitman and whispered something in his ear.

"It's a deal," the hitman said.

They all shook hands with the hitman. And then they all shook hands with the monkey. And then they all shook hands with each other.

Then they stood around, looking at one another and shuffling their feet.

The hitman said, after a while, "So where's my down payment?"

"Go fetch the cheque book," Anne told Bamber.

"I want cash," the hitman said.

"Don't have any," Anne said. "Leave cash lying around this place, one of these fellas'd nick it soon as look at it."

That wasn't true. But what was true was that they didn't have much money. They had heavy loan repayments, and it was hard to make a living growing turnips, in any case.

Bamber left to fetch the cheque book.

"So you've done a thousand hits?" Lester said.

"Yep. At least."

"You and the monkey?"

"Yep. Well, he's probably done more than me."

"Yeah?" Anne said.

"I just go along to help, usually," the hitman said. "He's the one who pulls the trigger. In fact, I've never actually killed anyone. No need. He's happy to do the dirty work."

"Isn't he scared of the noise?" Petey asked.

"Nah," the hitman said. "He uses a .22. Delicate little piece. Sounds no louder than a cap gun." He looked at his watch. "We have to go soon."

"Another job?"

"Nah. Got my dance class tonight."

"You dance?"

"Oh, yeah." He showed them. Nifty piece of footwork ending up with a 360-degree turn. The monkey applauded, so they joined in. "You want to see some more?"

AN HOUR LATER and the hitman had well and truly missed his dance class. But he seemed happy enough that he'd had the chance to entertain them and he'd forgotten about (or forgiven) the slap on the cheek. And the truth was, he was extremely good at dancing. All that spinning around and never once getting dizzy. Apparently, so he told them, it was all in the way you twisted your head to the side, focused on a particular spot, and let your body turn.

Like Petey had said, if the hitman was as good at killing people as he was at dancing, Dunlop didn't stand a chance.

Anne wrote the hitman his cheque and handed it over.

"If you don't cough up the rest when I'm done," the hitman said, "I'll have that fine-looking tractor I saw out in the turnip field."

Lester stiffened. Nobody was getting their hands on his tractor. "You'll get the money," he said. "When are you going to do it?"

The hitman looked at his watch. "Well," he said. "I've no other plans for the rest of the night."

"WHAT ARE WE GOING TO DO?" Lester asked, after he'd gone. "He'll be back for his money later."

"What do you mean?" Anne asked.

"We don't have any. He'll take my tractor."

"It's not yours," Bamber said. "It belongs to all of us."

"He's not getting it," Lester said.

Anne stroked his beard. "I don't know that we have any choice."

LESTER WENT BACK IN THE HOUSE and knocked on the door of the cupboard under the stairs.

The girl who lived in there opened it. She was about nine, wore clothes that were far too big for her, the sleeves of her jumper hanging over her wrists, trouser legs flapping over her feet. "What?" she said.

"I want to borrow your shotgun," Lester said.

She tilted her head, licked her lips. "Why?"

"Doesn't matter."

"What're you going to do with it?"

"Please just let me borrow it."

She stood there, hands on her hips. "You know what happened the last time I leant it to someone."

That was the time Dad had found Alf in bed with Mum.

"So?" Lester said.

"You going to shoot someone too?"

"Maybe."

"I can't let you do that."

Lester stared at her. "But this guy, he's going to take my tractor," he said.

"Oh," the girl said. "Oh, dear." She pouted. "That's probably for the best, don't you think?" Then she swivelled on the balls of her feet and closed the door.

WHEN THE HITMAN RETURNED, about eleven, he was covered in blood, and alone. They all went out to meet him. He climbed out of his Mini and they all wandered over to the barn together.

"Is it done?" Anne asked, once they were inside.

"Crazy coot, that Dunlop," the hitman said. "You people never told me. Just kept talking to himself."

"Is he dead?" Petey asked.

The hitman was out of breath. He held up a hand, then said, "Yeah."

"Where's the monkey?" Bamber asked.

Lester was glad Bamber had asked. He wanted to know too but was afraid of what the answer might be.

"Didn't make it," the hitman said, lowering his eyes. "Dunlop did something to him. He said, 'What are you doing here?' 'Oh, I've come to kill you.' 'That's nice. Why?' 'I don't know, it's what I do.' 'But you're a monkey.' 'And?' 'You shouldn't be shooting people. In fact, you shouldn't be talking like this.' 'I'll talk how I like,' the monkey said. And fired his first shot. Wide. The second got Dunlop in the leg. Dunlop said, 'You're a freak of nature.' 'I'm a monkey.' 'A monkey freak.' The third shot got Dunlop between the eyes and that was him. But the monkey wasn't finished. He looked at me and I told him no, he wasn't a freak, but he didn't believe me. He put the gun in his mouth and squeezed the trigger. That's how I got covered in all this crap."

"Bit of a mess, right enough," Anne said.

"Sorry about your monkey," Bamber told him.

"Never mind that," the hitman said. "Where's my money?"

Anne ran a hand through his hair, looked at Lester. Then away. "Don't have it. You'll have to take the tractor."

"Fine," he said.

But it wasn't fine. It wasn't fine at all.

Lester lunged towards Petey. Grabbed the fence post from him and swung it down, two-handed, on the hitman's head. There was a thunk and the hitman reeled. Lester whacked him again. And again. The hitman dropped to his knees and groaned. Lester hit him again. Kept pounding his skull with the fence post.

Thunk.

Thunk.

Thunk.

When Lester's arms hurt too much, he stopped.

Nobody spoke for a while.

Then Petey said, "Can I have it back?"

Lester held out the fence post. It was covered in blood, and bits of hair and scalp were stuck to it.

Petey started to cry.

Lester said, "He's not getting my tractor."

"No," Anne said. "He's not."

Anne took the hitman's arms and Bamber took his legs and they carried him over to the freezer. Lester helped them lift him inside.

When they closed the lid, it was as if nothing had changed.

"You okay?" Anne asked.

LESTER GOT UP AT 4:30 THE NEXT MORNING. He washed, brushed his teeth, dressed, and was outside by 4:45. The sky was cloudy and drops of rain fell on his face.

In the field, the turnips poked through the soil like rows of naked scalps. He didn't want to touch them. Didn't want to go anywhere near them.

He tiptoed through the field towards his tractor. He opened the door, climbed inside the cab.

He sat there, shaking.

Then he got out again and ran back into the house. He stopped outside the cupboard under the stairs and thought about asking the girl once again if he could borrow her shotgun. But he walked on, upstairs, into his mum's bedroom where he took his clothes off and climbed into bed beside her and Petey.

Mum woke up, stroked his hair.

Birds chirped, Petey snored, and his mum kept stroking his hair. He thought he might stay here for a long, long time.

The Footjob
Christa Faust

Have you ever done one?"
Lula asked me this while standing on a man's chest. I was standing on his face.

"No," I told her. "Have you?"

We were talking about footjobs. Know what a handjob is? Same deal but with your feet.

"Sure I have," she said with a lazy smile.

She shifted her weight and brushed her bare toes across the shape of the guy's hard dick under his jeans. His breath was hot against my arches. I reached out and pressed my palm against the wall for better balance.

"Footjobs aren't allowed here, you know," I said, feeling like somebody's mom, suddenly paranoid, like we were about to get busted for even talking about it.

"Here" was a monthly foot fetish party. It was only my second. Lula had been to every single one since the first, nearly ten years ago. The concept is simple. It's kind of like a strip club, only there's no nudity and instead of lap dances the girls give foot fetish sessions. Ten minutes for twenty bucks. These sessions can include anything from trampling, like we were doing, to toe sucking, licking or sniffing, foot massage, tickling, high heel or boot worship. They do *not* include footjobs. In fact any sort of contact between foot and dick is strictly forbidden, even through clothing. Trampling was an exception but Lula was always pushing it, always bending the rules. Always just a little bit naughty, but you could never stay mad at her. Everybody loved Lula. It was hard not to.

Lula and I were both petite and both natural redheads, but that's where the similarity ended. Lula had ten extra pounds in all the right places. Where I'm boyish, she was va-va-voom. She was a dark redhead, all thick unruly curls that would never stay pinned up. A sly little pixie-slut with a generous mouth and mischievous brown eyes. She was impulsive, mercurial. The best kind of bad girl.

I, on the other hand, am a good girl. A little bit shy, always careful and practical. I'm more of a strawberry blonde, with baby fine hair cut in a choppy bob and pale blue eyes set in a waspy sort of plain-jane face. A slender build, not much in the tits and ass department. We both have freckles, but mine seem more disorganized, scattered all over instead of just a neat decorative spray across the bridge of the nose like Lula had. Of course, there was one other thing we had in common. We both had beautiful feet.

My feet are sixes, narrow and elegant with long, expressive toes and delicate arches. Hers were fives and cute as kittens. Sky high arches and tiny rounded toes with perfect crimson nails. We both seemed to stay pretty busy at the foot parties and were often chosen to do doubles together. Like that trample session.

"I know you can't do footjobs here, silly," Lula said, shifting again and stepping with her full weight on the guy's crotch, gripping her bare toes like a monkey. One foot on the head of his dick and one on his balls. "I'm talking about *private* sessions."

She rocked from one foot to the other, alternately crushing his dick then his balls. Dick, balls. Dick, balls. He responded by grunting and then sucking in a deep breath with this repetitive rhythm that sounded like a choo-choo train. I giggled and moved from my perch on his face to the flatter and more stable ground of his chest.

Lula stepped off the guy's junk and joined me on his chest. She was very close to me, her foot planted between mine and her left thigh brushing against my right as she reached out to steady herself against the wall. She wrapped her other arm around my waist and spoke low and close to my ear.

"I know this guy," she said.

That's how I wound up doing my first and only footjob.

THE NIGHT BEFORE the private session I was kind of nervous and kind of excited and more than a little horny. I dragged my boyfriend away from the computer and into bed and when he took his pants off, I stretched out my leg and ran my toes along the underside of his half-hard dick.

"Weirdo," he said, laughing and pushing my foot away. He gripped his dick at the base, steering it towards my mouth. So much for that.

I thought about the footjob while he fucked me, wondering what it was going to be like. I also thought about Lula and the way she smelled when she put her arm around my waist. I don't always get off during sex, but I did that night.

The next day seemed particularly long and meaningless. The dayjob more soul-crushing. The traffic more intolerable. I couldn't wait for nine PM.

As usual, I arrived ten minutes early. I can't stand the thought of being late. People who are always late just don't know how to plan ahead. I'm always early, because I always give myself a little bit more time than I really need. You know, just in case. I figure if you expect the worst, you'll never be disappointed.

I decided to wait in my car, parked down the curvy street from the guy's huge, beautiful house. The guy's name was Mark, no last name that I knew of, and he lived up on the hill above the reservoir in Silver Lake. Big money moviestar house with turrets and bougainvillea all over. Automatic gate. Million dollar view. It was only two miles away from my place but might as well have been on another planet. I live on the other side of the 101 in what is now being billed as "Historic Filipinotown." The ad on Craigslist called the place "Silver Lake

Adjacent." Instead of a view of the "lake" for which Silver Lake had been named, I had a view of the ass-end of the Rampart Division police station. At least it was safe. Nobody was dumb enough to try and break into an apartment right next door to the police station.

Nine o'clock sure took its sweet time but when it finally arrived I checked my lipstick in the rearview, slid my feet into my strappy, high-heeled Italian sandals and got my skinny ass out of the car. I looked at my phone to check the time again and saw that my boyfriend had called. I turned the phone off without calling him back.

I know they say if you're going to do a private session at a guy's house, you should always make sure someone knows where you are, what time you got there and when you will be done. That's excellent advice and I'm usually so careful about that kind of thing, but that night I was really glad I didn't tell anyone where I was going.

There was a buzzer sort of thing outside the gate. I rang and waited. I was expecting a voice to come on asking who was there, but there was just a muffled click and the gate swung wide to let me in. The front door was already open when I got there. The guy, Mark, was waiting in the doorway.

He wasn't a big guy, maybe five foot six or so. Thinning brown hair. European nose. Decent build, fit and symmetrical. Faded jeans that probably cost more than everything I had on. He was barefoot.

"Nice," he said, his gaze locked on my feet. I had the feeling I could have been wearing a big red clown nose and he wouldn't have noticed. "Why don't you come on in and we can get acquainted."

I stepped into a large, airy living room. The décor had a tasteful but generic flavor, like an upscale hotel lobby. To my right was a massive picture window that would have overlooked the reservoir and all the surrounding hills if not for the heavy raw silk curtains.

"Is Lula here yet?" I asked.

Mark smiled, a chilly flexing of the facial muscles that seemed to have nothing to do with his eyes. His gaze never left my feet.

"Lula is always late," he said. That figured. "Can I get you a drink?"

I shook my head, thinking roofies and date rape. You never knew.

"Well then," he said. "Let's go down to the playroom."

Mark led me down a flight of narrow stairs to a door at the end of a long hallway. The door was locked with an expensive deadbolt and Mark unlocked it with a single key alone on a fancy gold key ring, stepping aside to let me into the large rectangular room beyond.

Wall to wall white carpet. A pair of stripper poles, improbably placed about four feet apart in the center of the room. Ultramodern white leather couch against the far wall. Subtle, recessed lighting. To the left and right were floor-to-ceiling shelves. The shelves to the left held women's high-heeled shoes and the ones to the right held what at first glance appeared to be bloodlessly severed feet, cut off a few inches above the ankle. When I looked closer, I saw that they were silicone life-casts. There had to be over a hundred pairs, each utterly individual and somehow weirdly intimate. The windows were covered with closed black miniblinds.

"I'd love to cast your feet," Mark said, handing me a sweaty wad of cash. "I guess you can say I'm a sort of collector."

The wad added up to five hundred dollars. I stuffed the money into my purse.

"Do you have Lula's feet?" I asked, scanning the shelves.

"Of course," he replied. "She's one of my favorites."

He reached out and pulled down one of a pair and once I saw it I couldn't believe I hadn't recognized it sooner. It was a perfect replica of Lula's curvy, kittenish foot, down to the flawless crimson nails. He handed it to me and I was surprised by how heavy it was. It was disturbingly soft and fleshlike on the surface but I could feel that it was actually articulated by some kind of complex bone-like structure beneath the silicone. I'd never actually held a freshly severed foot before, but I'm willing to bet it would feel almost exactly like that. It was more than a little creepy.

"It's nice to have Lula here with me," he said. "Even when I don't have time to book a session."

Again, that strangely disconnected robot smile, only now he was staring at the fake Lula foot instead of mine. It suddenly occurred to me that he probably jacked himself off with these fake feet and I couldn't hand it back to him fast enough. It was tough not to wipe my hands on my skirt. I really wished that Lula would show up.

"Why don't you try on some shoes for me while we're waiting?" The guy asked after he put the fake Lula foot back on the shelf beside its mate.

"Sure," I said, walking over to the white couch and taking a seat, setting my purse close beside me.

It was extremely quiet in that room, almost as if it had been soundproofed. His bare feet made no sound at all on the cushy carpet as he browsed the shelves, selecting shoes for me to try. He didn't ask my size. Apparently, he didn't need to.

He brought me three pairs. Classic black patent pumps, red sandals that were barely more than a spike heeled sole with the thinnest, most minimal strap to hold them on and clear plastic stripper platforms. He set them in a careful row on the carpet and then abruptly lay down on his back with his head between my feet.

"Try them on," he said, apparently speaking directly to my feet. "And take your time. When you have each pair on, stand up and slowly walk around my body starting on the left side and coming back around to the right. When you're finished with each pair, tell me that you don't like them and throw them on my chest. I'd like you to act kind of bitchy and stuck up from now on, all the way through the session."

I did what he asked. It wasn't so bad. He had his dick out of his expensive jeans before I finished the first lap around his prone body, but that was easy to ignore.

"I hate these shoes," I said, throwing the pumps down on him.

He moaned, jacking faster. His face was turning red, but still had no real expression. I was starting to feel like I didn't exist above the ankles. Where the hell was Lula?

I was just slipping on the clear stripper shoes when a jarring buzzer sounded, making me jump a little.

"That's Lula," Mark said, fumbling in the crumpled pocket of his jeans. He pulled out a small remote like the kind you use to get into your car and thumbed the button. "Keep going."

About halfway through my third orbit around Mark, Lula appeared in the doorway. She was wearing white leather fetish pumps with six-inch steel heels improbably paired with a cheap white rayon sundress that was pretty much completely see-through. I don't have to tell you she had nothing on underneath. I shave my bush but Lula doesn't. That bright red tuft was like a traffic light shining through the flimsy fabric. Instead of a purse, she was carrying an ugly yellow duffle bag that sagged like it was mostly empty.

"Hello, beautiful," she said to me, sliding her arm around my waist again and pressing a kiss against my hot, blushing cheek. "I see Mr. Impatient has put you to work already."

"Yeah," I said with a shrug. I never really knew what to say around Lula.

"Take your clothes off, Mark," she said, like it didn't really matter. Then, to me, "Did he show you Candy's feet yet?"

"Candy?" I arched an eyebrow, curious. "You mean Candy Box?"

Lula nodded, winked.

In case you've been living under a rock, Candy Box is that porn star who was murdered three years ago. Strangled. They pinched the boyfriend but he swears he didn't do it. There are plenty of people who believe him. Anyway, she did a lot of foot stuff. She used to do the foot parties too, but that was before my time.

"Mark," Lula said, setting the duffle on the couch beside my purse. "Go get Candy's feet."

I hadn't even noticed the safe. It was shoebox sized, sitting in the far corner of the bottom shelf on the foot cast side of the room. I don't know what I was expecting. Maybe I thought he was gonna pull out a real pair of dead, mummified feet. Of course it turned out to be just another pair of silicone casts. He brought the feet over to us one at a time, handing the right to Lula and the left to me.

"Wow," I said, holding the dead girl's foot. Another bon mot from the wittiest, most articulate girl in the world. Sheesh.

"I just *love* these feet," Lula said hefting the right foot and rubbing her cheek against the sole. "Candy was so hot. She had the most beautiful feet of all time."

I looked down at the foot I was holding. Sure it was nice, symmetrical and well proportioned. High arches. Small, flawless toes. But to tell the truth, I thought Lula's feet were better.

"Another collector once offered Mark fifty thousand dollars for Candy's feet," Lula said, using the foot's big toe to rub her nipple through her dress. "But he wouldn't sell."

"Forty-five," Mark said absently. He was naked now and jacking off again, gaze locked on the fake foot in Lula's hand.

"Whatever," Lula said with a smirk. "Let's get started."

The session itself wasn't really all that different from the sessions at the foot parties. Trampling, toe sucking, the usual routine, except the guy was naked while this was happening and beating off like a caveman trying to start a fire. He was laid out on a clean white towel between the two stripper poles and Lula and I used the poles for balance while we worked. Lula kept Candy's feet nearby and used them frequently, joking that Mark was lucky to get a triple session for the price of a double. It wasn't until the very end that we got around to the footjob.

It was actually harder than you'd think. Awkward. Of course Lula was a total pro. She made it look so easy. Laughing, she squirted more lube on him and told me use one of my feet together with one of hers. I was frowning like a kid learning to write my name, concentrating on getting the rhythm right when she leaned over and kissed me on the mouth.

Just a little kiss, sucking gently on the corner of my lower lip. I kind of lost track of what I was doing for a second, lost track of everything really. Then she stood up, slipped her sticky feet back into her white heels and winked.

"Time to finish him off," she said.

She stood back up on his chest and face and left the downstairs work to me.

He was almost there when it happened. That still makes me feel a little bit bad. Like it would have been better somehow if he'd gotten off first. Lula was looking right at me, balancing with one high-heeled foot on his face when she suddenly stepped down hard and to the left. The six-inch heel of Lula's shoe punctured the soft spot just beneath his ear.

"Oops," Lula said with a smirk.

Remember that nice white carpet? And Lula's white dress and white shoes? Man what a mess.

When Mark finally laid down and died, I felt this cold bubble of anger rising inside me. It was always hard to stay mad at Lula, but I was doing a pretty good job so far.

"What the hell were you thinking, Lula?" I asked.

"Dump your boyfriend," Lula said. She grabbed Candy's feet and stuffed them into the duffle bag. "We can split the money fifty/fifty."

Naughty little pixie, bright eyes glittering like she was suggesting we cheat on our diets and go for ice cream. She was so damn beautiful. So beautiful and so stupid.

"So what exactly is your plan here?" I asked, the cold spot spreading rapidly through my whole body. "Just murder this guy, steal his rare, collectable feet and leave him laying here with your shoe sticking out of his neck?"

"I wasn't gonna leave the shoe, silly," Lula said.

She came slinking towards me and I backed away. My brain was working overtime, desperately searching for a scenario in which we were anything but fucked.

"Did you tell anyone where you were going tonight?"

She shrugged.

"A couple friends, maybe."

I walked over to the couch, carefully avoiding the spreading puddles on the expensive carpet. My purse was right were I left it. I picked it up and unzipped the inner pocket.

"Did you tell anyone that I was doing this session with you?" I asked.

She shook her head.

"Of course not, beautiful," she said, working that bad girl smile. "Don't be such a worrywart. Come on, let's get the hell out of here."

Another thing you probably ought to know about me is that I'm at my best under pressure. I can rapidly evaluate any complex emergency situation and eliminate all unacceptable options until only one clear course of action remains. Running away with Lula like this, appealing as it might have been, was not the one remaining course of action.

I pulled a pair of thin leather driving gloves from my purse and put them on. Then I shot Lula.

I have an earthquake kit in the trunk of my car. I have a small flashlight on my keychain. And I carry an unlicensed, untraceable handgun in my purse. Good girl scout that I am, I'm always prepared. I expect the worst and I'm never disappointed.

Lula died much faster than Mark. When she was finished, I put the gun in Mark's dead hand and used his finger to put a few more bullets into Lula's body. I quickly wiped down everything I'd touched, put my own shoes back on and left Lula's duffle bag where she'd dropped it.

It was hardly an ideal solution, but I was betting on the cops' desire to go with the easy answer: kinky hooker tries to murder and rob a client but he shoots her before she can get away. I figured the longer it took for some neighbor to complain about the smell, the smoother my setup would go down. It would have been nice if I could have taken Candy's feet myself, but that would leave open-ended questions. To be honest, I was happy to walk away with my five hundred dollars.

I never did another footjob, but I did end up dumping my boyfriend.

destroy me

*69
Blake Crouch

At nine thirty on a Thursday evening, as he lounged in bed grading the pop quizzes he'd sprung on his eleventh grade honors English class, Tim West heard footsteps ascend the staircase and pad down the hallway toward the bedroom.

His wife, Laura, appeared in the open doorway.

"Tim, come here."

He set the papers aside and climbed out of bed.

Following her down the squeaky stairs into the living room, he found immense pleasure in the architecture of her long legs and the grace with which she carried herself. Coupled with that yellow satin teddy he loved and the floral tang of skin lotion, Tim foresaw a night of marital bliss. Historically, Thursdays were their night.

Laura sat him down in the oversize leather chair across from the fireplace, and as she took a seat on its matching ottoman, it struck him—this fleeting premonition that she was on the verge of revealing she was pregnant with their first child, a project they'd been working on since last Christmas. Instead, she reached over to the end table beside the chair and pressed the blinking Play button on the answering machine:

Ten seconds of the static hiss of wind.

A woman's voice breaks through, severely muffled, and mostly unintelligible except for, "… didn't mean anything!"

A man's voice, louder and distorted by static: "… making me do this."

"I can explain!"

"… late for that."

A thud, a sucking sound.

"… in my eyes." The man's voice. "Look in them! … you can't speak … but … listen the last minute … whore-life … be disrespected. You lie there and think about that while …"

Thirty seconds of that horrible sucking sound, occasionally cut by the wind.

The man weeps deeply and from his core.

AN ELECTRONIC VOICE ENDED THE MESSAGE WITH, "Thursday, 9:16 PM."

Tim looked at his wife. Laura shrugged. He reached over, played it again.

When it finished, Laura said, "There's no way that's what it sounds like, right?"

"There any way to know for certain?"

"Let's just call nine-one—"

"And tell them what? What information do we have?"

Laura rubbed her bare arms. Tim went to the hearth and turned up the gas logs. She came over, sat beside him on the cool brick.

"Maybe it's just some stupid joke," she said.

"Maybe."

"What? You don't think so?"

"Remember Gene Malack? Phys ed teacher?"

"Tall, geeky-looking guy. Sure."

"We hung out some last year while he was going through his divorce. Grabbed beers, went bowling. Nice guy, but a little quirky. There was this one time when our phone rang, and I picked it up, said, 'Hello?,' but no one answered. The strange thing was that I could hear someone talking, only it was muffled, just like that message. But I recognized Gene's voice. I should've hung up, but human nature, I stayed on, listened to him order a meal from the Wendy's drive-through. Apparently, he'd had our number on speed-dial in his cell. It had gotten joggled, accidentally called our house."

One of the straps had fallen down on Laura's teddy.

As Tim fixed it, she said, "You just trying to scare me? Let's call your brother—"

"No, not yet—"

"No, you're saying that a man, who we know well enough to be on his speed-dial list, was killing some poor woman tonight, and he accidentally … what was the word?"

"Joggled."

"Thank you. Joggled his phone, inadvertently calling us during the murder. That where you're going with this?"

"Look, maybe we're getting a little overly—"

"Overly, shit. I'm getting freaked out here, Tim."

"All right. Let's listen once more, see if we recognize the voice."

Tim went over to the end table, played the message a third time.

"There's just too much wind and static," he said as it ended.

Laura got up and walked into the kitchen, came back a moment later with a small notepad she used for grocery lists.

She returned to her spot on the hearth, pen poised over the paper, said, "Okay, who are we close enough friends with to be on their speed-dial?"

"Including family?"

"Anyone we know."

"My parents, your parents, my brother, your brother and sister."

"Jen." She scribbled on the pad.

"Chris."

"Shanna and David."

"Jan and Walter."

"Dave and Anne."

"Paul and Mo."

"Hans and Lanette."

"Kyle and Jason."

"Corey and Sarah."

This progressed for several minutes until Laura finally looked up from the pad, said, "There's thirty names here."

"So, I've got an unpleasant question."

"What?"

"If we're going on the assumption that what's on that answering machine is a man we know murdering a woman, we have to ask ourselves, which of our friends is capable of doing something like that?"

"God."

"I know."

For a moment, their living room stood so quiet Tim could hear the second hand of his grandmother's antique clock above the mantle and the Bose CD player spinning Bach up in their bedroom.

"I've got a name," he said.

"Me, too."

"You first."

"Corey Mustin."

"Oh, come on, you're just saying that 'cause he took me to that titty bar in Vegas, and you've hated him ever—"

"I hate most of your college friends, but he in particular gives me the creeps. I could see him turning psychotic if he got jealous enough. Woman's intuition, Tim. Don't doubt it. Your turn."

"Your friend Anne's husband."

"Dave? No, he's so sweet."

"I've never liked the guy. We played ball in church league a couple years ago, and he was a maniac on the court. Major temper problem. Hard fouler. We almost came to blows a few times."

"So what should I do? Put a check by their names?"

"Yeah ... wait. God, we're so stupid." Tim jumped up from the hearth, rushed over to the phone.

"What are you doing?" Laura asked.

"Star sixty-nine. Calls back the last number that called you."

As he reached for the phone, it rang.

He flinched, looked over at Laura, her eyes covered in the bend of her arm.

"That scared the shit out of me," she said.

"Should I answer it?"

"I don't know."

He picked up the phone mid-ring.

"Hello?"

"Tiiiiiimmmmm."

"Hi, Mom."

"How's my baby boy?"

"I'm fine, but—"

"You know, I talked to your brother today and I'm worried—"

"Look, Mom, I'm so sorry, but this is a really bad time. Can I call you back tomorrow?"

"Well, all right. Love you. Kisses and hugs to that pretty wife of yours."

"You, too. Bye, Mom." Tim hung up the phone.

Laura said, "Does that mean we can't star sixty-nine whoever left the message?"

"I don't know."

"You think there's some number you push to like, double star-sixty—"

"I don't work for the phone company, Laura."

"Remember, I suggested we buy the package with caller ID, but you were all, 'No, that's an extra five bucks a month.' I think it's time to call the police."

"No, I'll call Martin. He'll be off his shift in an hour."

A FEW MINUTES SHY OF ELEVEN O'CLOCK, the doorbell rang.

Tim unlocked the deadbolt, found his brother, Martin, standing on the stoop, half-squinting in the glare of the porchlight, his uniform wrinkled, deep bags under his eyes.

"You look rough, big bro," Tim said.

"Can I come in or you wanna chat out here in the cold?"

Tim peered around him, saw the squad car parked in the driveway, the engine ticking as it cooled.

Fog enveloped the streets and homes of Quail Ridge, one of the new subdivisions built on what had been a farmer's treeless pasture, the houses all new and homogenous, close enough to the interstate to always bask in its distant roar.

He stepped to the side as Martin walked into his house, then closed and locked the door after them.

"Laura asleep?" he asked.

"No, she's still up."

They walked past the living room into the kitchen where Laura, now sporting a more modest nightgown, had put a pot of water on the stove, the steam making the lid jump and jive.

"Hey, Marty," she said.

He kissed her on the cheek. "My God, you smell good. So you told him about us yet?"

"Never gets old," Tim said. "You think it would, but it just keeps getting funnier."

Laura said, "Cup of tea, Marty?"

"Why not."

Martin and Tim retired to the living room. After Laura got the tea steeping, she joined them, plopping down in the big leather chair across from the couch.

Martin said, "Pretty fucking quaint and what not with the fire going. So what's up? You guys having a little crumb-cruncher?"

Laura and Tim looked at each other, then Laura said, "No, why would you think that?"

"Yeah, Mart, typically not safe to ask if a woman's pregnant until you actually see the head crowning."

"So I'm not gonna be an uncle? Why the hell else would you ask me over this late?"

"Go ahead, Laura."

She pressed Play on the answering machine.

They listened to the message, and when it finished, Martin said, "Play it again."

After the message ended, they sat in silence, Martin with his brow furrowed, shaking his head.

He finally said, "I know you're too much of a cheap bastard to have caller ID or anything invented in the twenty-first century, so did you star-sixty-nine it?"

"Tried, but Mom called literally the second I picked up the phone."

Martin undid the top two buttons of his navy shirt, ran his fingers around the collar to loosen it.

"Could just be a prank," he said. "Maybe someone held the phone up to the television during a particular scene in a movie."

"If that's what it is, I don't recognize the movie."

Martin quickly redid the buttons on his shirt, said, "What do you think you've got there?"

"I think someone's phone got jiggled at the worst possible moment, and we were on their speed dial."

"You call nine-one-one?"

"Called you."

Martin nodded. "There's gotta be a way to find that number. You know, something you dial other than star-sixty-nine."

Tim said, "Star-seventy?"

"I don't know, something like that."

"We tried to call the phone company a little while ago, but they're closed until eight AM tomorrow."

Martin looked at Laura, said, "You okay, sweetie? You don't look so hot."

Tim saw it, too—something about her had changed, her face seasick yellow, hands trembling imperceptibly.

"I'm fine," she said.

"You sure? You look like you're about to blow chunks all over your new carpet."

"I said I'm fine."

Martin stood. "I need to use the little girl's room."

Laura watched him walk out of the room and down the first-floor hallway, and only when the bathroom door had closed, did she look back at Tim and whisper, "Did you see it?"

"See what?"

"When he unbuttoned his shirt a minute ago, it exposed his white t-shirt underneath."

"So?"

"So I saw blood on it, and I think he saw me looking at it, because he buttoned his shirt up again real fast."

Tim felt something constrict in his stomach.

"Why does he have blood on his shirt, Tim?"

The toilet flushed.

"Listen, when he comes back out, you say since you aren't feeling well, you're going to bed." The faucet turned on. "Then go upstairs and wait several minutes. I'm gonna offer Martin a drink. We'll sit in the kitchen, and you sneak back down and go outside, see if you can get into his squad car."

"Why?"

"I don't think he brought his cell phone inside with him. He usually keeps it in a little pouch on his belt. Probably left it in the car. Get it, and look back over the outgoing history. If he called our house at 9:16 tonight, we'll know."

"And then what?"

The bathroom faucet went quiet.

"I don't know. This is my brother for Chrissakes."

TIM OPENED ONE OF THE HIGH CABINETS above the sink and took down a bottle of whiskey.

"Old Grandad?" Martin asked.

"What, too low-shelf for you?"

"That's what Dad used to pass out to. Let me see that." He grabbed the bottle out of Tim's hands, unscrewed the cap, inhaled a whiff. "Jesus, brings back memories."

"You want ice or—"

"Naw, let's just pass it back and forth like old times in the field."

They sat at the breakfast table, taking turns with the fifth of Old Grandad. It had been several months since the brothers had really talked. They'd been close in high school, drifted in college, Martin only lasting three semesters. Tim had come home two years ago when Dad's liver finally yelled uncle, found that something had wedged itself between him and his brother, a nameless tension they'd never acknowledged outright.

And though all he could think about was the message and Laura, he forced himself to broach the subject of Mom—hostile territory—asked Martin if he thought she seemed to be thriving in the wake of Dad's passing.

"That's a pretty fucked-up thing to say."

"I didn't mean it like—"

"No, you're saying she's better off without him."

Beyond the kitchen, Tim heard the middle step of the staircase creak—Laura working her way down from the bedroom—and he wondered if Martin had heard it. The last two steps were noisy as well, and then came the front door you could hear opening from Argentina. Nothing else to do but get him riled and noisy.

"Yeah, Martin, I guess I am saying she's better off without him. What'd he do these last five years but cause us all a lot of heartache? And what'd you do but step in as Dad's faithful apologist?"

Another creak.

"Ever heard of honor thy father, Tim?" Martin's cheeks had flushed with the whiskey and Tim wondered if he'd intended to raise his voice like he had. His brother's back was to the archway between the kitchen and the living room, and as Tim saw Laura enter the foyer and start toward the front door, he tried to avert his eyes.

"You know he beat Mom."

"Once, Tim. One fucking time. And it was a total accident. He didn't mean to shove her as hard as he did." Laura turning the deadbolt now. "And it tore him up that he did it. You weren't here when it happened. Didn't see him crying like a goddamn two-year-old, sitting in his own vomit, did you?" Tim could hear the hinges creaking. "No," Martin answered his own question as the front door swung open, cold streaming in. "You were in college." Laura slipped outside, eased the door closed behind her. "Becoming a *teacher*." Any curiosity Tim had harbored concerning his brother's opinion of his chosen profession instantly wilted.

"You're right," Tim said. "Sorry. I just … part of me's still so pissed at him, you know?"

Martin lifted the bottle, took a long drink, wiped his mouth.

"Of course I know."

Tim pulled Old Grandad across the table, wondering how long it would take Laura. If the cruiser was locked, there'd be nothing she could do but come right back inside. If it was open, might take her a minute or two of searching the front seats to find the phone, another thirty seconds to figure out how to work Martin's cell, check his call history.

He sipped the whiskey, pushed the bottle back to Martin.

"Wish you'd come over more," Tim said. "Feel like I don't see you much these days."

"See me every Sunday at Mom's."

"That's not what I mean."

Tim wanted to ask Martin if he felt that wedge between them, met his brother's eyes across the table, but couldn't bring himself to say the words. They didn't operate on that frequency.

A FRIGID MIST FOGGED LAURA'S GLASSES, and with the porchlight out, she took her time descending the steps, the soles of her slippers holding a tenuous grip on the wet brick. The fog had thickened since Martin's arrival, the streetlamps putting out a glow far dimmer and more diffused than their normal sharp points of illumination—now just smudges of light in the distance.

She hurried down the sidewalk that curved from the house to the driveway.

Martin had parked his police cruiser behind the old Honda Civic she'd had since her junior year of high school, over two hundred thousand miles on the odometer and not a glimmer of senility.

Laura walked around to the front door on the passenger side, out of the sight-line of the living room windows. She reached to open the front passenger door, wondering if Martin's cruiser carried an alarm. If so, she was about to wake up everyone on the block, and had better prepare herself to explain to her brother-in-law why she'd tried to break into his car.

The door opened. Interior lights blazing. No screeching alarm. The front seat filthy—Chick-Fil-A wrappers and crushed Cheerwine cans in the floorboards.

She leaned over the computer in the central console, inspected the driver's seat.

No phone.

Two minutes of leafing through the myriad papers and napkins and straws and stray salt packets in the glove compartment convinced her it wasn't there either.

She glanced back through the partition that separated the front seats from the back.

In the middle seat, on top of a Penthouse magazine, lay Martin's black leather cell phone case.

"Yeah, I was seeing this woman for a little while."

"But not anymore?"

Martin took another long pull from Old Grandad, shook his head.

"What happened?"

"She wanted to domesticate me, as they say."

Tim forced a smile. "How so?"

"Tried to drag me to church and Sunday school. Anytime we'd be out and I'd order an alcoholic beverage—her term—she'd make this real restrained sigh, like her Southern Baptist sensibility had been scandalized. And in bed ..."

LAURA OPENED THE DOOR behind the front passenger seat and climbed into the back of the cruiser. Wary of the interior lights exposing her, on the chance Martin happened to glance outside, she pulled the door closed.

After a moment, the lights cut out.

She picked up the leather case, fished out Martin's cell phone, and flipped it open, the little screen glowing in the dark.

"... I'D GOTTEN MY HOPES UP, figured she's so uptight about every other fucking thing, girl must be a psychopath between the sheets. Like it has to balance out somewhere, right?"

As he sipped the whiskey, Tim glanced around Martin toward the front door.

"Sadly, not the case. When we finally did the deed, she just laid there, absolutely motionless, making these weird little noises. She was terrified of sex. I think she approached it like scooping up dogshit. Damn, this whiskey's running through me."

Martin got up from the table and left the kitchen, Tim listening to his brother's footsteps track down the hallway.

The bathroom door opened and closed.

It grew suddenly quiet.

The clock above the kitchen sink showed 11:35.

LAURA STARED AT THE CELL PHONE SCREEN and exhaled a long sigh. Martin's last call had gone out at 4:21 PM to Mary West, his and Tim's mother.

She closed the cell, slipped it back into the leather case, sat there for a moment in the dark car. She realized she'd somehow known all along, and she wondered how she'd let Tim know—maybe a shake of the head as she crept past the kitchen on her way up the stairs. Better not to advertise to Martin that they'd suspected him.

She searched for the door handle in the dark, and kept searching and kept searching. At least on this side, there didn't seem to be one. She moved to the other door, slid her hand across the vinyl. Nothing. Reaching forward, she touched the partition of vinyl-coated metal that separated the front and back seats, thinking, *You've got to be kidding me.*

TEN MINUTES LATER, flushed with embarrassment, Laura broke down and dialed her home number on Martin's cell. Even from inside the car, she could hear their telephone ringing through the living room windows. If she could get Tim to come outside unnoticed and let her out, Martin would never have to know about any of this.

The answering machine picked up, her voice advising, "Tim and Laura aren't here right now. You know the drill."

She closed Martin's cell, opened it, hit redial—five rings, then the machine again.

The moment she put the phone away, Martin's cell vibrated.

Laura opened the case, opened the phone—her landline calling, figured Tim had star-sixty-nined her last call.

Through the drawn shades of the living room windows, she saw his profile, pressed Talk.

"Tim?"

"Thank God, Laura." Marty's voice. "Someone's in the house."

"What are you talking about? Where's Tim?"

"He ran out through the backyard. Where are you?"

"I um … I'm outside. Went for a late walk."

"You on your cell?"

"Yeah. I don't understand what's—"

"I'm coming out. Meet me at the roundabout and we'll—"

Martin's cell beeped three times and died.

THE WHISKEY HAD MADE TIM THIRSTY, and Martin was taking his sweet time in the bathroom.

Tim went over to the sink, held a glass of water under the filter attached to the faucet.

He heard the creak of wood pressure—Marty walking back into the kitchen—and still watching the water level rise, Tim said, "Let me ask you something, Marty. You think whoever left that message knows they left it?"

"Yeah, Tim, I think they might."

Something in Martin's voice spun Tim around, and his first inclination was to laugh, because his brother did look ridiculous, standing just a few feet away in a pair of white socks, a shower cap hiding his short black hair, and the inexplicable choice to don the yellow satin teddy Laura had been wearing prior to his arrival.

"What the hell is this?" Tim asked, then noticed tears trailing down Martin's face.

"She'd gone to the movies with Tyler Hodges."

"Who are you talking—"

"Danielle."

"Matson?"

"Yeah."

"She's a junior in high school, man."

"You know what she did with Tyler after the movie?"

"Marty—"

"She went to the Grove with him and they parked and the windows were steamed up when I found them."

"Look, you can have the tape from our answering—"

"They'd trace the call," Martin said. "If you were to encourage them."

"We wouldn't."

"I can see the wheels turning in your eyes, but I've thought this through quite a bit more than you have. Played out all the scenarios, and this is—"

"Please, Marty. I could never turn you in."

Martin seemed to really consider this. He said, "Where's Laura?"

"Upstairs."

Martin cocked his head and shifted into his right hand the paring knife he'd liberated from the cutlery block.

"Don't fuck with me. I was just up there."

"You need help, Marty."

"You think so?"

"Remember that vacation we took to Myrtle Beach? I was twelve, you were fourteen. We rode the Mad Mouse roller coaster eight times in a row."

"That was a great summer."

"I'm your brother, man. Little Timmy. Look at yourself. Let me help you."

As he spoke, Tim noticed that Martin had gone so far as to put on black glove liners, and there was something so clinical and deliberate in the act, that for the first time, he actually felt afraid, a sharp plunging coldness streaking through his core, and he grew breathless as the long-overdue shot of adrenaline swept through him, and it suddenly occurred to him that he was just standing there, leaning back against the counter, watching Marty shove the curved paring knife in and out of his abdomen—four, five, six times—and he heard the water glass he'd been holding shatter on the hardwood floor beside his feet, Martin still stabbing him, a molten glow blossoming in his stomach, and as he reached down to touch the source of this tremendous pain, Martin grabbed a handful of his hair, Tim's head torqued back, staring at the ceiling, the phone ringing, and he felt the knifepoint enter his neck just under his jawbone, smelled the rusty stench of his blood on the blade, and Martin said as he opened his throat, "I'm so sorry, Timmy. It's almost over."

THE TASTE OF METAL WAS STRONG IN LAURA'S MOUTH, even before she saw the shadow emerge from the corner of the garage, the floodlight sensor triggered, Martin jogging toward the cruiser.

She ducked down behind the seats and flattened herself across the floorboards, her heart pounding under her pajama top.

The front driver's side door opened.

Light flooded the interior.

Martin climbed in, shut the door, sat motionless behind the wheel until the dome light winked out.

At last, Laura heard the jingle of keys.

The engine cranked, the car backing down the driveway and tears coming, her eyes welling up with fear and something even worse—the uncertain horror of what had just happened in their home while she was locked in the back of this car.

She reached up, her fingers grazing the backseat upholstery, just touching the leather cell phone case.

When Martin spoke, it startled the hell out of her and she jerked her arm back down into her chest.

"Hey guys, it's Marty. Listen, I'm really concerned based on my conversation with Tim. I'm coming over, and I hope we can talk about this. You know, I still remember your wedding day. Been what, eight years? Look, everyone goes through rocky patches, but this ... well, let's talk in person when I get there."

Laura stifled her sobs as the car slowed and made a long, gentle left turn, wondering if they were driving through the roundabout at the entrance to the subdivision.

Under his breath, Martin sighed, said, "Where the fuck are you?"

She grabbed the leather case off the seat, pried out the phone in the darkness.

The screen lit up. She dialed 911, pressed Talk.

The cruiser eased to a stop.

"Connecting ..." appeared on the screen, and she held the phone to her ear.

The driver's door opened and slammed, Laura's eyes briefly stinging in the light. She heard Martin's footsteps trail away on the pavement and still the phone against her ear had yet to ring.

She pulled it away, read the message: Signal Faded Call Lost.

In the top left corner of the screen, the connectivity icon that for some reason resembled a martini glass displayed zero bars.

The footsteps returned and Martin climbed back in, put the car into gear.

The acceleration of the hearty V8 pushed Laura into the base of the backseat.

Martin chuckled.

Laura held the phone up behind Martin's seat, glimpsed a single bar on the screen.

"Laura?"

She froze.

"You really have to tell me what that skin cream is," he said. "Whole car smells like it."

She didn't move.

"Come on, I know you're back there. Saw you when I got out of the car a minute ago. Now sit the fuck up or you're gonna make me angry."

That lonely bar on the cell phone screen had vanished.

Laura pushed up off the floorboard, climbed into the seat.

Martin watched her in the rearview mirror.

They were driving through the north end of the subdivision, the porchlights as distant as stars in the heavy midnight fog.

Martin turned onto their street.

"What'd you do to my husband?" Laura asked, fighting tears.

The phone in her lap boasted two strong bars and very little battery.

She reached down, watched 9-1-1 appear on the screen as her fingers struggled to find the right buttons in the dark.

"What were you doing in my cruiser?" Martin asked. "Looking for this?"

He held up his second cell phone as Laura pressed Talk.

Through the tiny speaker, the phone in her hand began to ring.

She said, "When did you know?"

"When you played the message."

Martin turned into their driveway.

"I'm really sorry about all this, Laura. Just an honest to God …"

He stomped the brake so hard that even at that slow rate of speed, Laura slammed into the partition. "You fucking bitch."

Faintly: "Nine-one-one. Where is your emergency?"

Martin jammed the shifter into Park, threw open the door.

"Oh, God, send someone to—"

The rear passenger door swung open and Martin dove in, Laura crushed under his weight, his hand cupped over her mouth, the phone ripped from her hand, and then the side of her head exploded, her vision jogged into a darkness that sparked with burning stars.

LAURA THOUGHT, *I'm conscious.*

She felt the side of her face resting against the floor, and when she tried to raise her head, her skin momentarily adhered to the hardwood.

She sat up, opened her eyes, temples throbbing.

Four feet away, slumped on the floor beside the sink, Tim lay staring at her, eyes open and vacant, a black slit yawning under his chin.

And though she sat in her own kitchen in a pool of her husband's blood, legs burgundy below the knees, hair matted into bloody dreads like some demon Rasta, she didn't scream or even cry.

Her yellow teddy was slathered in gore, her left breast dangling out of a tear across the front. She held a knife in her left hand that she'd used to skin a kiwi for breakfast a thousand years ago, Tim's .357 in her right.

The front door burst open, footsteps pounding through the foyer, male voices yelling, "Mooresville Police!"

She craned her neck, saw two cops arrive in the archway between the kitchen and the living room—a short man with a shaved head and her brother-in-law, wide-eyed and crying.

The short man said, "Go in the other room, Martin. You don't need to see—"

"She's got a gun!"

"Shit. Drop that right now!"

"Come on, Laura, please!"

"You wanna get shot?"

They were pointing their Glocks at her, screaming for her to drop
the gun, and she was trying, but it had been super-glued to her hand,
and she attempted to sling it across the room to break the bond, but
even her pointer finger had been cemented to the trigger, the barrel
of the .357 making a fleeting alignment on the policemen, and they
would write in their reports that she was making her move, that
deadly force had been the only option, both lawmen firing—Officer
McCullar twice, Officer West four times—and when the judgment
fell, both men were deemed to have acted reasonably, the hearts of
the brass going out to West in particular, the man having found his
little brother murdered and been forced to shoot the perpetrator, his
own sister-in-law.

All things considered, a month of paid leave and weekly sessions
with a therapist was the very least they could do.

Dinner For Toby
Simon Wood

"I'm going to make dinner for Toby," Barnett announced.

"What, Corn Flakes on toast?" Mike joked.

"No, I can cook. Like He-Man, I have the power."

Mike's smile faded. He checked over his shoulder and saw Toby sitting at a table by himself. Toby always sat alone during breaks between lectures. He clutched a can of Coke and stared at the canteen table. His gaze threatened to burn a hole clear through.

"Why?" Mike asked.

"Why not? He needs cheering up and a good meal wouldn't go amiss, I'm sure."

It didn't make sense. Intelligence-wise, both Barnett and Toby were on the same level, but personality-wise, they were at extreme ends of the scale. Barnett was bold and reckless, whereas Toby was so introverted he was on the verge of imploding. Toby's introversion probably had a lot to do with his dire acne. The overwhelming number of angry, pus-filled breakouts distorted his face and they didn't end there. Sores littered his arms and blighted his neck—his whole body had to be pock ridden. His paper-white skin and ginger hair only made his sores stand out more. The stench of prescription-grade acne lotion permanently surrounded him.

To say Mike disliked Toby was harsh. He felt for the guy, but Toby's presence made him uncomfortable. Toby was so excruciatingly self-conscious about his acne, it was painful to be around him. Unlike Mike, Barnett wasn't an empathetic person. His brash personality meant Toby shouldn't even have registered on his radar for this act of kindness.

"What are you up to?" Mike asked.

"Why would I be up to anything?" Barnett failed to look innocent.

"Because, when Toby transferred to this college six months ago, you bitched that he buggered up the class' harmony. So why the big change? C'mon, you ain't fooling anyone."

Barnett checked his watch. "We'd better get back to class."

Mechanical science defied the laws of time and the class dragged longer than it normally did. Mike's thoughts and gaze wandered in Toby's direction. Toby diligently took notes and worked through the class problems. Mike noticed Barnett's gaze was on Toby too. Barnett was close to salivating. There was something more to his philanthropic plan and Mike didn't know what it was, but he was sure he wasn't going to like it.

Mercifully, the class ended, drawing the college day to a close. Mike got tangled up with a homework assignment and Barnett went ahead. When Mike caught up with Barnett, he was deep in conversation with Toby outside the engineering block. Toby looked distinctly uncomfortable.

"Hey, Toby," Mike said.

Toby nodded awkwardly.

"You think about it and let me know," Barnett said.

"I'll do that," Toby said nervously. "I'd better go. Things to do. Catch you later, yeah?"

"Yeah, later, mate," Barnett said, and Toby slipped away.

Both Mike and Barnett watched Toby scuttle away to his beaten up Ford Escort and race away as fast as the tired engine would allow.

"What are you playing at?" Mike demanded.

Barnett winked. "I'll give you a ride home and I'll tell you all about it."

Halfway to Mike's flat, Barnett's restored VW Beetle was still managing to produce an arctic breeze from its heater. Barnett wiped at the continually fogging windscreen with his hand. Mike cracked open the window.

"I want to fuck a guy," Barnett announced.

If Mike knew Barnett to be anything, it wasn't gay. His dangerous personality attracted women by the armful. His coming out wasn't credible.

"What?"

"I've screwed chicks—blow jobs, anal, the works. I've done it and had it done to me, but I've never done a guy."

"I've never been shot in the head, but I don't think I need someone to shoot me to know it hurts like a bastard."

"See that's where you and me differ. I need to experience everything before I die."

"And you need to fuck a guy to accomplish that?"

"Yep." Barnett grinned at Mike. "Don't look so worried. You're not my type."

"But Toby is."

Barnett mulled the thought over and nodded. "I think so."

This was wrong—very wrong. But Mike couldn't come out and say it. If he did, Barnett would dig his heels in and do the opposite of what he was told. No, Mike would have to play it careful. If he planted enough seeds of doubt in Barnett's head, then he might axe the idea.

"How do you know you're his type?"

"I don't, but I'm sure I can bring him around to my way of thinking."

"Barnett, you don't even know if he's queer."

"I'm not, but I'm willing to give it a try."

"So your sudden interest in Toby is so you can see what it's like to fuck a guy?"

"Yeah."

"You can't force him to have sex with you."

"I won't force him." Barnett grinned. "I'll coerce him."

"Why him?"

"Why not?"

Barnett dropped Mike off outside his flat. Barnett disturbed Mike. His blasé plan to wine, dine and sodomize Toby disgusted and shocked him. It was unfair. Mike knew why Barnett had chosen Toby. Barnett was a predator, and he sensed Toby's overt weakness. He hadn't been joking when he said that Mike wasn't his type. Mike wasn't invincible, but he would fight back. Toby, however, had victim written all over his acne-pocked skin. It was obvious Barnett sensed he wouldn't put up a fight. It was all academic anyway; Toby hadn't agreed to Barnett's dinner date.

Yet …

"HE SAID YES," Barnett said, grinning, and sat in the lounge chair opposite Mike.

Mike put his book down. Arthritic fear paralyzed his body. He didn't have to ask who had agreed to what.

A couple of weeks had passed since Barnett had first mentioned his sodomizing scheme. Mike knew he'd had a couple of more tries at Toby, but to Mike's relief, Toby had cringingly declined each time. Mike thought—hoped—Barnett had given up on the idea, or at least on Toby as his prey.

"When?" Mike asked.

"Thursday night at eight. He's going to help me with my differentiation problems."

Mike leaned forward to give them some privacy. "Barnett, I can't let you go through with this."

"It's got nothing to do with you," Barnett said matter-of-factly.

That stumped Mike. It didn't. Barnett was a friend, but Mike wasn't his keeper. The same was true of Toby. Mike wasn't obliged to look out for him. Barnett could do whatever he wanted and Toby was adult enough to stand up for himself, but Mike was compelled to get involved. Barnett's morality disturbed him and Toby wasn't strong enough to survive his onslaught. Barnett's plan didn't involve two consenting adults. Yes, it didn't have anything to do with Mike, but he couldn't walk away from this situation.

"Barnett, you can't invite Toby round just so you can bugger him. That's rape."

"Not if he agrees."

"What makes you think he'll agree?"

"I'm a persuasive person."

Mike knew all about Barnett's persuasive powers. He'd witnessed them up close. Barnett was a great guy—if you were one of his friends—but he did have his vicious side if you weren't. A year ago, he'd jammed a classmate's face an inch from an operating lathe over a minor disagreement. Two years ago, he'd kicked a girlfriend from a moving car after he'd found she'd been cheating on him. If Toby didn't naturally warm to Barnett's advances, then Barnett would make sure he did.

"Don't you think, Mike?"

This kind of remark would have normally come with a smile and a twinkle in the eye, but these charming characteristics were absent. Barnett was irritated. Mike's protests were pushing him to the limit. If Mike wasn't careful, he was in danger of pissing Barnett off and losing any sway he had over his friend and the situation.

"Look Barnett, you can't go through with this. Fuck a guy by all means. Pick up a gay guy, but not Toby. It's wrong, mate."

"You don't have any say in the matter."

"I believe I do," Mike said, knowing he had crossed the line with his friend.

"So what do you think you're going to do about it?"

MIKE HAD GOTTEN TO BARNETT and he hoped it was enough to change his friend's mind, but in his heart of hearts, he knew it wasn't. Barnett became quiet and distant. Their conversation had dwindled to nonexistent on the run-up to Thursday, resulting in a lot of unreturned calls and avoidance in college.

Thursday evening arrived and Barnett seemed to be going through with everything. Leaving college, Mike glimpsed him chatting with Toby in the parking lot. At home, he watched the time zero in on eight o'clock. He felt like a death row inmate receiving the last rites. He couldn't help himself and snatched up the phone and dialed Barnett's number another time. He listened to the phone ring until the answering machine kicked in. He hung up. There was nothing for it. He had to go round there.

Mike rang the doorbell for the third time. No one was answering, but Barnett was inside. The lights were on and an ambient trance beat spewed from within.

"C'mon, Barnett," he thumped on the door, "answer the bloody door."

His request was answered. The door opened, but Barnett didn't answer the door—Toby did.

Toby, as impossible as it seemed, was whiter than his anemic skin allowed. His breakouts looked about to burst all at once. Three missing buttons from his shirt exposed scratch marks raking his skeleton-thin chest. His belt hung from one belt loop and his shirt tail poked through his open fly. Blood soaked his groin and a kitchen knife ran red in his grasp. Mike froze.

"Toby," Mike managed.

"Hey, Mike." He sounded a million miles away.

"Where's Barnett?"

"In the kitchen." He jerked the knife in the direction of the kitchen.

Mike eased past Toby and headed for the kitchen. Toby followed. Mike's steps were awkward and unpracticed. He had the terrible sense that Toby would use the knife on him.

Barnett was indeed in the kitchen, face down on the vinyl in front of the sink. An alarming amount of blood had emanated from his stomach and had blossomed across the floor, encompassing him from head to toe. All color, as well as life, had drained from his face. His eyes were open and a confused expression consumed his features. It hadn't gone the way he'd expected. He hadn't been persuasive.

"I don't understand it," Toby said. "We made dinner and we talked about everything—college, music, films. It was great. It was the first time since I transferred to this college that anyone treated me like a friend. It was going so well until we started cleaning the dishes. I said I'd wash and he said he'd dry. But he didn't. He came behind me and pressed up against me and whispered in my ear that he wanted to make love to me. I didn't know he was gay."

"He wasn't," Mike mumbled. "What happened?"

"I told him I wasn't like that. He said he didn't care. I told him I was going and he slammed me against the sink. I tried to push him off and he ripped at my trousers."

Mike winced at Toby's account. He lived every moment. He knew how Barnett would have sounded. He'd seen the seamless ease he exhibited when shifting from the compassionate to the vicious when events weren't going his way.

"I was washing the carving knife when he forced himself on me. I spun around and stabbed him. I didn't mean it. It just happened."

Mike studied the blood. Barnett hadn't been stabbed just the once. There was too much blood for a single wound.

"How many times did you stab him?" he asked.

"I stabbed him over and over again. I don't know how many times. What are we going to do, Mike?"

We? When did this become his problem to solve? He hadn't killed anyone, but he was just as guilty. He could have prevented this, if he'd handled Barnett differently. It was his problem to solve. He was culpable. Toby was innocent.

"Don't worry, we'll sort this out."

Mike turned the music down to a less obtrusive level. Now wasn't the time to draw attention to themselves.

"What do you want me to do?" Toby asked.

Mike turned to him. The knife was still in his hand, blood dripping from the tip. "Stand still. Don't move."

Mike tiptoed around Barnett and dug out a self-sealing bag from a kitchen drawer. He slipped the bag over the blade, took the knife from Toby without touching it, and sealed the bag. That was the weapon taken care of for now. He glanced over at Barnett. That was a totally different problem. He wouldn't be so easily dealt with.

"Mike, I've got blood on me."

"I know." Mike eyed the splatter. "Take a shower. Put your clothes in this." He snatched up a bin liner from under the sink. "We'll burn them."

"What will I wear?"

"You'll have to wear something of Barnett's."

Toby nodded and took the bin liner. He trudged into the bathroom. Mike waited until he heard the hiss of water striking the bath before moving. He scoured the small apartment for more bin liners or plastic sheeting. He found neither but he did find an old blanket that would smother a body easily. He laid the blanket out next to Barnett, careful not to allow the material to touch the blood. He was wondering how to move Barnett's body without making a mess when Toby wandered into the living room.

Mike recognized the clothes from Barnett's nightclubbing collection. They looked sharp on Barnett, but not on Toby. Everything hung badly on him. The pair of black trousers was too long in the leg. The pale gray shirt he wore was misbuttoned and half-tucked into the trousers. The cuffs were too long, exposing only his fingertips. Mike wasn't sure if Toby was still in shock or totally inept for all occasions.

"Help me put him on the blanket," Mike instructed.

Robot-like, Toby did as he was told.

"Turn him as we lift him."

Mike grabbed Barnett's wrists without thinking. His mind had been on how to dispose of him. It never entered into his head that he was handling a dead body. His hands were locked around Barnett's wrists when it hit him; he was holding a corpse. His grip tightened with fear, then his hands snapped open, dropping Barnett's arms.

"What's wrong?" Toby asked.

Mike blushed. "Nothing."

He retook Barnett's wrists. His friend was still warm, not normal body temperature warm, but warm enough not to feel like a corpse. Mike was reminded of an old girlfriend he'd had in school. She blamed her cool touch on poor circulation. It couldn't be any worse than Barnett's.

They lifted and flipped Barnett onto his back in one fluid move. His dead weight was too much for them and they dropped him onto the blanket with a thud.

He saw Barnett in all his slaughtered glory. His stomach was a mass of puncture wounds. Toby had to have stabbed him at least twenty times. Barnett had really met his match.

"Jesus Christ," Mike muttered.

Mike glanced at Toby. He had a hand to his mouth, just as shocked to see the carnage as Mike was. Mike supposed the horror was just sinking in for him.

"Let's wrap him up," Mike suggested after a long moment.

Mike padded Barnett's stomach with a pillow to help soak up the blood. They swaddled him in the blanket and bound it in place with packing tape. He looked mummified after they were finished.

"I'll bring Barnett's car round," Mike said.

"What about the blood?"

"We'll clear everything up when we get back. I just want to get rid of Barnett first."

Mike brought Barnett's Beetle as close as he could to the apartment. Before leaving the apartment with the corpse, Mike sneaked a look for passing neighbors. Luck was on their side, the coast was clear. They manhandled Barnett's corpse over to the Beetle and into the backseat. It was an awkward fit, and Mike would have been better off putting Barnett in his van, but he didn't want any traces of him in his vehicle.

Mike drove out to the reservoir in Barnett's Beetle and let Toby drive his van. He rarely stared at the road ahead. He kept his gaze locked on the glare of the van's headlights in the rearview mirror. He didn't want to lose sight of Toby. Toby was barely keeping it together. The last thing Mike needed was Toby going AWOL on him while he was stuck driving a car with a corpse in it. He could have made Toby drive Barnett's Beetle, he was that malleable, but it seemed the lesser of two evils to let him drive the van.

Mike wondered what this experience would do to Toby. Would tonight force him to take deeper refuge inside himself than he already had? Or would he blossom, flushed with the confidence of killing a man? Mike feared either outcome. Both mindsets drew attention to Toby, as would Barnett's disappearance. People knew Toby was having dinner with Barnett and they would ask questions. If he cracked, Mike knew the cops would end up at his door. Accessory after the fact had a sour taste to it. Maybe he'd made the wrong decision. If he had, it was too late now. He turned the bend and the hourglass-shaped lake came into view.

Mike pulled up on the bridge that crossed the lake at its narrowest point. Campers and fisherman used the road, but it was out of season, so it was deserted. They unloaded the body next to the railings and drove off the bridge to stash the cars. They trotted back to the corpse, each of them carrying makeshift weights to keep the body on the bottom. They bundled Barnett over the side, and the last Mike saw of his friend was the bubbles left as he descended below the surface.

"Now his car," Mike said.

Mike had thought about leaving it in a bad neighborhood with the doors unlocked or just torching it, but both options ended with eventual police involvement. No, the car had to simply disappear. They wiped it down and dropped it off outside a scrap yard. He knew someone there who would take care of it for a backhander.

Mike drove his van back to Barnett's. It was after one and sleep was taking a grip on him, but he couldn't call it a night yet. There was still the mopping up to do.

"Remember, use paper towels first," Mike instructed. "They'll burn easier."

They soaked up the blood. There was no mop, but Mike found a sponge in the bathroom. He was filling a bowl with soapy water when Toby spoke. He'd been quiet up until then, doing as he was told, and his question startled Mike.

"What?" Mike asked.

"Why did you come here tonight?"

Mike hemmed and hawed. He didn't have a lie on tap and didn't want to answer. "I was passing."

Toby's eyes were black beads.

Sweat broke out on Mike's brow. He turned the tap off and lifted the bowl out of the sink.

"You knew, didn't you?" Toby demanded, an edge in his voice.

"Knew what?"

"You knew what Barnett was planning to do tonight."

"I don't know what you're talking about."

Mike plonked the bowl on the floor. Water slopped out onto the linoleum. He soaked it up before the suds went too far and scrubbed at the bloodstains.

"You do know what I'm talking about. You knew this was a setup. Barnett wasn't interested in being friends; he just wanted to fuck me."

Mike swallowed hard. Toby's manner was changing. Barnett had ruined him. He'd destroyed his innocence and naivety. Barnett had broken Toby and what was spilling from him couldn't be put back. Mike scrubbed harder at the stains, his fear manifesting itself as elbow grease.

Toby tied a knot in the top of a bin bag he was holding and dropped it on the floor. "What did you come around for, Mike?"

"You're right. I knew what he had planned. I didn't like it and I came here to stop him. Alright? He got the idea into his head that he had to fuck a guy, not because he was gay, but because it was something he had to experience."

"Why me?" Tears shone in Toby's eyes. He brushed them away.

Mike sighed. "Why do you think? Because you're weak and you wouldn't put up much of a fight."

"Well, he was wrong, wasn't he?"

"You've got that right." Mike wrung the sponge into the bowl. Rose-colored water poured between his fingers and turned the bubbles in the bowl the same color.

"Did you think it was funny?"

Mike threw the sponge into the bowl, splashing water everywhere. "What do you think, eh? Of course I didn't think it was funny. I've been trying to talk him out of it for weeks."

"You've known for weeks and you didn't do a thing about it?"

"I did my best."

"Well, it wasn't good enough."

"Yeah, well, Barnett is a man unto himself. You don't tell Barnett. He tells you."

Mike finished cleaning the floor and picked up the bowl. He took it over to the sink and poured it down the drain. Toby was on him in a second, knocking the bowl from his grasp. Toby pinned him against the sink with his body and held him in place with the knife he'd stabbed Barnett with, still sheathed in its plastic bag. Even through the plastic, Mike felt the blade cut into his throat.

"Did you really try that hard, Mike?"

"Of course I did."

"Or did you think to yourself you wouldn't mind a piece of that action too?"

"No." Mike's answer was emphatic.

"Are you sure, Mike?" Toby ground his groin against Mike's backside. "Are you sure you weren't tempted? Are you sure you didn't want a taste?"

Even though Toby had showered, he still stunk of that damn medicated acne cream. The guy had to have had the stuff oozing from his pores.

"I didn't want a taste. I just didn't want him hurting you."

"Ah, I didn't know you cared," Toby mocked. "If I didn't know better, I'd think you have a soft spot for me, even a queer thing for me. Hmm? Am I on to something?" Toby pumped his hips against Mike again.

"Don't flatter yourself. I don't give a shit about you other than I didn't see why you should be hurt. And if you really want to know, I tried to stop him because I pitied you."

It was rough stuff to say to someone with a knife pressed against your throat, but Mike didn't care. He was pissed off. He'd made a mistake by not doing more, but he'd made up for it as best he could. Toby pressed the knife harder. It pierced its plastic skin and pricked Mike's flesh.

"Maybe you don't care for me, but maybe I care for you. Maybe Barnett has awakened something in me that I didn't know existed. And maybe I need to explore it." Toby reached around Mike's waist and fumbled with his belt and fly. "Maybe you're the man who can help me discover that something."

"Why are you doing this? Haven't you been through enough?"

"I have, but you haven't. You need to learn a lesson. You can't treat people like this. I promise I won't be as brutal as Barnett, but I can't say it won't hurt. Consider it my gift to you."

"Don't do it, Toby," Mike instructed, his words slow and carefully spoken.

But Toby wasn't listening to Mike anymore. Mike had lost his control over him. Toby had grown into his own man—a man like Barnett. He finished uncoupling Mike's jeans, yanking them down with his underwear, before working on his own trousers.

"Toby, you know this is wrong."

Toby cut Mike's breath off with the knife, forcing his head back. "How can it be wrong, if I haven't done anything yet?"

Toby was in shock and in pain, Mike understood that, but this had to stop. Toby deserved justice but this wasn't it. It was revenge.

"Toby, please stop," Mike pleaded.

"No," Toby snapped.

Toby didn't back down and Mike knew he never would. He wished things could have been different, but there was no other way. He couldn't play the victim for Toby. His hand found the knife block and curled around a knife handle.

Cow Palace
Talia Berliner

He was looking for The Moment. It had started with the cow. Before the cow there was the man in Italy who was a chair. Before the chair there were pieces of bodies, first on paper, and now again, in the flesh, all around him, part of the furniture, encased in resin or hidden behind cement walls.

SOMETIMES, WHEN HE COULD NOT WORK, when he reached a block, when he felt uneasy, he watched the cow for peace and inspiration. In fact, the fifty-seven-second Turkish video was such a frequent Internet destination for him that he'd bookmarked it as a favorite on his personal toolbar—nickname: *cow* (between *x* and *y*, chromosomal letters representing extreme porn sites)—changing the URL whenever the clip was taken off YouTube, forcing him to locate it again. This happened regularly.

cow

Clicking that word took him directly to the page on which the creature currently looped in bovine perpetuity. There was some debate as to whether the cow was alive or dead when the giant metal fork pitched it onto the shredder, a pink-chunk-filled room-sized version of the shin-high black mesh canister he'd bought at Staples for disposing private documents. Even though the video was introduced with a declaration stating that the footage portrayed a dead, diseased animal (lime powder, in fact, seemed to fall from its body in the trough), there were accompanying sounds—effects perhaps—but very convincing, and he liked to believe that the beast was quite alive at the onset. And still living for a while, struggling with the device, against its monstrous unforgiving wheel, having the life shredded from her, bit by bit. The cow was there, and then at some point was not; just another half ton of shredded rosy meat—no bones, oddly—lining the rectangular metal container.

He was interested in that moment of non-being, when the animal went from Here to There, from one form in the here, to another, elsewhere. He kept trying, over and over, to determine exactly when that point occurred. The animal was whole and mute, heaped onto the mechanism. Then, something was activated—a growling of engine gears—and she did a little automated jig, as if dancing in fetlock tiptoe on a rolling log. For a second things appeared equal between cow and machine and then there was an imperceptible shift, an instant where she was caught, with audible protest, by the irreversible forward-moving process, and started being ripped apart—a portion of shank here, a wide swath of loin there—until, gradually, the apparatus sucked her in, absorbed her, taking whatever there was to the other side of the blades, and all that could be seen was a random hoof and the bobbing witless head until those, too, became part of the fleshy undertow. But *when* did it happen—the exit, the transmogrification from Here to There? *That* is what he wanted to know. He clicked Replay repeatedly, mesmerized, attempting to isolate that flash between being and nothingness, but the more he watched the more he could not tell.

LITTLE DETAILS CAUGHT HIS EYE: the curve of a wrist and hand forming a caraway seed comma; a constellation of proximal beauty marks on alabaster skin, to be connected like a geometry diagram; the bend of an elbow, at once sharp jutting exterior and soft at its inner fold;

the architecture of an instep. It had been this way since art school figure drawing class. The instructor would eyeball his rough sketch, un-
failingly critiquing his apparent inability to "plant the foot," that there
lacked gravity, a sense of flesh—the naked limb, toes-to-ankle—
meeting solid ground. But her pedestrian concerns were of no interest to him. He only saw disembodied parts, not the sum of the whole.
A model would assume a pose and he'd focus on the hands—the finished drawings resembled sign language charts. He completed a double major in furniture design and sculpture, supplementing his formal
study with hours digesting the nearby medical school library's offer-
ings, and, whenever he could, by sneaking into lectures on anatomy
and dissection, death and dying.

TWO YEARS LATER, in the small Italian town where he'd been in a year-
long apprenticeship to a master woodworker, his enthusiasms improbably and accidentally converged. One night, riding home through
empty streets, he saw a monumental chair, perfectly upright with right-
angled extensions, being lifted from the backseat of an automobile by
several men and offloaded onto the unpeopled sidewalk. As his bus
passed the scene he realized that this chair had clothing and a head;
it was not a piece of furniture but a dead man fully rigor-mortised, set
like a mold into the seated position in which he took his final breath.
The bus was going too quickly for him to witness the aftermath—it
was like watching a Zoetrope strip—but what he did see, the beautiful spectacle, would never leave him, and he hoped that someday he
could match its vision.

THE FIRST EFFORT, and his one close call, had been with Elfi and Elsi,
zaftig twins from Leipzig—as wide as they were tall—three of whose
piano legs, the trio still dressed in fishnet stockings and black patent
leather little girl shoes, now supported the eviscerated baby grand in
the middle of the loft; like everything else, just for show. He'd bought
it at auction, a shell, not even an octave of ivory and ebony on which
to practice arpeggios. He found the Leipzig twins at the Coney Island
Sideshow New Year's Eve gala, where, despite their robust corpulence,

they performed anatomically impossible contortions with precision, their considerable weight resting implausibly on tiny puppet hands; Elsi also swallowed swords. They were exceedingly ravenous all the time, especially post-show. He lured them home with the simple bait of free-flowing beer and thick bloody steaks, which he fed them big top-style—insisting they be naked like animals, though he allowed them the stockings and shoes—throwing the almost-raw meat at their heads as they crouched on all fours, blonde-maned lions with gaping, frothing mouths. In return, Elsi swallowed his entire knockwurst until it burst its casing inside her; Elfi thanked him by peeling down her fishnets and letting him overflow her dimpled rear, his cock a needle in a giant pin cushion.

He'd only required three legs for his Potemkin village Steinway. The orphaned fourth limb was recycled in his bathroom as a towel rack, shooting out from the wall in an eternal can-can high kick, a brown velour rectangle neatly draped, bridging knee to thigh, a matching washcloth corner-looped over the big toe, its fishnet captivity carefully snipped away. He couldn't resist the quartet of small manicured hands, so delicate, so gracefully articulated; now drawer pulls on the antique vanity; forty fingers spanning eight hands, reflected wrist-to-wrist in its mirrored plate-glass. The twins were at Coney on the last stop of a farewell world tour, and he'd caught their swan song. It was anyone's guess where they might be. No embassy came calling.

HE MOUNTED THE BODIES in a freestanding resin monolith, a tableau made even more beautiful by the daylight reflecting against the material's golden surface. They floated in a silent ballet, buoyed in permanent slumber from the drug he'd administered, blood swirling around them like galaxies, his own semen here and there caught forever in a Morse code trajectory. By Elfi's ass, it looked like a tampon string. She loomed gigantically—upside down, breasts lopsidedly adrift—near her twin, one virtually touching the other as they'd done in the womb, errant helium parade balloons, handless arms at sides, almost perfectly rounded, being divested of their legs; the flesh, muscles, veins, arteries and bones hanging shaggily, despite his attempt to wrap them nicely in duct tape. He could make out Elsi's cunt between the mess. He was sorry he hadn't treated her to a proper fucking, he thought, as he tugged himself. Given her profession he wouldn't have been surprised had his prick emerged from her mouth on the other end. He imagined the chewed slabs of steak and gallons of beer within their bloated stomachs.

HE OWNED THE SINGLE-STORY INDUSTRIAL BUILDING where he was the sole tenant, by the West Side Highway in the Meatpacking District. An appendage to a beef-processing plant taking up the adjacent city block, it revealed a quirky miscellany of interior architecture, a configuration falling somewhere between carnival spook house, crawl space, claustrophobium and repository. A meandering ramp curled towards a low-ceilinged partial-basement grotto while the loading dock on street level opened into a central loft flanked by an odd warren of cavities: diminutive enclosures and a sampler of uniquely-shaped niches, alcoves, storage recesses and long-unrefrigerated meat lockers. He'd adapted the commercial space for living, painting it all—thick concrete walls and floor—a gray one notch below white, achieving an austere but elegant quasi-sanctified atmosphere, like a museum. Rusty meat hooks dangled from swerving conveyer line tracks above, unaltered. There were no windows in this fortress-bunker. Pyramid skylights, fitted with opaque wired glass, punctuated the layout, providing even illumination. He lived completely hidden from the outside world, inhabiting his own universe of perfectly diffused light.

BOOKS FILLED VARIOUS NICHES, documenting a non-linear path of do-it-yourself postgraduate study and engagement: Gray's Anatomy; tomes on embalming, the Mortuary Arts and taxidermy; medical textbooks, with an emphasis on amputation surgery; dentistry fundamentals; handbooks of homeopathic poisons and anesthetics; jewelry and metalsmithing guides; catalogues of Weegee photographs. He slept in a horizontal wall cut-out, as if entombed, a skeleton on a catacomb shelf, cocooned inside a purple down sleeping bag, over a foam rubber mat. He subscribed to *Martha Stewart Living* and *Real Simple* for bedtime reading—both as a calmative balm and to immerse himself in images of beauty, so that they would be the last things he saw each night before his eyes closed. Gaston Bachelard's *The Poetics of Space* leaned on his bedroll, much of its text underlined in the red pencil also serving as a bookmark.

HE FOUND BETTINA aka the Human Bowling Pin, mid-February, via Craigslist, in the "Events" category, a participant on an evening-long fetish panel, held in a windowless, damp black-walled sub-basement S & M dungeon in his neighborhood. Sprouting a neon-orange buzz-cut, she was all torso (courtesy of Thalidomide), flat of chest, boyishly narrow, lusty of lip and 100 percent infertile: in short, the perfect woman. After paying her wrangler a large sum of money, he took Bettina home in a plastic shopping bag from The Container Store. Her sexual appetite was enormous and even had she said *no*, which she never did, it was impossible for her to prevent his access—from taking her and enjoying those portals sufficiently elastic to accommodate him. He rolled her around the bed like a baker kneading pizza dough. He played spin the bottle with her limbless form, making use of whatever hole landed between his legs. He sat her on his lap—a plush toy—and discovered that simply by bouncing his left leg, trousered knee in direct contact with an ever-swollen clitoris, he could make her come in only a few minutes, screaming like a non-stop #2 Express train running on the local track.

He kept Bettina naked when not in use, sitting atop the mahogany highboy on a doily like a vase—now and then placing a flower in her yawning mouth and pouring a little water in, just for chuckles—and whenever he felt the urge he took her and had her, sometimes pacing the room with his cock a skewer piercing her insides, a wide belt clamping her body to his like a marching band drum. Having her absorb his semen was great fun but less so was Bettina's hygienic maintenance and feeding. Tired of weeks spooning the bowling pin cans of baby food and tuna fish (her preferred diet) and tending to their transformation on the other side of her bowels, he ultimately disposed of Bettina as well. Now she topped a resin totem pole, the hovering dot of an *i*, a lost balloon, untethered—the skylight washing her singular form in a chromatic glow. Bettina had been an exception, fascinating him as a whole with the sum of her parts even though she had none. And he thought if he stared long enough he could find her locked in The Moment between Here and There, that instant fixed everlastingly in the resin.

THE REST WERE MOSTLY NEW YORK CITY'S HOMELESS, fortunately for him in seemingly limitless supply. They would not be missed as they were already gone:

The ancient black man sleeping outside a delicatessen at Spring Street's western rim near the UPS depot, one frigid March night, spread across cardboard flats arranged over the warmth of sidewalk grate steam—disheveled, putrid, drunk and out cold, skin wrinkled and compressed in accordion folds. Amid the disarray, lounging from his untended fly like a pointer: a massive, soft pink cock that appeared to have led another life, untouched and unharmed by age, circumstances of hardship or cold Manhattan winters; the dormant penis of a sheltered suburban teenager on the body of a desiccated bum. It would make a beautiful coat hook. And after a single modeling session, easily contracted with the promise of a meal, cash and a roof for the night, it did.

He tilted the castrated bleeder into an alcove, a slumped altar angel. He made a wall of brick, niche-edge-to-niche-edge, pouring cement in so the mixture covered the man. He troweled his wall flush with the one into which the bay was carved until it seamlessly matched the surroundings, leaving no sign that a negative space had ever been there.

WITH THE HOMELESS generally came their possessions. So many of them. Caravans of shopping carts—autobiographies on wheels—cloaked with blue tarpaulins, multiple bulges and totes of who-knows-what fastened to their metal grids, wooden poles carrying more sacks, dirty white sneakers hung by tied laces, surrender-flag-style, at the shafts' tips. These objects were now separated from their owners, their accumulation stilled. He did not bother going through anything; usually the stench was a deterrent.

He rolled the fetid carts down the ramp to the basement vault where one could barely stand. He started at its far end, building floor-to-ceiling walls using the brick and mortar, encasing each wagonful of hopelessness within a compartment—joining the remains of whoever it had attended—sealing off the closeted inventory of flesh, bone and useless anthropological debris with the cement and trowel. Over the next few months he reached the ramp itself, carts lined up in supermarket rows, four abreast, until they met the entryway threshold where he erected a double-layered wall, effectively obscuring the very existence of ramp and crypt, containing, three dozen strata deep, a history of failure hidden behind a surface finished in smooth concrete. Then he returned to the main living space.

HE NOTICED THE YOUNG JUNKIE couple one summer evening, sprawled on the sidewalk, illuminated by the fluorescent display window of the all-night drugstore on Fourteenth Street near Union Square. A Dalmatian they called Lou Reed—probably stolen from a firehouse, ornamented with a red bandana—squatted beside them, panting and drooling in the July heat. A scrap of cardboard pled their dubious case. He blatantly ignored their comrade, a gaunt older man wearing ripped camouflage gear, sitting cross-legged as if meditating. Of no particular aesthetic appeal—one hand, freakishly oversized in proportion to the rest of him, was gnarled, webbed and missing two digits—there was also the accompanying riddle of tics and twitches. He couldn't tolerate such annoyances for one minute. The girl, in a very pregnant state, had an oblong mole, a large plump raisin where her pierced upper lip met pallid skin, underneath a small cerulean raindrop tattoo permanently dripping from her studded nostril. He wondered how the boy could restrain himself from biting the mole off when they were high and fucking. A use could be found for it, surely. Indeed, his doorbell had been disemboweled and a replacement was in order. Of course, her almost-lactating nipples could be repurposed for that but it would be nice to have a choice. The three nomads, eight legs total, followed him home at midnight, to model risqué poses. They got high the way they always did, he gave them tainted liquor and they fucked on the floor, on a moving pad—he even made the boy have the dog fuck her—as he watched, masturbated, and sketched the scene he'd orchestrated, the girl drifting into a stupor, at which point he commanded the crying boy to bite the mole off before he, too, lost consciousness. For a while he stood above them, watching closely, to see if he could recognize The Moment when they went from being Here to being There, like the cow. It was impossible. When all was done he excised the still baby from the girl's torso—unborn skin so soft and versatile. There was nothing much he wanted from the boy, except of course his teeth—he'd been pulling them for some time as a matter of course with an ongoing project in mind—half of which were rotten anyway, so it wasn't a very productive yield. He picked a suitable alcove for the lot, built up a wall, and when it was waist-high—once completed there would be no trace of the indentation—he hoisted the bleeding wanderers behind it and poured the cement in, adding the yelping canine, too. He was not a fucking pet person.

WEEKS AFTER HIS ENCOUNTER with the vagabond addicts, their ragged flak-jacketed friend called out to him from the regular spot, now his alone, inquiring as to their whereabouts. He replied that they'd gotten the help they so desperately needed, that nobody should be living on the streets of New York City, especially a woman in delicate condition, and that keeping an animal when one hasn't the ability to properly take care of oneself was as idiotic as it was inhumane. Although this man utterly offended every artistic sensibility, he momentarily toyed with violating his own standards, merely to put the crippled soul out of his tic-tocking misery. Maybe that deformed hand could work as a claw foot on his bathtub. He made his usual offer: overnight accommodations and an Andrew Jackson in exchange for easy figure modeling. The twitching man extended a digit, making an obscene gesture with his three-pronged hand—the middle finger was one he still possessed—and, just in case the digital semaphore had been unclear, hacked up a column of phlegm and spat at his would-be benefactor. In its airborne trajectory the helixed gob skimmed its target's cheek and landed—a shucked oyster—the bulk on his red sweatshirt hood, the rest on the sidewalk embedded with flattened black circles of petrified gum.

Suit yourself, you disgusting prick, he thought, as he stalked away, yanking the fleece beyond his head in a swift maneuver, wiping the slime off his face and heaving the garment into a green metal trash receptacle on the corner, emptying discarded plastic bags of dog shit over the cloth, to ensure that no one would take the thing. He did not believe in handouts.

ON NIGHTS WHEN HE FELT A CERTAIN unnamed restlessness he got behind the wheel and cruised the highways and service roads, "dumpster diving," hoping to come upon a vehicular accident before the police or fire department. Sometimes he was lucky, like when he spotted the overturned yellow SUV on a Long Island Expressway exit ramp bordering Flushing, at 4:15 AM one October Saturday, just after a thunderstorm. Five people were strewn about the automobile—on its back like a playful elephant, wheels still spinning; signal lights in endless rhythmic blink, alarm trilling—an Asian family: man, woman, three children. The man was clearly dead; his headless armed torso lay beneath a tree—a Halloween scarecrow's stuffed shirt—his severed legs nearby; jumbo chopsticks, one crossed over the other as if to indicate the end of a meal. His head was lodged between tree branches—a giant coconut—alas, irretrievable; his left hand rested on the pavement amid broken glass. The woman was still alive, lying under the half-hinged pinging passenger-side door, her right arm and both legs ten feet away. The children were scattered in pieces across the road and partially thrown onto the grass, each lifeless. One was hamburger meat, having been trampled by the vehicle, and as such useless to him. He snapped on a pair of micro-thin latex surgical gloves and harvested the two remaining children—girls—porcelain dolls in shards, depositing the flotsam within one of the large heavy-duty black plastic Hefty waste bags kept in his trunk for these "search and rescue" missions.

Before leaving the scene—he was surprised that no police or ambulances had yet arrived—pumped up with the adrenaline of potential discovery and aroused by the sight of the semi-conscious woman's parted labia, welcoming him, spread in such a flirty pout, the rosy lips made redder by the blood escaping her insides flanking the natural gash, he peeled off a glove and slid its longest finger over his cock as an improvised condom, the four uninhabited sections dangling like a rooster's wattle. He lowered himself into that slippery opening, excited by her moans of loss and pain, and, holding onto the narrow broken hips, fucked her with the blood of her children until he'd emptied all he had into the latex, noting the momentous occasion in his head: My First Asian Pussy. He put the glove back on his hand, its middle finger warmed by his own semen, and left her there—she could still do a lot with one arm, he thought—but gathered her portable limbs and those of her husband, loading them into additional Hefty bags, casting the two bloody surgical gloves in as well, and massaged the leftover ejaculate through his wavy salt and pepper hair. Unfortunately, there was no time for pulling teeth. Driving off with his bounty, his balls calm and drained, seeing the red whoop and twirl of the sirens in the far distance of the rearview mirror, he was practically electric-dizzy at the notion of the many things he could do with the materials from this one haul. The woman's arm, for starters. It would be the perfect door handle on his Oriental armoire, attached akimbo as if knuckles rested on hip.

THE BETH TORAH HOME FOR THE HEBREW AGED stood on a cliff ninety minutes from Grand Central Terminal via Metro-North and was divided into five parts, beginning with independent living and ending with that exclusive portal to death's door, the hospice. He would not find The Moment here but he would find the pieces. He made a visit under the pretext of checking out the facility for an elderly parent. After a perfunctory tour he was given free rein to look around and assess whether it would be a good match; the cheerful brunette and her clipboard left him alone with a glossy pocketed brochure. He ambled through the Community Room where freshly-coiffured women, overly made-up like cadavers, and a sprinkling of men, all in and out of wheelchairs, crafted an art project he'd done in Kindergarten—tracing hand silhouettes on construction paper to form Thanksgiving turkeys. In one corner a young woman sat at an upright, hammering out show tunes from long-closed Broadway productions, a few of the residents trying to keep up with her. He roamed the halls, peering into any open doorways. Men or women, semi-veiled by striped ceiling-tracked curtains, were recumbent in padded chairs that seemed to engulf them, or propped languidly in bed, staring at nothing, and always, the clatter from the too-loud televisions, set to Nickelodeon, MTV, CNN, The Weather Channel. It made no difference; it was company. He moved through the varied care levels, nodding to intermittently passing staff personnel. He pushed the double-porthole doors—like those in restaurant kitchens or operating rooms—and entered the final zone: the hospice.

It was there he had hoped to find them, in this abandoned outpost, quiet except for an out-of-sync chorus tinkle of beeps emanating from dozens of medical attachments and monitors. In otherwise dim silence they lay, hooked up and breathing, according to the machines, but semi-conscious, ready and waiting to go. Pieces of beige masking tape stuck to the doors as if the chambers were temporary offices—which, in a sense, they were—each strip thickly block-lettered in blue Bic pen, announcing the identity of the occupant: Lapinski, Cohen, Jacobson, Kleinfeld, Steinberg, Moses, Rabinowitz …

He began systematically, from the beginning of the first corridor, working counterclockwise, passing a picture window overlooking the November-chilled Hudson River and the railroad tracks, retracing his steps up the other side of the hall. He had brought his sharpest X-ACTO knife, the one with the finest blade. It only took a few minutes, and no resistance, thanks to Morphine drips, to cut the chunk of skin, gossamer-like from years of being alive. He lightly grazed the left forearm's epidermis, scoring an outline framing the tattoo, then delved deeper on the second go, swiftly slicing and lifting the flesh in one Band-Aid-sized piece, its number—sometimes prepended by a letter: A or B—stretching slightly with removal.

They resembled primitive lottery tickets, which, in a sense, they had been. And these chosen were the winners. By the end of Corridors E-203, 204 and 205, among the dozens of residents, he had amassed the eighteen patches needed, each of which he slipped into a minute glassine envelope and then each envelope between facing pages of a small reporter's notebook, so nothing would adhere. Once the pad was closed and wedged in his back jeans pocket the pieces would flatten and be almost ready to use. He liked the idea of bringing together so many people from such disparate places merely by carrying slivers of them, each an ambassador representing the countries they'd hailed from and the sights they'd seen: Germany, Lithuania, France, Austria, Hungary; Auschwitz, Birkenau. He was doing them a great favor. They had not come into this world numbered and, as a result of his efforts, they would not leave it with these brandings.

The shoji screens would be stunning, more alluring than those he had seen at the Metropolitan Museum. He would cut the tattooed strips into tiny squares—each bearing a single letter or numeral—and embed them in the paper mold's pulp, using one strip per sheet, the blue ink ciphers scattered throughout, pointed in every direction. Eighteen sheets; one person embodied in each. When the paper was dry he would attach it to the screens' wooden structure, a grid with eighteen rectangular divisions. So much better than the typical enmeshed leaf and flower bits, he thought, these enigmatic translucent calligraphic cryptograms.

AFTER FILLING THE BASEMENT, most niches, storage recesses and meat lockers with his subjects, he'd progressed to the central loft, constructing wall upon wall, shoring up the volume of sad belongings and their owners, or what remained of them, sealed and neutralized in cement, excepting a few favorites and their corresponding parts. Those were confined within a series of mobile resin monoliths, on casters to easily slide from view like pocket doors—disappearing into hollow new walls erected for that purpose—fist knobs mounted on their tapered ends.

By Christmas it was practically a full house. He had brimmed so many nooks, made so many expansions to hold his inanimate depository, that most of the building's square footage was now dedicated to what he had concealed, the walls of disguise finely finished, smooth and painted, giving an illusion of having always been there. The living area, already constricted, had gradually become smaller and smaller, ultimately only allowing for his creations and himself, a walk-in storeroom. With his sleeping burrow occupied he bunked under the table on a thin black vinyl runner, rolled and stored during waking hours. He did not need the comfort of sleeping bag or foam any longer. He could lie on the concrete floor if necessary. He was paring things down.

The space, though crowded, was a jewel box, a showplace, something out of a model home. The piano; the side table on four women's feet, two light-complected, two dark; the salad bowl made from the bronzed uterus of the mole-lipped girl; the accompanying fork and spoon, her fetus' hands ornamental holders at their tips; the leather-like checkerboard, alternating brown and beige quadrants of flesh; the rug crafted from pubic hair (of those he could bear to touch, even with rubber gloves); the cartoonish working clock with, literally, a big hand and a little hand—one from the Asian man at the Flushing wreck; the other from his daughter—each pointing to a number; the Oriental armoire with the mother's bent arm as its door handle; the red velvet couch, its weight evenly balanced over six masculine fists.

He reclined in his favorite chair, a replica of the long-ago marvel in Italy starting it all: an entire body within resin—a stocky man, nude and kneeling, bent into the sharp zigzag angles of a chair, a Mies van der Rohe cantilevered style, its perpendicular arms supporting his own, his palms on upturned resin hands, meeting as if in prayer, his head brushing that encased behind his, a genuine headrest if ever there was one. Hanging above the display, a masterpiece in perennial progress: the chandelier, its abundantly cascading strands of teeth—baby and adult, illustrating the spectrum of dental enamel—casting geometric shadows on the advancing walls.

The favored models and their parts soared in the monoliths, caught like insects in amber—one-by-one, toothless, with pubic triangles skinned—suspended, dead-man-floating in a motionless dance, playing "Statues" *ad infinitum*. They exhibited an encyclopedia of anatomy, like the drawings he once made, but wholly dimensional, interrelated puzzle pieces: each body or part gesturing to the next in a voiceless signage.

As the sun crossed the skylight, different shapes were illuminated, singled out, brought into sharp focus. It was as close as he could get to a perfect vision. He sat admiring his production—the furniture, objects and the monoliths' composed tableaux of bodies and parts— in the back of his mind, as ever, the shredded cow.

HE WANDERED THE STREETS when the city was at its quietest, to clear his head, often terminating in the subway where he traveled a route back and forth continuously from end station to end station. The vibration of the ride made him hard. The system was mostly deserted at this hour, somewhere between today and tomorrow—in this case New Year's Day and January 2. He had just missed a train; three club-hopping girls, laughing and drunk—probably still from New Year's Eve celebrations twenty-four hours ago, coats dropping off shoulders in slovenliness—listed up the stairs as he descended. Their outfits angered and titillated him. Had there been only one of them he wasn't sure which he would do: pull the skimpy tube top down or lift the short skirt up; both options were tempting. He definitely would have considered a track-push, if they weren't a group. He'd enjoy following the path of a round head, punted by sharp metal wheels, a soccer ball ricocheting from beam to beam, its bloody comet tail-whip braiding into straight flaxen hair.

At these times the trains were normally empty except for the sleeping homeless, each figure stretched across contiguous orange, yellow and tan plastic seats, customarily one sleeper per car, distributed through the train like a suspended broken line; it was an optimum opportunity for selecting models. His proposition of a stationary quiet dormitory trumped riding the "berths" of New York City Transit's rolling stock, and sleepers tended to have fewer articles with them to manage; shopping carts were not permitted underground.

He liked the wee hours. The schedule was limited but he was happy for the idle time, to be alone with his incessant bovine conundrum, looping the video clip in his head, trying, as always, to discern that elusive magical moment while he waited for a train. Some of them didn't stop now; the industrial yellow work convoys, out-of-service ghost runs speeding back to the rail yards on deadhead trips.

He stood cross-armed, leaning against a forest green steel column, his black combat boots touching the warning rumble strip—the bright-yellow safety paving cuffing the platform edge in a cushiony Braille-like dotted topography.

After about twenty minutes a pair of wildly blinding eyes emerged from the tunnel, getting larger in diameter as the rollicking segmented serpent—a white numeral 2 on a red circle the third eye, heralding a stainless steel Cyclops—approached the station rapidly, horn blowing. By its velocity he could tell that this one was just passing through, an express running on the local track. A cylinder of dank air, disturbed by the barreling monster, blasted him from the tube's darkness.

He did not feel the twitching hand—oversized, gnarled, with three webbed fingers; a shadow between his shoulder blades, stealthily making light contact with the skin of his brown leather jacket—not even when it thrust him, forcibly, into the shrieking blur of metal and decibels and onto the tracks. It took an incalculable interval for his body to be shredded—for him to go from the Here of being to the There of nothingness. He couldn't have pinpointed the transition himself. The conductor, in his cab cringing behind goggles, was unable to stop, despite braking, until all eight cars had rattled over the body. And there it was, what remained that hadn't been thoroughly masticated or stuck along the chassis underbelly: one leg, divided into chunks of meat and bone, the other launched across the rail bed to the

Uptown side like an Olympic javelin, a fleeting Hermes; two hands, one aimed at a curious rat next to a relinquished Coke bottle, and its mate, still with forearm, a bloody exclamation mark resting palm up in a black puddle collecting a slow, rusty drip—a floater in a vacation pool, a hand having its fortune told. The head was sliced in half and lay between railroad ties—an open-faced Reuben sandwich, the left eye missing, the right staring into the middle distance. And, poised atop the guard shielding the electrified third rail: one naked foot, toes-to-ankle, flesh firmly planted, meeting solid ground.

We Mate in the Dark
Maxim Jakubowski

Darkness comes in all shades of black.
And then comes the darkness inside.

His love for her was like a cancer. Eating away at his insides, every day a bite further, a stab beyond the limits of pain. An illness for which there was no cure.

Even when they were still together, he could not manage to enjoy the moments fully, too busy thinking of all the million reasons their relationship could not last: his ugliness, the inevitable fading of his sexual potency, her blinding beauty, the difference in age, their conflicting cultural and linguistic backgrounds, the geographical distance that normally separated them, the essential contrast between their respective personalities—he glass half empty, she glass half full.

He even privately made lists enumerating the arguments for and against their affair lasting. A man with imagination. Not a pessimist, he argued with himself, just a realist.

Just as he would send her frantic e-mails whenever they spent more than a week apart, for reasons of work or study. Listing around one hundred things that he wanted to do with her still, ranging from

the disgustingly romantic to the outrageously pornographic. Wild
fantasies, galaxies of tenderness, marathons of yearning and desire
and such.

She would jokingly reply that at least half of the things he fever-
ishly detailed she would willingly agree to, but that some of the others were out of the question. For now.

"You're just too melodramatic, sometimes," Julie would say.

"I know," he would reply, chuckling gently. "Isn't that why you
like me?"

"I just don't know."

And then one day, she broke it off.

She could no longer accept his unavailability, his cautiousness,
his public distance. Yes, she knew he loved her; she loved him too.
But, inside, Julie guessed that love must be something more, surely,
than stolen time, sharing him with others.

"I'd like to just be able to phone you when I feel like it and ask
you to meet me in town to simply have a coffee, and talk," she said.
"But it's not possible, is it? You are in a different country, with another
life."

"Oh, Julie …"

"I want a normal boyfriend, with whom I could do normal
things," she added as he struggled for words.

"I know," was all he could say.

"I want life, I want adventures," Julie said. Implying that he had
lived his life already, traveled, had children, and that was a part of
him he could no longer offer her.

He pleaded for her to change her decision. Rang her several times
a day. Wrote her letters full of passion and beauty. His literary version
of stalking. Flew to her city and roamed its streets, seeing places they
had been together with a new clarity, realizing how strong his love for
her was, reassessing the relationship. She discovered he was in town,
but by then it was too late as he was on his way to the airport. She got
angry with him.

Finally, after a whole month or so of verbal siege, she demurred.
Yes, she would see him again.

No other promises.

No guarantees.

A mercy fuck. A good-bye fuck. A last few days together for old time's sake, he realized. An act of charity to provide him with closure, he knew.

They settled on a time and place.

On foreign shores.

The story of their ten-months-long relationship.

WE MEET AT THE RAILWAY STATION. A cavernous bowl milling with people, all invisible to me, anonymous, a crowd in which I have no interest. She is the focus of my attention. Her smile is tentative but she is as beautiful as ever, wearing a flowing long white skirt that finishes below her ankles and a tight grey t-shirt top. Her usual scuffed trainers have seen better days.

We kiss.

Do I detect a shadow of hesitation in her embrace?

Her shoulder bag is bulging.

We purchase tickets to the resort. They are surprisingly cheap, but then it's Spain and not England …

The thirty-five-minute journey down the rugged coastline takes place in part silence and part banalities. The other passengers barely look at us, although I guess they are unsure as to whether we are father and daughter or man and lover.

Fuck 'em.

The hotel she has booked is barely half a mile from the smaller train station so we don't take one of the rickety taxis lined up on the piazza outside, but walk in its direction. Her smile is now warmer, the white skirt billows like a cloud as she walks alongside me. Does her ass look a touch bigger in this skirt, I wonder? No matter, as my fingers discreetly run down her side in a gesture of infinite affection, as we head down the small hill. She does not object.

We check in.

The reservation we have made is for two nights. She has lectures to attend on Friday.

The room is well-lit but a bit spartan and the large bed stands at its center like an inescapable monument. The main window overlooks the port, sailing boats and speedboats bobbing gently in the water. At night it must be blissfully silent.

I open my bag and give her the small necklace I had bought for her back in London. She tries it on. A couple of dark blood cherries and green leaves against the pallor of her throat. It looks good on her. A veil of gentleness has returned to her eyes.

We sit on the edge of the bed now, knees touching.

We talk.

"This is the last time," Julie says.

"I know,"

"Nothing you can say or do will make me change my mind," she adds.

The chill reaches my heart and grips it in a vice. She has always been an obstinate sod, never deviating from any promise and assurance she makes.

I sigh.

"Stand up," I ask her.

She does.

"Give me a twirl."

The sharp Mediterranean light pouring in from the window reveals the shape of her legs through the thin cottonish material of the white skirt. She turns on her axis. Almost like dancing.

"You're so beautiful."

She says nothing.

Shimmies a little for me.

Somehow, the movement around her thighs and arse makes the material even more transparent and I focus on the dark patch between her legs.

I squint.

"Aren't you wearing panties?"

Her smile is impish.

"No."

"All day?"

"I slipped them off in the washroom while you were checking us in downstairs."

"I can see your bush."

"I know."

"You're wonderful."

"Like that day in London."

"Yes ... wanton, tender, available ..."

"I knew you'd like it," she says, her sketchy dance moves coming to a slow halt.

"Come here," I beckon.

We embrace.

The softness of her body is like a balm.

I undress her until she is bathing in a pool of light.

My gaze focuses on the lower reaches of her stomach.

Her pubic area is swamped by a dark forest of curls, each single one blacker than coal. I lower myself and smell her essence. Look up towards her face.

"I want to trim you."

There is a look of hesitation. Then she finally nods in agreement.

"Not all of it," she begs.

"OK."

Later we make love, with an unspoken agreement between us not to discuss the future or our feelings, let alone the total absurdity of the current situation, even though it floats above our sweating bodies like a wreath.

Out of breath, we finally call a halt to our sexual exertions, quickly shower separately (where once we did together), slip some clothes on and agree to go out and have a coffee.

"Come on, you can't wear that shirt," she remarks as I slip on a colorful Hawaiian shirt. "You're too old for that. You'll look ridiculous."

"Oh, I like it. It's one of my favorites."

"Well, I'm not going out in public with you if you insist on wearing that thing."

I put on another, plainer shirt and we walk to the seafront where we have our coffees in a bar in the shadow of an old gothic church.

We lack conversation and at one stage she cries. I try to console her, but my words somehow no longer have the magic they once had.

"Hungry?"

"Yes," she sniffs.

We sit at an outside table at a restaurant on the promenade. Night is falling over the sea, a pale moon peering like a hiccup between passing clouds. The food has no taste, even though I remember how much I enjoyed it on the last occasion we ate here.

As we walk back to our hotel, the resort is awakening, readying itself for the bacchanalia of the night, noise growing louder as every kind of music filters out from a hundred bars and conversations in the narrow street reach a new pitch, as we nudge our way through the growing crowds of drinkers, revellers and holidaymakers.

Once back in the room, I furtively swallow a blue pill in the bathroom. My guilty secret.

"What are you doing?"

"Just a bit of a headache."

When I return to the room, she has already shed her clothes and is under the covers.

"Oh, you know how much I like to undress you," I object.

"It's not important," she protests. "Another time."

But will there be another time, I wonder.

I move to the bed, pull the cover away from her body. Unveiled, she stretches her long limbs in a semblance of crucifixion. I become hard again. I hoist myself onto the bed and straddle her and offer my cock to her mouth.

The next hours are a sheer catalogue of lust as our frustrations are set loose, and the anger inside us is given free rein and love and hate coexist in the silent light of the moon.

I hurt her.

She hurts me.

We do things we have never done before in a frenzy of limbs, body parts and uncontrollable emotions.

Outside, above the port, the weather has turned. As if in response to us. The night sky falls into the water.

We fall asleep, still embedded in each other somehow, raw flesh joined at skin level, sewn together with secretions and perspiration, intimately blended at a primeval level.

The next morning.

Skies outside blue again. Not a shadow of a cloud. Sea birds chattering in the distance.

"I love you."

"You said you would never do that. You knew I didn't want it there."

"I know."

"But it's OK. A first time for everything, eh?"

"Does it hurt?"

"Still a little."

"I'm sorry."

"You were like a savage."

"You too … Look, those are teethmarks there …"

"Looks who's talking … Those bruises will take weeks to fade."

I sighed as the tenderness rolled over me like giant surfing waves and my stomach tightened at the knowledge that this was going to be our last day together and that one day other men would enjoy her as I had, do those terrible things to her too. Worse, that she would enjoy it. Forget me.

I held back a tear.

Looked at her. Her dry lips were twisted in an indecipherable grimace, as if she was thinking the same things as me.

Her eyes filled with water.

I followed suit.

And we fell into each other's arms, hanging on to each other with desperation.

Half an hour of silence later.

"What are we going to do?" one of us asked. It could have been either of us.

"Do you think the hotel has room service?"

"Maybe."

They didn't. Not outside of season. We would stay in that room all day, surviving on mineral water and fruit juice from the mini-bar and odd biscuits and nuts.

Fucking.

With gentleness.

Like animals.

Accompanied with a waltz of smiles.

In sadness.

Abetted, of course, by the blue herbal pills I had stashed away in my shaving kit in the bathroom.

On our second night we just slept. Passion spent. Bodies at the point of exhaustion, stretched, gaping, throats dry, skin drawn taut and sensitive.

In the morning, under grey skies, we finally awoke, adhering to each other, spooned, with the weight of the new day's silence weighing heavily over us. I wiped sleep away from my eyes.

"Morning …"

"Hmmm …"

We lazed for a while.

Finally, she shook off her torpor, turned towards me, her left nipple peering impudently over the edge of the crumpled sheet.

"I should get up," she said, with little expression in her voice.

"Not yet?" I asked.

"There's a train for the city at 10:15."

"Time for …" I lowered my hand on her shoulder.

"I'm not sure," she said.

"Please."

She responded with silence.

I caressed her arm, while my other hand moved to her stomach, my fingers following the thin trail of fuzz that descended from her navel to her cunt.

She squirmed.

"Enough," she said.

"No, I still want you."

"But you'll always want me," she answered. "That's the way you are."

"You have a cold heart," I said.

"Maybe."

But she made no move to exit the bed.

Soon, her nipples were hard again.

I motioned her onto her knees and positioned myself behind her and entered her in one swift movement. She was still sufficiently lubricated from our earlier excesses. It felt hot inside her, like being home again. She moaned gently as I dug deeper into her innards.

I closed my eyes, banishing the terrible sight of my cock ravaging her bowels because all it evoked to me now was the premonition of other men fucking her in the same way, once I was no longer around. Was it jealousy? How could one be jealous of men who didn't even exist for her yet?

I was out of breath, drained of energy. It felt as if her whole body was now inert, suspended on the end of my penis as I impaled her with a metronomic rhythm.

The bile began to rise up through my throat and for a moment there I thought I was actually going to be sick, an abominable conclusion to our affair. But I succeeded in keeping the bitterness down, lodged at the back of my mouth.

No, not another man. Men. Boys. Others.

I screamed.

Her whole body tensed under me as she came, assuming from the fierceness of my sound that I was about to explode too, flooding her insides with my warmth.

But that scream was no form of blessed relief. It was anger. Undiluted rage. At losing her. At her betrayal, her new-found indifference, at the world.

Somehow, out of my direct control, or was I just deluding myself, my hands moved slowly from her butt cheeks where my fingers left pink parallel indentations, towards her head. Still in the blissful throes of her orgasm, her body straightened and I took hold of her long, ebony hair. Pulled hard. My cock moved even deeper inside her.

By now the bile floated like lead inside the roof of my mouth, poisoning me alive.

I closed my eyes and my fingers circled her neck.

She was too weak to resist the sudden pressure.

She struggled a little but my grip was firm. Madness had provided me with the extra strength required.

My cock went limp and flopped out of her, a pitiful puppet now abandoned by the gods of lust.

I don't know how long it took her to die. I was elsewhere altogether, in a world where thoughts had no sense or logic. A merciless universe where no other man would ever touch her, or be loved by her. A world where I was the only one she would ever love.

HE WRAPPED HER LIFELESS BODY between the sheets they had spent so long making love in. It felt right.

She looked peaceful in death, even younger than she was.

He washed her face, then with infinite care and attention, her body. Wiping away all traces of sin and sex, all the smells of him.

Then left the room, after putting the Don't Disturb sign on the door handle, and impressing on reception his instructions that she should be allowed to sleep as she was unwell and that room cleaning was not necessary today, thank you.

He spent most of the day mostly wandering up and down the promenade, lost in thought.

He returned to their hotel room by early evening. His request had been obeyed and the room, and her dead body, had not been disturbed.

As night fell, he kept on staring at her growing pallor but the tears wouldn't come. Which made him angry at himself. Surely, now was the time for mourning?

He unzipped his traveling bag and pulled out the laptop—a MacBook Pro, all matte aluminium—he never journeyed overseas without. Connected to the Internet. Researched for an hour or so, until he found what he was looking for. Then posted an ad on the clandestine site he had hunted down. Making a proposal. Maybe it would find no takers.

He lay down on the bed next to her cold body and snuggled up to her and dozed off. The pockmarked moon outside the window rose above the bay and the port.

At around two or so in the morning, the bell on his laptop pinged repeatedly.

Someone had read his posting.

He pulled the laptop over from the bedside table and placed it on his knees.

It only took thirty minutes to make the arrangements.

He moved to the bathroom and emptied his wash bag and placed a brand new blade in his razor, stripped, showered and then meticulously shaved away all the hair above and around his penis, testicles and anus until he was as smooth as a new born baby. Fully naked. Vulnerable if not quite innocent.

He returned to the bedroom.

His safari jacket was hanging from the hotel room door. He pulled the paper bag from one of its many pockets. He had purchased the flick knife this afternoon during the course of his aimless ramblings. This was a good place to buy leather goods and steel souvenirs.

Tested the tip of the knife against his finger and quickly drew a drop of blood. Which he wiped away against his bare thigh.

Then undraped her body, stood in silence facing it as if in prayer.

He whispered her name.

Once.

"Julie."

Twice.

"Julie."

And wielded the knife with a steady hand, carving her open with all the delicacy he could summon and cut out her heart.

One hour later, he had walked to the furthest reach of the southernmost beach. This end of the town was deserted and the silence around was only broken by the shy lapping of waves against the fine sand beach. He had found a broken deck chair made out of wood and with a few judicious kicks and pulls it had come apart.

He kneeled down and placed the heart on the criss cross trellis of the deck chair section, and poured a whole tube of lighting fluid over it, then stepped out of his clothes and waded naked into the sea holding the sinister platter and a disposable lighter until the water reached his waist.

He set fire to the fluid and pushed the miniature raft away towards the open sea, watching impassively as the small funeral pyre bobbed away over the waters, its light reflected in concentric circles as it slowly advanced. Soon, the fire becalmed and the fragile floating edifice began to sink. In an instant, it sank, and the horizon of the sea was empty again.

"Good-bye," he whispered into the darkness.

And retraced his steps towards the shore.

Once there, abandoning his cast away clothes on the sand, still fully nude, he made his way further south towards the area where the beach intersected with the railway tracks. There was no one around. This was the zone of town the guide books and web sites warned people away from. The gay cruising grounds the town was also notorious for.

He walked over the tracks. There were not many trains at this time of night. Passed by the tunnel dug into the mountain and into a labyrinth of bushes and tree stumps. Then remembering the map he had studied earlier on his laptop screen, he took a sharp left and arrived at a small, totally isolated cove. Not the sort of place you would ever come upon by accident.

In the shadows, he could already see a few shapeless groups of men in the distance, where the small beach met a crop of sharp seemingly unpassable rock formations that extended into the sea, segregating the area from the rest of the world.

He advanced.

Reached the first group of men. There were four of them. All tall and muscled. One was naked, studiously stroking an elongated cock, the others still clothed, in jeans or shorts and vests.

"I am here," he declared.

The time for thinking was over, he knew.

He had succumbed to the cancer of love. Now was the time to expiate, he realized.

Behind the first group of men he had approached, an amorphous shape neared, as if emerging from the very sea, monsters from the deep, three more men, each fiercer in appearance than the other. Hungry with lust.

One of the men in the initial group, probably the one he had exchanged emails with on the Internet earlier, spoke:

"Good."

The bulky stranger looked him up and own, checking no doubt that he had shaved where instructed.

"Are you ready?"

He nodded silently.

The two groups merged. Circled him.

"On your knees, slut," he was ordered.

He obeyed.

The sand below him was still wet from the night. All he could hear was the sea and its million echoes of loneliness.

A hand moved across his face and a piece of material was tightened around his head, blinding him instantly. All he could now experience was his own nudity. He felt himself getting slightly hard, as if the anticipation and the fear had an aphrodisiac effect.

A cock, hard and unwashed, was shoved deep into his mouth as another hand held his jaw wide open. He gagged and was almost sick on the spot. A hard, sudden slap against his butt cheeks felt like fire. The cock inside his mouth reached for the back of his throat. His tongue mechanically began to lick it, caress it, suck it, service it.

Things accelerated steadily, like a film being cranked at ever faster speed. His legs were kicked out from under him and he fell flat on his stomach onto the damp sand, releasing momentarily the penis that had been forcing his mouth and throat. Hands pulled him up and adjusted his position so that the cock, or was it another one altogether, invested his mouth again and his rear now presented itself to the predators. Two fingers were forced into his sphincter, stretching him painfully then he heard and felt someone spitting into the newly-receptive orifice and before he could even catch his breath he was violently sodomised.

The initial friction burned intensely but as the man relentlessly pumped inside him, he somehow managed to get used to it, busy as he was having to satisfy the succession of cocks taking turns inside his mouth. The man inside his rear quickly came, and it was like a torrent of lava spreading within him. There was barely an instant to pause and another man had taken the relay, even larger this time, from the feeling in his bruised flesh.

He had difficulty breathing as the unrelenting assault continued.

Maybe daylight would come and he would be reprieved, he briefly thought.

A foot kicked him the ribs. A surge of pain coursed through his body.

He choked on another ejaculation spurting below his tongue. Tasting bitter.

Each man took turns with him, both orally and anally. Some even came back for seconds.

He felt broken now, like the shadow of the man he had once been. Turned into an object, a fuck doll for all to abuse.

Which, with a twisted sense of morality, he knew he deserved.

And more.

There was a lull.

The men were resting but he could still smell their hunger in the sea air.

He lay there, gasping, gaping at every extremity, probably bleeding from the sexual attacks, leaking unholy cocktails.

But he was also serene, finally at peace with himself.

The blindfold was removed.

Somehow it was still night.

And at that moment, he knew it would be night forever.

The leader leaned over his prostrate body.

"You're a good slut," he remarked.

"Thank you, sir," he managed to blurt out. His lips were numb, his tongue heavy.

"So ...," some seconds can last a lifetime, "are you ready?"

He nodded as best he could.

"Perfect."

The other men were all standing, cocks at the ready, leering, fists clenched.

A foot suddenly made violent contact with his face, breaking his nose.

Then another, connecting with his balls.

The flash of pain was unbearable.

The sky disappeared as the men all moved closer.

He felt something (a fist?) being forced into his anus, tearing him forever, while a storm of punches landed on every square inch of his chest and stomach.

He fainted briefly.

When he came to, shaken back into consciousness by the heat of urine pouring from all directions above across his face, they had pulled his body to the edge of the lapping sea. Where matters would be less messy and the water would wash away the blood. The men surrounded him. Both his arms were stretched and firmly held back as were his legs, as if he were about to be quartered by a team of wild horses. His sinews screamed.

He caught a flash of metal in the pale moonlight.

Closed his eyes and remembered how once she had loved him.

They castrated him and shared his genitals between themselves.

They were in no hurry.

He died from loss of blood.

Then they ate the rest of him.

Terrible things happen in the dark.

Spin the Bottle
Pearce Hansen

The butane was sparked and poised in front of the straight shooter when Leo started pounding on the garage door.

"Open up Redd. We gotta talk."

"Shit," Redd muttered as he put the lighter and the crack loaded pipe in his pocket. "Hide," he ordered Shondra. "Don't say nothin'."

Shondra: his neighbor from around the corner. Like Mix-A-Lot admired, she was 36-24-36 and only a smidgen over five feet. A little while ago she'd seen Redd hurrying home after copping from Felix, and had known with womanly intuition that he'd been holding.

"You know that shit makes all the girls horny," Shondra had said, leering gap-toothed at the pocket Redd had his hand parked in as if to protect the three Gs of crack concealed there.

"Like who?" Redd asked.

"Like me," Shondra had said, planting one hand on top of the pocket where his rock was stashed, planting the other on Redd's crotch and giving it a friendly squeeze.

But right now Leo was still pounding on the garage door. The radio by his bed was tuned to KKSF, 103.7, and cool jazz filled the garage like refreshing water—Redd's Dad had loved jazz, and the beat-up little clock radio was all he had left to remember the old man by. Redd gently, reverently turned the broken knob to Off, and headed toward the garage door to open up. He saw the look in Shondra's eyes as she smiled down at the rocks spilled out on the battered coffee table, and he scooped it all up and put it in his other pocket.

"Get hid," he ordered her again, and she obeyed though with a disappointed look on her face.

Redd removed the stick he'd jammed the inside latch with; the springs screamed as he lifted the garage door up and open to reveal Leo standing there moping at him.

Leo: they'd never been all that close but Redd had burned every other bridge since beginning his last, latest run. Leo was a sap, all Redd had had to do was play the "Remember when?" game with him and he'd been nodding and smiling in good fellowship, eager to help out an old homie down on his luck.

Leo sniffed the air a bit as if testing for the acridity of lingering crack smoke. Was it disappointment that filled his face when he didn't smell any?

"Who you got back there?" Leo asked with a hopeful look as he stared back into the dark interior of the garage Redd was currently calling home; the garage under Leo's house actually.

"Oh, you know," Redd said, puffing up like some kind of player for Leo's jealous admiration. "How's Jeanine?" he asked, knowing she probably had to be listening from upstairs, probably with the window cracked just enough to hear while she kept her ever widening girth safely out of sight.

The hopeful look left Leo's eyes with a snap, and the mopey expression filled his face again. "We gotta talk," Leo said, in the tones usually reserved for a doctor telling his patient very bad news.

Leo paused, as if waiting for Redd to take some of the conversational burden off of him. But Redd just stared at the cracked cement of the driveway sloping down into the basement-level garage, waiting for the hammer to fall.

"It's like this," Leo said. "You know I got those warrants, right? I mean, it's just traffic stops, but they'll still haul me in if I get pulled over. I can't do time, bro—you know I've got jobs."

Redd nodded. Leo was an under-the-table construction sub-contractor; he'd just about gotten on Redd's last nerve constantly griping about how he had tendonitis in his forearm from swinging that framing hammer all day.

"It's like this," Leo said again, licking his lips with a sly gaze that didn't really fit with his piggy gimlet eyes. "Jeanine figures you should pay back rent to get me off the hook. One hand washes the other, right?"

"Right," Redd said.

"It'll only take two hundred dollars to pay off the tickets. You got more than that in your GR check today, right?"

"I haven't cashed it yet," Redd said, though with a sinking feeling. Of course he had, and of course he'd spent it immediately on the three Gs of crack currently residing in his pocket.

Leo leaned in, his palms facing Redd in placation. "It's not me, it's Jeanine," he said, voice low to defend against his wife's eavesdropping, making her the heavy.

"How soon you need it?" Redd asked, looking as helpful and sincere as possible.

Leo looked relieved, as if all his troubles were over now. "ASAP, bro. But by tomorrow at the latest." Leo hurried upstairs to let Jeanine know just how wrong she'd been all along about her husband's good buddy.

"Let's do it up now," Shondra said as she came up to join him. "Let's walk outside and smoke it right out in the open so they can see. Fuck 'em, what they gonna do?"

Part of Redd wanted to do just what Shondra said. Another part wanted to do up anyways, but only down here, only after the door was safely closed. He needed a hit, bad.

But he stepped toward the back of the cement-floored garage and examined what he'd been calling home for the last few months. Like any drowning man, he was clasping tight to whatever flotsam promised to keep him from sinking beneath the surface forever.

He didn't have much keeping him afloat here: The one lone naked bulb on the wall, controlled by the short pull string. The exposed un-sheet-rocked interior walls, two-by-four framing backed by peeling tarpaper. The plywood coffin-sized inset box built into the interior wall that Redd slept in, on an air mattress in a greasy sleeping bag. The snowdrifts of dirty clothes carpeting the floor.

The (almost empty) sack of food hanging from the rafter so that the vermin that rustled through the garage whenever the lights were out wouldn't be able to steal Redd's meager sustenance. Redd took pride in cutting his food intake down to about two cans of beans a week. The hunger button wasn't quite working right for him anymore, but every few days, like clockwork, he'd open a can of whatever was in the sack and eat it cold. He didn't mind it cold, but it wouldn't've mattered if he did mind—the garage had no cooking facilities and no running water.

And in the cubby up by where he laid his head, the only possession Redd cared about in the world: the decrepit old AM/FM clock radio that Dad had given him so long ago. It was missing a button or two, the clock wouldn't keep straight time anymore, and it was basically held together by duct tape and wire—it wasn't even digital ferchrissakes. But he always smiled when he looked at it—it brought back memories from long ago, from when life was . . . something else.

He turned it on with reverence. KSFX was fading and popping, and he moved the old radio around until it caught the signal.

Out of the corner of his eye he saw Shondra rubbing her palm all over the coffee table to wipe up whatever hubba dust might be left from the rocks Redd had scooped up. But Redd didn't object—hell, he'd never minded cockroaches after all.

He looked down at the clothing heaped around on the floor and picked out all the articles he thought might be worth something: three Pendleton shirts, a pea coat, and a couple of other things. He wouldn't have any cold weather clothes after this, but he had to raise that two hundred dollars.

He shooed Shondra out ahead of him with the double armful of clothing held in front of him, then laid the clothes down as he turned and reached up to grab the garage door to pull it down. He looked in at the radio, still playing that fine, mellow jazz. There was no way he'd ever sell it no matter what—and nobody would give him anything for it anyways, it was worthless to anybody but him.

He caught Shondra following his gaze to look at the radio as he lowered the garage door. "I'll come by later and give you a taste," Redd said.

"Of course you will," Shondra said. He carefully snapped the padlock shut in the hasp as she watched. He yanked it several times to ensure it was latched before stepping up and away.

The used clothing store was up off of West MacArthur, a long hump from Leo's house up by Adeline; especially when you were lugging a double armful of clothes. Redd got out of breath a couple of times and had to stop; he was weak now—maybe he needed to eat a little more often.

At the clothing store, the Asian behind the counter looked with distaste at the clothes Redd piled on the counter. But his grimace turned to a pursed lipped nod when he saw the Pendleton labels on the shirts, the Derby label inside the jacket. Redd waited patiently as the Asian inspected each article, looking for rips or stains, nodding as he put most of them on the table behind him, but pushing a few of them back Redd's way in rejection.

"Forty dollar," the Asian said when he was done.

Redd looked at his last non-raggedy items of attire, maybe worth five hundred dollars new. The forty dollars were a drop in the bucket toward the two hundred dollars he needed, but Redd took the two twenties the guy pushed his way across the counter, and left the store.

He was cramming the clothing into a trash can, not wanting to bother carrying them home, when he heard his name being called from down the street. Redd turned and saw Shannon, approaching from about a half a block away with another couple of guys attending him like the gutter prince he thought he was.

The sun gleamed off the skinz' shaved heads; they all wore uniform red suspenders, rolled up jeans, bomber jackets and Doc Martin boots. Redd saw that they were all carrying decks; it occurred to him to wonder why they were lugging their skateboards instead of riding them. He gave a tentative, deniable wave, which Shannon returned, smiling as he and his three henchmen reached Redd.

Shannon stood his longboard upright, butt on the sidewalk, as he looked at the clothes Redd had stuffed in the trash, and nodded his long horse face. "You gotta be on your last legs if you're selling off your clothes," Shannon observed.

Redd couldn't deny the obvious, but he couldn't figure out why Shannon even cared.

"This one's a likely stray," Shannon said over his shoulder to his little brother Chatter. Chatter and the other two skinz laughed.

"Hey, puppy," Shannon said to Redd. "Wanna come hang with the big dogs?"

Shannon's crib was three garbage strewn flights up in an apartment building off San Pablo. Shannon rapped his knuckles on the chewed-up blue door and it was opened instantly.

NIN was playing on the stereo. A bootwoman with a lit cigarette dangling from her mouth was cooking something that smelled like spaghetti in the kitchenette in the far back corner; an overflowing garbage can stood next to her.

Redd's mouth watered and his stomach knotted at the smell of the cooking food, and the silent dog pack of skinheads inspected him without shyness. Even the bootwoman cook stopped stirring and turned her burner down, then turned to stare at Redd as she tapped the ash off the end of her smoke.

The apartment walls were covered in spray-painted obscenities and flyers for punk shows, mainly for gigs across the Bay in the City. There were about a dozen skinz and bootwomen in the studio apartment, either standing or sitting at one of various mismatched castoff chairs or couches. Redd glanced over to see a row of baseball bats leaned against the wall next to the door: a ready arsenal for when the crackheads living in this building raised any objection to the behavior of the only white people living in it.

"Make room for our new friend," Shannon ordered, waving his hands apart palm out like he was separating the Red Sea. A couple of skinz hurried off of a couch, one almost spilling his beer.

Shannon and Redd sat next to each other on the vacated couch space. Shannon smiled at Redd. "We've known each other a long time," Shannon said, voice warm and gentle. "You are hurting, aren't you?"

Redd nodded reluctantly. "Yeah. I gots to scrape up about one hundred and sixty dollars or I'm on the pavement tomorrow."

Shannon nodded at all the unspeaking skinz surrounding them, as if to say "See?" to an unasked question. "Maybe we could help each other out. I got something I need help on, and if you do it we'll let you hang with us."

"Yeah?" Redd asked, his dust-covered hopes raising for the first time in many moons.

"Yeah, we'll take care of you for sure bro," Shannon said. He looked at the ceiling. "Unless you just want your end so you can cover your rent?" Shannon's eyes widened as if he'd just happened to remember something. "Say, you wouldn't happen to have any of that shit, would you?"

Redd's mouth opened a little but he was tongue tied. He could still pretend that he'd been planning on selling his stash of rock to get Leo's money, couldn't he? *I wasn't going to just do it all to my head in one last blast,* he told himself.

Shannon chuckled at the look on Redd's face. He gestured around at his entourage of skinz. "See, it's like this. Here in the East Bay Skinz, we're like Robin Hood, you know? Share and share alike."

Shannon's eyes narrowed as he saw Redd's continued uncertainty. "If you really don't want in with us, just call it a front before you get your cut of the job. What's the matter? Don't you trust me?"

"I want in," Redd said hurriedly, and brought out his rocks and his straight shooter.

Redd went on autopilot then, the addict brain watching sweaty faced as his pipe was passed around the room, his rocks were steadily smoked, every skin and bootwoman in the East Bay Skinz took turns filling their lungs with Redd's rapidly evaporating stash. It all seemed to be over in seconds, like on fast forward. And, out of three grams of hubba, Redd got to hit maybe one nickel rock out of his own (final?) stash.

The fogbanks of crack smoke filled the apartment thick enough for a contact high, and Shannon blew on Redd's overheated straight shooter before tossing it on the coffee table, where it audibly cracked.

Redd hurriedly scooped up his broken pipe. "Time to go for a little drive."

They headed up Ashby, Redd and Shannon and Chatter and another skin, in an old green Valiant. "See, it's like this. I know these people," Shannon said from up where he was riding shotgun. "These Satanists. They do things for me sometimes, I do things for them—you know how it is, right?"

Redd nodded in the backseat as the skin driving hung a right on College. Redd said "Right," as he realized Shannon wasn't even looking at him. Shannon's little brother Chatter was sitting sideways on the other side of the backseat, facing Redd with a wrinkled nose.

Shannon continued. "Sometimes they want something more nasty than usual. I mean, hey, they're all like 'Hail Lucifer,' right?"

"Right," Redd said. Chatter opened his window and made a big production of sticking his head out into the fresh air like a dog.

"Don't draw attention," Shannon ordered his little brother as they turned east up toward the Hills.

"He stinks," Chatter blurted, the words coming out of him like he'd been holding them in for a while. "When's the last time you bathed?" Chatter asked Redd, his round face knotted up in a scowling sneer.

"Chatter," Shannon said, voice raised.

Chatter sank back in his seat, but he left his window open and his profile was sullen.

"Here we are," Shannon said, and the skin driving pulled up to a dark, tree-shadowed stretch of curb by a wrought iron fence. On the other side of the fence Redd saw row after row of tombstones and monuments, mausoleums and sepulchers, as far back as he could see into the murky, enfolding darkness. There were no lights on in there that he could see.

Redd hurried after Shannon as he shimmied up over the low hanging bough of a willow tree growing next to the fence, and jumped off the bough and over. Redd followed with Chatter and the driver close behind him.

As he stood on the bough preparing to make his leap, Redd stopped as he looked down at all the spear points topping the wrought

iron fence, imagining coming up short on his jump and landing on
the fence top, imagined all the spearheads stabbing through him at
waist level and out the other side . . . Shannon hissed, Redd success-
fully jumped, and the other two followed.

"See, it's like this," Shannon said as he walked amongst the plots
with his arm around Redd's shoulder; if he thought Redd stank, he
gave no sign of it. "Like I say, these Satanists pay good, and they do
me enough other favors I like to keep them happy. But sometimes
they ask for extra."

Chatter and the driver were walking ahead, muttering to each
other as they furtively splashed the beam of a small pocket flashlight
on various monuments and landmarks, as if retracing a path previ-
ously trodden.

"Here we are," the driver called back softly, and Shannon and
Redd hurried up to join them in front of an old, weather beaten mausoleum. The driver flashed the pen flash on what looked like a brand
new padlock holding the ends of a rusty, ancient chain together
through the mausoleum's ornate bronze door handles. Shannon pulled
a shiny key from his pocket and unlocked the padlock.

The mausoleum doors shrieked as they swung open, and they all
froze for a minute to see if anyone anywhere had heard. "Should have
used oil," Shannon muttered as he led the way inside.

The pen flash jerked from place to place within the crypt, not
supplying enough light to entirely illuminate the bone-cold house of
death. The walls were covered in green bronze plaques long enough
to conceal the oblong boxes Redd figured were behind them.

"This one," Chatter said, gesturing at one of the bronze plaques.
Chatter hurried up, pulled a stubby little jimmy crowbar from his
waistband. He pried up one corner, grabbed it with his other hand
and yanked; all the rusted screws holding up the plaque snapped, but
Chatter couldn't hold the entire weight of it one-handed, and the
plaque dropped to the floor and bonged like a bell as it hit and
bounced a couple of times.

"Shit," Chatter muttered, as Redd cringed. Chatter reached into
the now exposed niche and grabbed one end of the moldy old coffin

lying lengthwise, safe in the niche's embrace as it had been for many decades.

"Help him," Shannon ordered Redd, and Redd grabbed the other end of the box and helped Chatter lower it to the floor of the vault. The four men eyed each other furtively for a few moments; then, like a squeamish rapist steeling himself to rob his victim's virginity, Chatter rammed the end of his jimmy under the lid of the cobwebby coffin and pried upward. The lid cracked, the ancient rotted wood surrendering into several pieces. Like kids at Christmas, all four of them yanked clinging pieces of lid away, and exposed what lay within.

It didn't look real, this withered black mummy dressed in rotted black lace. The leather-fingered hands were crossed at the chest over bulges of material on the bodice that suggested they once enclosed breasts before those fragile hidden tatas had sagged away into whatever they looked like now under the dress. Redd wasn't about to grope under the dress and get to second base with this dead woman.

Her head was thrown back and her mouth had fallen wide open in an eternal scream, exposing long, yellow teeth jutting from her black gums in an enviably perfect grill. The once blond hair looked like it belonged on a doll; it was especially surreal to see that wavy coif of tarnished gold rooted in that dead scalp.

Redd heard a click and saw that Shannon had opened his foldie; Redd considered just what close quarters the inside of the mausoleum was, of how hard it would be to run if Shannon started swiping around with that blade.

But Shannon just tossed his knife in the air and flipped it so that he was holding it by the blade, offering the hilt to Redd.

"We need the head, Redd," Shannon said with a smile. The driver grunted, perhaps at the rhyme.

Redd stared at that knife without touching it. After a moment, Shannon said, "They're paying a grand, and they're picking it up in an hour. Hell, I was gonna make my little brother Chatter do it before I saw you today. You wanna chop it off Chatter?"

"No fuckin' way," Chatter said with firmness.

"You see?" Shannon said, arching his shaggy brows at Redd. "You do it, and you're either in with us, or you get two hundred dollars for your troubles."

Plus the three hundred dollars for the rock I fronted you, Redd wanted to point out, but it didn't feel like the right time.

Redd took the knife and squatted next to the coffin. The other three men watched as he dug his left hand into that thick mass of hair and grasped it in a tight fist. He pulled to get some tension on the neck, and the ancient vertebrae within the mummy neck creaked audibly.

As he was placing the edge of the blade against the corpse's wrist-thin neck, the driver seemed to be having technical difficulties with the pen flash: he couldn't seem to keep the light on the subject at hand.

As Redd watched the light jerking around, shadows danced across the corpse's face, making it look like the sunken sockets were rolling their eyes at him in mockery. Redd's blood ran cold at the sight; he imagined all the other dead in this cemetery, whose buried faces he'd walked across getting here, were writhing in their coffins laughing at him as well.

You cannot disrespect us, the dead said silently. You will be with us soon enough.

"If you're shy, we can always leave and let you do it alone in the dark," Shannon suggested.

Redd's head whipped up, and he stared at the three other men with such rage blazing from his eyes that they were taken aback; even Shannon, this Joe Cool Prez of the East Bay Skinz.

"Hold the light fuckin' steady," Redd ordered the driver.

The pen flash's beam held solid as a rock as Redd sawed at the throat rapidly. It felt like he was cutting through a huge desiccated roll of beef jerky, though he had to repress a gag at associating food with this object he was dismembering. The blade clicked against the vertebrae and he wiggled it till he found the seam between two of the neck bones; a pry and a digging chop and the spine was separated, and he pulled on the hair a little tighter as he sawed through the last bit of leathery mummified flesh and then the head was loose in his hand.

Redd stood, and held the dead woman's head up as if for everyone's inspection. It was surprising how heavy it was; something so old and desiccated—something no longer useful to its former owner—shouldn't weigh so much.

"Nothing to it," Redd said. "Decapitation 101."

"Damn," Shannon breathed as he pulled a pillowcase from his back pocket and held it open for Redd to drop the head into. Looking around at the awed looks on the other three men's faces as he dropped the head in the pillowcase, Redd felt closer to triumph than he had in a long time.

When they got back to Shannon's apartment building and Redd made to follow them inside, Shannon put a hand on Redd's chest and physically stopped him.

"Listen, bro, you did good," Shannon said. "But these Satanists are shy people. They ain't gonna want to see any strangers when they make their appointment here and pick up their fucking head."

Shannon chuckled as he followed the other two skinz through the apartment building entrance. "Trust me Redd—you don't even want these people to know you exist."

Redd just stood there in front of Shannon's building, feeling naked as he waited to be invited back inside—either to get his head shaved and become a member of the East Bay Skinz, or to get his cut and continue living in Leo's garage. After a few minutes, a chopped, maroon Impala low-rider cruised up, but slowed as it came opposite Redd. He saw a carfull of silent blobby heads inside there, no more than unspeaking black silhouettes in the dim side street lights—Redd couldn't even say what race they were, but all those dark cardboard cutout figures in the car were looking right at him as the low-rider passed.

Redd looked down at the pavement and tried to think of other things as the Impala sped up down the block and around the corner. He looked around and saw a thick, overgrown bank of shrubbery down the side of the apartment building; it looked like it hadn't been touched by clippers in years. Redd hurried over to it, turned sideways and scuffed along between the shrubs and the gritty stucco wall.

About twenty feet down he squatted and hid there in the musky dark that smelled of sap and cobwebs.

He heard the low-rider engine chugging closer again, and he glimpsed its headlights then its taillights for an instant as it rolled past the narrow gap between the shrubbery and the apartment building. It stopped in the street, out of Redd's sight around in front of the apartment. His heart pounded as he listened to it idling invisible up there, listening for voices or slamming car doors.

After a good solid minute he heard the Impala move out and away again, but he just squatted there in the dark, shivering at the rank pre-dawn mist that had arisen to cling to him as he hid there.

He judged he'd been there maybe an hour, and the sky was beginning to lighten, a distant bird began singing and he heard footsteps coming his way along the outside of the shrubbery. A big black dude suddenly stood swaying in front of the patch of shrubbery where Redd squatted.

The black dude was breathing hard, his exhalations smelling of expensive gin. As he fumbled at his fly preparatory to taking a leak, his bleary gaze looked down to meet Redd's looking right back at him. The black dude's eyes rolled in surprise, and he took a step back, almost tripping and falling on his ass.

"I'm just waiting for somebody," Redd called out softly from inside the bush. But the dude just made a drunken, dismissive swipe at the air in Redd's direction, before walking as steadily as he could down the shrubbery to relieve himself elsewhere.

As Redd gingerly crawled his cramped body out of the shrubbery and back into the dawn, he could hear the black dude's sigh of relief and the splash of his piss.

"What?" Shannon asked as he opened the door to Redd's quiet knock. Shannon's entire body was a sneer.

Redd sagged inside as he saw how every skin in the apartment was grinning at him in contempt and mockery. A joke had been told in Redd's absence, one that wasn't going to be shared with him other than to make him the butt of it. He'd been the night's entertainment, no more.

"My cut at least," Redd mumbled, knowing it was no good, but still having to ask to observe the forms.

"I don't know what you're talking about," Shannon said, menace oozing out of his eyes like toothpaste starting to squeeze out the tube.

For a moment, despite the scene's inherent humiliation, Redd almost weakened enough to ask what he'd wanted to before: if he could just crash here out of the wet and the cold. If he could just couch surf with them and pay his rent by being their whipping boy. By being their punk.

Shuddering in self disgust, Redd turned and walked away. Behind him Shannon's door closed and Redd could hear the muffled chorus of laughter even out in the hall as he walked away with his head down.

It was dawn when Redd got home, and he was ready to lay down even if he wouldn't be able to sleep for days. He stopped when he saw how the padlock had been pried open, how the garage door wasn't closed all the way.

Going into the basement with his heart pounding, Redd sparked his butane in his trembling hand as he went straight to the milk crate next to his air mattress and verified that Dad's clock radio was gone.

He was so, so tired, but he stepped rapidly as he rounded the corner to Shondra's. She was living above a dry cleaner's, and she buzzed him up. He took the stairs two at a time, and rapped on her door.

"You still holdin' that, baby?" Shondra asked as she opened the door. "You gonna share a little taste with me an my man DeVron?"

Behind her a big, ebony golem of a dude sat on her couch with both feet flat on the floor and his hands on his knees as he watched the flickering tube as if hypnotized. His face looked like it had a few divots knocked out of it from time to time.

"Her man." Shondra's sex life was none of Redd's business, but he'd noted before that he never seemed to see her with the same dude twice and he didn't figure this DeVron blood to be Shondra's life partner neither.

"Naw, I'm tapped," Redd said, and watched the welcoming smile fade from her face. "Someone broke into my crib. My radio's gone."

"You saying I did it? You calling me a thief?" Shondra asked in a raised theatrical voice, her head swaying from side to side like she had a snake neck. Behind her, G-Thug Unit DeVron stood up from the couch to tower. His mashed-up face was aimed Redd's way, but there was as little emotion on it as when he'd been parking his gaze on the TV screen. Now that DeVron was standing, Redd could see his clock radio brazenly sitting on the end table at the far end of the couch.

Redd beat a hasty retreat. He could live without his Dad's radio; it was a beat-up antique piece of crap anyways; it had been dying for a long time.

Despite the early hour, Leo was standing outside when Redd got back to the house, almost as if he'd been waiting. Jeanine stood up on the porch with her arms crossed.

"You don't have the money, do you?" Leo asked. Redd shook his head, studying how the garage door was shut with a new padlock on it. He knew his key wouldn't work on it, and he knew it would be a waste of time to ask if he could snag his earthly possessions. But all Redd's stuff was a bunch of crap anyways; none of it was even worth the effort of lugging it around.

Leo leaned in. "How come you never offered me any of that shit?" he asked in a lowered voice. Leo glanced over his shoulder at Jeanine, who Redd noticed was sporting a black eye this morning.

"I would have smoked it with you anytime," Leo said accusingly. Then he and Jeanine were arm in arm going up the front steps toward the warmth of their loving home, and Redd turned his back on his garage squat forever. It'd been a hole anyways—saying goodbye to it was no big.

Redd walked up Prince Street toward Martin Luther King Junior Way, not really heading anywhere, but figuring one direction was as good as another right now.

A slanger rolled up to accost him as Redd passed a grimy looking apartment building. Redd recognized the slanger, the blood named Felix that Redd had copped off yesterday and had copped off of many times before. Redd looked at Felix with the hopeful look all addicts have when they're broke and think that maybe, somehow, the milk of human kindness might be extended their way just this once . . .

But Felix recognized Redd right back. As there was no money in Redd's hand and Felix knew by heart the crackhead beggar's posture Redd was displaying. Felix snorted in disgust and headed back to his station in the shadows of the shrubbery without a word. Redd had no credit left in the hubba community; he'd lost any credibility with Felix and his brethren a long time ago.

Redd turned south after he hit MLK, again mentally flipping a coin without bothering to even stop and think about it. Maybe he'd catch an AC Transit trunk line bus, 51 or 63, ride it back and forth till kicked off by the driver at each end of the line. He could catch a few catnap winks sitting upright as long as he wasn't obvious about it.

As he was coming up on a liquor store, a burly young brother spilled out the door, with a TEC-9 in one hand and a bulging paper bag in the other. The brother was grinning as he started to turn in Redd's direction and they made full eye contact. The brother's lips parted, either to yell a boisterous racial epithet in passing or to give voice to post-211 exuberance. Redd figured the guy was in too much of a hurry to stop and gab, but he kept his eye on the TEC, ready to dive out of the way if it started swinging up his way.

Three gunshots rang out, and the brother sailed forward through the air with a puzzled look on his face, and then hit the pavement, the bag and gun spilling from his hands.

The liquor store owner stood with one foot outside the doorway, a .45 in his hand as he looked down at the squirming robber. The liquor store owner kicked the brother in the head and his writhing stopped. He grabbed the robber by the ankle and commenced dragging him inside to make it a legal kill.

"Please don't leak," the liquor store owner ordered the blood pooling on the brother's back. "Don't leak on the ground." His eyes raised and he stopped dragging the corpse as he saw Redd standing there watching from a few feet away. A look came into his eyes; a look that Redd imagined might've been in them the instant before the guy shot the robber in the back.

"I'm not a witness," Redd said hurriedly, watching this guy's .45 as closely as he'd watched the robber's TEC. "I didn't see nothin'."

After a few seconds that gleaming look faded from the liquor store owner's eyes, and he nodded as dragged the body the rest of the way inside so this upstanding Citizen could claim to the indifferent cops it'd been self-defense instead of retaliation. Redd turned and started walking away fast in the direction he'd come from.

"Wait," he heard from behind, and he froze with shoulders hunched before slowly turning.

The liquor store owner stood holding a bottle of Johnny Walker Red outstretched Redd's way. Redd made sure the gun wasn't in the guy's other hand before warily approaching.

But the guy pulled the bottle of Walker back out of reach just as Redd stuck his hand out to grasp it. "You're not a witness," the liquor store owner reminded him firmly. "You didn't see nothing."

Redd nodded in agreement to close the deal. The liquor store owner handed him the bottle, reached down to scoop up the grocery bag of cash that the robber had died for, and went back inside his liquor store to call the Man. Redd saw the dead brother's TEC-9 in the gutter, picked it up, and hurried away before the pigs showed up to shut everything down as a crime scene.

"Wait," the liquor store owner called again from behind him. But Redd just grinned, all assholes and elbows as he commenced running toward the corner—he knew the guy wanted the TEC, but it was Redd's property now, finder's keepers.

As he turned the corner Redd looked back and saw the liquor store owner still standing in front of his liquor store, staring at Redd wide- eyed as strobing cop car lights appeared in the distance behind him. Redd giggled as he ran, imagining how the guy would try to play it when he couldn't produce a weapon to go with the dead robber's body.

Some time later Redd was swigging from the bottle in an alley around the corner from the Ashby BART Station. He had his ass planted on a piece of cardboard he was using as a provisional seat, and his back was against the cold, hard brick wall with his legs stuck out straight on the filthy alley. None of it was what you'd call ergonomic, but it would have to do.

The bottle of Walker was half empty as Redd carefully set it down next to him on the cardboard; he had a mellow, powerful buzz going, and he didn't want to spoil it by spilling this one last bit of comfort. This warm glow would last forever—or, if not, Redd didn't want to consider anything past when it ended.

He picked up the TEC-9 and considered it. He kicked out the magazine to admire the rounds all stacked and ready; he worked the action and ejected the round that had been loaded in the pipe to say hello at the very first squeeze of the trigger.

Redd swayed to his feet and dragged the cardboard to the center of the alley one-handed, flinching as the bottle almost toppled. He staggered as he stood upright again, but the TEC was still solid in his grip.

He placed one hand against the cold, damp alley wall as he knelt and placed the TEC in the center of the cardboard on its side and gave it a little spin. It turned like a top, that murderous barrel doing a full three-sixty. Redd smiled as he realized it was threatening the whole world around it, him included.

He remembered back when he was a kid and Dad was still alive. What had he been, nine? Ten? Him and Beth Arney and her little sister, and that goofy kid down the block, what had his name been again? Didn't matter.

He remembered the cool of her grandmother's basement, remembered sitting next to Beth, the most beautiful girl in the world, he'd thought at the time. Playing Spin the Bottle, watching that empty pop bottle spin as rapidly as the TEC-9 was spinning now in front of him. Waiting for the bottle to stop so he could deliver a kiss to whoever it was pointed at.

He shut one eye to make the double vision go away, and looked around the alley. He picked up a crumpled-up empty pack of smokes and set it down in what he figured was the direction to Shannon's coven of skinz. An empty fries container pointed the way to Leo's, and close beside that a used syringe represented Shondra's hovel.

He looked at the array, feeling something missing, sensing the lack of balance—three was never enough for Spin the Bottle after all.

Redd laughed as realization came and he fumbled his straight shooter out of his pocket and set it down midway between Leo and Shondra, and Shannon. The pipe would stand in for himself.

The TEC-9 would be delivering the last kiss the brother who had formerly owned it had failed to give the world. Whoever it stopped at was who Redd would point the TEC at and squeeze the trigger. And if it didn't point at himself, Redd would spin it again after the first visit, as many times as it took.

Redd whipped the TEC around hard and watched it spin, looking on with great interest as it spun, then slowed, and then finally stopped.

Acknowledgments

This book would not exist without Jon and Ruth Jordan, Clair Lamb and the B&A of BHB.